CRYSTAL
BLOODS

CRYSTAL BLOODS

AERIN APELTUN

Elsewhen Press

CRYSTAL BLOODS
First published in Great Britain by Elsewhen Press, 2025
An imprint of Alnpete Limited

Map copyright © 2024 Aerin Apeltun and Alison Buck

Elsewhen Press, PO Box 757, Dartford, Kent DA2 7TQ
www.elsewhen.press

British Library Cataloguing in Publication Data.
A catalogue record for this book is available from the British Library.

ISBN 978-1-915304-64-3 Print edition
ISBN 978-1-915304-74-2 eBook edition

Designed and formatted by Elsewhen Press

This book is a work of fiction. All names, characters, places,
monarchies, empires, religious orders, and events are either a product
of the author's fertile imagination or are used fictitiously. Any
resemblance to actual events, priestesses, royal families, evil emperors,
places or people (living, dead, or astral projections) is purely
coincidental.

Contents

To my husband and daughter
for all their love and support

To all the dreamers, continue to dream because sometimes dreams do come true

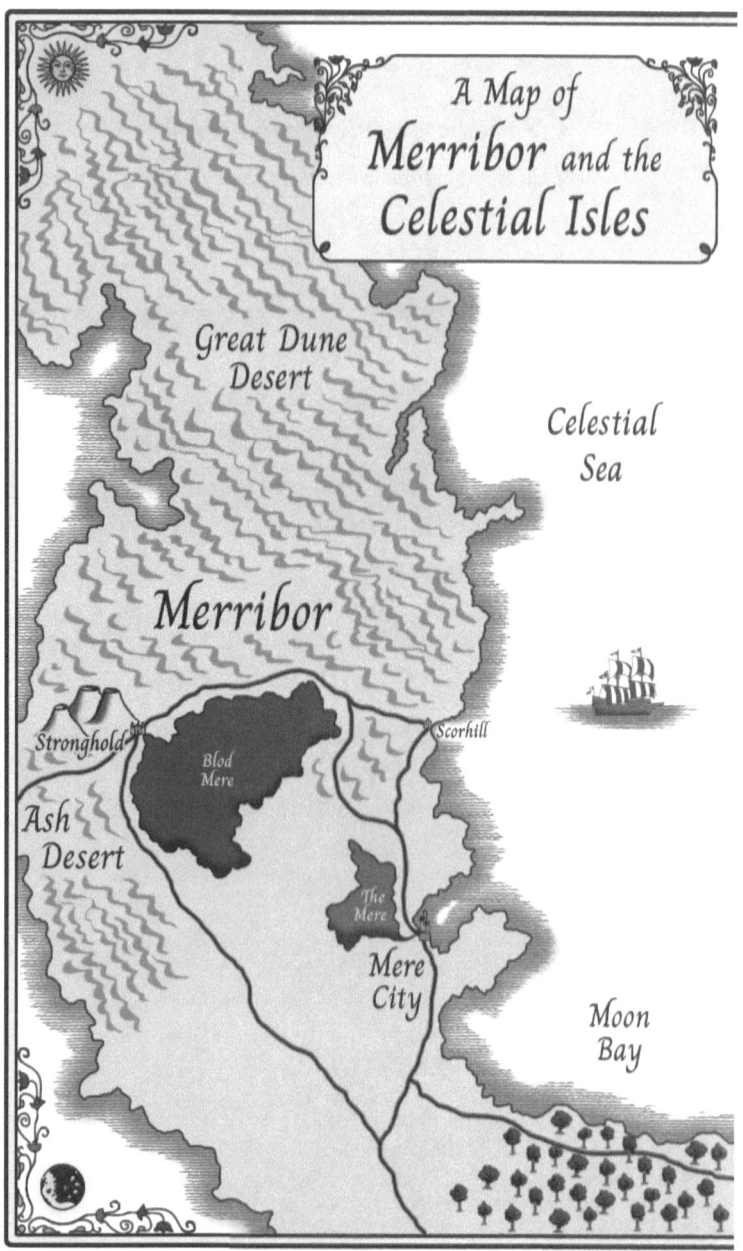

A Map of
Merribor and the
Celestial Isles

Great Dune
Desert

Celestial
Sea

Merribor

Stronghold

Blod
Mere

Scorhill

*Ash
Desert*

The
Mere

Mere
City

Moon
Bay

Celestial
Temple

N

Planetae

Galatae

W   *E*

S

Asterion
Archipelago

Solis

Helios

Starlight
Citadel

Steorra

Moon City

Luna

◄► 100 Miles ►◄

Fairfield

The Celestial Isles

Dunton

Chapter One

My blood could kill me, especially if I fell into the wrong hands.

It would grant someone power. Control. My blood would be so dangerous, so coveted by others that if they knew about it, knew about *me*, they'd want the dominion it could offer. And they would bleed me dry to get hold of it – literally.

Staying hidden was my only option.

I opened the letter my mother had sent to me before I'd left my uncle's house on the coast, and sighed. The third on this particular subject, that had a little voice screaming in my head.

Mother had always promised me she would do everything she could to stop me from being Pledged. She'd failed. Her letter was yet another pleading forgiveness, assuring me she'd found a suitable match. A suitable husband. A lesser prince, a sixth child, still with Royal Blood, but far removed from the throne and not destined for it, so I'd never have to worry about responsibilities. A decent, kind young man, but a prince who would pay me little attention. One who would never need to know my secret.

I folded the letter and slipped it back into my saddlebag, catching my finger on the buckle as I secured it. *Starlight*, what had I done? A single, small drop of blood beaded on my pale skin and fell into my palm – but it was no longer a drop of blood as it landed, but a small, clear crystal that glittered in the sunlight. I quickly slipped it in my pocket and grabbed a handkerchief, halting the flow of blood. Idiot. I should've been more careful.

'Are you all right, Sorsha?'

I turned to see my best friend, Kit, back astride his chestnut horse, his beautiful dark sepia skin sparkling with sweat in the warm late spring sun.

'I'm fine,' I said, pressing on the handkerchief to double check the bleeding had stopped.

'Did you catch your finger? The way you freak out every time you cut yourself is mad. No one likes the look of blood, but you take it to extremes.'

He had no idea.

'Sorry, it just makes me feel a bit queasy,' I lied, glancing down and shielding my eyes from the sun as it reflected off the sea. The water was as blue as my eyes, today, sparkling in the noon sunlight. I squinted in the bright light as I chewed on a ginger-coloured curl that had come loose from my ponytail, resting my other, bandaged hand, on the hilt of the sharp knife at my hip.

'Stop fussing about it, Sorsh. You really don't need to panic. Now, come on, or we'll never get there at this rate,' he said, his black hair shifting in the wind, his deep brown eyes saying *Starlight, would you get a move on*.

'That's rather the idea,' I said. I retied my long, wavy hair into a rather messy ponytail and mounted my horse, the twin short swords on my back catching uncomfortably. My horse flicked its ears at me in an irritated fashion, and whinnied as if chastising me.

Kit gave me a long look. 'You only have to go to the Starlight Court once a year. You're lucky. You could be living there.'

I sighed. He was right. As a Royal Cousin I had the honorary title "Starlight Princess". The Seventh, to be exact, not because of age, but because of my place in the line of succession. As Seventh, I was furthest removed from the throne; consequently, and thankfully, ignored. Not important. I had a permanent place at Court – if I wanted it – but unlike my other cousins I didn't live there, it was too dangerous for them, and for me. Not that they knew it, and not that I think they particularly wanted me there, the awkward, sword wielding princess with few manners. They thought I was odd. Weird.

But I wasn't the anomaly they all thought: the standoffish, quiet, cold Starlight Princess, with a reputation for stings and prickles. I just couldn't allow myself to relax, to be myself without fear of giving myself away. It was a burden I had become used to. But that didn't mean I liked it.

Even Kit didn't know my secret. That privilege belonged only to my mother and her brother, my Uncle Stanos, who I lived with at his estate on the coast, a day's ride from the capital. The estate where Kit's family lived and worked. But for how much longer would I be able to hide there? I'd hoped it would be forever. Having lived away from Court for so long its social scene was not something I felt comfortable with. Balls and banquets brought me out in a rash, or at the very least, made me hyperventilate. The thought of being Pledged now, having to socialise at Court, made me sick to the stomach.

'Anyway, your mother will be dying to see you again,' Kit continued unperturbed.

'She only visited us a couple of months ago,' I said, adjusting my reins, noticing my skin already beginning to burn in the sun.

'Even so–'

'As long as she doesn't try to pour me into one of those hideous silk gowns she likes to find for me to wear, it'll be fine.' They were always so difficult to hide a knife or two in.

'But you look beautiful in those dresses,' he said, a twinkle in his eye. 'You're well-endowed enough to look quite gorgeous in them.'

I scowled at him. 'They're horrible, I can't move let alone breathe in them, and I feel like a dessert on display. And you don't care if I look beautiful or not, you're too busy eyeing up the princes.'

'Like sweets in a sweet shop. All decked out in their finery but up on the top shelves. Out of my reach,' he said, a wistful note to his voice. He looked at me.

We both roared with laughter. 'All completely true though,' I said.

'Oh, yes,' he nodded, kicking his horse into a trot.

I followed after him, wiping the perspiration from my

3

brow. My deep teal suede britches were proving warm attire in the sun, and I'd already removed my dark purple suede coat, leaving just the sleeveless lilac tunic and thin white silk shirt under. And I was still hot. Our horses kicked up dust from the dry roads, insects chirped in the long grasses stretching away on either side of us as we left the coast taking a shortcut inland, birds swooping low, calling to their mates.

The day wore on, and as we rode along I mulled over my predicament. I lived out of the limelight of the Court, which suited me fine, but I'd never have the chance to be free to live as I wanted. Too dangerous. If I was injured – it didn't bear thinking about. That was one of the reasons my parents had sent me away in the first place once they knew what I was, shortly before Father had died. Uncle Stanos, a retired general from the Steorran Army, had taught me to defend myself, to fight, so if the need ever arose I could protect myself and not spill any of my blood. Because when I did, that's when all hell broke loose. I'd been lucky just now. Only one Crystal. It could've been a lot worse. Kit might have seen.

'We're here, Sorsh,' Kit said, turning towards me in his saddle. 'Sorsha, wake up. We're at the Citadel.'

I shook myself from my reverie and looked out on the sparkling white quartz city. The Starlight Citadel. Named for our Starlight Order, on our home island of Steorra. The walls surrounding the city shone in the afternoon sun, making the whole Citadel look like a gigantic pearl nestling in a velvet green shell of hills that rose behind it. The azure water of the Celestial Sea lapped against it, reflecting the sun and scattering its rays across the land like doves. The towers of the palace rose high into the sky at the centre of the Citadel, reaching for the stars themselves. My home for nigh on eighteen years.

Well, sort of.

Sometimes the isle itself felt like a safe haven from those outside, from the other islands, but on an increasing number of occasions, a gilded cage. I had to keep a low profile, stay away from excitement, from danger. From normality. But that didn't mean a part of me didn't long to escape this golden prison, long to leave this emerald island in the surrounding sapphire sea. I just couldn't, and never would.

Whatever I may want.

There were four Orders amongst the isles, each with their own ways and their own islands, known collectively as the Celestial Orders. The Moon Order to the south-west, the Sun Order to the north and the Planetary Order to our north-north-west. Historically, we hadn't always got along, so at regular intervals there were strategic unions between the Royal Families and their wider cousins, just to make sure everyone remained friends.

We Pledged ourselves to one another, rather like they got married in Merribor, and we took it very seriously. A Pledge was for life and very rarely broken; if it was, you became a kind of outcast amongst your Order. Being Pledged was the important part, viewed as being the actual exchanging of the vows between the two people, called the Pledging Oath – the legalities were secondary, unless you were of noble birth which made the signing of documents also important. And, of course, it was usually an excuse for a party. As soon as you'd both agreed and exchanged Oaths, it was official. No going back. You didn't even need a witness. Before then, being truly intimate with someone was frowned on to the point of expulsion from your family, and depending on who you were, your Order. Although, of course, you had to be found out first.

Pledging myself to someone was something I'd always intended to avoid at all costs, but it appeared my position as a Starlight Princess meant I had no escape.

Beyond our islands lay the great land of Merribor where Emperor Taliesin ruled. He didn't bother us, we didn't bother him – although we did trade our salt, fish, quartz, and precious metals with his merchants, and they provided us with food, cloth and other goods. We all got along well enough.

Sea salt lingered in the air as we trotted towards the

city gates, passing the Soul Tree. I glanced at it, and the quartz baubles glittering in the sun, placed there to remember loved ones lost at sea. One hung there for my father. I shivered as we passed it, just as I always did. The quartz came from the salt quarry not far away, and not from a Crystal Blood like me. Thank the Starlight.

We rode into the city streets, past shops where vendors yelled about their wares, and the smell of freshly baked cinnamon bread drifted into the street replacing the salty air. The reek of stale beer mixed with stew seeped out of the inns we passed, adding to the heady scent of the Citadel. At the palace we quickly dismounted, the stable boys running over to tend to our horses, our bags immediately taken to our rooms. I looked at the great steps leading up to the palace door, my palms breaking out in a cold sweat as my heart skipped in my chest like a fish trying to escape a net. I took a deep breath and led the way, heading to the throne room to find my mother. At this time of day the whole Court assembled there to catch up on the latest gossip, as well as important news.

'Would you stop gawping at all the young men? It's embarrassing,' I said quietly, digging Kit in the ribs as we entered the great chamber and looked around to see who was here to pay homage today. Cream marble covered the walls of the throne room arching up to the ceiling where silver and gold leaf shone in the early evening sun reaching in from the glass skylights. The black granite floor glistened with flecks of white quartz that caught the light and sparkled like stars, making you feel as if you walked amongst the very galaxies themselves.

'You're having a fairly good look yourself,' Kit said, an indignant note to his voice.

'That's different – I don't know why, but it is,' I said primly. 'Besides, I've not been here for a year and there're some new faces.'

I scanned the room. Right in the middle stood my cousins, the Starlight Princesses Aster and Phoebe, chattering away and smiling sweetly at a gaggle of young men that stood in thrall around them. The princesses were dressed in lovely silver silk dresses that caught the light and shimmered like starlight. Aster's beautiful, wavy brown hair was piled high on top of her head, while Phoebe held herself gracefully, laughing lightly at the young men's jokes. I glanced down at my clothes and dusty boots, an errant curl falling in front of my eyes. They both put me to shame. I screwed my nose up at their beauty and grace. I'd never be anything like them. I didn't have an elegant bone in my body.

Making sure we kept to the edge of the room, I didn't want to be drawn into any unnecessary conversations, we skirted the courtiers. I glanced around the throne room wondering where Mother was; perhaps she was still in her rooms, maybe I should go and see, although if I did I'd find one of those damn dresses waiting for me.

'That's Prince Etienne,' Kit said, stopping and pointing.

'Who?'

'Prince Etienne of the Sun Order. I wonder what he's doing here.'

'The heir?' I asked, trying to get a look between guests in the direction Kit was indicating. There on the periphery stood a tall, broad shouldered, proud looking young man. He was maybe a year or two older than me – a couple of years younger than Kit. He brushed his tousled, dark blond hair from his eyes, hair that was quite long enough to rake your fingers through with ease, although not quite long enough for him to tie back. His tanned skin spoke of time spent outside, and shone in the sunlight cascading down from the skylights. He was richly dressed and looked incredibly handsome, in fact, he was probably the most handsome young man I'd ever seen, even outdoing my cousin, Prince Taran, and that was saying something.

I narrowed my eyes as I looked at him. The Orders may be friends now, but we still treated each other with a certain amount of suspicion, or at least I did, but I had good reason to treat everyone with suspicion and keep them at arm's length.

'No, the youngest son,' Kit said. 'Rumour has it he's a Red.'

'A Red? A Red Crystal Blood?' My heart froze. *Starlight*, would he sense me?

Kit nodded vigorously. 'Although there's no proof. I imagine he'd want to keep it a secret if it was true.'

'It's an amazing power to have, if you can use it,' I said.

Kit frowned. 'Wouldn't that make him want to keep it secret even more? I mean, wouldn't people want to exploit it? Exploit *him,* if it were true?'

I gave a little shrug. 'Not really. A single colour Blood like him wouldn't be in particular danger – no one can use his blood unless they have a Pellucid Crystal.'

'You're well informed.'

'I'm a princess, Kit.' I grinned smugly at him.

'I forget so easily,' he said, grinning back at me as his gaze drifted to my paired swords.

'I wish they all would.' I nodded at the crowd around us.

'Not much chance now, I'm afraid. What's a Pellucid Crystal, anyway?'

I winced, shifting uneasily. I'd hoped he wouldn't ask. I'd probably said too much already. 'Pellucids are rare,' I said eventually. 'You can only get them from Double Bloods.'

'I've heard of Double Bloods, but I didn't know about Pellucids.' He shuffled his feet and rubbed his left eyebrow. 'Doubles are supposed to be mythical, now, aren't they?'

If only he knew.

'That's what they say. Anyway, a Single Blood is useless without a Double Blood's Pellucid.'

'Then it's a good thing they don't exist anymore,' Kit said. 'Being a Double Blood would be incredibly dangerous. I guess Prince Etienne's fairly safe, then.' He jabbed his chin in the direction of the Sun Prince.

I looked back towards Etienne. 'Yes, he's safe.'

Prince Etienne glanced my way, and I realised he was

speaking to Taran. My blood ran cold. Taran looked at me, grinned a rather unpleasant grin even by his standards, and guided Prince Etienne towards me. My cousin obviously thought he'd sport with me again, but I really wasn't in the mood.

'Taran's bringing Prince Etienne over,' I hissed to Kit, searching for a way out amongst the throng as my heart hammered in my chest like a blacksmith at his anvil. The room became slightly shimmery, sparkly even – I hated it when that happened. 'I have to get out.'

Kit shuddered. 'It's too late to run.'

I groaned.

'Cousin, how lovely to see you again,' Taran said, his eyes sparkling with glee as he took my hand and kissed it with his thin lips, his long, black hair falling forwards, brushing my fingers. I swiftly stepped back, my skin crawling at his touch. He may like to assume an air of charm, but he never ceased to be cruel and vicious to me. Always had some game he was playing, usually one that involved teasing and taunting me in some way for his own amusement.

Although we were cousins, the connection was quite a distant one. He was twenty, still to be Pledged – Starlight Princes were Pledged later than the princesses – and a very handsome young man. What's more, he knew it. He liked to flirt with all the eligible girls, and a few of the ineligible ones too. His efforts always fell flat with me, which only helped to encourage him, but I never had any intention of melting into a giggling heap to massage his ego. He definitely wasn't my type. Not that I was entirely sure what my type was. I mulled it over for a second as I ran my gaze slowly over Prince Etienne. My chest tightened.

'It's been too long – a year, again?' Taran asked. 'We miss you at Court so much, you should really move back here, a beautiful ornament to enrich our humdrum everyday lives.'

'Still alive, Cousin? I thought the Planetary Order might have caught up with you by now, after your latest little stunt,' I said, relishing the look of annoyance that flickered in his eyes. Yes, I'd hit a nerve but it served him right. Even at my uncle's, news of my cousin's exploits filtered through – besides, he shouldn't smuggle.

'No need to be so prickly, Sorsha,' he said, eyes narrowing, vein fluttering in his neck. 'May I introduce Prince Etienne of the Sun Order,' he said, regaining his composure and moving his hands with a flourish. 'Prince Etienne, this is my most adorable cousin, the Starlight Princess, Sorsha.'

The Prince raised an eyebrow. 'One of the Seven Starlight Princesses?' he asked, taking my hand and kissing it.

The smell of Purple Vetiver Grass swept around me. The bunchgrass, that grew all across the Celestial Isles, gave off a scent like cut-grass that was both rich and warm, with woody notes that made it quite intoxicating. This time, as Prince Etienne kissed my hand, tingles swept up my arm. I snatched my hand away in surprise. My heart skipped as he looked at me through his blond hair – a completely different sensation to the one I'd just experienced with Taran.

'I can't say you're dressed like a Starlight Princess,' the Sun Prince continued, a lopsided grin appearing on his face reaching to his turquoise eyes that would have sparkled in quite an alluring fashion if he hadn't annoyed me with his slightly haughty, proud manner.

'Don't worry. She's just been away from Court for a while, that's all. Once her mother gets hold of her she'll be dressed like all the other princesses here, hair done, and looking as beautiful and painted as any doll in this chamber,' Taran said, a mocking look in his eyes as he waved his hand around the room.

I glowered at him. He knew full well that even with a dress on and my hair done, I'd still look nothing like the other princesses. They were all far more poised, elegant and of course, practised, than I was. I was socially awkward and graceless in comparison, and a little bit of me was embarrassed by it – and Taran didn't just know that, but took as much advantage of it as he could.

'Unfortunately, I'm sorry to say you've caught me on my day off, Prince Etienne,' I said, giving the Sun Prince a wan little smile.

'Prince Etienne is being Pledged to one of the Starlight Princesses,' Taran said. 'I hear the one chosen for you is graceful and beautiful beyond compare, Your Highness, you'll have no worries there,' he said, smiling at Etienne and waving his hands around again in an extremely irritating fashion. 'She'll be exquisite.'

'You must both excuse me,' I said. 'I need to find my mother. I haven't seen her since my return to Court and she'll be keen to see me. Let's go, Kit.'

'Not so quick, Sorsha,' Taran said, grabbing my left wrist. 'Rumour has it your mother has arranged your Pledging, too.'

I tensed. Did everyone know?

'I wasn't aware it was common knowledge yet,' I said stiffly.

He grinned the smuggest grin I'd ever seen. 'I have my spies. What I can't begin to imagine is where she found someone stupid enough to take you on.'

I caught Etienne frowning at Taran – he obviously didn't approve of the Starlight Prince's behaviour.

Kit took a step forward. 'Take that back.'

I threw my free arm out to stop him from getting any closer to Taran. He may be good with a sword, but my cousin was better.

Taran chuckled. 'Worried you're going to lose your job, Kit?'

'I suggest you stop now while you still can, Cousin,' I said, getting more annoyed by the moment, especially as his grip on me seemed to be intensifying. If he carried on like this I'd have a bruise.

Taran looked back at me. 'I'm trying to work out who would willingly and knowingly take on a sword-wielding, awkward, country bumpkin-princess like you. I bet whoever it is doesn't know it's *you* who he's being Pledged to,' Taran continued. 'How delightful. I can't wait to fill him in on all the delicious details about you once we

11

know who he is.' He leant towards me. 'By the time I'm finished giving him the particulars, he'll loathe the thought of being Pledged to you. He'll hate every single minute he has to endure in your company, let alone in your bed.'

I snapped.

My right hand still free, I slipped my dagger from my waist and swiftly held it to Taran's throat, the muscles under my blade now quivering as his eyes widened with shock and his face blanched. He let go of me.

'I suggest while I'm at Court you stay away from me from now on,' I said, steely voiced. 'I also suggest you never, ever speak to the man they Pledge me to or your life expectancy will be greatly reduced, and that will be without any help from the Planetary Order.'

Taran swallowed. 'People are looking,' he hissed.

'Let them. Now, have we reached an understanding?'

He tried to nod, but gave up with the knife resting at his throat. 'Yes, Cousin.'

'Excellent.' I slipped the knife back into its sheath. 'Well, this was an unpleasant diversion and I can't say it's been nice to see you again, Taran dear, but I must go to my mother now,' I said, giving him one final scowl before turning to the Sun Prince, whose eyes looked as if they were about to pop out of his head. 'Prince Etienne, it was lovely to meet you.'

The prince's turquoise eyes clouded, then began to sparkle as he looked at me, one side of his mouth quirking up in a little lopsided smile. 'And you, Princess,' he said, nodding and giving me a little bow. Taran should take notes from the Sun Prince.

I turned and headed towards the garden door, Kit following in my wake.

'I'm impressed at your restraint,' Kit said. 'I'd have killed him for that.'

'Which is why I held you back,' I said.

'He gets worse every time we see him,' Kit muttered.

'I don't know why. I've done nothing to him,' I said, scratching my head in frustration.

'I just think he enjoys winding you up. But being

chastised like that in front of the whole Court? I think that will have him backing off for at least a while.'

'Let's hope so.'

'Princess Sorsha. Good, you're here!' Dexan, the King's Chamberlain, swept towards me.

My heart lurched. All I wanted to do was get out of here and escape to the peace of my mother's rooms.

'Princess, the King requests your presence in his Council Chamber immediately.' Dexan turned away from me and scurried over to Prince Etienne who stood with a bemused expression on his face as he stared after me. 'Your Royal Highness,' he said, bowing to the prince. 'King Finnar will see you now.'

'Thank you, Chamberlain.' The Prince nodded as Taran raised an eyebrow.

'This way.'

Now what? I didn't wait. Casting Kit a pained sidelong glance, I headed straight for the Council Chamber, threading my way through the richly dressed courtiers who gave me slightly disapproving looks as they noticed my attire – or was it my weapons?

What did Finnar want with me? The King hardly ever asked to see me, and why now when this foreign prince was here?

I hadn't even seen Mother yet.

I marched into the Council Chamber, Kit pausing at the door, and walked over towards where my cousin, Finnar, stood. To one side sat the King's desk, covered in papers and books, and on the left of it, wedged between a heap of parchment and a scroll, sat a small rose made of silver with sparkling purple crystals covering its petals.

The Amaranthine Rose.

One of the Steorran Relics. Rumour had it the crystals were from a Blood, but I had no idea if that was true or not. What I did know was that I'd been attached to it since I first laid eyes on it as a four-year-old child, mesmerised by its beautiful deep purple gemstones that twisted light around them making it appear as if they glowed with some sort of internal light in their silver setting. It was the oldest and greatest Relic of the Starlight Order.

King Finnar stood at his grand central table, studying a map. A noise on the other side of the room made me look over. An official was ushering my mother out the far door. She had a frantic look on her face, which only magnified when she caught sight of me. She began to gesture, but the official firmly steered her out the door. I glanced back to Kit who nodded, and disappeared into the throng of courtiers.

'Sorsha, good to see you,' Finnar said, turning and giving me a hug.

'Finnar, you look well,' I said, flinching as his short goatee beard scratched my cheek.

He grinned at me, his brown hair glistening in the sun streaming in the windows. 'I think I might have a job for you.'

My blood ran cold. 'A job? For me?' He'd never asked anything of me before – how could I refuse?

He nodded, then looked towards Prince Etienne who had entered the chamber. 'Prince Etienne, it's a pleasure to finally meet you in person.'

The prince bowed, moving his hair from his eyes as he stood straight. 'Your Majesty. My grandmother spoke of you often.'

'She was my grandfather's favourite sister,' Finnar said. 'We should have met before.' Dexan closed the chamber door and the noise from the Throne Room receded. 'Now, you're having trouble contacting the Moon Order?'

Etienne hesitated a moment, glancing at me.

'Sorsha is here to help – please, tell me what you know,' Finnar pressed.

I was there to help? I was there to visit Mother and pay my annual visit to the Court, not help with some diplomatic job and some foreign, slightly haughty, prince.

Etienne nodded. 'My aunt was supposed to visit from the Moon Order over two weeks ago, now. Sometimes things are delayed – bad weather, logistics – there were storms around at the time, so we weren't surprised by a short delay of a few days but, hell, we've heard nothing from the island at all in that time. They aren't that sociable normally, I know, but Luna do trade with us and we usually have a merchant vessel reach Helios City once a fortnight, but there's been no sign of any Lunan ships for a while. My father's starting to worry. Have you heard from them, Your Majesty?'

Finnar scratched his beard. 'No. It's been a similar length of time since we heard from them. I'd begun to get concerned myself – as you say, they like to keep themselves to themselves, but we still trade with them as well. There have been no ships putting in here, either.'

'I see.' Etienne nodded, chewing his lip. 'My father tasked me with visiting Luna to make sure all was well, but I thought I'd stop in here on the way to see if you had any news.'

'Unfortunately not,' Finnar said, shaking his head. 'In fact I was already thinking of sending a small delegation – a couple of people – to check things were well. If I sent many more the Moon Order could take offence.'

'Indeed.' Etienne smiled. 'Which is why Father sent me and one other to "visit" my aunt to check she was well.'

'In that case I suggest you continue on your journey, and if I may, I will send Princess Sorsha with you to act as my representative – our cousin, the Second Starlight Princess Ephyna, may be in need of assistance.'

'Princess Sorsha?' Etienne asked, raising a questioning eyebrow.

'We will present it as a family visit, so the Moon Order won't query it,' Finnar said.

Etienne nodded. 'I suppose that is true – a young princess visiting her cousin is of no threat.'

Really? I'd like to have a moment alone with this prince and show him exactly how I was no threat.

'Although, as it happens, Princess Sorsha has a particular skill set that may be of use,' Finnar said.

'Diplomacy?' Etienne asked, raising an eyebrow as he looked me up and down.

'Hardly,' I muttered under my breath. Diplomacy wasn't a word people tended to use around me.

Finnar gave me a long look before turning back to Etienne. 'She can fight better than any man on this island.'

'She can?' Etienne looked at me in surprise, glancing at the swords on my back. 'Maybe I should've guessed.'

I shrugged. 'Misspent youth,' I said.

'If you get into a tight situation you'll be glad she was with you,' Finnar said.

Damn. How could this be happening? I'd been trained so I could stay *out* of trouble, not get into it. Mother would have kittens – but perhaps she already knew; she had given me a very funny look when she left the Council Chamber.

'Take Kit with you, Sorsha, he can help,' Finnar said. 'I suggest you all rest tonight and leave first thing in the morning.'

I nodded. It didn't matter what Finnar had said, Kit would come with me whatever.

Etienne bowed to Finnar and turned to me. 'I look forward to seeing you in the morning, Princess Sorsha.'

I sighed. This wasn't supposed to be happening.

Chapter Two

'Starlight, I don't know why he's asked you to go now,' Mother said, her braided hair glistening in the morning sunlight streaming through her chamber window. 'I tried to persuade him not to send you, but he wouldn't listen. Instead he said it would be good for you.'

Overnight I'd come to view my impending voyage with a mixture of annoyance, terror and excitement. Escaping the island had always been an impossible dream, but it had become a sudden reality. A reality I now wasn't sure I wanted, yet craved in equal measure. I'd always got on well with Ephyna, so seeing her would actually be quite pleasant, as long as I could navigate any Moon Court nonsense.

'It'll be fine,' I said. 'We won't be gone long, although I had hoped to spend some time with you properly.'

Mother smiled. 'You want to try more dresses?'

I cringed. 'No. I just miss you, that's all. Uncle's wonderful, but I miss being able to talk to you about things. You know, girl things.'

'I miss that too,' she said with a little sigh. 'But we both know this has been the safest thing for you.'

I nodded. 'Maybe we'll get some time together once I get back.'

'Hopefully, at least a little while. There are things I'd like to tell you before you're Pledged. I hadn't expected this to happen, that Finnar would even consider sending you off like this, but we have to accept his decision. He *is* King of Steorra. I just don't like it.'

'I'm not sure I do either. I'd rather be here with you, even if it does mean wearing dresses,' I said, scrunching my nose up.

Mother frowned. 'Dresses aren't that bad, and you look lovely in them.'

I snorted. 'They just highlight my lack of elegance.'

'Rubbish. You give yourself too little credit.'

'Maybe,' I shrugged.

Mother suddenly grabbed my hand. 'Promise me you'll be careful, promise me you won't take any unnecessary risks.'

'Of course I won't,' I said. *I'm not stupid.* I knew full well what was at stake here. Me.

Mother nodded slowly, letting go of me. 'Kit will look after you.'

'I have a feeling it'll be the other way around,' I murmured, adjusting my weapons and picking up my pack.

'I've received another letter about your Pledging,' she said, lifting up a piece of parchment from a side table. 'It's all settled. The Pledging documents have been sent to the priestesses at the Celestial Temple for their Official Records. As soon as you get back here from Luna Isle you'll need to get ready to leave for your new home.'

I froze. 'My what?'

'You'll still be living on Steorra, don't worry,' Mother said. 'I've arranged for the prince to live here, rather than you going back to his island, as is the usual custom. I said I couldn't do without you, and I think it will be safer for you to remain on Steorra, so we'll still get time together. Finnar's found you a lovely country villa a few miles out of the Citadel, so you can still safely avoid the majority of Court life.'

And the prince agreed to that?

'Nothing about this is safe for me,' I said, clenching my teeth. 'Why do I have to be Pledged at all?'

'You know it's our custom. By eighteen all Starlight Princesses must be Pledged. There's no way out of it, even for you in your position, and time is running out for you. I tried to stop it. Believe me, I did, but there was nothing I could do, especially not without revealing your secret.'

'And I'll have to keep it from my husband too? How do you propose I do that?'

'I'm hoping the prince will leave you alone as much as possible. I'm arranging for Finnar to give him a position at Court that will see him kept busy and off the island as much as possible.'

'How can I be Pledged to someone I don't even know?' I asked, balling a fist. 'I mean, I might not even like him.'

'We've been through this before, Sorsha,' Mother said, giving me a chastising look. 'You have no choice in the matter. You'll have to make the best of things, and in time, you may come to like him – love him, even.'

'I highly doubt that. I don't see why I can't be left alone, find my own husband in time. Someone I love.'

'A love match?' Mother laughed. 'No Starlight Princess has had a love match in two hundred years. Like me and your father, you will marry as your mother and the prince's parents, see fit; you both will. And you will learn to accept it, the same way I did when I married your father without knowing him at all. We met the day we were Pledged. At least you'll have an advantage.'

I looked at her and frowned. 'Advantage? What do you mean?'

Bare knuckles rapped at the oak door.

'Yes?' Mother called.

'Is Princess Sorsha ready?' Kit asked, peering into the room. 'It's time to go.'

'Coming, Kit,' I said. 'Mother, did you and Father ever love each other? *Really* love each other?'

Mother looked at me, a little frown on her face. 'To begin with, no. It took us several years before we fell for one another. By the time you arrived… yes. We were truly in love.'

I chewed my lip and nodded.

'Now, stop worrying,' she said.

I twirled an errant curl around my finger before hefting my pack over my shoulder. 'Who is he? The prince? Where's he from?'

She stepped towards me and took my hand. 'I can't tell you yet. Finnar wants to wait until your return, then I'll explain everything to you.'

'Whoever it is, it better not be Taran.'

Mother laughed. 'Of course it's not Taran, girl, you

know you're being Pledged to a prince from another isle. We don't want intermarrying going on within the family. When they last practiced that they had to put a stop to it – the children started going a little funny.'

'Hmm.'

'You might like your prince, you know.'

'I might not.'

'Try and keep an open mind, and when you return, I'll introduce him to you properly.'

Kit coughed. 'We need to get going, Sorsh, or we'll miss the tide.'

Mother bit her lip; never a good sign. 'Everything will be fine, Sorsha.'

I sighed. Maybe Taran was right. Marrying the mysterious Seventh Starlight Princess who was never at Court, and had the manners of a near peasant, wasn't every Celestial Isle's Prince's dream of a lifelong partner. I just hoped he wouldn't hate me once he found out who he was being Pledged to. If he had any sense at all he'd try and get out of it as soon as possible, for both our sakes.

'Sorsh!' Kit tapped his fingers on the door.

'All right,' I nodded and turned back to Mother. 'I'll be back before you know it,' I said, kissing her on the cheek.

'You better be,' Mother said, patting my shoulder, her face pale and creased. 'And don't worry… I really do think you'll grow to like him. Maybe even love–'

'Let's hope so, because I'm going to have to spend the rest of my life with him,' I muttered, before walking over to the door.

'*Try* and get on with Prince Etienne, won't you?'

'It'll be a long journey if she doesn't,' Kit said, screwing his face up.

I scowled at him, then gave Mother a little wave before following Kit out into the labyrinth of passageways of the Starlight Palace.

#

The open sea and I were not friends.

Could I swim? Yes, in fact I was quite good.

Could I sail around the inlets of Steorra in a little yacht? No problem.

Could I sail out in open water? Forget it.

The moment a ship went out beyond the inshore waters my stomach twisted and I hurled up everything in it. It wasn't content until it was totally empty.

'It's all psychological,' Kit had told me helpfully when I was twelve and we'd been out on a serenely calm sea in my uncle's yacht and my stomach had rebelled.

'Nonsense,' I'd said, and I still firmly believed this. It was seasickness, pure and simple.

The open sea and I were not friends. Psychology had nothing to do with it.

I tore my eyes from the breaking waves where I stood at the bow of the ship, and glanced back over towards the main cabin entrance. Etienne stood talking to a young woman, a sword at his waist, dark blond hair shifting in the breeze. He glanced at me, and nodded. His companion's golden skin glistened in the sunlight, her braided, light blonde hair shining, and her grey-blue eyes as clear and piercing as a mountain lake. On her finger she had a silver ring with a deep blue stone in it, as blue as the sky on a summer's day, that she twisted absently around her finger. Her tunic and leggings were highly embroidered with silver and gold thread; despite the rich colours of my own clothing, I looked a little less than regal next to her. Who she was, I didn't know, didn't really care, but she carried a sword and dagger and hadn't left Etienne's side since I'd first seen them arrive on deck. They were obviously close, whoever she was.

The ship's captain, Lucian, walked over to them and started talking. I turned away and watched the pearly Starlight Citadel disappearing in the distance as we followed the coast south-west. I stood on deck watching the shoreline slide by as the sun rose high in the sky, gulls soaring and crying a song of longing overhead, the bow of the creaking wooden ship cutting through the gentle waves like a knife, salty spray lifting into the air so I could taste it on my tongue. Being out on deck helped me to feel better than being stuck down below in the cabins as the ship gently rolled and the wind filled the great sails. My breakfast had long since disappeared overboard, and my empty stomach ached, although that could've been more due to the retching than being empty.

I adjusted the weapons on my back, the scabbards catching on each other. The training with my uncle had been relentless. He'd made me practice over and over until my movements had become ingrained into my mind and into my muscles to the point where I didn't have to think and my responses were instinct. I didn't have to think what to do in any given situation. I just did it.

I'd learnt to fight, learnt not to freeze when attacked, learnt to ignore the pain of a punch or a kick, learnt to push through it, learnt to use kicks, how to use elbows, learnt to hit nothing higher than the waist – no point in overbalancing yourself or making it easier for your opponent to knock you over. I'd learnt to endure bruises and strains; above all learnt when not to fight, and when to run.

'How's the stomach, Sorsh?' Kit asked, joining me at the rail as the sun began to reach for the horizon.

'How you'd expect,' I said, suddenly realising the coast had vanished while I'd stared into space, and water now surrounded us on all sides as far as I could see to the very horizon. The blue cloak of the sea welcomed us into its midst.

'Do you fancy any supper?'

I shook my head, screwing up my nose. 'Don't think I'll risk it. Thanks though.'

'All right,' Kit said, nodding. He looked out over the water. 'Have you spoken to Prince Etienne or Lady Amalia yet?'

'No.'

'You should. They're both really quite nice…'

'For the Sun Order?' I asked, a grin playing on my lips.

He smiled. 'Something like that.'

'Who is she, this Lady Amalia?'

'She's the prince's cousin and bodyguard.'

'Bodyguard? They must be more enlightened on Solis than Steorra.'

Kit raised an eyebrow. 'And what about you, Sorsh? Stood there in your britches and swords?'

'That's entirely different,' I said turning away. 'I'm different.'

'Well, maybe she is, too.'

I shrugged. 'Perhaps.'

'She's a lady, not a princess, though.'

'What about him, what's he like? A haughty, stubborn, self-centred Sun Prince?'

Kit looked at me. 'You really don't like him, do you?'

'I don't know him,' I said, sighing. 'I just know our collective history.'

'He's not at all haughty. Maybe a little suspicious of us, being from a different Order. Rather like you in that way. But he doesn't come across as entitled. You may have misjudged him.'

'We'll see,' I said, sniffing. 'You know your problem? You like everyone.'

Kit buffed his fingernails on his tunic. 'So? I think it's better to give people the benefit of the doubt. Innocent 'til proven guilty.'

'Hmm, maybe'.

'Try it, Sorsh. You may be surprised. Try and be more open to people. Trust them more, wherever they're from.'

'Maybe.' *But he didn't have to protect my secret.* 'Does that include Taran?' I asked slyly.

Kit grinned. 'I make an exception in his case,' he said, wandering off chuckling.

I sighed, watching him go. Not for the first time I wished I could be more like him – relaxed in company, easy-going and laid-back. Something I'd never achieved and probably never would.

I managed to avoid the two Solisians until the following morning when they came out on deck. I tried to hide at the stern, but it didn't last long before they cornered me.

'Prince Etienne,' I said, giving him an awkward half curtsey, my palms breaking out in a cold sweat.

He bowed. 'Princess, I'd like to introduce my cousin and bodyguard, Lady Amalia,' Prince Etienne said, gesturing to the young woman beside him. Up close I judged her to be a year or so older than the prince. There was a fierceness to her eyes, or maybe the protectiveness of an older cousin.

'It's a pleasure to meet you, Princess Sorsha,' Amalia said, nodding. 'I've heard a lot about you.'

'You have?' That made me nervous and my heart started to nudge uncomfortably at my ribcage, trying to get out.

'Your friend, Kit, has been telling us all about you.'

I bet he had. I'd be having a word with him later. Sometimes he could be a little loose-lipped. 'Really? I'm not particularly interesting, I'm afraid.'

'On the contrary, a princess who lives away from the Court and instead of taking part in Royal activities learns to fight, is very interesting,' Prince Etienne said, a strange look in his deep turquoise eyes.

I looked into them, trying to work out if he meant it or was being facetious like Taran.

'Another woman who can fight is something I'm pleased to see,' Amalia said, her icy eyes softening. 'I've never met another.'

'Neither have I,' I said. 'Anomalies in a male-dominated world.'

She grinned. 'Aren't we? Although I hear there's a land far to the east where the women rule over the men.'

'Really? I quite like the sound of that,' I said, warming to this young Solisian woman.

'You're impossible,' Prince Etienne said, elbowing his cousin in the ribs. 'It's just myth.'

'Poppycock, and not necessarily, Eti,' Amalia said, an indignant note to her voice. 'And one day I intend to find out.'

'I'll come with you, Lady Amalia,' I said, grinning.

'Call me Amalia,' she said, shifting her sleeve, a tattoo

of the sun poking out on her left wrist. 'And call him Etienne – all this formality when we're alone is plain daft.'

Prince Etienne raised an eyebrow.

'What?' Amalia asked, looking at Etienne. 'We're not at Court, we're not in a formal setting, relax.'

Etienne shrugged. 'Fine.'

'Then you'd better call me Sorsha,' I said – no point in being deliberately stand-offish, even if I was still suspicious of them. I had no basis for this other than Order history, and Amalia appeared nice enough. There was something about Etienne, though, something I couldn't put my finger on that made him seem somewhat reserved, distant; holding back in some way that Amalia wasn't.

I spent the day watching the breaking waves, swooping gulls and chatting to Kit. The Solisians stayed mainly below deck and I didn't see them again until the next morning, which suited me fine. Talking with Kit was like talking with close family, with a brother – or what I imagined talking with a brother would be like – but anyone else, particularly in a formal setting? My palms would break out in a cold sweat, my heart would start to pound, the room would go all shimmery and sparkly, and sometimes I'd get this weird out of body experience as if I were watching through a pane of glass, not really there, and yet still interacting with the conversation. I didn't like the sensations. So I did my best to avoid social situations or having to talk to strangers. Hence my once a year, and once a year only, visits to the Citadel. I grinned and bore it for two weeks a year, returning home to my uncle's estate drained and exhausted. I hated the visits really, but I did it for Mother; she was convinced that otherwise the Court would forget who I was, not that I minded much, but I was a Starlight Princess after all. I had no choice.

Amalia came out on deck and stretched. She noticed me at the rail, smiled, and came over towards me. Looked like I was going to have to indulge in some polite conversation.

'Good morning,' she said, looking out over the water. 'Not sure I like the look of those clouds out there.'

I followed her gaze. Out on the western horizon huddled a group of black clouds, dark and foreboding.

'Perhaps they'll just drift off,' I said, hopefully. My seasickness was bad enough without a storm.

'Maybe.' She leant with her back against the rail. 'How many Starlight Princesses are there?'

'How many?' I asked, surprised at her question. 'Seven.'

She nodded slowly.

'Why?' I asked.

'Eti is about to be Pledged to a Starlight Princess.'

I nodded. 'I'd heard that. Do you know which one?' I asked. I knew Lyra's match was about to be announced – perhaps it was her.

'One of the younger ones, I think, I'm not sure which,' Amalia said. 'Although I think he does, her title at least, but he's been sworn to secrecy until it's made public. You know what Royalty are like with their Pledges – great secrets until they're formally announced.'

I nodded. It couldn't be Lyra, then. Of the seven of us I was in the middle, age wise, Lyra a couple of months older than me. Rather like me, she'd resisted being Pledged for as long as she could, but now her eighteenth birthday was upon her and she'd finally had to give in to the pressure. Her intended was quite handsome, by all accounts, but I didn't know who.

Selene and Phoebe were the youngest, but I hadn't heard it was one of them, and they were a year younger than me, and although not unheard of to be Pledged at that age, they were still a bit young. Then there was Aster. She was six months my junior. She was the most likely candidate.

I knew Etienne couldn't be *my* mystery prince – Taran had made that quite clear by indicating he knew who the Sun Prince's match was – and anyway, the Royalty of the Sun Isle had always been quite particular about who their sons were married to. Not a chance in all of Starlight that it would be the infamous Seventh Starlight Princess; it must be Aster.

'He hasn't even told you?' I asked, surprised.

Amalia shook her head. 'No. It's more than his life's worth. Not that I think it really matters much, it's being announced soon, anyway. He's not looking forward to it at all. Dreading it, in fact. But he has no choice, in his position, and because of that position, knowing he'd have his Pledging arranged one day, he's never looked at a girl. At least not in that way. You can't really, can you? When you know your life is going to be arranged for you – there's no point. Not to mention the fact his father would have hit the roof.'

'What about you?'

'Me?'

'Shouldn't you be Pledged by now?'

She grimaced. 'I'm not a princess like you, so the Royal Rules don't apply to me in quite the same way. I have until I'm twenty-two, so I've still got a couple of years to find a love-match before they find me someone instead.'

I sighed. 'That would be nice. To be Pledged to someone you actually loved.'

She raised an eyebrow. 'You're being forced into it?'

I laughed a bitter little laugh. 'Of course I am. I'm almost eighteen. My time has run out.'

'I'm sorry,' she said, bowing her head. 'Being a Sun Prince, Eti has until his twenty-first birthday to be Pledged, like all the Celestial Isle Princes. He's just under two years from that, but his father decided to do it early so all his sons were Pledged and he didn't have to worry about arranging any more unions... It's a bit cold out here, I'm going back to the cabin. See you later.'

I nodded and she disappeared into the ship. I turned back to look at the black clouds. There was a reason why small boats never made the crossing from Luna to Steorra; the weather and the currents. The weather was unpredictable and the currents too much for small vessels, even if they took a roundabout route. They were torn to shreds out on the water, and so only larger ships like Captain Lucian's ever made the journey.

I leant on the rail. I sympathised with Etienne and his predicament. From what Amalia said I could narrow down my possible future husband to a Prince of Luna or Planetae, seeing as Etienne's brothers were already Pledged and he was destined for one of my younger cousins. I knew nothing much about the princes of either Order, and I now regretted paying such little attention when Mother had spoken of them. However, from what she'd said, I wouldn't have to wait long to meet him. A little shiver worked its way down my spine.

'Are you always this prickly?' Etienne asked from behind me making me jump. He came and stood beside me, a lopsided grin on his face that made my heart do some strange little flip.

'Sorry?' I asked.

'You don't go out of your way to be friendly,' he said.

I took a long breath. 'Depends on who it is,' I said. 'Kit says I should be more tolerant.'

A smile crept into Etienne's eyes. 'Maybe you should.'

The wind ruffled his hair as the sun set it alight, making his gorgeous eyes almost seem to glow. My heart skipped a beat, and not because of anxiety. What was I thinking? Being more tolerant was one thing, but I couldn't afford to let my guard down that much.

'I was beginning to think you were avoiding me,' Etienne said, gripping the ship's rail as we hit a big wave.

He'd seen straight through me. 'No, of course not, I just feel better out on deck, that's all.'

'Hmm... I thought you were staying away from me?'

'Now why would I do that?'

'I don't get the impression you like to talk much, at least, not to people you don't know – and sometimes even to those you do,' he said, glancing at me. 'I thought you handled Prince Taran very well, by the way. I heard what he said to you – I'm sure your Pledged won't loathe being with you. Taran is just a real bastard.'

I raised an eyebrow. 'Really? Most people think

Taran's the most charming and affable person they've ever come across.'

Etienne shrugged. 'It's a veneer. He's the sort who takes in most people he meets.'

'But not you?'

Etienne grinned. 'No, not me. I realised what he was like the moment I met him.'

The Sun Prince's perceptiveness unnerved me slightly. What else could he see?

'Good for you.' I paused, glancing out at the slowly dissipating clouds. 'It's true I'm not the most outgoing of people – I guess I just enjoy my own company.'

'Me too, I'd rather keep to myself,' he said, leaning on the rail and gazing out to sea. His hair shifted into his eyes and for some strange, brief moment, I wanted to reach out and move it away. 'Much better to stay on the fringes, don't you think?'

It was a place I knew well, one I usually rejoiced in, but sometimes, wished I didn't.

I frowned. 'How can you do that when you're a king's son?' I asked.

He shrugged. 'I'm one of many. Not the heir. Neither am I one of the older sons. They were all given roles, but not me. I think I was an accident. My parents never meant to have me, and so I honestly think I was a bit of an embarrassment to them. I got pushed to one side quite quickly. Guess I've become used to it over time, and it suits me now.'

'Being at the edges of things? I know how you feel,' I murmured.

He turned and looked at me. 'Yes,' he said, his eyes searching mine. 'I think you do.'

Chapter Three

I hated every minute of the rolling ship's voyage. This was our sixth day at sea, and I was loathing each sickening moment of it. I'd managed to eat, but I had to do it little and often. Despite my difficulty, Etienne and Amalia had proved to be engaging companions, and I'd got to know them a little now, as well as something about their home isle. Kit spent his time looking smugly at me.

The coastline of north-western Luna was finally coming into sight, but all I could see across the horizon were angry clouds rolling towards us.

'Sir, sir, bad weather ahead, Captain!' one of the sailors shouted, running past me as he saw the same advancing storm. A bolt of lightning stabbed at the sea like a fisherman stabbing into the water with his spear, desperate to catch his next meal.

'Starlight, that's all we need,' I muttered.

'Doesn't bode well, does it?' Etienne asked, squinting at the clouds. He'd been standing beside me, silently watching the clouds for a while.

My stomach churned at the prospect of a storm. 'No, it doesn't.'

Captain Lucian came over to us. 'I don't like the look of that weather,' he said. 'I'm going to put in on the north-west coast – there's a fishing town with a small harbour where we can wait this monster out. It's the only harbour on Luna Isle that can take a ship our size, other than the capital. With any luck we'll make it there before this thing arrives, in fact, we might manage to miss it entirely.'

Etienne nodded. 'By the Sun, I'd rather not be out at sea in a storm like that.'

'No indeed, Your Highness, it's not a pretty sight.' The Captain strode off across the deck issuing orders as he went.

'Let's tell the others,' Etienne said, moving back towards the cabin.

#

A short while later, we'd reached the small fishing town that Captain Lucian had spoken of, and the ship lay safely inside the arms of the harbour walls. Out to sea, roiling black clouds jettisoned their lightning into the water with ferocious regularity. From the look of the distant waves, I was glad to be in the harbour. A curtain of rain swept across the sea and inland, shrouding everything in its gauzy veil. We would be stuck here until high tide tomorrow morning now.

I sat listening to the rain tapping away on the deck above my head, for a while hammering down like a relentless blacksmith at his forge, punctuated by blue-white flashes that lit the main cabin where we'd all taken refuge as angry rumbles of thunder echoed around us.

'The Captain says that we're the first ship to put in here for almost three months,' Etienne said, staring out of the cabin window.

'I can't think this is a busy port,' Amalia said. 'Not for big ships, anyway.'

'No. They do get some passing through from the capital, but apparently none for a while now.'

A flash lit the cabin and a few seconds later, a crack of thunder reverberated around us, making the window rattle.

'Well, this is lovely,' Kit said, his face ashen.

'Don't you like storms?' Amalia asked.

'No, not one bit.'

'What about you, Sorsha?' Etienne asked.

I shrugged. 'They don't bother me too much as long as they're not right overhead, then I'm not so keen.'

'At least we're not out on the open sea,' Kit said, grunting at the prospect. 'You'd be needing more than one bucket out there right now,' he said, turning to give me a grin. A bright flash filled the cabin and an almost instantaneous clap of thunder reverberated around us. Kit ducked, eyes wide; I flinched at the sound.

We rode out the storm and by early evening it had

passed the town, the sky a clear blue once more as the sun headed for the horizon. I decided to go for a short walk along the beach past the harbour walls. Kit still looked a little tense from the storm and, although I asked him to join me, he decided to stay behind.

I headed out of the ship, along the harbour wall and to the soft sandy beach beyond. I wandered along for some time, watching the waves racing up the beach, the humid air making little beads of perspiration spring out on my forehead. I wiped them away, glancing back towards the town, now quite a distance away. Etienne was walking along towards me. What did he want?

I sighed. I'd hoped to have a little time alone, seeing as Kit had stayed behind, but it obviously wasn't to be. Still, I didn't find the prince quite so disagreeable now: in fact, I was slowly warming to him.

'It's a beautiful evening, considering the storm earlier,' Etienne said, flicking his gorgeous hair from his eyes as he reached me.

'I'm surprised it's cleared up quite so quickly,' I said.

'Guess it depends which way the wind's blowing.'

'Hmm.' I looked towards the setting sun. 'Probably time to head back,' I said, at least that way I wouldn't have to talk to him for too long.

'We've got a little while yet. It's really warm. How about a quick paddle in the sea to cool down?' He sat on a large rock and started pulling his boots off.

'What, now?'

He nodded, standing up again and turning his britches up.

'You'll get them all wet – the waves are still quite big from time to time,' I said, looking out at the water.

'I'll dry,' he said, grinning at me. 'Coming?'

The smile on his face and the sparkle in his eyes made my heart do a little flip. I swallowed, gazing after him as he moved towards the water. The sunlight caught his tousled, dark blond hair, almost setting light to it as a gentle breeze ruffled it about.

'I'll watch,' I said, moving over to sit on the rock.

Suddenly, he yelled out in pain.

'Dammit! What the hell's that?' He started hopping around on one foot, swearing.

What, *by Starlight*, had he just done? I jumped up and ran over to him. 'What is it?'

'By the Sun, my foot's on fire!'

I looked at the sand where he'd been standing at the water's edge. There, partly camouflaged by the golden grains, lay a Moonweever Fish. The long, brown fish buried itself a little more in the sand. I swore. They were renowned on Steorra for the pain they could inflict – they didn't kill, but the fearsome pain was legendary. Most people passed out, the rest cried out in pain for hours, up to a day, before it finally subsided. Etienne was in for a very rough time.

'Come and sit down, but whatever you do, don't put that foot down or you'll drive the spines in further,' I said, ducking under his arm and helping him hop back towards the rock.

'What was it?' he asked, pain filling his quavering voice.

'A Moonweever Fish. They have venomous spines, and once their venom gets into your system it can be very painful.' No point in worrying him with the full truth, or the fact that it would get worse in the next few hours.

'You're telling me,' he said as he sat back on the rock. He groaned in pain, his face pale. 'I've never felt anything like this before.'

'I don't suppose you have,' I said, kneeling on the sand in front of him and resting his injured foot on my knee. The spines from the fish were quite obvious. Ideally, a pair of tweezers would be my weapon of choice to pull them out, but that wasn't an option here, so I went for the next best thing. 'You're going to have to stay still while I do this,' I said, getting my knife out.

His pain-drowned eyes almost popped out of his head. 'You're going to cut my foot off?'

'Don't be ridiculous,' I snapped. 'I'm going to use the edge of the blade to remove the spines. It might hurt a bit.'

'More than it does already?'

'I hope not. Now stay still.'

I held on to his foot with one hand and used the other to carefully draw the edge of the blade across his skin to remove the spines. He groaned as I worked, gripping onto the rock, all his muscles tense, his knuckles white and eyes tightly shut. He was doing well to stay conscious – the pain had to be ferocious, and a lesser man would've passed out. I glanced up at him, feeling a deep respect for the Sun Prince I hadn't up until now. By the time I'd finished, his skin was red and his foot beginning to swell, which was only to be expected – from what I knew.

'You have these monsters on Steorra?' he asked, teeth gritted.

'The odd one gets washed up from time to time, but the local people try to remove them where they can. They're much more common here, hence their name. I understand that they're quite a delicacy, if you know how to prepare them.'

'I think I've gone off fish.'

'I don't blame you.'

He opened an eye. 'I'll never get my boot back on with my foot swollen like that – how long before it goes down?'

'Usually in an hour or so.'

'Great. And the pain?'

I flinched. I couldn't lie to such a direct question. 'Twenty-four hours, maybe, if you're unlucky.'

'What?' He stared at me, then glanced back towards the harbour. 'There's no way I can walk on it, and you can't exactly carry me on your own. I'll never make it back tonight. Maybe you should go back alone, come and fetch me tomorrow.'

'Don't be daft, I'm not leaving you.'

'Really?' he asked, relief in his voice. 'I wasn't sure if…'

'You need looking after. I can't leave you here overnight – besides, Amalia would probably kill me if I did,' I said, looking at him sideways and giving him a little grin.

He grunted. 'She probably would. She's very protective of me.'

'It must be nice having someone like that.'

'You have Kit, don't you?'

'He's not family. He's paid to accompany me – although he is my friend now too.'

'Amalia's paid too, but she volunteered. I guess it's similar with her as it is with Kit.'

'So both our companions are mercenaries? Nice.'

Etienne shrugged. 'Although they'd both do it willingly, now.'

'I suppose.'

I looked down at his foot. The swelling had increased, his skin tight and bright red – everything I'd expected to see. The harbour sat a fair distance away. I stifled a little sigh. Despite what I might want, I really didn't like to leave the prince alone on the beach, particularly as it was getting cooler; not good for someone in his condition. I wasn't sure the King of Solis would take kindly to me leaving his son to hypothermia.

'Let's give it a little while for the swelling to calm down,' I said, cleaning my knife in the sand. 'Then we'll see how you are.'

He stifled a little moan of pain. 'I think I'm dying.'

'You're being dramatic. You won't die, but it's going to hurt for a while.'

'Help take my mind off the fire in my foot – talk to me some more. Give me something to think about other than this pain.'

There were worse things I could be doing than talking to the Prince, although I did rather wish Etienne had never come out here.

'All right,' I said, sitting beside him and resheathing my knife. 'Tell me about your family.'

'My family?' He grimaced. 'I have my parents, the King and Queen, and my brothers.'

'Brothers? I don't even have one sibling. I'm quite jealous. What are their names? Are they older or younger than you?'

'They're all older. Quite a bit older, actually. Sol is the eldest, he's thirty-eight, and heir to the throne – not to mention a real bastard. Then it's Haul, he's almost as bad, Apollo, Sunne and finally Tyr. The only one I've ever been close to is Tyr. He's twenty-nine. The rest used to gang up on me, growing up, and tease me relentlessly – Tyr was the only one who stood up for me. The others did their best to get me into trouble whenever they could.'

'They sound like a load of bullies.'

'They were, and still are. The problem is, Father and Mother have never realised. Whenever Tyr and I went to them to complain, the others would always say we were making it up. They were always the favourites because they were older, and therefore to be believed – at least that's how it seemed. Tyr was more popular with my parents than me, too.' He paused and rubbed his forehead. 'You see, I believe I was a mistake. That's why there's ten years between me and Tyr. I think every time they look at me, my parents are reminded of it. I'm not important, just a nuisance.'

'I'm sorry,' I said, feeling genuine sympathy for the Sun Prince. 'It can't have been easy.'

'It wasn't – isn't. My parents sent me away to school in Merribor, to Dunton where they have a centre of learning. I thought I might get some peace there, but the other boys treated me like dirt because I was from a foreign isle and they just saw me as a pampered prince,' he said, a wry look on his face. 'If only they'd known, but they never bothered to find out the truth of it. I didn't make a single friend while I was there. I came back after three years and Amalia became my bodyguard.'

The Sun Prince had obviously not had an easy time of it. My life had been quite smooth in comparison.

'My brothers have all been Pledged for a while now, of course. Other than Tyr, they're all still as obnoxious as ever and their wives aren't much better. Other than Amalia, it's been quite lonely.' He winced. 'This pain is getting worse, not better.'

'And now you've been Pledged too?' I asked, trying to jolly him along.

He nodded. 'To one of your Starlight Princesses. I don't know what her name is, though, but I do know the Pledging Records have now been sent to the priestesses at the Celestial Temple, so it's all official – whoever she is. I was hoping I might find out when I got to the Starlight Citadel, but I didn't. Maybe I'll find out when we return.'

'Maybe. I'm surprised Taran didn't tell you who it was – he seemed to know.'

'Perhaps he's been sworn to secrecy too.'

I snorted. 'That would make little difference to him if he thought he could make some gain from it. Or some mischief.'

A wisp of a frown crossed Etienne's face. 'He really does sound like a true bastard.'

'That's because he is... Well, I hope, whichever princess it is, she's a good match for you.'

'We'll see,' he said with a shrug. 'To be honest I'd far rather I had a choice so it could be a love match. But none of my brothers have had one, so I won't be any different. Sol and Apollo hate their wives. Sunne and Tyr tolerate theirs. Haul, I'm not sure about, but he's always going around with a glum expression – she's besotted with him, but he doesn't appear so keen. Tyr's still trying to work his out, but she's very demanding – I think she'd have preferred to be closer to the prospect of being Queen, but being bound to Tyr she doesn't stand a cat in hell's chance.' He paused a moment, getting his breath back. 'None of them had a choice, any more than I do. I hope, whoever I get, we can at least get on. I just hope we don't loathe each other, but I guess I'll have to make the best of it like everyone else.' He sighed, staring wistfully into the distance. 'It would just be nice to get to know her a little first before we're officially Pledged, but that won't happen. It's likely I won't meet her until our Pledging Day – that'll be the first time I ever talk to her, maybe even see her.'

I shuddered. A similar fate probably awaited me.

'Have your brothers all had children?' I asked.

He shook his head. 'Not one of them, and Father is getting a little fractious about it. I'm not sure if there's a problem or they just don't get on with their wives well enough to do *that*, but Sol will have to soon because the Order needs heirs and Father isn't getting younger.'

I snorted. 'Well, I'm not surprised your father's getting anxious. Of course if they'd been allowed to choose their wives, he might have been surrounded by grandchildren by now.'

Etienne nodded, a wan little smile appearing. 'Quite possibly.'

'You know, this Pledging business is a nightmare.'

'Not looking forward to it?'

I shuddered. 'No. Mother has arranged it all, though, and just sent the formal documents off to the Celestial Temple. She's going to introduce him to me when I get back to Steorra. Apparently he's a prince, but far removed from one of the Celestial Isle's thrones. She's arranging with Finnar for him to be given a job at the Starlight Court so that I won't have to see him much.'

Etienne laughed. 'You might find you like him – he might even like you, want to spend time with you.'

I screwed my nose up. 'And we might loathe each other, rather like you're fearing with your match. Anyway, once he finds out he's being Pledged to *me*, he'll probably make a run for it, and I wouldn't blame him. No one wants to be bound to an enigma, let alone a princess who carries weapons and has as much poise and grace as a log.'

'You might be surprised,' he said with a grin. 'Your mystery prince might fall head over heels in love with you and never want to leave your side.'

'Surprised? I'd be shocked if that happened, and probably never recover.'

He let out a little laugh, then sucked in a breath of pain. I glanced at his face. Sweat beaded on his brow, sticking his hair to his forehead. His tanned skin looked pasty in the golden rays of the setting sun. I was beginning to worry he might pass out after all – I hadn't mentioned to him that he hadn't just had one or two spines in his foot, but a good dozen. To have remained conscious this long he must have a very high pain threshold, but even he was now beginning to fade.

'My parents grew to love each other, I think,' I said.

'Mine too,' he said, his voice raspy. 'They didn't love each other to begin with, but I think over time they learnt to. Not the way I'd like to do it. I'd rather be in love first.'

'So would I,' I murmured. 'But we won't get the luxury of that choice, will we?'

I looked back towards the distant town. I chewed my lip as I thought. I could only come up with one thing to do to relieve his pain and get us back to the ship before we ended up stuck for the night on the rapidly cooling beach. Something I'd never done willingly before. But the only option I had was very risky. If he realised what I was doing, I'd be in real trouble. The worst.

Would he keep my secret if he found out, this Sun Prince of Solis, that I barely knew? I glanced into his eyes, turquoise eyes that, although full of excruciating pain, held an honourable, trustworthy look. For some reason I had a feeling about him, that even if he found out, I could trust him, but that didn't mean I wouldn't try and keep it secret from him just in case.

I did have to do something, though. From the way his hands clung to the rock, knuckles white, he was in tremendous pain. I couldn't let him endure it like this when I could help – and after all, he wasn't really as bad as I'd first thought in the Starlight Palace when I'd met him. He was definitely growing on me.

He stifled a groan and screwed his eyes shut with the pain.

I got up and walked down to the water's edge, pulling my handkerchief out, wetting it, and wringing it out a little. I started to slip my knife from its sheath, then paused. I suddenly remembered I didn't need to – I already had what I needed. I stood up and returned to the prince. He opened his eyes, an eyebrow arched in confusion. I took a long breath and knelt down beside him. I reached out and gently placed his foot on my knee once more. The swelling had begun to go down, but I knew the pain would only get worse.

'What are you doing?' he asked, flinching as I gently ran my fingertips over his inflamed skin.

'Close your eyes and take deep breaths,' I said. 'I'm going to see if I can do something for the pain.'

'I wish you would,' he pleaded, 'because I don't know how much longer I can take this.' He squeezed his eyes shut. 'So what are you going to do?'

Making sure his eyes were fully closed, I pulled the small Pellucid Crystal from my pocket that I'd shed days ago.

'I'm going to put this wet handkerchief on it to try and cool it and reduce the pain,' I said, wrapping the crystal in the edge of the handkerchief.

He opened an eye.

'I told you to keep your eyes shut,' I said, hastily making sure he wouldn't see the Crystal.

'Why?'

'Because it helps with the pain if you're not looking at your foot.'

'You think so?'

'Just do as you're told.'

He snorted. 'That's something I'm used to doing.'

I winced. 'I'm sorry. I didn't mean–'

'It's fine, it was meant to be a joke, it was just in very poor taste. Do you really think that wet handkerchief will do something to help?'

I shrugged. 'It's worth a try, unless you don't want me to.'

He swallowed. 'No, do it. I don't care what you do, just try something. Anything. This is too much,' he said, his voice cracking with the pain. He shut his eye again and gritted his teeth.

For a moment my heart flipped as I took in his distressed expression.

'Hold on for a little longer, and keep your eyes shut,' I said.

'All right,' he said, jaw set, a muscle quivering in his neck.

I gently wrapped the wet handkerchief around his foot, making sure I placed the Pellucid Crystal over his wounds from the Moonweever's spines. Keeping a finger under the cloth and on the Crystal, I shut my eyes, concentrating on his injury. The Pellucid wasn't a healing Crystal – they were Orange – but I knew it could reduce pain. I opened my eyes. My hands glowed a soft white where they rested around Etienne's foot. The sun broke through a cloud, a final blast of sunlight masking my work, before it disappeared below the horizon.

'The pain… it's easing,' Etienne said, his voice full of relief.

'Stay like you are,' I said, continuing to focus on his foot, willing it to feel better for him. The light from the Pellucid slowly faded away. They didn't last long, and I'd done what I could without shedding blood to create more and letting him see me, and that was something I was not prepared to do unless absolutely necessary. Hopefully this would be enough to get him back to the ship.

'How's it feeling now?' I asked, removing the handkerchief from his foot and slipping the spent Crystal into my pocket.

He opened his eyes, the strain on his face gone, his muscles relaxing. 'Much, much better,' he said. 'Not gone completely, but nothing like it was. I think I can probably walk on it now.'

I nodded and gently put his foot back on the sand. 'Good. I think the swelling's gone down enough so you can get your boot back on.'

I stood up and started to move away, but he grabbed my arm.

'Thank you, Sorsha. I couldn't have borne that for much longer.' He looked up at me, his eyes so sincere I couldn't help but smile at him.

'You'd be surprised what you can bear when you have to, but to be honest, you were doing far better than most in your situation. It would only have got worse.'

His eyes widened. 'Worse than that?'

'I've heard it peaks at about six hours after treading on the fish.'

He swallowed. 'Well, whatever you did was magic.'

'Not quite,' I murmured.

'What did you do?' he asked, frowning.

'Nothing special, I'm just good with my hands,' I said grinning, hoping I'd avoid any further interrogation. I couldn't tell him the truth. 'See if you can get your boot on and we'll head back.'

He nodded and gingerly slipped his boot back over his foot. He winced, but managed to get it on, then stood up and tested his foot.

'It's not too bad,' he said. 'I can limp back as long as I take it slowly.'

I nodded, ducking under his arm so he could put some of his weight on me.

He looked at me, something flickering deep in his eyes, and smiled. 'Thanks.'

'Let's get you back.'

It took us three times as long to get back to the ship as it had taken to walk out to the rock. Etienne limped along, doing a good job, despite the fact I knew he was still in quite a bit of pain – but at least the pain wasn't killing him now, like he'd said it was before.

By the time we got back darkness had fallen. Amalia and Kit came running down the gangplank, questions flying in all directions. The prince's cousin immediately took charge of him and helped him into the cabin with Kit's assistance. Etienne glanced back at me, that same strange flicker in his eyes. I smiled at him, then headed straight for my cabin and bed.

#

The next morning we set off for Luna's capital, the sky a

clear azure blue, and the wind in our favour. I stood at the bow, not feeling too queasy as we were pretty much hugging the coastline, and watched a small pod of dolphins that played beside the ship. Etienne came out of the main cabin and limped over to me. His gait was much better than the previous evening, and only because I knew it was there did I really see it. He leant on the rail next to me, looking out over the waves.

'How's the foot?' I asked.

'Much better, thank you,' he said. 'There's no swelling. It still twinges a little, but it's nothing much now, and certainly fine compared to yesterday evening. I'm limping a little just in case, rather than because I need to.'

I nodded. 'I'm glad it's improved.'

He turned towards me, giving me a smile that spread right across his face and had his eyes sparkling like turquoise diamonds, if there are such things. 'Thank you, Sorsha. If you hadn't been there yesterday, I don't know what would have happened to me. You didn't have to help and, well, I really appreciate it.'

He stared into my eyes and for a few seconds I met his gaze. His turquoise eyes were mesmerising, and for a moment I lost myself in their depths. Was kindness something he wasn't used to? I'd done what I'd thought right. I swallowed and looked down. This was awkward.

'Glad I could help,' I said.

He smiled. 'Amalia can't understand what you did to kill the pain like that.'

'Like I said, I'm good with my hands.'

He raised an eyebrow. 'But–'

'Next time, keep your boots on,' I said, trying to end his questioning.

A wisp of a frown slipped across his face. 'Don't worry, I will, and another time I'll… by the Sun…'

His sudden silence made me look up.

'What is it?' I asked, frowning.

'Oh hell, look at that,' he said, rubbing his forehead, an agitated edge to his voice as he stared out over the ship's rail and pointed.

Moon City had come into view while we talked, but now I could see what had got Etienne so jittery. The city appeared to be in ruins. A cloud of thick black smoke rose from a hill beside the ravaged capital. Shouts started around the ship as others saw the smoke and shattered city. Captain Lucian started barking orders as we sailed towards the broken harbour where half sunken ships reached out of the black water like hands desperately grasping for help that would never come.

Chapter Four

'Starlight, what's happened here?' I looked around at the devastation. Grey stone streets spread out before me, wooden doors broken from their hinges – smashed like driftwood on the tide – charred remains of thatched roofs dangling from the apex of buildings, some with walls partially collapsed from the heat of fires, personal belongings scattered around like chaff. The worst was that the city itself wasn't too dissimilar to the Starlight Citadel, and it made me a little homesick as I shuddered at the sight.

'I don't know,' Etienne said, his voice shocked, his hand on his sword hilt. 'But it happened a while ago, by the looks of things.'

'I don't like it one bit,' Amalia said through gritted teeth. 'The place has been attacked and ransacked.'

'But by who?' Kit asked, his usual jollity long since gone, replaced by a slightly wild look in his eyes. 'Who would do this? And why? Not one of the other Orders, surely?'

I glanced away from a building where a decomposing corpse lay, dark blood splattered against the kitchen wall. I'd seen a dead body once before, or at least the remains of one. An old shepherd who'd become disorientated one night after a little too much wine, had fallen into a small ravine on uncle's estate. By the time we found him two weeks later his body was mainly bones due to rats and wild animals, and a cheesy smell hung in the air around him, which took me weeks to forget. That same odour wafted in the air here too.

I swallowed. 'This didn't happen in the last couple of days,' I said, resisting the urge to throw up.

Etienne glanced enquiringly at me.

'The smell – and the state of that body back there. The local rats have been at it.'

He raised an eyebrow. 'Life away from Court hasn't been dull?'

'Not always.'

'How long, would you say?'

'Maybe a couple of weeks.'

The few people we came across acted more like mice than humans, taking one look at us and fleeing, not giving us the chance to speak to them before they disappeared into any hiding place they could find. We continued on along the main street, the smell of ash and death hung heavy in the air as we made our way towards the palace. My stomach churned at the sights and smells, nausea in my throat as I tried to take in the destruction of Luna's capital.

'Why haven't they dealt with all the dead?' Kit asked, his voice quiet.

'Probably because there were just too many of them,' Amalia said. 'I'd say most of the citizens have been killed – that doesn't leave many to bury the dead.'

I glanced at the layer of ash on some surfaces, made thick and mud-like from rain, but now dry and cracked.

'So why haven't we heard about this?' Kit asked. 'Surely they'd have sent word. I know they can be a bit unsociable, but I would have thought–'

'Poppycock, didn't you notice the harbour?' Amalia asked, looking cautiously around a corner, recoiling at the sight of a decaying body a few feet away slumped behind a barrel. 'There were no seaworthy ships. They were all scuttled, or sunk, and small boats can't make the crossing. This is the only harbour deep enough on Luna Isle to take ships that can make the voyage, other than the town we stopped at.'

'And I heard someone there comment on the fact they've not seen any ships for some time.' Etienne glanced at her. 'You think they've been deliberately cut off?'

Amalia shrugged. 'I don't know, but that would be my guess, and the reason we haven't heard from them for a while.'

'I wonder if Ephyna's all right,' I murmured. Kit's hand slipped into mine.

'I'm sure she is,' he said quietly. 'They'd have got her to safety.'

Etienne glanced across at me, worry flickering in his eyes. I wondered if his aunt was still alive, and shuddered.

'Only a very few survived. Those that could run or 'ad weapons to fight back. The rest were slaughtered.' A voice came from a broken down house.

I turned. An old man, his clothes not much better than rags, held on to the doorframe, his white hair shifting in the breeze from the salty docks.

'A few of us 'ad hiding places – but some were burnt alive in them. I was lucky,' he said.

I took a deep breath.

'And the smoke from the hill? What's that?' Kit asked.

'Funerals?' Etienne asked.

The man scoffed. 'Most don't have anyone to mourn them to have a proper funeral. They're just trying to collect up as many of the bodies as they can and cremate them in mass fires. Even after all this time there are still many to gather up.'

Amalia blanched.

'The King of Luna, 'e died in the attack,' the old man said. ''e's being entombed with his wife today – as tradition dictates after two weeks.'

I shuddered.

'Most of the surviving city-folk are up there paying their respects. Alas, my foot prevents me from getting up the 'ill,' he said, waving his right foot at us.

'So the Queen of Luna died too?' Kit asked.

'No, no, the Queen didn't die in the attack,' the old man said shaking his head. 'She escaped, but they're entombing 'er with the King today – it's tradition, you know.'

Etienne bristled. 'A hell of a stupid one, if you ask me.'

The old man shook his head. 'It's always been like that – the Queen entombed with the King when 'e dies.'

I swallowed. I'd heard of this before, but we didn't do it on Steorra anymore. As far as I knew only the Moon and Sun Orders continued what I felt to be a barbaric custom. A ritual as old as the Orders themselves, the queen buried with the king to travel with him to the afterlife. In reality, left to starve to death in homage to "His Majesty", or at least that's how I saw it. A noble act, some still said at home. The whole idea left me wanting to throw up. No way did I ever want to become a wife of a Moon or Sun King, left to rot when he died. A little shiver worked its way down my spine.

'Who attacked you?' I asked, trying to throw off the images of tombs and death.

The man shrugged. 'Don't know. It 'appened at night, no warning, just carnage. But I think they were looking for something.'

'In your homes?' Amalia asked, frowning.

He shrugged again.

'Let's get up to the palace,' Etienne said. 'Thank you for your help, sir.' He nodded to the old man and led the way, heading towards the palace at the top of the hill.

The walk quickly became one I wanted to forget. The destruction was close to absolute, barely a building untouched by fire or violence. They may had been cremating the unfortunate dead people of the city, but they'd not found them all yet, not by a long way.

As we reached the palace I glanced to the south-east where the King's Tomb stood proudly, dark grey marble shining in the sunlight, and beyond it on the hill, a roiling black cloud of smoke from the funeral pyres of the dead citizens. The sight had a kind of mesmerising look about it.

'Come on,' Etienne said from beside me, placing a hand on my shoulder steering me towards the palace. Normally I'd have shaken him off, but today, so unnerved by what we'd seen, by what had happened here, I welcomed it as a kind of calming sensation spread through me.

I nodded and walked with him through the broken palace gates and into the courtyard. Burnt stables stood on one side, torn gardens on another and ahead the white marble palace of the Moon Order, stained with black sooty swirls. A richly dressed, although slightly bedraggled, man came running out of the open palace door, his dishevelled grey hair moving in the breeze coming off the sea.

'Prince Etienne? Prince Etienne of the Sun Order? You're so welcome, so welcome,' the man said shaking hands with the prince.

'Chamberlain Mare? We'd heard nothing from you – we were worried,' Etienne said.

'We were attacked, Your Highness, attacked unprovoked. The King murdered, the people slain,' Mare said, his eyes full of horror and fear. 'With our ships sunk we were trapped here on the island with no way to contact the outside world. We couldn't call for assistance or warn anyone. We were totally alone, until now, until you.'

'But who did this?' I asked, looking around at the devastation, the smell of destruction clinging to my clothes and refusing to leave my nose even when I tried breathing through a sleeve.

The Chamberlain looked towards me then at Etienne.

'This is Princess Sorsha of the Starlight Order,' Etienne said, nodding towards me. 'These are our companions-at-arms,' he said, gesturing to Kit and Amalia.

Mare nodded. 'It's not for me to say, Princess Sorsha, but for King Linus to speak to you about this sorry state of affairs.'

'King Linus?' Amalia frowned and looked at Etienne.

'Isn't it King Lunan?' Etienne asked. 'He's the heir, isn't he?'

'He was killed defending the Queen,' Mare said, bowing his head. 'Only princes Linus and Artem survived. The other princes were killed in the raid bravely defending the palace and the Royal Family as the others escaped. Our new King Linus and his wife, Queen Terza, both survived with Prince Artem.'

I took a deep breath. Did this mean that my Pledged prince was dead? Only Artem had survived. Was it him?

51

Or was it some prince from the Planetary Order? I glanced around. The destruction and murder here was absolute, low or high-born, it didn't matter; the attackers didn't care.

'Please, come this way, the King will be back from the funerals shortly. We'll make you as comfortable as we can, in our current circumstances. It will take years to rebuild…' Mare said, his voice trailing off as he looked over the ruined city.

#

'They came at night.' The haunted expression in Linus' eyes would stay with me forever. His younger brother, Artem, probably around his twentieth year, stood at the window, looking out over the huge black cloud of smoke as the sun set. 'We had no warning, nothing to give us any idea they were coming.'

'But why did they attack?' Etienne asked. 'It wasn't the island they wanted or they wouldn't have left.'

'They were searching for – art.'

'For what?' Had I misheard him? Art?

'It seems Emperor Taliesin of Merribor was after our priceless works of art – sculptures, paintings, books, jewellery,' Artem said, brushing his floppy black hair from his eyes. 'He sent his son, Prince Cynric, at the head of his raiding party and they took every last one they could find.'

'The Emperor?' Kit's eyes widened even as he frowned.

'But why?' Amalia asked. 'What would the Emperor want with Luna's art?'

Artem shrugged. 'Maybe Taliesin wants to increase his private art collection.'

'Artem, this is not the time for levity,' Linus said, glaring at his younger brother. 'Our parents and brothers are dead, our people dead, our city razed to the ground, and our priceless and most valuable Relics stolen from us for no reason.'

'There must be a reason,' I said quietly.

'Whatever it is, Princess Sorsha, it's beyond our grasp, at least for now,' Linus said, rubbing his chin in thought. 'I have no answer for you.'

'Can you tell us – my aunt, Princess Penelope, and Princess Sorsha's cousin Ephyna – are they alive?' Etienne asked.

My heart pounded, waiting for Linus' response. Out the corner of my eye I thought I caught Artem smirk, but it could have been a trick of the light.

Linus bowed his head. 'They died when the palace was attacked. I'm sorry. I was very fond of them both.' He sighed. 'What we need now is supplies. We're painfully short of food and medicines.'

Etienne nodded, and glanced at me.

I bit my lip, not sure how to take the news. Ephyna and I hadn't ever been close, but as one of the Starlight Princesses, and my cousin, we'd spent some time together when I was little, before I'd been sent away from Court by Mother. I felt Kit come up beside me, and he slid his arm around my shoulders. The whole thing had me on edge. How and why this could be happening, I didn't understand. The Emperor had always kept clear of the Orders, why he'd now attack Luna was beyond me – and for their art? Unimaginable.

'We'll do as you ask and send aid,' Etienne said. 'It'll be a few weeks, but we'll do what we can.'

'Thank you, Prince Etienne,' Linus said. 'I know our Orders haven't always got along, but I hope we can put all that behind us in this terrible hour – the Starlight Order too,' he glanced at me – I nodded.

Linus was right. Whatever we'd fallen out about in the past was now irrelevant. We had to work together, help each other and try and figure out what Taliesin wanted. And stop him from taking more.

'I think it may be advisable for me to go with them, brother, coordinate the aid from Steorra,' Artem said, his left eyebrow twitching.

Linus frowned for a moment, then slowly nodded.

'Yes, I think that would be a good idea. You can arrange things from the Starlight Citadel, send food and shelter, as well as building materials and manpower to help us rebuild. We'll need all the help we can get.'

Artem smiled. 'Of course, I'll do my best.' Even the golden rays of the setting sun spilling in the window couldn't add warmth to his skin, the colour of freshly fallen snow. 'I suggest we leave on the early morning tide.'

'It was strange,' Linus said, staring into the distance. 'But we had no word from any of the other Isles for a while before the attack.'

'That's one of the reasons we came to check on you, because we'd heard nothing from Luna for a while,' Etienne said.

'Maybe Prince Cynric cut off communications first to make sure you couldn't call for help,' Kit said, frowning.

'Maybe,' Linus nodded, his gaze steadying in the room. 'They were headed in the direction of Merribor when they left. Those of us that were able to flee didn't dare return to the city for several days until we were sure they were gone and weren't going to come back.'

'Let's hope they've gone back to Merribor permanently and don't intend to travel north anytime soon,' Artem said.

'To Steorra and Solis?' Etienne asked, raising an eyebrow. 'Why would they do that?'

'Perhaps they didn't find what they wanted here.'

'I'm sure you're wrong, Artem,' Linus said.

'I'm just saying they could head for the other Isles in due course,' Artem said, his eyebrow twitching again.

'True, I suppose. All I can do is suggest that the other Orders are warned at once, just in case Taliesin and Cynric are preparing to attack them, too.'

I shivered, glancing at Etienne. He looked back at me, his eyes a mystery. Something felt wrong.

Chapter Five

A keen salty wind blew us towards Steorra. Despite the comfortable bed at the palace I'd slept little and I was relieved to be back on the ship, heading for home. This hadn't been the trip I'd expected. What my cousin would say when we got back and reported to him, I didn't know. Mother would have proverbial kittens, then introduce me to my prince. I shuddered at the thought. I was heading back to a prison.

Once again I did my best to stay out on deck during the journey. Captain Lucian would walk past and nod to me, a grim expression on his face as he kept his sailors and ship in order – I liked him. Although I'd warmed to Etienne and Amalia, and in fact got on well with them both now, I still preferred to be alone, or with Kit. Artem never appeared on deck once, preferring to stay below, and had barely uttered a word to us since leaving Luna.

On the third day of the journey I stood on deck looking out over the water, watching the waves breaking gently around us, salt on my tongue and the wind in my unruly hair, whipping it into my eyes. I retied my hair back and watched a pod of dolphins swimming elegantly beside the ship as the sails flapped and the reassuring sound of creaking rigging swept around me.

'You really don't like being below, do you?' Etienne asked, walking over to join me.

'I get seasick and being out on deck makes me feel better – and it's easier to throw up,' I said ruefully.

He nodded. 'I understand.' He leant on the bow-rail, watching the dolphins.

'Do you really still entomb your queens with your kings when they die?' I asked, staring out over the water.

Etienne took a deep breath. 'Yes,' he said, a sick look on his face. 'I don't know why the hell my father still allows it. The Entombing Law was passed hundreds of years ago – the ancient people had a belief that for the queen to travel into the afterlife with the king she had to be entombed with him. Most people are more enlightened now, but the Royal Family still follows the tradition, although not for a while. My grandmother and great-grandmother both died before their husbands. I fear for Mother though, because she's several years younger than Father. Maybe they'll have stopped it by the time Sol dies. They don't do it on Steorra anymore?'

'No, they do not,' I said emphatically. 'I'm surprised the Moon Order have continued the tradition. The Queen was quite young, wasn't she? I mean, she was the King's second wife, not the princes' mother?'

Etienne nodded. 'In her late thirties, I think.'

I shivered. 'Still, I don't think it's something that will bother me. Not on the outer fringes of the Court.'

'Stay at the edges,' he murmured, nodding. 'Not something that will bother my wife either.'

I turned to look at him. Pain flickered in his eyes for a moment, taking me by surprise – maybe he wasn't the proud prince I'd thought.

He glanced at me. 'Staying at the edges isn't my choice, Sorsha, any more than being sent away to school was, but sometimes people and circumstances push you there.'

Was this the reason for his reserve?

He glanced down at his hands, wiggling his fingers for a moment. 'I never wanted to be irrelevant. When I was small I tried to make myself wanted, but everything I tried failed,' he said quietly. 'Quite often because Sol or Haul put a stop to it. But in truth, my parents were more interested in my older brothers than me – I didn't matter so much. Amalia was much the same, pushed to the fringes because the Court disapproved of her father – a noble from the Planetary Order.'

'One of the strategic Pledge matches?' I asked.

Etienne nodded.

'Did it work?'

He sighed. 'To an extent. But you know how these things are. The strategic matches are meant to strengthen bonds between the nobility of the Orders, but there's still an element of mistrust on the part of the Order you marry into. It made life hard for Amalia's parents, and when Amalia was born she, too, was looked on with some suspicion and kept out of the main Court life. Bit like me.'

I hadn't been deliberately kept out by the wider Court, but kept away by my mother because of my secret; my blood. Because of that the Court became somewhat wary of me. It seemed we were all on the edges of the Court, treated with suspicion – or in Taran's mind, an object of amusement and ridicule. I, at least, was an aberration.

'That's why you and Amalia are so close?' I asked.

He smiled. 'We've kept each other sane over the years. Amalia trained as my bodyguard while I was away in Dunton, partly to have an excuse to be with me, but she's always been protective of me in a big sister kind of way. Anyway it kept us together and away from everyone else.'

'Makes sense. A bit like me and Kit.'

'But the Starlight Court didn't treat you like the Sun Court treated us. Kit says you were always welcomed there, so why did you choose to live away?'

'You spoke just now of choices – living away from Court wasn't one of mine,' I said – which was true, at least to begin with. 'Mother wanted me away from all the Court machinations,' I lied, looking down. 'Sent me to live with her brother, a retired army general, at his coastal estate. I just never came back to Court, other than my yearly visit to remind everyone I still exist. I like the peace and quiet, no gossip to contend with, no fashion to keep up with, no new hair styles to worry about – or social functions, for that matter.'

'Not a social butterfly then?' he asked with a smile.

I shook my head. 'Definitely not. Social events bring me out in hives.'

He chuckled. 'You and me both.'

We stood watching the water slide past for a while as the breeze rustled the sails, making them flap with a cheery and somewhat calming noise, punctuated by Captain Lucian's shouts. The salty tang in the air was strong today, and a huge albatross suddenly glided low over the water, matching the ship's speed. I shuddered. Albatrosses were birds of ill omen, of burden – my secret was burden enough, I didn't need another. As quickly as it had arrived, it flew off, up, high into the sky towards the sun itself. Etienne shifted, an anxious look in his eyes for a moment after it'd gone.

'So you don't know where the prince you're being Pledged to is from?' he asked suddenly.

'No. I haven't a clue. I did wonder if it might be one from Luna, but having been there now I think it can't have been because I would have thought Linus would have said something. Maybe it's a prince from Planetae. I really don't know, but then, no one ever tells me anything,' I said, a slightly acerbic note to my voice which I hadn't intended.

'What about Kit?'

'What about him?' I laughed. 'He's no prince and he's more likely to want to Pledge himself to you than to me,' I said with a big grin.

'Oh, sorry, I didn't realise,' Etienne said, a rosy blush appearing high on his cheeks.

'Doesn't matter.'

'I just wish Father didn't want me Pledged and out of his hair just yet. I still have time, but "as soon as possible", were his exact words,' Etienne said, a sour look on his face.

'Not looking forward to it at all, are you?'

He grunted. 'I can't imagine spending my life with anyone at the moment, let alone someone I've not met before. I mean, how can you... you know, when you don't even know them. I just can't get my head around it. Makes me feel sick.'

'No love matches for us,' I said bitterly.

'Love,' Etienne scoffed. 'Love doesn't even come in to it as far as Father's concerned. I'll probably end up being Pledged to some brainless bore.' He glanced at me.

'Sorry. It's one of your cousins, I shouldn't have said that.'

'Don't worry, I know how you feel,' I assured him. I just hoped he'd not been Pledged to Aster, or poor Etienne would be in for a really wretched life. She'd drive him to distraction with her head stuffed full of hairstyles, clothes and shoes.

Etienne turned to me, a wistful look in his eyes. 'If only we could choose.'

'Choose?' I laughed. 'Never. As soon as we get back to Steorra, that'll be it for me. My freedom will be at an end and I'll be made to live with this prince.'

He looked away before he spoke. 'I was hoping to spend more time with you, get to know you better, before that happened.'

'I...' What could I say to that? A little shiver of warmth swept down my spine. 'It doesn't mean we'll never meet again.'

'True,' he said, looking back at me. 'Maybe I'll have to make a special visit to see you at Court, or wherever your new home is.'

'You'd do that?' Etienne constantly surprised me. Someone who actually wanted to spend time with me for being *me* was a new experience. 'Really?'

He smiled. 'I'd like to keep in touch with my new... friend.'

'I'd like that too.' I smiled back, meaning every word, then screwed my nose up. 'As long as whoever my Pledged prince is doesn't mind.'

'And if he does?'

I turned and grinned at him. 'I've never done as I was told. If he doesn't like it that's his problem.'

Etienne laughed. 'You really aren't like any other princess I've ever met.'

'Which I hope is a good thing?' I asked, suddenly worried he might decide not to like me anymore.

'It's definitely a good thing,' he said with a smile, gently resting a hand on my shoulder. 'A very good thing.'

The more time I spent with Etienne, the more I talked to him, the more comfortable I felt in his company. I was beginning to feel like we'd always known each other, always been friends, which was ridiculous in a way, but with some people, it seemed, things were like that. It just hadn't ever happened to me before. Not until now. Not until Etienne.

'Eti! Dinner!' Amalia shouted from the cabin.

Etienne waved to her. 'You coming?' he asked me.

I shook my head. 'No, I'm avoiding as many big meals on board ship as I can. I'll try and have a snack during the evening.'

He nodded. 'Of course. I'll see you later,' he said, heading into the cabin.

#

'Sail ho!' shouted the sailor in the crow's nest.

On the horizon a fleet of ships sailed north, the morning sun reflecting off their sails. Whether they'd sailed past Steorra or from it I couldn't be sure at this distance, but the hairs on the back of my neck stood up and I felt nausea rising in my throat, and this time not from the sea voyage.

Kit came running up beside me, squinting into the distance. 'The sailors said something about a fleet.'

I nodded. 'They're sailing north.'

He sucked in a breath. 'The Emperor's ships?'

'Too far away to tell the colour of the sails, but they're the right shape,' I said, shivering despite the warm breeze.

'What do we do?'

'There's nothing we can do,' Etienne said, joining us with Amalia and Artem. 'If they are the Emperor's ships we can't stop them.'

'Maybe we could get ahead of them, outrun them and warn Solis,' Amalia said.

'Warn them about what? We don't know what's happened yet – if anything,' Artem said.

Amalia huffed.

'We have to go to the Starlight Citadel,' I said, looking along the coast towards the city, still well out of sight, and it would be for several more hours. A shard of ice rested in my chest as I thought of my mother. My stomach churned. Maybe they weren't the Emperor's ships, maybe they hadn't stopped at the Starlight Citadel, maybe…

I stood at the rail, straining to see the horizon, willing the coast to rush past, but the ship continued steadily as morning slipped into afternoon. Etienne had remained beside me the whole time.

A wisp of dark cloud drifted up from the horizon in stark contrast to the green of the coast and the blue of the sea. A chill hand grasped at my heart.

'What is it?' I swallowed.

Etienne squinted, looking out at the horizon.

'What's what?' Kit asked, frowning at me as he walked across the deck with Amalia just behind him.

'Smoke,' Etienne said finally, his voice quiet. 'I'm sorry.'

'Are you sure, Eti?' Amalia asked.

Etienne nodded.

Artem appeared, watching the cloud intently, his eyes bright. 'He's right – it's definitely smoke.'

For the first time during daylight on this voyage, I turned from the sea and headed down to my cabin. For some time I sat on the chair that stood in one corner, as waves of hot and cold swept over me. I wiped my clammy hands on my britches, my mind racing as it presented me with all manner of images of death and destruction. I took a deep breath. I had to get a hold of myself – at the moment I didn't know whether the city had been sacked or whether it might be the forest to the north on fire. But I feared it was the former.

A knock at the door broke my train of thought.

'Yes?' I said, getting up. It would be Kit, checking up on me.

The door opened and Etienne stepped in. 'I wanted to make sure you were all right,' he said.

'Not really,' I said, sitting back down, 'and I won't be until we get home and know for certain.'

Etienne nodded. 'I wish I could tell you now – but I don't have a Pellucid.'

'Sorry, what?' I asked, looking up at him.

He shut the door and sat on my bed. 'You've probably heard the rumours, that I'm a Red Crystal Blood?'

I nodded.

'Well, the rumours are true. And if I had a Pellucid Crystal I'd give you a Red to find out what you need to know. Red Crystals are Psychic Stones, they can form Astral Projections, so you can speak to someone far off. But there are no Double Bloods anymore, and so no Pellucids.'

I nodded again – so, Kit was right. 'I'd heard something of the sort about you,' I said. 'I'm sorry you can't use your Crystals, although if you could, you'd be in danger from others.'

'Maybe. But being a Blood, able to use our Crystals, would be a gift,' Etienne said, his turquoise eyes gleaming.

'To you, maybe,' I muttered.

'What?'

'Nothing.'

'I really wish I could use my Gift,' he said, his eyes far away. 'I wish I could help you.'

I gave him a wan little smile. 'Thank you… How long have you known about it?' I asked.

'Since I was seven,' he said. 'You tend to find out before you're ten, that's the latest the Blood Gift takes effect.'

I didn't like to say, *yes I know… I've known about Crystal Bloods since I was six, since my own Gift, if you can call it that, appeared.* The day I'd been playing in the palace gardens and cut my knee quite badly. As the blood oozed from my leg, instead of dripping onto the ground and landing in great red splodges, two Purple Crystals and one large, clear round Pellucid Crystal hit the ground. The colour drained from my mother's face until she looked like a ghost. She grabbed the Crystals, clasped my wound to stop it bleeding – so tightly it hurt and brought tears to my eyes – scooped me up and had me back in our chambers before you could say "Starlight". I shed two more Pellucids back in our rooms before she could get the bleeding to stop.

'My Crystals will never be of any use because Double Bloods don't exist anymore,' Etienne said, pulling a red gemstone from his pocket and holding it up to the light. It sparkled a deep, crimson red. Beautiful and mesmerising. 'My First Crystal. Said to be the most powerful you shed. I keep it for good luck, rather than because I think I'll ever be able to use it.'

I nodded, trying to look interested and not anxious. 'You don't think there are any Double Bloods anywhere? Not even one?'

'Not even one.' He smiled, then frowned. 'Of course if we had a Yellow Crystal and a Pellucid we might be able to find a Double Blood – Yellow Crystals vibrate when they're close to another Blood, or so I've heard, but I've never come across a Yellow and a Pellucid to find out if it's true.'

And hopefully he never would, at least not while I was around.

'Sorsh!' Kit burst into my cabin, pausing to give me and Etienne a funny look. 'Captain Lucian says we'll reach the Citadel by evening.'

I nodded. 'Then we'll know what's going on,' I said, glancing at Etienne.

The Sun Prince nodded. 'Then we'll know.'

Chapter Six

Fires burnt throughout the Starlight Citadel casting foul
and frightening shadows as acrid smoke filled the streets,
hanging low over the bodies of the dead. If I hadn't
already had an empty stomach from the sea voyage then
that would've been rectified within moments of stepping
ashore. The smell of salt and fish at the harbour mingled
with smoke from the burning ships left in the same state
as the Moon City's, all sunk or scuttled. I led the way
through the streets, hurriedly leaving the hulking corpses
of the ships behind me, up towards the palace. From what
I could see in the city, none of the Emperor's soldiers
remained here, just the evidence of their handiwork and it
made my blood light with a fire I'd never known in my
life.

The skirts of night swept around us only helping to
enhance the grisly and shocking scenes playing out
before us. Some of the folk had survived and were
tending to the injured, but many lay dead and their
loved ones lamented their passing with loud wails of
heartrending anguish. Taliesin had a lot to answer for –
and all this for pieces of art? I could think of few other
acts of such heinous and wanton destruction. He was a
bastard, plain and simple. And one day I would see
that he paid for the lives of my countrymen with his
own.

Although at the moment, I wasn't quite sure how I'd
visit my revenge on him – but I swore that I would.

We reached the palace, burning buildings and roofs
lighting our way as the stars came out, their beautifully
twinkling lights in stark contrast to the carnage and
horror revealing itself beneath them. The courtyard area
lay strewn with broken barrels, boxes and bodies of both
horses and men. Kit's ashen face said it all. Never would
either of us ever have thought to bear witness to
something like this in our homeland.

My heart pounded in my ears as we walked up the steps to the broken palace doors. Inside, the destruction and death continued. I took a torch from the wall and lit it from a small pile of burning wood that had once been a table, the others following suit. Only then, in the light of the torches, did I see Artem's face. A kind of twinkle of fascination and curiosity rested in his eyes, unlike Etienne and Amalia, who both looked sickened by what they saw. The Moon Prince fumbled with something in his hand and tucked it under his shirt.

I frowned; what was he doing? Not that I cared as my home lay in ruins around me.

Etienne glanced towards me. 'Where do we go?'

'My mother's apartments,' I said. 'She spends most of her time there.'

Silence surrounded us as we made our way through the palace corridors, broken intermittently by groaning and sometimes punctuated by a cry that chilled me to the core. We climbed a red carpeted staircase to the upper floor. A deep moan of pain came from along the landing – I looked across, my torch forming a pool of golden light. Taran lay crumpled on the carpet, a dark shadow of blood surrounding him on the floor. I'd never liked him, but neither had I wanted him to meet his end this way. I ran over to him and crouched beside him, moving his hair from an ugly cut on the side of his face.

His eyelids flickered and he looked at me, his gaze unfocused for a moment. 'Sorsha?'

'It's all right, Taran, we'll look after you,' I said, although quite how, I wasn't sure.

'No, no hope for me,' he said, grabbing at my hand. 'Find Finnar, he went to the West Tower. The Refuge.'

I swallowed and nodded. 'I will.'

'They were Emperor Taliesin's men. They wanted–' He coughed, his lips flecking with scarlet. 'Our art. They wanted our art!' Taran almost laughed, but it came out as an incredulous gurgling as blood welled in his throat. 'And our Relics.' He struggled to breath. 'Sorsha, I'm sorry I teased you, I'm sorry for a lot of things…'

'Don't worry about...' I stopped speaking as Taran's hand slipped from my arm and he went limp. I glanced up to see Etienne, forehead furrowed.

Kit swore from behind me. 'Taran was a great swordsman. To best him would have taken some doing.'

'Or he was simply overpowered,' Amalia said, staring at the dead prince, her hand resting on her dagger.

'Let's go,' I said, getting up and heading towards my mother's chambers. We passed other bodies along the way, some I recognised, and fear swept through me at what I'd find in my mother's apartments. We reached the door, the lock broken, the scene within one of broken furniture and dishevelled possessions.

I glanced at Kit. His face had turned even more ashen. He looked sick, his face strained. My mother was almost a mother to him too, and I knew he didn't want to see what lay beyond the door anymore than I did – he wouldn't be able to handle it. I wasn't sure I could, either, but I had no choice.

'Kit, go and see if you can find Finnar,' I said. 'I'll be fine on my own.'

'Are you sure, Sorsh?' he asked, resting his hand on my arm. 'I'll stay if you want.'

'No,' I said, shaking my head. 'You go, we need to know what happened to him – I'll catch you up.'

He nodded and the others moved away after him, all except for Etienne. He stood rooted to the spot. I glanced at him in surprise.

'You shouldn't do this alone,' he said, slipping a hand on my shoulder. Amalia paused, frowning at him, her hand still on her dagger. 'Don't worry, Amalia, we'll be fine. You go with Kit, find the King.'

'If you're sure, Eti,' she said, moving after the others.

'Thank you,' I murmured to Etienne, and stepped into Mother's chambers.

Bookcases had been emptied of their contents, pictures stripped from the walls, clothes lay in crumpled heaps, including the dress she'd been preparing for my return, a gorgeous white silk creation I'd now never get to wear –

was that to be my Pledging Dress? I shivered and raised my torch. Next to a chair by the window that looked out onto the gardens, lay Lyssa. I moved over to her and crouched beside her body. Her eyes were open in horror, her throat cut, congealed blood on her skin that had stained her gown black as if she had spilt wine on it. I reached out and closed her eyes, her skin cold to my touch.

I stood up, and Etienne looking at me enquiringly. 'Lyssa, my mother's maid.'

He nodded.

A sound from the bedroom had me running. I swept into the room leaving Etienne lingering at the bedroom door. Mother lay on the floor, the moonlight illuminating her body long before my torchlight reached her. A dark stain still glistened wet on her chest.

'Mother!' I ran over to her, dropping my torch which Etienne hastily retrieved before stepping back towards the door to give us some privacy. 'Mother?'

'Sorsha?' She opened her eyes and smiled. 'I thought never to see your dear face again.'

I looked at her wound, and for a moment as my palms sweated and my breathing became fast and shallow, my mother looked as if she were on the other side of a pane of glass, not right beside me. 'We'll save you, Mother, make you well again.'

'You don't have an Orange Crystal, otherwise perhaps you could.'

For only the second time in my life I wished to use my Gift, as Etienne had called it, to shed blood, to produce a Pellucid that I could use to heal my Mother. But she was right, I needed an Orange, a Healing Stone, and neither I nor Etienne could produce one of those. His Psychic Stones would be of no use, and neither would my Purple Shields. I was helpless. Useless to her in her hour of need, not that I entirely knew how to use the two stones together. I'd only ever used a Pellucid for pain, the first time by accident when I cut my hand slicing vegetables and clenched my fist because of the pain, trapping the Pellucid. The glow from my hand had almost scared me to death. Since then I'd only done it a couple of times, and, of course, for Etienne on the beach.

'Sorsha, they took art, the Relics, jewellery, the paintings, the books. Some they burnt, but they didn't find the Starburst Necklace – you know where it is. Take it with you.'

'I don't need the Starburst,' I said, thinking of the necklace, famed for its two amethyst crystals set between two outer diamonds and at the centre, a larger diamond that shone like the brightest of stars. The purple amethysts glowed with a kind of internal light like the depths of night that no one could explain. What use would a trinket like that be to me with my mother dead and my home destroyed – other than to sell?

'You must,' she said, taking hold of my hand and squeezing it in a most uncomfortable fashion.

'I don't understand.'

'The gemstones within it… they're not gemstones.'

'What do you mean?'

'They're your First Crystals.'

My blood ran cold. My First Crystals? The first Blood Crystals I'd shed in the garden so long ago?

'I hid them in plain sight,' she continued, her voice beginning to falter. 'They are the most precious and most powerful stones you'll ever shed, my child. Get them… take them with you… you may have need of them.'

I nodded, speechless, my heart hammering against my ribcage, my stomach feeling as if it had just dropped out of me.

She glanced towards the door where Etienne waited. A little smile formed on her face. 'Ah, so you k…' She groaned and took a deep shuddering breath. She reached up to my cheek, her voice cracking. '… will look after you. Stay hidden, as you have been. Stay safe, keep your secret safe, don't let anyone else but him kno…'

Him? 'Let who know, Mother?'

Her hand dropped.

'Mother? Mother! No!' I pulled her to me, felt her

heartbeat cease as a little gasp escaped her lips – her final breath.

I'd been so young when we lost Father, I didn't really understand. This time I understood. I understood Taliesin had murdered my Mother, Taran and countless other of my people for what? Art? I didn't have words for how ludicrous, how pointless this all was. So many lives for paintings and sculptures? Why?

Fury welled in my heart, anger lit my veins, rage like a storm swirled inside me as I held her, rocking back and forth as if that would bring her back. My heart clamoured in my chest, breaking in two until the ache consumed me and tears took me. I let her go, let her rest on the carpeted floor of her chamber and sobbed until my whole body shook with it. A hand rested lightly on my shoulder, turning me around. Etienne crouched behind me and pulled me close, gently holding me in his arms as he whispered words of comfort in my ear. I continued to weep and the woody, rich smell of vetiver engulfed me as I rested my face on his shoulder and in his hair. Eventually I pulled back and clambered to my feet with his help, my swords catching on my back.

The torches on the wall illuminated Etienne's ashen face and glassy eyes, wrenching my heart. 'What can I do?' he asked quietly as he stood in front of me.

'Hold me,' I said, numb from grief and shock. He took hold of me again, enveloping me in his arms.

'Why is he doing this? Why is the Emperor plundering and killing the Orders?' My voice came out weak and crackly like autumn leaves.

Etienne shook his head. 'I don't know,' he said. 'For the art's value?'

'He must have more treasures in Merribor than the Orders have put together,' I said. 'No, that's not it, there's something else, I can feel it.'

'I think you're right, but what it is? I can't even begin to guess.'

We stayed like that for a few minutes more, until I felt composed enough to leave the room.

'We can't just leave her here,' I said miserably, glancing back at my mother's broken body.

'We won't, we'll come back, but for now we'd better find Kit and the others,' Etienne said, taking my hand and leading me towards the door. 'Find King Finnar.'

'Just a moment,' I said, slipping my hand from his and moving to Mother's bed. I knelt down and felt underneath the bedframe, finally reaching the small wooden box in its hiding place that sat wedged in the base of the bed. I pulled the walnut box out and rested it on the mattress.

'What is it?' Etienne asked, standing behind me.

I opened the lid, the necklace immediately bursting into life as the moonlight hit it.

'The Starburst Necklace,' I said, lifting it from the box. My fingers tingled at its touch and I wondered if that was me or the power I knew it contained – I hadn't held it in years. The Purple Crystals glistened with their strange internal light and the Pellucids scattered the milky light into a thousand rainbows of dazzling colours. I desperately hoped the prince hadn't heard what Mother had said to me.

A little gasp escaped his lips as he saw the necklace. 'That's beautiful. If I didn't know better…' Etienne's voice trailed off as he gazed at the gemstones – at my First Crystals.

Had he guessed what they were?

'My Mother had it made for me when I was small,' I said, watching the rainbows. 'I never took it with me to Uncle's – not much use for it there – but I can't leave it here now, Mother's right about that. *Was* right,' I said, glancing at her body. The question was, what to do with it. Leave it in its box? But then I'd have to lug it around with me and hope I didn't lose it. No, I had a better idea. I undid the clasp and slipped the necklace around my neck, but my fingers fumbled as I tried to do it up. Only then did I realise I was shaking.

'Let me,' Etienne said, gently taking the necklace from me and doing up the clasp as I held my hair out of the way. Did he feel the tingling too?

'Thank you,' I murmured, standing once more. I tucked it under my tunic out of sight. As the Crystals rested on my skin, warmth spread through me and a sensation of, not power exactly, but a kind of confidence I'd never felt before. But confidence was no good in the presence of grief and suffering. Confidence wouldn't help me cope with my mother's death, with what had happened here in the Citadel. Shield Stones were no good to me now, even if I dared use them and reveal myself to the world. They wouldn't save Steorra and they wouldn't bring Mother back. 'Let's head for the tower, see if we can find Kit.'

Etienne nodded and passed me my torch before grabbing his and we left the chamber, heading back out into the palace corridors.

I felt as if I were in a fog, a mist of grief, as we walked along picking our way over bodies, around broken furniture and past burning rooms. Never in a million years could I have imagined anything like this, and for a moment the corridor shifted around me, starting to spin and I thought I might fall until Etienne steadied me.

'Take it slowly, you've had one hell of a shock,' he said, his eyes serious and worried.

We continued on, his arm around me for support, my heart thudding and my palms sweating as we headed for the West Tower and Finnar's last stand.

Artem's eyebrow started twitching. 'By the time we get underway tomorrow they'll have a good day's head start.'

'No, not tomorrow, you must leave tonight,' Finnar said. 'Can I count on you and Princess Sorsha to warn the other Orders, Prince Etienne?'

My heart froze as Etienne nodded.

'You want me to go too?' I asked, at once horrified at the prospect of leaving Steorra again so soon, and yet at the same time relieved to be continuing in the company of the Sun Prince.

'I do,' Finnar said. 'Sorsha, I need you to raise the alarm. Etienne will no doubt stay in Solis with Prince Artem who will coordinate Steorra and Luna's needs – we cannot help Luna now we have our own troubles – you will need to sail on to Planetae to warn them.'

I swallowed. This was the last thing I wanted to do. I wanted to bury Mother and go home, leave the world to itself – although I was increasingly finding the presence of Etienne a calming and reassuring thing. The fact he'd said he'd visit me in the future had filled me with a sensation I'd never felt before. To know someone wanted to see *me* was a new feeling. One that left me warm and happy. Knowing I'd be leaving him when we reached Steorra had begun to bother me. Now though, the thought of travelling with him was the only thing that would get me on board that ship again.

'If that's what you command,' I said, slightly stiffly.

'I do,' Finnar said firmly. 'I suggest you leave now and head straight for Solis.'

'But Mother–'

'I'll see to it she has a proper burial,' Finnar said, looking at Dexan.

'Of course, Princess, she will have all the proper rights performed,' Dexan nodded.

'But I want to be there,' I murmured. I had to say goodbye properly.

'There's no time, you must leave now,' Finnar said.

I looked out of the study window, out over the burning Starlight Citadel where the stars shone benignly down on the scene of devastation. Pale moonlight rippled on the distant sea like a milky carpet leading me away from home. I swallowed and nodded, turning back to the spiral staircase.

I started to follow the others down the steps.

'Sorsha, how are you getting on with Prince Etienne?' Finnar asked.

I frowned. 'I'm sorry?' I asked, pausing.

'How are the two of you getting along?'

I shrugged. 'All right, I suppose. It was a little rocky to begin with, but we're getting there.'

'Good,' Finnar nodded. 'I'm glad, particularly in the circumstances.'

What circumstances?

'We may need his help when this is all over, so don't do anything to upset him,' Finnar continued.

Oh. I raised an eyebrow as I looked at the King. 'Me upset him? What about the other way around?'

'Just try to at least be friends. It'll be better in the long run if you are.'

'Yes, Your Majesty.' What a strange thing to say. After all, I wouldn't deliberately try to upset the Sun Prince. I turned towards the stairs.

'And Sorsha. They took the Amaranthine Rose.'

I swore. Of all our Relics it was the most precious. 'Bastards.'

'We will get it back.'

'Damn right.'

'I'll come down to the docks shortly to see you off.'

I nodded and followed the others down the steps.

#

We gathered in the main cabin as Captain Lucian set sail.

'I guess you're off the hook with your Pledging now, Eti,' Amalia said quietly, toying with the hilt of her dagger.

Etienne looked at her. 'Well…'

I looked up through the mist of grief that threatened to

envelop me but still lapped around me, not quite taking me completely into its grasp. 'Do you know who it was going to be?' I asked him.

He chewed his lip. 'Father never told me her name, but–'

'It was probably Aster, from what Amalia said. And Taran did say she was beautiful.'

'I can't see that's going to happen now. I mean, there are more important things happening in the world.'

'Than being Pledged?' Amalia asked, raising an eyebrow. 'I think continuing the Royal Line will be seen as a priority, don't you?'

'Maybe,' Etienne murmured, an uneasiness to his voice as he shot a glance in my direction. We were both in a similar position, and I knew how he felt.

'If it was Aster, you won't be being Pledged to the Fifth Starlight Princess now,' Kit said, his face bleak.

'Aster was the Fifth Starlight Princess?' Etienne asked, raising an eyebrow. 'I wasn–'

'She's dead. I saw her in one of the corridors,' Kit said, cutting in in a sick voice. 'They'd… she'd been… she's dead,' he said finally.

I looked sharply at him, and my greatest fears for her were written in his eyes. I suddenly felt nauseous. That could've been me, if I'd been at the Palace, and Kit's expression said he knew it. Strangely, so did the look Etienne gave me.

'You were lucky you were with us,' Amalia said, glancing at me. I nodded slowly, although anyone who'd tried attacking me would have got more than they'd bargained for in response.

'I saw the other two younger princesses dead as well,' Kit murmured.

Etienne frowned. 'I'm so sorry.' He glanced at me, concern clouding his eyes.

Kit's words were like a dagger to my heart. I'd lost not only my mother today, but so many cousins too. I needed fresh air. I needed to throw up.

I bolted from the cabin.

#

The mist of grief hadn't left me.

It swirled about me as I stared out over the ship's rail, the fires of the Starlight Citadel fading into the distance before dawn even broke. It was a couple of hours before the sky, stained with silver and gold, began to lighten as the ship cut through the salt air and the white tipped waves, gulls crying plaintively above. My red eyes, puffy and achy, found it hard to focus as spray swept into the air, stinging them.

Kit stayed below deck, finding his own way to deal with his grief. I sat on a barrel, wondering if the anguish twisting inside me would ever cease, or be as raw as this day forevermore. The searing pain only went away in brief moments of overwhelming numbness, when I had no feeling at all.

I still couldn't believe Finnar had sent me on this mission, especially after Mother's death, but he'd been insistent and we'd left him and Dexan to start rallying the remaining people and sort out what food and shelter they could. Not being at Mother's funeral bothered me most, but just before we left the docks Finnar pointedly, if not slightly callously, told me the living were now more important than the dead and the other Orders had to be warned. I knew he was right, I just didn't see why I had to be the one to do it – Kit could've done it alone, or Etienne could have sent messengers from Solis. At the same time, escaping the ravaged Citadel didn't entirely upset me; seeing it in such a state of devastation broke my heart.

Like Mother's death broke my heart.

I didn't even bother to go below decks to try and sleep – what was the point? When I shut my eyes I only saw fire, death and Mother's pale face. I didn't need to see that again any time soon, so I stayed put at the rail, throwing up intermittently, and not all of it due to seasickness.

The sun rose above the horizon, its rays warming the cold blue surface of the sea, casting glittering diamonds across the water. Late morning Amalia appeared on deck and came over to me.

'How are you doing?' she asked.

I shrugged. 'Hard to say, really.'

'King Finnar should've let you stay,' she said, fiddling with the blue gem ring on her finger. 'Eti and I could've sent messengers on from Solis.'

'It doesn't matter, I'm glad I can help,' I said, although my heart certainly didn't mean it.

Amalia's piercing grey-blue eyes looked into me. 'I'm sorry for your loss, Sorsha. Eti told me everything.'

I gave her a half smile. 'Thanks.'

After a while she returned to the cabins, leaving me alone once more but for the sailors scuttling about the deck and up and down the rigging like mice, Captain Lucian keeping things in order. His calm, measured way helped soothe me a little. By late afternoon Kit still hadn't appeared and I started to wonder if he was all right. As the sun began to set a wave of fatigue and tears washed over me. I slumped down behind the barrel for some privacy and buried my face in my hands as tears rolled unchecked down my cheeks as my heart twisted painfully in my chest.

'Sorsha?' Etienne's voice broke through the cloud of fog surrounding me.

I looked up at him through my tears, finding it hard to focus on the prince's face. He crouched down beside me, his warm hand coming to rest on my cheek. A hot spark lit inside me, quivering in my chest for a moment at his touch. I started to shiver – until he'd touched me I hadn't realised how cold I'd become, and shaking overtook my whole body.

He frowned. 'I need to get you inside,' he said, pulling me to my feet. 'I shouldn't have left you for so long, but I thought you needed the time alone.'

'I did,' I murmured. But I didn't want to be alone now.

'Come on.' He put his arm around me and guided me below deck to my cabin. 'Do you want anything to eat?' he asked, pouring me a mug of sweet mead which I dutifully drank.

'No, thank you, I couldn't stomach it at the moment.'

'Then get into bed, you need to warm up.'

I slipped my boots off and got under the blankets still fully clothed, still shivering.

He rubbed his forehead a moment before speaking. 'Do you wa–'

'Will you stay with me? For a while, anyway, until I've warmed up?'

His turquoise eyes softened. 'If you want me to,' he said softly.

I nodded. 'I don't want to be alone,' and I meant it whole heartedly. Never had I wanted company more than at that moment – and other than Kit I never normally wanted company. Etienne had changed that. He'd wormed his way into my affections in such a short, traumatic time that I knew deep down I didn't want to be without him. I needed his company tonight. I needed a friend. 'I want you to stay.'

He smiled, pulled his boots off and joined me under the blankets. He hesitated a moment and then, allowing me time to pull away if I wanted, slowly slipped his arms around me. But I didn't pull back. I was quite happy to let him hold me tonight.

'Is this all right?' he asked.

'Yes, thank you,' I said, snuggling against him.

'This is all new to me,' he said quietly as he rested against me. His voice had a slightly husky, emotional quality to it I'd never heard before and I turned to look at him in the light from the gently rocking oil lamp hanging from the cabin wall.

'What, being in bed with a girl?' I said, and couldn't help the wan little grin that forced its way onto my face.

'No – well, yes, actually, but what I mean is: being wanted.'

I looked into his gorgeous turquoise eyes, trying to understand what his life had truly been like as a Sun Prince forced to the edges of his Court.

He rubbed his forehead before he continued. 'Actually having someone who isn't Amalia who wants me to be with them and isn't just saying it because it's their duty or because of some formal occasion where they have to put up with me out of tradition, is new to me.'

I touched his warm cheek, noticing his eyes glistening as he spoke. 'Well, this definitely isn't a formal situation, Prince Etienne, and I don't want you here out of any sense of duty. I want you here for you, because you understand, somehow.'

'Amalia says I have empathy like no one else she's ever met,' he said, looking back at me.

I nodded. 'I think you do, not to mention you're considerate and caring.'

I shouldn't have said that – I immediately felt blood rushing to my cheeks, and my heart started racing even as a little lopsided grin appeared on his face. I couldn't get involved with him. I was promised to a prince who was out there somewhere, even if Etienne was no longer bound.

A shock ran through me even as the thought crossed my mind. The prince I was bound to might well be dead already, or under attack by the Emperor's fleet – and Etienne's Pledged had been...

He spoke before I could fall entirely into that deep, dark pit.

'And you, despite your initial prickles, are the most loyal and courageous person I've ever met. Not to mention kind and compassionate.'

I snorted. 'Courageous?' Me? I spent my life hiding, dodging anything half dangerous to keep my secret safe. 'I'm not sure that's me.'

'Maybe no one's got close enough to you before to point it out.'

Was he right? I still didn't think courageous was a word to describe me. Although I suppose loyal was – I was loyal to the Crown, my family, to Kit. Maybe now to Etienne. He looked at me, his pupils dilating slightly.

He kissed my head. 'Try and get some sleep,' he said, settling beside me.

I hadn't realised how tired I was, and as these new thoughts circled in my mind I quickly drifted off to sleep.

Chapter Eight

Flames licked at the walls around me, their red-gold fingers reaching for anything that would burn – for anyone. The smell of smoke and burning filled the air and threatened to choke me as it poured down my throat, yet I didn't cough. The great four-poster bed burst into flame, the heat searing as the fire consumed the mattress. On the floor lay the body of my mother, her face deathly white, her broken body with scarlet blood soaking into her silken dress, dripping onto the floor as she reached impotently for me with a blood covered hand, her eyes dead.

'Stay hidden. Stay safe, keep your secret safe, don't let anyone know, but him,' she intoned over and over again until my ears rang with her words.

'Let who know, Mother? Who?'

I stood rooted to the spot, unable to move, unable to help her, unable to leave this horror. I tried to shut my eyes, to block out the scene, but I couldn't. I'd been too late to save her. If I'd arrived earlier could I have stopped this? If I'd had the Starburst Necklace could I have protected her with its Crystals? Or would we both have died?

My heart thudded uncomfortably, smashing against my ribcage, a cold sweat all over my body and nausea rising in my throat. I could do nothing. I was helpless and I hated the feeling.

The flames swept from the bed, forming a wall between me and my mother, and still I couldn't move. My skin reddened in the heat but try as I might I couldn't leave, still couldn't move. One of the posts of the great four-poster bed collapsed, the flaming tester fell towards me and I screamed.

I awoke, my heart racing, sweat plastering my hair to my head. Etienne had gone. A sudden wave of nausea had me bolting for the deck, leaving my boots behind as I sprinted up the steps, out the door and over to the ship's rail; but there was nothing left in my stomach, all I had was bile. Even so I retched and retched, my throat burning like my dreams. A wave of lightheadedness swept over me, telling me I ought to try and eat something, and soon.

'Sorsh.' Kit came running over. 'Are you all right?'

I nodded. I didn't know if this was seasickness or the dream, but it didn't really matter much. 'Yes. Sorry.'

'Don't be,' he said, putting his arm around me. 'I'm sorry I didn't come and see you yesterday. Seeing home like that… it's taken me a while to process it. I should've been there for you. I'm sorry,' he said again, bowing his head.

'It's fine, Kit, this isn't just about me,' I said, noticing Prince Artem at the prow of the ship talking to Amalia, or rather, listening to Amalia. 'I fear we're all going to be touched by this before it's over. Anyway, I was glad to be alone myself, at least for a while.'

'Etienne?'

'What?' I felt the blood rushing to my face.

'You like him.' It was more accusation than anything.

I swallowed. 'He's all right.'

'I think you've changed your feelings towards the Sun Prince. I told you he wasn't what you thought.'

'Maybe,' I mumbled. 'I might have misjudged him a little.'

'A little?'

'If you haven't got anything helpful to say you can go,' I said nudging him gently in the ribs.

He smiled. 'That's my Sorsh,' he said.

'And that's my Kit,' I said, hugging him. 'Have you seen Etienne?'

'Amalia says he's still asleep. Apparently you were rather restless last night. Kept him awake.'

The whole ship knew about last night? Even though nothing inappropriate had happened my face turned the same colour as a ripe strawberry.

Kit chuckled.

'Go away,' I said, this time meaning it. As soon as he left

I went in search of some dry biscuits to take the edge off my hunger and give my stomach something to throw up.

As the morning wore on I stood watching the waves, my grief alternating with the fire that had lit in my veins when Mother died. That need for justice began to clamour inside my head. I couldn't let this go unpunished, couldn't leave it. I had to do something. It may be the only way I could get some sort of closure on my Mother's death, particularly as I wasn't even going to be at her funeral. I'd have to get my solace elsewhere.

In revenge.

Late morning Etienne came out on deck and stretched. On seeing me he smiled and walked over to the rail. That smile, well it could probably melt glaciers.

'How are you feeling?' he asked.

'Not too bad,' I said, aware my eyes were still puffy and rather unattractive, not that he seemed to notice. 'How did you sleep?'

'On and off. I left you at dawn and went back to my cabin.'

I nodded. 'Kit said I was restless.'

Etienne smiled. 'You could say that.'

'Sorry.'

'You don't need to apologise. I'd have left sooner if it bothered me, and besides, I think you may have slept better with me there anyway.'

'I think so too.'

#

'Sail ho!'

'What is it?' I asked, squinting as I looked up, raising my hand against the sun. We'd been chasing the Emperor's fleet for several days but had, despite Lucian's best efforts, been unable to catch them. A change in wind direction had slowed us down for a while, stringing out my nerves. Etienne was as least as anxious as I was, if not more so, and my dreams hadn't been helping.

'Not sure, come on,' Etienne said, taking my hand and

leading me towards the bow where the others stood with Captain Lucian, his spyglass open and raised. 'What's happening, Captain?'

Captain Lucian continued his observation for a moment before lowering the spyglass and closing it. 'Solis has just come into sight, Your Highness – the harbour at Helios City is full of Merriborian warships.'

My heart fell at his words. I looked at Etienne. His face was pale and strained.

Lucian passed the spyglass to Etienne. 'There's smoke, Prince Etienne. What do you want to do?'

Etienne let go of me and took the spyglass, opened it and lifted it to his eye. I tried to see what he was looking at, but even squinting I could only just make out the distant coastline. I glanced at Amalia who was gazing out over the sea, her face taut, hand unconsciously on her knife. As he lowered the spyglass Etienne's eyes had a haunted look about them – were his parents dead or alive? And what about his brothers? I feared the worst, and from his ashen face, so did he.

'I don't believe our presence will change the tide of what happens there today,' Etienne said, his muscles tight. 'We could get ourselves killed if we try and land. That'll help no one, and one ship can't make any difference to Helios City now. What we can do is warn the Planetary Order, maybe spare them from the same fate.' He took a deep breath. 'We have to assume the fleet will continue on as it did from Steorra, rather than return to Merribor like before. We sail to Planetae Island.'

Lucian nodded. 'Come about,' he shouted, and started giving orders as he moved down the ship, sailors quickly adjusting sails and rigging, noise and calls filling the salty air.

I turned to Etienne as he passed the spyglass to Amalia, and slipped my hand into his, squeezing it. He looked at me, his eyes full of unshed tears as his home city began to burn, just as mine had, bringing everything back in one huge wave of grief and loss. I bit back the tears that filled my eyes as anger raged inside me.

'If we can save even one person on Planetae, then it's worth it,' he murmured.

I nodded – spoken like a true prince. 'I know.'

By the evening we'd made good time, but this would be a longer journey than the ones between the other isles had been; it would take many days to reach Planetae's capital, Galatae. A stiff breeze moved us swiftly along through the white horses, slicing through the water like a dagger. For once I joined the others for the evening meal, glad of the company and distraction from my own internal storm. I ate little, spoke little, but their company meant a lot, even if it was subdued after seeing their home succumbing to the same fate as Moon City and the Starlight Citadel. The others kept the conversation light, away from our troubles, discussing Planetae Island. Only Artem had been there before, and he seemed quite excited at the prospect, more excited than I'd have thought, in the circumstances.

As the evening drew on I settled in my cabin, but sleep took a long time to claim me. I heard Etienne enter his cabin next to mine not long after I'd retired, and Kit and Amalia went down to their cabins. I thought I heard Artem go out on deck, but I could've been wrong. I considered going to see Etienne, but after today he probably needed his rest, so I tried to sleep, but tears soon filled my eyes, guilt weighing heavily in my chest. Could I have done something if I'd been at the Citadel? I squeezed my eyes tight shut, tears leaking out as I buried my face in my pillow, my chest aching with grief. I really wanted company. Etienne's company. His calm, reassuring presence. But I stayed where I was and in the early hours, eventually drifted off into a fitful sleep.

#

Gold and red fingered flames licked at the walls around me as the smell of burning filled my lungs. Once again the great four-poster bed burst into flames sending ghastly shadows over the chamber. My mother lay on the floor, her dress soaking with crimson blood, her lifeless hand reaching towards me.

'Stay hidden. Stay safe, keep your secret safe, don't let anyone know, but him.' The words spun in my head like a child's top.

Again I couldn't move, couldn't help, and still didn't know who she was referring to. I was useless.

My heart thundered in my chest as a cold sweat sprung up covering my body.

The flames sprang from the bed, keeping me from my mother's body as the heat scorched me, forming a wall between me and my mother, and still I couldn't move. My skin reddened in the heat, but try as I might, I couldn't leave. The bed collapsed, burning curtains suddenly surrounding me.

I screamed.

'Sorsha? Sorsha! It's a dream, only a dream,' Etienne said, kneeling at the side of the bed as I woke.

The scream was fresh on my lips, my throat sore. I looked at him, my eyes wide, sweat making my clothes and hair cling to me.

'It's all right, just breathe,' he said gently, his hand resting on my shoulder.

I burst into tears.

'Hey, it's all right,' he said, sitting on the edge of the bed.

I sat up and he pulled me into a hug as I continued to weep. Calming vetiver surrounded me taking me into its warm embrace as he held me to him while I sobbed.

The Starlight Citadel. Helios City. Moon City. Why was this happening? I couldn't understand it.

I pulled back a little. 'I'm sorry, I didn't mean to wake you,' I said after a couple of minutes, my voice croaky. 'Have I woken anyone else?' I asked, glancing to the door.

He shook his head. 'No, I don't think so, they're all fast asleep.'

'Weren't you?'

'No. Can't drop off to sleep for some reason. I just can't settle.'

Maybe there was a solution for both of us. Maybe... we just wanted each other's company.

I took a breath. 'Want to stay with me?'

'Is this going to become a habit?' he asked.

I shrugged and lay back down. 'We'll see – I guess it depends on how many more horrors we come across.'

He gave me a wan little smile and climbed into the bed, lying beside me looking up at the ceiling. 'I can't get what happened in Steorra and Luna out of my mind, or what might have happened at home. I wish I knew exactly what's happened to Helios, to my family – but I suppose not knowing still lets me hang on to hope, however false it may be.'

'Hope I don't have,' I murmured.

'Sometimes not knowing is better than knowing.'

'Perhaps. I just wonder if Mother would still be alive if I'd been there, if I could've saved her.'

He turned towards me. 'You can't think like that anymore than I can. In all likelihood we'd have been killed too if we'd been there with them. This way, at least we're still alive. At least we can do something.'

We lay there for a while listening to the creaking of the ship's hull and the sound of the waves outside the cabin window.

'They may have survived, like Finnar,' I said.

'We don't have a Refuge room like you. But I'll change that when I get home.' He hesitated for a moment. 'Do you mind me asking, what happened to your father?'

'No, I don't mind. Father was a diplomat, and spent a lot of time travelling around Merribor and Faerland for the King. He died when I was seven, so I don't remember a huge amount about it, other than he was on a diplomatic mission to western Merribor when his ship went down in a storm. I cried for days whe–when Mother came to Uncle's and told me. Father was very dear to me, I just wish I could remember him more.'

Etienne nodded, taking my hand. 'I'm sorry it happened when you were so young.'

'We placed a quartz bauble on the Soul Tree outside

the Citadel to remember him. I wonder if it's still there after...' Tears welled in my eyes as my thoughts drifted back to Steorra.

'If it's not, we'll replace it one day, don't worry.'

We lay silently for a bit.

'Have you ever met any of the Planetary Royal Family before?' I asked.

'I met the King and his son, Prince Vergil, shortly after the prince had become the heir. They visited a couple of years ago, just after his eldest son died. They went to all the isles.'

So this Prince of Planetae couldn't be the one Mother had found for me. Maybe there was another, a distant family member instead, that she had arranged for me.

'You?' Etienne asked.

I shook my head. 'When it came to Royal Visits, being at my uncle's, I tended to miss them all – thankfully.'

Etienne chuckled. 'I rather like the sound of your life,' he said. 'I wouldn't have minded missing all of that, too.'

The very thought of a Royal Visit made my palms sweat. Visiting Galatae City and the King, even in these circumstances, wouldn't quell my anxiety when we actually got there, and I knew it. Deep down I dreaded it, but it had to be done, we had to warn them, and then...

I lay on my side facing Etienne. 'What do you think's going to happen?'

He took a deep breath. 'We'll warn Planetae, help them defend the city then go home and rebuild.'

'And Taliesin and Cynric?'

He turned to me and frowned. 'What do you mean? What about them?'

'Do we let them get away with whatever it is they're doing?'

'What choice do we have? We don't have great armies like the Emperor.'

'No, but there are other ways of getting revenge.'

'Revenge?'

'Maybe they should experience what happened to our people themselves.'

His forehead furrowed. 'You'd kill them?'

'I think we need justice for our people. Their heinous crimes can't go unpunished,' I said, the fire from my nightmare still filling my veins. 'We need to know what they're doing and stop them. It's up to us, Etienne, we're the only ones who can do this. We're the surviving Royal Families of the destroyed Orders – don't we owe it to our people, to our families – to ourselves?'

He looked at me, his eyes pools I could drown in. 'There you go, what did I say?'

I frowned. 'What did you say?'

'You have more courage than anyone I've ever known.'

'Courage or stupidity?'

'Definitely courage,' he said with a smile. 'Let's get to Galatae City, then see what we can do to avenge them and bring justice.'

Chapter Nine

The voyage to Galatae City passed relatively uneventfully, if you ignored my nightmares and the rain that hammered down on us solidly for several days keeping me below decks more than I'd have liked. The weather slowed us down a little, but eventually the emerald green coastline of Planetae Isle came into sight and one fine morning we rounded a massive headland and sailed in towards Galatae City. The city itself sat at the far end of an inlet, at the head of a great long U-shaped valley where the sea reached inland like a long arm, the valley pulling us in even as the impossibly steep rock walls rose up either side of us, almost seeming to close in on us as we went. Here and there a hanging valley nestled high up the rock wall, waterfalls gently cascading down towards the sea like white wispy veils. I'd never seen anything like this before.

Etienne didn't appear to appreciate the view. He sat on a barrel and, rather than admiring the scenery, had his nose firmly in a small book. Maybe not so much book, as a work of art. Each vellum page had gold edging, the words written in what looked like iron gall ink, probably imported from neighbouring Faerland down to our south-east across the Straits, with highly swirling, intricate characters – some in red – which weren't easy to read. Colourful initials, decorative illustrations and dense text filled the pages, but the outside of the tome was what impressed me the most. The red leather-bound book's cover was embellished with gold and silver painted symbols and inset with gemstones of what looked like emerald, golden topaz and diamond, or maybe they were quartz. The coloured stones, of varying shapes and sizes, ran around the outside edges of the cover, with the five smaller quartz stones decorating the spine. It was the most magnificent book I'd ever seen – we had nothing like that in the library back at the Citadel.

'What is it?' I asked Etienne, coming over to sit beside him.

'Hmm? Oh, this? It's a book of poetry and myth,' he said.

'Poetry? I didn't see you as a poet.'

'By the Sun, I'm not a poet, but I enjoy the lyrical writing – it can help take my mind off things...' He gazed out over the water and valley for a moment as if suddenly seeing them for the first time.

'Have you had it long?'

'My mother gave it to me some years ago. A birthday gift. Can't say I thought much of it at the time, but I guess it's come to mean more as time's gone on – particularly now with... you know,' he said glancing at me and then back at the book, the wind catching his tousled hair.

I knew what he meant particularly now, with everything that'd happened and him not knowing whether his parents and brothers were still alive.

The ship hit a rogue wave, lurching to one side. Etienne made a grab for the barrel beside him to steady himself, losing hold of his book in the process. It fell towards the deck next to me. I bent down to catch it, just missing. I leant down further to pick it up just as Etienne reached out for it.

Our hands touched, both grasping the book at the same time. I looked up to find Etienne's face barely an inch from mine. I gazed into his deep turquoise eyes for a moment. His eyes moved from mine to my lips, lingering before he smiled at me, a look of almost... longing, in his eyes. I tore my eyes away, face hot, as I let go of him and the book, and moved back. I swallowed.

'Sorry,' I mumbled.

'Not your fault,' he murmured back. 'Thanks for trying to catch it.'

My heart pounded, pulse loud in my ears. 'You'd better take care of it,' I said, glancing across the deck. 'I think our dear, silent Prince Artem has his eye on it.'

Etienne looked up and over to the Moon Prince who

stood at the side of the ship, watching. Artem quickly moved away towards the stern.

'Don't worry, it never leaves me,' Etienne said, placing it in a pocket inside his clothes. 'He won't get his hands on it.'

'What do you make of him, you know, Artem?' I asked.

Etienne shrugged. 'Not sure really, it's hard to make someone out when they hardly ever speak, but there's something about him I can't quite put my finger on.'

'I know what you mean.' A sudden thought slammed uncomfortably into my mind. 'How many siblings does– did he have?' I asked, as a chill as cold as winter swept through me – was he the sixth child? Please, Starlight, don't let him be the sixth. 'Were they older or younger?'

Etienne frowned. 'Why?'

'Just wondered.'

'Err, three, I think. Linus and one other older, and another younger.'

I nodded. 'Good.'

The Sun Prince raised an eyebrow. 'Care to elaborate?'

'It's nothing,' I said, shaking my head. 'Nothing at all.' Thankfully.

The ship sailed through a narrow channel. At either side of the valley sitting on headlands, rose two squat stone towers, with huge rusty chains running from them into the water.

'What are they for?' I asked no one in particular.

'For the defensive nets,' Captain Lucian said coming up beside me on his rounds of the deck. 'The chains are attached to great metal nets that can be raised in times of war. They were last used fifty years ago, or so I heard, but they maintain them and check them regularly in case they ever need them.'

'They might be needing them soon,' Etienne said sourly, gazing at them as we slipped serenely past. 'We have no way of installing anything like that at home.'

'Neither do we,' I said.

Lucian nodded. 'They do have an advantage of terrain

here,' he said. 'Just up ahead, those barges tied to the shore, they're ready to place across the channel further up where it narrows so they can be sunk, stopping any ships from passing closer to the city.'

I smiled. 'You've been here before, haven't you?'

'A few times, Princess,' Lucian grinned. 'My grandmother was from here,' he said, before walking off and shouting orders to the men up the rigging who wrestled with the sails in the stiff breeze.

'Have you seen a city like this before?' Kit asked coming over with Amalia.

'Made of wood? No, never,' Amalia said, her blue jewelled hand resting on her knife as usual.

'Wood?' I turned to look at the city that now finally made an appearance at the end of the inlet. Sure enough, rising up the hillside beyond a great wall of grey stone blocks, sat wooden buildings, brightly painted in vibrant reds and blues and greens, with yellow accents. High above them a great building rose – the palace? – just as colourful.

'Nothing like home, is it?' Kit said quietly from beside me, a momentary pang of grief shifting inside me at his words and I bit my lip to stop tears from forming.

'No,' I said. 'Nothing like home.'

Captain Lucian brought the ship safely into the docks and we disembarked at the harbour where the smell of dead fish threatened to overwhelm me for a moment, before making our way up through the twisting streets, past the jewel-coloured houses and towards the palace. As we reached the open gates, a tall young man about Amalia's age, with shining, dark sepia skin, a little darker than Kit's, walked out to greet us. His beautiful dark brown eyes studied us as he came toward us, two soldiers at his back.

'Prince Etienne, this is an unexpected pleasure,' the young man said, smiling so his eyes lit up. 'We had no idea of your visit.'

'It's not so much a visit as an urgent need to speak with you and your father, Prince Vergil,' Etienne said, shaking the prince's hand.

Vergil frowned. 'Bad news?'

'You could say that,' Amalia said, looking at Vergil through her long eyelashes.

'Lady Amalia,' Vergil said, taking her hand and kissing it as he gazed into her eyes. He cleared his throat. 'It's good to see you again.'

'And you,' she murmured a pink tinge colouring her cheeks.

I glanced at Kit and raised an eyebrow. He smiled back.

'Prince Artem,' Vergil said stiffly, turning to the Moon Prince. 'I'm surprised to see you with a party from the Sun Order.'

'Needs must, Prince Vergil,' Artem said, his eyes cold.

'May I present Princess Sorsha from the Starlight Order and her companion, Kit,' Etienne said, breaking the awkward silence that had taken hold.

'Princess Sorsha, the mythical Starlight Princess?' Vergil asked, kissing my hand and frowning.

'Mythical?' I asked, confused.

'You were mentioned when my father and I visited the Starlight Citadel,' Vergil said. 'Apparently your yearly visits to the Court have become legend.'

Kit laughed. 'There you go, Sorsh. You're a legend.'

I gave Kit a long look. 'I prefer life away from Court, Your Highness, that's all.'

'If you're all here, then your news must be urgent indeed.' Vergil scratched his head, looking at us.

'We need to see your father immediately,' Etienne said with a nod. 'Planetae may be in grave danger.'

Vergil narrowed his eyes in thought, then turned to the soldiers behind him. 'Start making preparations for the defence of Galatae.' The soldiers looked at each other, shocked expressions creeping over their faces, then nodded and ran off. 'Come with me. Father's waiting for us in the Great Hall.'

We followed the Planetary Prince up to the entrance of the palace that sat up on the hill. I glanced back. The view over the sea out towards the open water was extraordinary. The sunbeams scattered off the water like sparks from a fire even as one side of the valley began to disappear into shadow. I turned back and followed the others into the palace and to the Great Hall. As we entered the huge chamber my hands broke out in a familiar cold sweat and my heart began to pound. I could see the King on his throne at the far end of the hall, and the thought of what we were about to tell him only increased the horrid sensations. I swallowed as we stopped in front of the throne and the Planetary King, Saros.

'Father,' Vergil said bowing. 'Prince Etienne of the Sun Order, Prince Artem of the Moon Order and Princess Sorsha, the Starlight Princess, are here with urgent news.'

We bowed, although I did some half-bow, curtsey thing, my hands trembling.

'Indeed,' King Saros said, scratching his white beard, a stark contrast to his dark skin. 'Princes, Princess, welcome to the Isle of Planetae. What is your news?'

'Moon City, the Starlight Citadel and Helios City have all been raided by Prince Cynric on the orders of Emperor Taliesin to steal our artworks,' Etienne said.

'Artworks?' Vergil frowned. 'Did you say artworks?'

'Go on,' Saros said, his knuckles turning white as his fingers curled around the arms of his throne.

'They have stolen anything of value, killed the citizens and put the cities to the torch,' Etienne said.

'The Royal Families?'

'Many members are dead,' Etienne said, bowing his head.

'Your parents?'

'I don't know, the city was under attack as we arrived back, so we sailed on to warn you.' The Sun Prince's eyes had that haunted look again.

'Prince Artem?' Saros asked.

'My parents and other brothers are dead,' Artem said, his voice unemotional. 'My brother Linus now rules.'

Saros had an appalled look in his eyes.

'Princess, how did Steorra fair?' Vergil asked.

'King Finnar lives,' I said, my palms sweating and for a moment Vergil appeared to be on the other side of a pane of glass. 'My mother and my cousins are dead.'

'I'm sorry.'

Saros clenched his jaw. 'Taliesin has no right, we agreed years ago they would remain sacred.'

'Your Majesty?' I asked – what was he talking about?

'Each Order has five sacred Relics, artworks, that are of great sentimental significance to our peoples. They were never secret, but then Taliesin expressed an interest in them for their value. The Orders came to an arrangement with him, a monetary one, that would see the Relics remain with the Orders. Despite this agreement, many of the Orders hid their valued pieces in case he reneged on the deal. It's taken him a while, but it looks like that is exactly what he's doing.'

I now wished Finnar had hidden the Amaranthine Rose. If it really did contain Crystals their power now lay in Taliesin's hands – did he know what he had?

'But why now, Father?' Vergil asked, his voice perplexed as he scratched his head.

'Who can say, but we must make sure our Relics are well hidden before Prince Cynric gets here, and the inlet secured. Chamberlain Gaea!' King Saros thundered.

'I've already begun the preparations,' Vergil said.

Saros nodded as a Planetaean man, with long black hair and dressed in deep green velvet, came dashing into the Great Hall.

'Majesty,' he said with a low bow.

King Saros stood. 'Chamberlain, remove all our Relics to the ruined city at once, secure the inlet, raise the net and scuttle the barges, prepare the army for Merriborian raiders.'

'Sire?' Chamberlain Gaea's face dropped, his eyes grew wild and his skin ashen. 'The Emperor?'

Saros' jaw tightened. 'We are under attack.'

Chamberlain Gaea nodded, glanced at us and rushed out without another word.

'Vergil, you will take Prince Etienne's party north to

Anchorton, take a boat and sail to the Celestial Temple and warn the Priestess Athene of Taliesin's treachery,' Saros said.

I noticed Artem raise an eyebrow as Kit glanced at me. The Celestial Temple? I'd never been there, only heard stories about the priestesses and the graceful building they tended. Surely they couldn't have any art there that Cynric would try and steal? I rather thought Saros was keeping something back, but this wasn't the time to question him. We had to leave.

'But Father, I can help here, defend the city,' Vergil said, looking slightly aghast at his father's order.

'I know, my son,' Saros said, stepping forward and placing a hand on his son's shoulder. 'But this may be even more important than saving our city.'

'Can we not sail back down the inlet before you raise the net?' Artem asked.

Saros shook his head. 'From what you've said we have to assume that Cynric won't be far behind you – you won't reach open water in time. You must head north on land. Get your things from your ship. Vergil, come with me, you must prepare for the journey. My son will meet you all at the docks in an hour. And thank you for your warning.' The King left the Throne Room with Vergil trailing uncomfortably in his wake.

Amalia's eyes were full of concern, as were Etienne's, but as he looked at me a feeling of calm and warmth washed over me. Our journey together wasn't over. We still had much to do, and somehow I had the feeling this was only the beginning.

We went back to the docks and collected our packs. Etienne spoke to Captain Lucian to explain. The sailor nodded.

'You must escape that way, your father wouldn't want you trapped here,' Lucian said.

'I'm still sorry to leave you here like this,' Etienne said. 'Thank you for your service.'

'Any time, Your Highness. I hope we'll meet again one day,' he said shaking Etienne by the hand.

We said our goodbyes and made our way over to the meeting place.

'I hate horses,' Amalia said, rolling her eyes to the sky as Vergil appeared with a servant leading enough horses for us all. 'They stink.'

'So will you after a few days in the saddle, so don't worry about it,' Etienne said, walking over towards Vergil.

'Thanks, Eti.'

Kit grinned. 'I don't mind horses.'

'I'll just be glad not to throw up on this journey,' I said, following Etienne.

'You and me both,' Kit said.

'Shut up.'

We attached our packs to our horses and mounted up, riding out of the city and along the shore a short way before Vergil led us along a path that wove its way up the side of the valley in a series of hairpin bends. We climbed ever higher until we reached a ribbon of water cascading out from a hanging valley above us in a torrent of spray and noise.

'Not far now,' Vergil called back over the sound of the waterfall, shifting the axe that sat on his back into a more comfortable position.

'Not far until what?' Amalia yelled back.

'Until we reach the valley up there,' he said pointing.

'We're going up there?' she asked, her eyes wide.

'It's fine.' Vergil grinned at her.

I hoped it would be, but the rugged pathway became little more than an animal track with scrubby plants at either side, and before long we had to get off our horses and lead them up the slippery side of the valley. Eventually we reached the top of the falls and after clambering around some rocks, a wide valley opened up before us, totally hidden from the valley and water below. We remounted, sweating in the warm sunshine.

I looked back down into the valley. Far below, just visible around the distant headland entrance into the inlet, loomed the dark shapes of Cynric's fleet. I glanced back towards Galatae – the net stood in its raised position and the five barges had been sunk in readiness for the Merriborian Prince's attack.

'Maybe they can hold them off,' Etienne said from beside me, his horse shifting restlessly beneath him. 'They have the advantage of knowing what's coming.'

'Let's damn well hope they can.' I nodded. 'I'd rather like to stay and watch the Emperor's men getting a bloody nose.'

'Not spoken like a Starlight Princess,' he said with a grin.

'Didn't you know? Today's my day off.' I laughed, and we urged our horses on into the hanging valley.

Chapter Ten

Camping was something I was used to, but I don't think Artem had spent a single night out under the stars, ever. He looked decidedly uncomfortable, and I couldn't say I felt sorry for him. The others all seemed quite happy as we ate our evening meal of herb and dumpling stew Kit and Amalia had prepared. Artem hardly ate any of it. He'd probably have turned his nose up at it completely if it wasn't for the fact we hadn't eaten since breakfast. We settled down to sleep under the blankets Vergil had brought with him, beside the campfire which shed its warmth around us. We'd stopped in a little dip in the ground, quite sheltered and not far from a stream, far up the hanging valley and away from the city. On two sides of us lay thick undergrowth and on a third a few trees and ferns ran up the valley side. I lay on my back huddled under my blanket, gazing up at the stars, drinking in the night air that had an earthy edge of dampness to it as it nipped at my nose. We were high up in the hills and the climate here was colder than down by the sea, and the air temperature confirmed it.

'What's that?' Amalia asked suddenly.

To the south-west the sky had a distant orange-red glow to it. Fire?

'The city?' Kit asked, voicing what we all wondered.

'Could be the ships,' Etienne said, raising himself up on one elbow. 'I noticed your father had fire catapults down the valley, Vergil. They'd make one hell of a merry blaze if they could hit Cynric's ships. The fire would probably jump from ship to ship, if the wind's in the right direction.'

Vergil nodded with a smile, although a concerned look flickered in his fire-lit eyes. 'Those catapults can set light to a ship at a good three to four hundred yards on a good day. That's over halfway across the inlet where they're stationed, and they're quite accurate. It could well be Cynric's fleet that's alight and not the city.'

'Let's hope so,' Amalia said, smiling reassuringly at the prince.

'That's all we can do at the moment, anyway,' he said, his eyes taking on a faraway look.

I gazed back up at the stars and smiled. The idea it could be the fleet alight and not the city was a comforting thought, especially as Lucian and the ship's crew were still in port. After a while we stopped talking and I drifted off to sleep, but my dreams were filled with fire and blood, only this time I didn't just see Mother's face, but Taran's too, in turns mocking me and pleading with me to save him, blood smeared on his deathly pale face. I awoke, my heart thumping like I'd run a mile. I scrambled out of my blankets as quickly and quietly as I could, so as not to disturb anyone, and headed for the trees. Once a short distance from the camp, I fell to my knees, a cold sweat breaking out all over my body as I started to shake. The fleet arriving had probably been the catalyst for tonight's nightmares, but it was seeing Mother that unnerved me the most.

I began to cry, weeping turning into sobs that racked my body. I hadn't really had a chance to grieve properly, and at this precise moment, I found myself overwhelmed with emotion. A warm hand started to rub my back and I twisted around to see Etienne crouching behind me, his eyes worried in the starlight.

'I've got you, you're all right,' he murmured in my ear.

'But I'm not, am I?' I mumbled between sobs. 'And I don't know if I ever will be again, not now Mother's gone.'

He gently pulled me towards him, holding me in his arms, talking quietly in my ear as I wept, cradling me in his comforting embrace.

'Sorsh?' Kit appeared through the undergrowth.

'She's okay, Kit, she just had a bad dream,' Etienne said.

Kit nodded. 'If you're sure?'

'We're fine.'

Kit moved away through the plants, back to the campsite.

I sobbed my heart out, wave upon wave of grief hitting me, Mother's face there every time I shut my eyes, and when it wasn't grief, anger raged in my veins. Taliesin and Cynric wouldn't get away with this. I was still having trouble processing everything that had happened since I first left the Starlight Citadel, and the tears somehow helped, however embarrassed I was of them.

'You will be okay again, it'll just take time,' Etienne said, his embrace warm and strong. 'You need to be patient.'

I couldn't help but let out a bitter little laugh. 'I'm not sure patience is in my vocabulary. At least, I think Kit would say it isn't.'

Etienne moved back and smiled. He reached out, brushing my damp hair from my eyes. 'Everything will be fine. You'll see. Now let's get you back to camp. You're freezing.'

We walked back to the fire that Kit had put another couple of branches on before returning to his blankets. I lay back down under my covers, but my shivering wouldn't stop and Etienne realised it.

'Shall I sleep next to you, warm you up?' he whispered, so as not to wake the others.

'Please,' I said, my teeth chattering.

He threw his blanket over us both and got under mine, moving next to me. We lay there looking at the stars, my shivering slowly subsiding as his bodily warmth reached through to me. Going back to sleep wouldn't be easy. I didn't want those nightmares again – and yet with all the travelling, the lack of food due to seasickness, and now my dreams and the lack of sleep that went with them, I was more tired than ever, and yet I was still unable to nod off. Etienne turned towards me after a while and slowly, gently slipped his arm across my stomach. I didn't resist, just moved my head towards him as vetiver swept around me. The scent wasn't as strong as it had once been, now that it was mingled with the smell of travel, but it was still there in the background. That, and his comforting warmth, helped to dispel the bad thoughts, and I finally nodded off to sleep in his arms.

#

No one said anything when I woke the next morning to find Etienne still lying next to me. Kit just grinned. Amalia seemed too busy helping Vergil with the breakfast, laughing at almost everything he said. Artem was nowhere to be seen until the food was ready, when he reappeared. We ate swiftly. I managed to stomach a few mouthfuls, and we set off again, riding into a pine forest, the smell of the needles mixing with the loamy soil as we followed a path up the side of the valley and out onto a ridge with views north to the sea. I turned back towards Galatae, but it lay hidden behind a mountain – we were still none the wiser as to what had happened.

The chill air made me wrap my cloak tightly around me as the west wind blew over the bald hills and mountains towards us. Birds of prey circled high above and insects chirped in the long grasses on either side of us. The blue sky of yesterday was long gone, replaced with low scudding grey clouds that skimmed the peaks of the highest mountains way out to the west with their white, snow-capped tops grazing the dusky veil, intermittently disappearing before coming back into view.

We rode hard, keen to get to the northern fishing port of Anchorton as soon as possible. Time marched against us. How long Cynric would be delayed in Galatae, we couldn't tell, so we had to push on. We rode down from the ridge into grasslands, on into ancient woodland where birds chattered, squirrels jumped from tree to tree and deer raced into the ferns to escape us. The smell of the little woodland flowers peppering the spaces between the trees drifted on the air, sweet and light. The air warmed as we rode down onto the plains close to the sea and we even dared allow ourselves to push the horses into a gallop for a while. As night fell we rode into Anchorton, and not a moment too soon. Exhaustion racked me – a saddle was not my natural environment any more than a ship, but at least it didn't make me sick. I was in turns achy and numb from a day-and-a-half in the saddle.

'We'll head straight to the harbour,' Vergil said. 'Father always has a yacht on standby here in case of emergency.'

The street lanterns flickered, only recently lit, as we rode down to the harbour scattering strange shadows across our path. The only two inns turned out to be full to bursting with inebriated, and soon to be inebriated, patrons. The smell of stale drink mingled with the sea salt and fish coming from the little harbour. Not a great combination for someone not looking forward to their next sea voyage.

Vergil dismounted and we followed suit, waiting with the horses as he quickly made his way along a creaking wooden jetty to a decent sized yacht berthed near a couple of small fishing vessels.

'Vergil hates the water,' Amalia murmured from beside me looking after him.

'How do you know?' I asked.

'He told me last night. Something to do with his brother, but I'm not sure quite what.'

'You two are getting on well,' I said, glancing sideways at her.

She shrugged. 'We've met before and we became friends then, we even write to each other sometimes. He's easy to talk to and there's no pretence. I like him.'

'I thought as much.'

'I don't know what you're grinning at. I saw Etienne under your blankets with you this morning,' she said, giving me a long look.

'I didn't have a good night and he offered to keep me warm – I thought he was being chivalrous,' I said primly, keeping my voice low so he didn't hear, but he was deep in conversation with Kit.

'He's never been chivalrous with a girl in his life. You're the first. Just don't break his heart – he's very special to me and I'd take it rather personally.'

That was the very last thing I intended to do. 'Is that a warning from a cousin or a bodyguard?' I smiled.

'Both,' she said, her voice and face deadly serious.

'I don't intend to do anything of the kind,' I said. 'Although I'm not sure sharing blankets counts for anything much.'

'It does to him, believe me, it does to him.'

For some reason her words warmed my core, and I glanced over to Etienne. He looked up and smiled that lopsided smile and I couldn't help but grin inanely back at him. He was special and I was growing exceptionally fond of him.

Maybe I even...

I never finished the thought. It brought me up short. I had no space in my life for this. I'd been promised to another. The identity of that prince may still be a mystery to me, but until I knew his fate for sure, I wasn't in any position to view Etienne as anything more than a friend; a good friend, perhaps, but nothing more – even if he was no longer Pledged. I also had my secret to keep. That had to be my priority, just as Mother had said. I couldn't afford to let my guard down, and I'd unconsciously begun to do so. I had to stop whatever this was, now, before it became anything more. I couldn't risk my life, or his, if my secret came out. It wasn't that I didn't trust him – I did – but together we'd both be in danger because of my Crystals, and because of being Pledged to someone who wasn't Etienne. I wouldn't do that, not to him. I cared about him too much.

I swallowed. Sighed.

Stay hidden. Stay safe, keep your secret safe. Don't let anyone know, but him.

Mother's words echoed in my head. Who had she been talking about? Who was it that I could tell my secret to? She had to mean Kit. Who else was there? But I didn't want to risk telling him, and certainly couldn't tell Etienne. He could *never* know.

And I could never be with him.

I glanced over at where he stood talking to Kit. My heart sank. I'd have to finish this before it even started, and it tore at my heart. The realisation he was more to me than a friend now, that I cared about him, only made the decision even easier and yet more painful still. I'd have to push him away for his own safety.

I had to let him go, and it tore my heart in two.

Chapter Eleven

This time I really *was* avoiding Etienne, and on a yacht that's no mean feat. We'd slept in hammocks in a cabin below deck – not the most comfortable night I'd ever spent. The swaying of the ship only helped to add to, rather than quell, my nausea, but at least I wasn't being sick. As day broke I slipped out of my hammock and up the steps and out onto the deck. Vergil already sat perched on a wooden crate near the cabin door.

'Good morning,' I said, gazing across the water and at the sky filled with puffy white clouds.

'I suppose it is, isn't it?' he said, a little smile playing on his lips. 'You like to sail?'

'No,' I said emphatically, sitting beside him. 'I get really seasick – I definitely prefer land.'

'Me too,' he murmured.

'Seasick?'

'No. I…' he gazed across the deck. 'It's a long story.'

'We have time,' I said, wanting to get to know this young prince properly.

'My brother and I were out swimming in a mountain pool, heading for two years ago, now,' Vergil said, a pained look in his eyes, sadness too. 'He got into difficulty, caught on some weed, and drowned.'

I gasped. How awful.

'I tried to save him. I cut him free and brought him back to shore, but there was nothing I could do. Not even with my Blo… never mind.' He turned away, his face ashen.

I frowned. With what? A cold rush swept through me. 'Blood Crystals?' I whispered.

He looked sharply at me. 'What do you know of Blood Crystals?'

'More than you might think,' I murmured. 'Etienne is a Red Crystal Blood.'

Vergil nodded slowly. 'I did hear such a rumour, but thought that was probably all it was.'

'No, it's true, he told me himself. What are you? What colour?'

'Orange. The colour of the Healing Stones, but I couldn't save my brother. The Crystals on their own were no good – you need a Pellucid Crystal, you see, and I didn't have one. There haven't been any in years, there are no Double Bloods anymore.'

Yes, there are, but I couldn't reveal that, and anyway, it wouldn't help Vergil, or his guilt, to tell him.

'You did all you could – it wasn't your fault,' I said.

'Maybe not, but there's that nagging doubt I could've done more. If I'd realised what was happening sooner. If I'd been closer to him, could I have saved him?'

'Don't go there,' I said. 'I have the same thoughts about my mother. If we'd got back to the Citadel sooner, could I have saved her? If I'd never left in the first place would I have been able to do anything? Those thoughts can only make you go crazy. And besides, if he was already dead, a thousand Pellucid Crystals wouldn't have made any difference.'

'How have we never met before, Sorsha?' Vergil asked, a wan smile breaking out on his face. 'I have a feeling we'd have been great friends.'

I smiled back. 'As you know, I'm seldom at Court. I visit once a year so I'm likely to have missed any visits you've made over the years. But I can see that's my loss.'

Vergil's smile became bigger. 'And mine too,' he said, resting his hand on my arm. 'Well, maybe we can make up for it now.'

I nodded. 'Maybe we can.' I looked up to see Etienne coming out of the cabin. He took one look at Vergil and his arm resting on my shoulder and a little scowl formed on his face.

'Morning,' he said gruffly, and walked over to the bow of the boat.

'Good morning,' Vergil replied.

My initial reaction was to go to Etienne and tell him nothing was going on – but if I wanted to distance myself from him, perhaps spending time with Vergil would help, even if the thought made a knife twist in my chest.

'My brother had been Pledged,' Vergil continued, unaware of Etienne's reaction. 'Now Father is thinking of Pledging me to her instead, but they were in love and I don't even like her that much.'

'Can't you say no?'

Vergil shrugged. 'Have you ever tried saying no to your father?'

I swallowed. 'He's dead.'

'Oh, yes, I'm so sorry, I didn't mean–'

'It's fine,' I said. This time I was reaching out to him. 'It happened a long time ago. But I know what you mean.'

'The problem is, I'm now the heir and he'll want me settled down as soon as possible.'

Amalia stepped out on deck, smiled at Vergil and went to join Etienne at the bow.

'Maybe you should make your own choice,' I said, following his gaze towards the young bodyguard, 'before anything is formally arranged.'

Vergil glanced at me and looked away. 'How do you kno–' His face took on a pink glow. 'That would never be allowed. She's a bodyguard, and you know as well as I do these things are arranged by our families.'

'Vergil, she's of noble blood, what could be more proper?'

He sniffed as he thought. 'I hadn't looked at it like that before.'

'And she's of a different Order, which will make for a useful strategic match between Planetae and Solis. And what's more, her father was a noble of the Planetary Order. Surely your father couldn't find a better match for you himself, could he?'

He raised an eyebrow. 'I didn't know about her father.' He scratched his head. 'You really think we could do it?'

'Talk to her. See what she thinks about it. And of course, once you've exchanged Oaths...' I waved my hands about to make my point. 'Just present it to your father calmly and firmly.'

He grinned at me. 'Maybe I will. Thank you, Sorsha.'

It might not be an option for me – for me and Etienne – but Vergil and Amalia still had a wisp of a chance, and I hoped they'd take it while they still could.

Although staying away from Etienne proved a challenge, the fact that the yacht was small meant there was little chance of being alone with him. I made sure I was either with Kit, Vergil or Amalia. I drew the line at Artem. The Moon Prince continued to be standoffish, aloof and rarely spoke unless he had to. He spent most of his time below deck, brooding about something or other. He didn't even attempt to be friendly – in fact I was beginning to wonder why he was still with us. He could hardly coordinate aid for Luna from the Celestial Temple, but stay with us he had. And it sent shivers down my spine.

Every time Etienne smiled at me I tried to turn in a different direction, look away, talk to someone. Pain flickered in his eyes that cut me to the quick, but it was for his own good. And mine too. I'd already got in deeper than I'd ever meant, and every time I looked away my heart splintered.

During the afternoon of the second day at sea I looked out over the water scanning it for Cynric's fleet, but the sea remained clear of ships which gave me some hope we'd reach the Celestial Temple and Priestess Athene before them.

'Are you avoiding Etienne?' Kit stood beside me. 'Amalia's not pleased with you. She said you're making him unhappy.'

'How can I be avoiding him on such a small boat?' I asked, resolutely gazing out to sea.

'Has he done something wrong?'

'Don't be daft, of course not.'

'Then what is it? Sorsh, I'm your oldest friend. You can tell me.'

I bit my lip. No, I couldn't because it would mean telling him something I'd kept secret from him all these years. Trying to explain why I'd kept it secret all this time would be impossible. Growing up, if I'd been going to tell anyone, it would have been my dearest Kit.

'Have you gone off him?' Kit asked, his deep brown eyes searching mine.

'I was never *on* him,' I said.

'But I thought… Amalia thought–'

'Well, you both thought wrong. He's just a friend – I admit he isn't the arrogant Sun Prince I once thought, but he's only a friend, Kit, nothing more.'

'But Amalia said you were getting close. You're so well suited.'

'Kit, leave it. I've been Pledged elsewhere, you know that.'

'You wouldn't be reacting this way if you didn't like him,' Kit said, a sullen edge to his voice. 'You've always told me everything, Sorsh. Why not now?'

'Because there's nothing to tell. We're friends and that's it and it can't be anything else. Now change the subject or go away.'

He sighed. 'Did you know Artem spends his time looking out the cabin window? Looking back towards Planetae, muttering to himself?'

'What?' I twisted towards him.

'He's really weird. I don't think I really like him.'

'I'm not sure he's gone out of his way to be liked,' I said.

'I suppose he could be making sure we're not being followed,' Kit said.

'Maybe he's hoping we are,' I said in a low voice.

'What?'

'Nothing,' but a nagging doubt now wormed its way into my chest and wouldn't leave.

#

At noon the following day the Island of the Celestial Temple rose up out of the water before us, an emerald in the sapphire sea. Its sweeping golden beaches and aqua water looked like a quintessential paradise, and I wondered if there was ever bad weather here. As far as the Temple was concerned, the Orders took their particular Celestial Body very seriously. On Steorra we didn't exactly worship the stars, but we treated them with a certain reverence and respect. It was assumed at some point during your life you would travel to the Celestial Temple and pay homage to your Order's namesake. The Moon Order were the most fervent, and even had their own temple dedicated to the moon on the far side of Luna Isle where people congregated at certain times of the year. We didn't have such a focal point on our island, just looking up at the night sky was enough for us, but there was a Steorran tradition where you made a pilgrimage to the Celestial Temple in your twenty-first year to pay homage and learn from the Priestesses.

The yacht dropped anchor and a small rowing boat made two journeys to bring us all across the gentle azure waves to the beach where, unnervingly, two women stood in white robes, smiling benevolently. We climbed out the boat, splashing through the cool waves onto the hot sandy beach, the taste of salt on my tongue.

'Welcome, welcome,' the first, a blonde woman, said. 'I am the Priestess Arethusa and this is Priestess Erytheia,' she said indicating the other, long red-haired priestess. 'Your arrival is unexpected.'

'We're here on an urgent mission,' Etienne said. 'I'm Prince Etienne of the Sun Order, this is Prince Vergil of the Planetary Order, Princess Sorsha of the Starlight Order, and coming ashore is Prince Artem of the Moon Order. These other two are our companions Lady Amalia and Kit. We must speak with Priestess Athene as soon as possible – King Saros of Planetae has asked us to warn you.'

'Warn us?' Priestess Erytheia asked, her eyebrow raised in slight alarm. 'Come with me.'

Erytheia led the way along the beach and up to a path that wound its way through evergreen trees of pine and conifer where the smell of pine and citrus drifted on the air. The heat of the beach receded, replaced by the cool shadows of the wood that cast a dappled light around us as we walked. We left the sound of waves behind, replaced by the chattering of birds and the chirp of insects in the undergrowth.

Etienne moved up beside me. 'Are we ever going to talk about it?'

'Talk about what?' I asked, looking straight ahead.

'You really are avoiding me this time. For the last few days, you've barely spoken to me.'

'I don't know what you're talking about. We've just been at sea on a small boat together.'

'Sorsha, you know what I mean,' he said, grabbing my arm and pulling me to a halt. 'We were getting on really well – *really* well – and now you're hardly acknowledging me.'

'As far as I know we're friends,' I said, trying to ignore the look of hurt I caught in his gorgeous eyes when I dared glance at him. 'Nothing's changed.' I gently pulled away.

'But things *were* changing – at least I thought they were,' he said, his voice strained, a yearning in his eyes. 'I thought we were beginning to...' He left it hanging.

I shrugged. 'Not sure what you mean,' I said, and started walking. He pulled me to a halt again, waiting for the others to pass, then took hold of my shoulders, making me look at him.

'I don't know what's going on, but we were *so* close. Now, you're pushing me away like I'm some sort of filth.' His face was full of sorrow as he looked at me.

My heart twisted at his words. For a moment I couldn't breathe as his fingers dug uncomfortably into my arms.

'Why are you doing this, Sorsha? Why?' he asked, searching my eyes for an answer.

I clenched a fist, trying to hold back the tears that I knew were coming. 'You know why. And you're right. We were getting close. Too close. Your Pledged may be gone now, but as far as I know mine isn't, and I can't just pretend otherwise, go against the law and my mother's last wish.' My heart was racing as I spoke, bile rising in my throat. 'I've been Pledged, Etienne, bound to someone else, and I have to honour it. We can never be more than friends, so please, just let me be.' I tried to pull away, but he held me tightly.

'I understand that. I do. Really,' he said. 'You have no idea if he's alive or dead, and can't do anything until you know who he is and where he is, but–'

'But what?'

'But maybe we can find out. And then, once we know…'

I swallowed. 'Once we know, I'll either have to honour the Pledge Mother made for me, or go along with whatever match Finnar finds for me instead.'

He sighed, his grip on me lessening a little. 'I just so desperately wish things were different for us.'

'So do I,' I murmured. 'So do I.'

He let go of me, and I hurried after the others. This was killing me slowly inside. Pushing Etienne away was the hardest thing I'd ever had to do. A knife in the gut would be less painful, but I had no choice. Mother had Pledged me to a prince, and even though she was gone, I'd have to honour it whether I wanted to or not. The Pledging Records had been sent to the Temple, and that was that. I could do nothing about it even if I wanted to. And I did.

The path through the trees began to climb making me sweat as my pulse rate increased from the exertion. As we broke free of the wood the sunlight almost blinded me as the heat returned.

'By the Sun,' Amalia swore from somewhere ahead of me.

I shielded my eyes, and there in front of me stood the Celestial Temple rising majestically from the top of a hill. Made of pure white marble, the massive building and its gardens were surrounded by the bluest lake I'd ever seen, a marble bridge leading over to the temple. Brilliant white steps led up to the building's entrance, a series of huge white columns with small amethysts at each column's base, with the odd diamond, ran along the outside forming a peristyle porch around the main temple in the centre, and two large wings on either side. A large pediment sat below the cobalt blue tiled roof with a frieze of planets, stars, moons and suns running along it. The whole structure gave off a kind of calm grandeur, a regal magnificence.

Surrounding the vast structure were the most beautiful gardens, well-manicured with neatly cut hedges and well-tended, vibrantly coloured flowerbeds that exuded the most delicious perfumes and tall, thin trees of deep green rising like needles towards the sky. Peacocks squawked from the shrubbery, intermittently flashing their brilliant plumage as they patrolled the gardens. Small ponds with chattering fountains sent droplets of water into the air like a farmer sifting his wheat and chaff, scattering rainbows into the sky.

'This way,' Arethusa said. She led us across the bridge and through the gardens, up the steps, through the porch and into a bright hallway lit by the sun shining into a courtyard area with another peristyle and a pool with a turquoise mosaic floor, similar in colour to Etienne's eyes. Beyond that, a corridor took us through to a large hall where yet more columns, this time with golden highlights, stood away from the walls with statues of the personifications of the Celestial Bodies along the sides – Ouranos for the Planets, Apollus of the Sun, Mene for the Moon, and Aster, the Stars. Priestesses milled around in the hall, talking quietly to each other, parting as we walked towards them. At the far end stood a large marble statue of Aither, personification of the air, that rose to almost touch the ceiling a full fifty feet above us. A truly amazing sight.

Out from behind the statue of Aither came a woman, dressed in similar robes to the other Priestesses, with silver hair piled high on her head in an intricate design, her similarly coloured eyes running over each of us in turn. My palms began to sweat and my heart skipped at the prospect of meeting Priestess Athene. I glanced to Kit, but he seemed totally entranced by the place – I didn't dare look at Etienne.

'Welcome all, I am Athene,' the silver haired priestess said.

Chapter Twelve

'We're–' Etienne began.

'Don't worry, I know you all, Prince Etienne,' she said. 'Arethusa and Erytheia will attend to Lady Amalia and Kit's needs. The rest of you can follow me.' She turned and walked back the way she'd come.

Kit nodded to me and followed the Priestesses with Amalia in tow. I followed the others around the statue and into a room behind at the back of the great chamber. In the centre, on top of three round steps, stood a pedestal with a large gold dish at the top. Voile curtains hung at a large window at the far side of the room that overlooked the lake that surrounded the temple, shifting in the warm breeze.

'I know who you are, but all who come here must shed a drop of blood in the Sanguis Bolla – a sign of your pilgrimage here,' Athene said, gesturing to the bowl. Only now did I see the golden knife lying on the top of the pedestal. 'As you are royalty, you will take part in the ceremony first, your friends will join me later.'

My blood ran cold. I couldn't do this, and not in public. I took a step back, searching for the nearest exit.

'I don't see how this is necessary,' Artem said, the first time I'd heard him speak today. 'I'm not here on a pilgrimage.'

'But you would have come at some point, would you not, Prince Artem?' Athene said, her silver eyes hardening. 'To pay your respects to the Celestial Bodies?'

Artem shifted his weight from foot to foot. 'Well–'

'Fulfil the ritual now – it only requires a drop, then you may retire to rooms already prepared for you where you can rest and eat.'

'We have a lot to tell you first, Priestess,' Prince Vergil said, his eyes wide as he looked at the bowl.

'Go on,' Athene said.

Vergil looked at Etienne.

'Emperor Taliesin has sent his son, Prince Cynric, to raid the Orders for their art,' Etienne said. 'Their soldiers have burnt and murdered their way through our capital cities, stolen our art, destroyed homes. When we left Planetae the Emperor's fleet was just arriving – we fear they'll head here next.'

'Art, you say?' Athene said, turning to the window. 'Are you sure it was the art?'

'Yes,' Etienne said. 'Our paintings, sculptures, books, jewellery – anything of value.'

'And when do you think they could reach here?'

Vergil scratched his head. 'I'd guess the day after tomorrow, but it could be sooner, depending on the weather.'

'Then we have time to make preparations,' Athene said, turning back to us. 'I thank you all for your warning – seeing the four Orders working together warms my heart.' She walked back over to the Sanguis Bolla. 'Prince Artem, if you'd like to begin.'

I couldn't understand Athene's lack of concern. We may have time in hand, however that didn't mean we could afford to be complacent, but I had no intention of arguing. I was too busy taking deep breaths and trying to keep my heart rate under control.

Artem mumbled something and stepped up to the golden bowl. He took hold of the knife and pricked his finger. A drop of blood fell into the bowl, sizzled and vanished. As he put the knife down, there was no blood left on it, either.

'Is that it?' Artem asked.

Athene nodded. 'That is all that is required of you. Priestess Celeano will take you to your room,' she said, indicating the dark haired priestess who had silently appeared at a side door.

Artem nodded curtly and left the room.

'Prince Etienne.' Athene gestured to the bowl.

Etienne stepped forward and took hold of the knife. He sliced the end of his finger sending shivers down my spine; Vergil took a step back, his face taking on a sickly hue. A drop of blood fell from Etienne's finger, landing in the bowl as a beautiful deep Red Blood Crystal.

Athene nodded. 'Take your crystal, guard it well. You may go.'

Arethusa appeared and guided Etienne from the room, although he glanced back at me as he left. I watched him go, my heart heavy. If only my Pledged was dead, I could perhaps find a way to be with Etienne.

I stifled a gasp.

How could I think such a thing? Wish death on some poor young man just because I wanted Etienne instead?

I had to stop this.

I *had* to come to terms with the fact I couldn't have the Sun Prince.

'After you, Sorsha,' Vergil said, shaking me from my thoughts.

'No, you go first,' I said. 'I'll go last.'

'If you're sure,' he said, the reluctance evident in his voice. He stepped up to the bowl and took up the knife. He hesitated, his hands trembling. 'I'm sorry, I can't do this. I hate the sight of blood, even when it does turn to crystal.' He put the knife back down.

'Shut your eyes and allow me,' Athene said gently, stepping forward. Vergil firmly shut his eyes and held out his hand. The Priestess pricked the end of his finger. A single drop of blood fell towards the bowl, landing as an Orange Blood Crystal. She covered his hand for a moment before releasing it. 'Your finger is healed,' she said.

Vergil opened an eye, then the other, holding his finger up and looking at it in surprise. 'How did you do that?' he asked, picking up his Crystal.

Athene smiled. 'Go with Erytheia,' she said.

Vergil turned to me, his eyes wide, then followed Erytheia out the room.

'And now you, Princess Sorsha,' Athene said with a smile.

She wouldn't be smiling in a minute.

My heart raced. I didn't want to do this, but how could I get out of it? Even Artem and Vergil hadn't managed that. I looked at Athene who appeared to be behind a pane of glass, and I took several deep breaths.

'There's nothing to fear,' Athene said.

That's what you think.

I climbed the steps, everything taking on a shiny, sparkly hue. I took hold of the clean golden knife, my hands trembling. I looked at the priestess. She nodded to me, an encouraging look on her face.

I sighed and pricked my finger.

A large drop of blood hung on my fingertip for a second before landing in the bowl, quickly followed by another; but blood didn't hit the golden metal, instead a small Purple Blood Crystal skittered into the bowl to join the crystal clear Pellucid Blood Crystal already lying there.

A gasp from behind me made me spin around.

Etienne stood in the doorway, his eyes wide, a startled expression on his face. 'You're a Double Blood?'

I turned back to Athene in horror.

'Trust him,' she said, an enigmatic smile on her face as she left the room, heading back into the temple. 'He can know.'

He can know. Was Etienne who Mother had been talking about? It suddenly dawned on me that he'd been in the room when she'd said that. She'd seen him standing there?

I grabbed the two Crystals, bowing my head, trying to steady my breathing as I squeezed my finger to stop the bleeding.

'Now I see,' Etienne said. 'Although to be honest, I think I'd guessed.'

'You had?'

'I saw the way you acted when you caught your hand on the tower door back at the Starlight Citadel.'

'I didn't think you'd noticed that.'

I held on to the top of the pedestal as I struggled to keep myself upright. I turned towards him.

'You could've told me, you know.' Hurt lingered in his voice, and in his eyes.

'How? I couldn't. I couldn't tell anyone. It wasn't safe – for you or me. I had no choice but to keep it secret. Even Kit doesn't know about me.'

'He doesn't?' Etienne's voice softened at the news. 'Oh.'

'The only people who have ever known are Mother and my uncle. That's it. If anyone finds out it could put me in danger, and if you're with me and you know that makes you a target too. And being a Single Blood that puts you in even greater danger, because with my Pellucids your Reds could be used.' I hurriedly stuffed my Crystals in the same pocket that held those I'd shed the night of Mother's death.

Etienne cocked his head to one side, his eyes never leaving mine. 'I understand now. That's why you've been avoiding me?'

'That and the fact that Amalia said you were getting attached to me, and I realised I was getting attached to you, too, and I couldn't let that happen because I'm Pledged, and because that put us both in danger, Crystal-wise and because of the law, and I didn't want to put your life at risk too, and–'

'Slow down,' he said, laughing as he moved towards me and took my hands in his. They were warm against my cold fingers. 'You were trying to protect me from the law, and from getting involved in your secret?' he asked, a strange look in his eyes.

I nodded. 'I'm sorry, I should have told you it all before.'

He shook his head. 'No, you probably shouldn't. But I think Athene wanted me to know about you being a Double Blood – I was told I needed to come back here. I think this was why. Maybe she didn't want you to carry the burden alone. And as for us getting close–'

'Etienne, I…' I didn't know what to say.

'Come here,' he said, pulling me to him and giving me a hug. The faint hint of his body's natural vetiver scent

123

set my core alight, and I held him tightly, for a moment my cares melting away as we stood there, a gentle breeze caressing us from the window. 'Things *have* changed between us, haven't they?' he murmured.

I stepped back and nodded. 'I-I didn't know how to stop it. I just knew I needed to protect you from my secret, and from getting in too deep with me. I've been Pledged. There's nothing we can do.' My shoulders sagged.

'Just for now forget your Pledging. And I don't need protecting, Princess. What I need is *you*.'

I looked into his turquoise eyes wondering, not for the first time, if I could drown in them. 'I'm glad, because I need you too,' I said, stepping back into his embrace as he kissed my forehead. Having someone to talk to about everything, who understood and knew about my secret, was a blessing and I valued him all the more, silently thanking Athene. And for a little while I did exactly what he'd said to do, and forgot my Pledging.

#

The room I'd been given lay in the west wing of the temple, on the first floor next to Etienne's overlooking the lake at the side of the Temple. It was simply furnished, but comfortable, and the voile curtains shifted gently in the breeze coming in the window. We'd all been able to bathe before bed, and for once I slept well, the calm of the Temple rubbing off on me and although I had no nightmares, I woke early and couldn't get back to sleep. I glanced out the window – still an hour or so before dawn.

A coolness lingered in the last of the night air, and I decided to go for a walk in the gardens. There was hardly a breath of wind as I wandered between the sheltered moonlit hedges and ponds. The dark sky spread above me, the stars watched me benignly no cloud to hide them, and the full moon smiled down on me, lighting my way as it sunk towards the horizon. I paused, the moon at my back, a fountain giggling away in front of me. In the spray a bow of white light appeared, suddenly dancing with the colours of the spectrum as it wavered in the water droplets. I'd never seen anything like it before.

'It's a Moonbow.' Artem's voice made me jump.

I turned towards where he stood not far behind me. 'A what?'

'A Moonbow. Very rare. You only see them when the moon is full and at a certain angle just after moonrise or before moonset, and of course with rain or waterspray.'

'I've never heard of them before.'

'As I say, very rare. Rather like you.'

I coughed. 'Me, rare? I don't think so. There are seven Starlight Princesses,' I said, as my heart pounded on my ribs. Did he know? Did he see what happened yesterday? 'At least there were.'

'And yet you have a quality that makes you rare even amongst them, don't you?' He came over towards me and I took an involuntary step back. 'You don't like me?'

'I don't know you.'

'We've been together several weeks now, you and I. It seemed quite enough for you to get to know the others.'

'You don't talk much, so it's hard to get to know you,' I said warily. 'And I've been with most of the others for longer.'

He smiled a forced, half-smile. 'True.'

'And some people you don't truly know after a lifetime, whereas others you've recently met can feel as if you've known them your whole life.'

'Like Prince Etienne?' he asked, raising an eyebrow.

Yes, like Etienne

I just stared at him, my face a mask.

'Hmm. So, tell me, Princess Sorsha,' he said, running his fingers across the top of a hedge, 'have the arrangements been made for your Pledging yet?'

I wanted to bolt. Get away from him. To say he made me feel uncomfortable was an understatement and I'd stupidly left all my weapons in my room, not thinking I'd need them here, although they weren't strictly necessary.

'Well, actually…' I wasn't prepared for this.

'Ah.' His moon-bleached eyes looked almost dead in the light, his left eyebrow twitching. 'You don't know who it's to? It's probably all irrelevant now, so maybe, when we leave here, you can come with me.'

'Come with you? Why? Where to exactly?' My skin crawled as he stepped closer. I knew he wasn't the one I'd been Pledged to. I knew my supposed prince was a sixth child and far removed from the throne. Artem was not the sixth.

He looked at the hedge, his fingers still caressing the leaves. 'My brother is, how would you put it, sickly. I think in time, in a short time, I'll be needing a queen, and who more suitable than a Starlight Princess?'

'I'm sorry, Prince Artem, but that won't be possible. She's Pledged to me,' Etienne said, stepping out of the shadows.

Chapter Thirteen

I was Pledged to Etienne?

If only.

When did this happen? In a way I didn't care. The fact he was there gave me a comforting reassurance. Resorting to unarmed violence wouldn't have been my first choice.

Artem scowled at the Sun Prince. '*You* were Pledged to the Seventh Princess? What a shame,' he said, an edge to his voice as a strange little sound came from deep in Etienne's throat. 'I'd hoped her prince was dead.'

'Shame?' Etienne asked, regaining his composure and coming to stand beside me, slipping his hand into mine. 'Why do you say that?'

'Dangerous times, Prince Etienne, dangerous times,' Artem said. 'Let's hope you get to exchange vows back in Helios in public.'

'Is that some kind of threat?' Etienne asked, his jaw set.

Artem laughed a cold, hollow laugh. 'Of course not. Just an observation. I'll say goodnight to you both – or should it be good-day?' he asked as he turned on his heel and headed back to the Temple.

'Damn, what was that about?' I stood wide-eyed watching Artem walk into the building.

'Not sure, but I don't like it one bit,' Etienne said letting go of me, and for a moment a little tinge of regret slid through me. I glanced at him – his forehead was creased, and he looked far away somewhere, deep in thought as if pondering something. 'Did your cousin, Taran, lie much?'

'Taran?' Where was this coming from? 'Does the sun rise every morning?'

'He was that bad?'

'He was happiest spinning lies, and the more tangled he could make them, the better. I did my best to steer clear of him, but as you know, I didn't always succeed.'

'He did seem quite set on cornering you that day.'

I snorted. 'I think toying with me is-was one of his favourite pastimes.' But for all his faults, I had never wished Taran any actual harm. Thinking of him reminded me once more of home, and I shivered. 'And when did I become Pledged to you?' I asked, changing the subject and looking Etienne right in the eye.

'What?' he asked. Suddenly he appeared a little uncomfortable. 'I thought it would get rid of Artem, and it did.'

'Hmm. I can take care of myself, you know.' I hadn't wanted to use violence as a way of escaping Artem, but I would have – if pushed.

'But you have no weapons.'

'I don't actually need them – why do you think I was sent to my Uncle Stanos? He's an ex-general in the army. He taught me to fight, not just with weapons,' I said.

'Oh,' Etienne said, then frowned as a look of realisation dawned on his face. 'That's why you stayed away from Court? To protect your secret and learn how to fight, so if it was ever necessary you'd be less likely to spill your own blood and reveal your secret?'

I nodded.

He shook his head. 'It all makes sense now. It must have been a lonely, scary life with no-one to talk to about things except your uncle.'

'We never spoke about it – he knew, yes – but it was too risky to speak about it out loud, even there, so yes, I suppose it has been lonely. Kit was given the job of being my companion, after all, you can't have a Starlight Princess cavorting around without some sort of escort even on the outer reaches of Steorra, and he became like a brother to me. But I couldn't tell even him, it was too dangerous for both of us.'

'I'm sorry it's been so hard.'

I smiled. 'No harder than for you, just different.'

Etienne paused a moment. 'Would being bound to me really be so bad?' he asked. A little flicker of hurt danced in his eyes before he glanced away, a slightly fearful look in his eyes.

'I didn't say that,' I said, my face burning like the sun. 'Surely you'd want a courtly, poised princess, one that was elegant, like Aster, not awkward with the manners of a peasant like me. There are still other Orders with elegant princesses to choose from.'

'But none of them are you.'

I swallowed. Did he really mean that? 'I couldn't, even if I wanted to, and you know that. My prince could still be alive and looking for me.'

Etienne gazed at me, the lopsided smile returning. 'We'll see.'

'What's that supposed to mean?'

'Nothing.'

'The Pledging documents have already been sent here for the priestesses Pledging Records. It can't be undone, and you know the penalty for royalty taking the Pledging Oath with someone that wasn't arranged for them. And if he were to find out I was with you, you know what that would mean.'

'Imprisonment. Execution.'

'Exactly.'

'They wouldn't execute me.'

'You may be happy to take that chance, but I'm not.'

'So you really do have feelings for me?' he asked, raising an eyebrow.

Starlight, of course I did.

'Whether I do or don't is irrelevant. Nothing like that can happen between us.'

'Like I said, though, we'll see.'

'You're impossible, Prince Etienne,' I said, sighing.

'I do hope so,' he said, wrapping a warm arm around me.

I chewed on a stray lock of hair. 'Maybe I could ask the priestesses if I could see the Records, find out who I've been Pledged to.'

'That's not a bad idea. But do you think they'll let you look?'

'In the circumstances, they might.'

'Come on, let's go back in. I hear the priestesses are

renowned for the most delicious breakfasts they prepare just before dawn.'

I glanced at the sky, now tinged with gold from the rapidly approaching sun. 'We'd better get going then.'

#

I spent the morning with Etienne exploring the Temple. It was a vast complex with smaller shrines to the individual Orders, areas for contemplation, and a large library where I thought I might lose him. As well as the large guest area, there was the refectory where we'd eaten a delicious breakfast, just as Etienne had promised. We wandered up a staircase to look at the view over the gardens from a first floor balcony.

'You know I'm a little hesitant to stay here,' I said. 'Knowing that Cynric is probably coming.'

'He may never arrive – the Planetary Order might have succeeded in sinking the fleet,' Etienne said, leaning on the balcony rail and taking in the gardens.

'And they might not.'

'Hmm, I've been thinking the same. You might be right. So where do you want to go?'

I chewed my lip a moment. 'I guess we should go and see what happened in Helios.'

He continued to look over the gardens as his body stiffened. 'I know,' he murmured. 'Problem is, in some ways while we're away there's still hope. If we go back it'll become final.'

'But don't you want to know if your family is still alive?' I asked in surprise.

'Yes and no. If what's happened on the other islands is indicative of what's happened on Solis there's a good chance I've lost some if not all of them.' His eyes became glassy as he gazed into the distance.

I wormed my way under his arm as my heart tore a little for him. The only way I could help him was to be there for him, as he had been for me. Now he'd bathed, his natural vetiver scent once again filled the air as I snuggled into him.

'You smell of honeysuckle and jasmine,' he said quietly, gazing into my eyes, his turquoise irises dazzling me as his pupils dilated and his lips parted a little.

'I do?' I asked in surprise. 'You smell of vetiver, warm, woody and rich.'

He chuckled. 'No one's ever said that before.'

'Maybe they haven't got close enough to you before to find out.'

He pulled me closer. 'What would I do without you, princess?' he asked, his gaze lowering to my lips, making my heart lurch in my chest.

'Oh, you'd muddle along, I expect,' I managed to get out.

'Not anymore.' He kissed my forehead, sending little sparks dancing down my spine. I looked up at him, at his velvet lips wondering...

'Hey, Eti, have you seen this?' Amalia's voice broke through our moment.

Damn.

Etienne sighed. 'Seen what?' he asked, an edge to his voice as he turned to his cousin who didn't seem to notice that she'd interrupted us.

'In here, come and look,' she said, waving us towards a door back down the corridor.

'We'd better see what she wants or she'll never leave us alone,' Etienne said.

I smiled at the rosy blush on his cheeks and nodded. 'Come on.'

We untangled ourselves and walked back into the Temple and down to the door Amalia was indicating. Vergil already stood inside the room inspecting something.

'They're certainly Blood Crystals,' Vergil said looking up.

'Are you sure?' Amalia asked.

We moved over to where he stood next to a black granite block. At the top lay a smooth panel, with seven little indentations in it, one with a blue Crystal ensconced in it, another with a green and another with a yellow.

Four gaps remained in the first, second, fourth and seventh positions.

'They look like Blood Crystals to me,' Etienne said.

'What do you think it's for?' I asked, studying the panel.

'No idea,' Etienne said, giving it a good look.

I glanced around the room. It was plain except for a strange freestanding black granite arch which looked as though it should have a door, but didn't. It was just an ornately carved archway standing in the middle of the room. Very strange. Very odd.

'I can't say I've ever seen the like,' Vergil said, walking around the arch and then cautiously through it.

'Perhaps the priestesses use it for their rituals,' Amalia said.

'If they do, they haven't been keeping up with their devotions,' I said, running my finger along the top of the granite console accumulating dust on my finger. 'No one's been in here for ages.'

#

Later that afternoon Priestess Athene asked to see us.

'So you've made up with Etienne?' Kit asked as we walked through the Temple where the priestesses bustled about making preparations for the coming attack.

'Maybe,' I murmured, glancing back to where the Sun Prince walked with Amalia and Vergil.

'Good. I don't know what your problem was. If you're still worried about that prince you were being Pledged to I'd forget him. It's not going to happen now.'

'It depends who he is, Kit. The Records are here – I thought I might speak to Athene about seeing them, find out who it is.'

Kit nodded. 'Not a bad idea, actually. Well, at least Amalia is happier now.'

'I'm glad,' I said, not really bothered if she was or not – this was between me and Etienne. On the other hand, I'd rather have her on my side.

'I was wondering about leaving here. We need to go bef...'

I didn't hear the rest of what Kit was saying. I'd glanced down a side corridor and what I saw made me pause. Halfway down stood Artem with his back to me. I could see he was holding something, but what, I couldn't tell. A priestess started along the passage from the far end. Artem turned slightly. In one hand he held a Yellow Blood Crystal on a long gold chain hanging around his neck. He had something in his other hand that caught the light, but I couldn't see what. A Pellucid?

I stifled a gasp. He must know about me, and Etienne, and Vergil. But did he know I was a Double Blood? Artem quickly slipped the Crystal pendant into his clothes, his other hand sliding into his pocket, and moved off down another passageway.

'What is it?' Etienne asked, pausing beside me as Vergil and Amalia continued after a still talking Kit.

'He knows about us – about me,' I whispered.

'What?'

'Artem – he has a Yellow Blood Crystal and probably a Pellucid. He'll be able to tell we're all Bloods,' I said, my fingers cold. 'And if he knows...'

'We'll face whatever comes together,' he said, turning me to him. 'Together.'

'Come on, Sorsh. Athene wants to see us,' Kit said impatiently from the base of Aither's statue.

I gave Etienne a long-suffering look and we headed for Athene's chamber at the back of the Temple. She was waiting for us as we entered.

'I want to thank you for your warning,' she said. 'You've given us time to prepare.'

'We were thinking maybe we should leave before Prince Cynric gets here,' Etienne said. The others nodded.

'It may be wise of you to do so,' Athene said. 'But first I have things of my own I must tell you.'

'Shouldn't we wait for Artem?' Kit asked, looking to the door.

Athene shook her head. 'This does not concern him.'

I glanced at Etienne – did she know Artem had the Crystals? A little furrow appeared in the Sun Prince's brow.

'You all know of the existence of Crystal Bloods,' Athene began.

We all nodded.

'Each colour has a different use,' the priestess continued. 'Green Memory Stones allow for enhanced sight, and the ability to extract forgotten memories from yourself and others. Orange Healing Stones can save a life – but not bring back someone who has already passed,' she said, glancing at Vergil. He bowed his head. 'Blue are the Truth Stones that stop people from lying, compel them to speak true. Yellow Crystals are Finding Stones, they can detect other Crystal Bloods. Reds–'

'Reds are for telling the weather and warding off evil,' Kit said, looking pleased with himself.

Etienne frowned.

'No, they are not,' Athene said, looking slightly peeved at being interrupted. 'Reds are Psychic Stones, they can produce astral projections, create illusions and dermo-optical perception.'

'What's that?' Amalia asked, her eyes narrowing.

'The ability to see through things with your hands,' Athene said. 'Like through a wall or a door.'

Etienne glanced at me and shrugged. 'Not heard that one before.'

'Purple Crystals are Shield Stones with the power to repel magical and physical attacks, and Pellucid Crystals, only shed by Double Bloods, enable the use of the other Crystals. Sometimes if used alone they have been known to reduce pain, but not heal like Orange Crystals. Without a Pellucid the others do not work, and when used, depending on the size, their power only lasts for so long. Their power is not indefinite, and Pellucids drain the fastest. The power fades, weakens over time. But the Crystals cannot be destroyed, only used up after which they become ordinary gemstones.'

I sighed. Of course, that's why the priestesses weren't too worried – the columns surrounding the Temple didn't contain amethysts and diamonds, but Purple and Pellucid Crystals. They would protect the Temple and those inside. Cynric could do what he wanted, but he'd never breach the Temple.

'These days there are few Single Bloods, even fewer Double Bloods,' Athene said. 'The Orders realised the importance of the Crystals and so over the years they collected them and placed them in their most precious Relics – in the frame of a painting, in the cover of a book, in a piece of jewellery, in the stone or metal of a sculpture. Each Order took five Relics, all embellished with Crystals, and hid them amongst their artworks, some in plain sight, others in private collections and yet more buried. These Relics are the only way of getting hold of a large number of Crystals. There are a scattering of other Crystals in the world from those who discovered their Gifts but never had the stones placed in Relics, but they are few and far between, hard to find as they are small in number. The only other place to get a supply of Crystals is to find Crystal Bloods themselves and use their blood – willingly or unwillingly.'

'Why are you telling us all this?' Kit asked. 'This doesn't affect us – well, Prince Etienne, maybe.'

'Emperor Taliesin has discovered the power of the Crystals from the ancient books in his library. He knows about the Relics and has sent Cynric to collect all possible artworks that may contain Crystals. He can then sift through them all to find the Crystals in amongst the ordinary gemstones. Using Yellows he can track down Crystal Bloods, imprison them for a steady supply of Crystals or kill them, bleed them dry for a good quantity all at once. Taliesin can use the Crystals to subdue everyone in the Empire, and then use them to corrupt the world.'

Chapter Fourteen

'So that's what he's been after all along?' Amalia asked. 'He wants our Relics for the Crystals?'

'Then use them to find the Bloods,' Vergil said, his eyes wide. 'Use their blood, bleed them dry...'

'And rule the world,' Etienne added, his eyes angry.

'If Taliesin managed that then no one could stop him,' Kit murmured.

'Then we have to stop him before he can get all the Crystals and start searching for Bloods,' Etienne said.

'But he's already started,' I murmured, glancing at Etienne.

'What?' Vergil asked.

'I think Artem is working for Taliesin – I just saw him with a Yellow and a Pellucid, and there have been other things.'

'Several other things,' Etienne said, nodding.

Kit's shoulders slumped. 'You're right. He's acted a bit shifty ever since we met him.'

Artem was a traitor. Many things now made sense – the Moon Prince's furtiveness, lack of concern for his people, interest in the burning cities, even his interest in me. Athene had obviously already had her suspicions; he hadn't been invited here.

'I will arrange for Prince Artem to be apprehended at once,' Athene said.

I took a deep breath. 'So we have to stop Taliesin, recover all the stolen Crystals and free any Bloods he may already have,' I said. Mother had died for this, Taran had died, and so had many others – and now, with the help of Kit and my new friends, I'd stop Taliesin and Cynric.

Etienne nodded.

'You have two Relics with you already,' Athene said. 'And some First Crystals that may be of use to you.'

My hand went instinctively to my neck where the

Starburst Necklace still sat under my tunic. Etienne frowned, then a look of realisation dawned on his face.

'Two Relics?' Vergil asked. 'Where?'

'The blue stone in Lady Amalia's ring,' Athene said.

'What?' Amalia's face drained as she looked at the ring, twisting it around her finger. 'It was given to me by my mother – I had no idea it was a Relic. So it's a Truth Stone?'

Athene nodded. 'And Prince Etienne's book.'

Of course, the old book Etienne had been reading on the way into Galatae.

'I didn't know,' Etienne said, his hand going to his chest pocket where the book still sat.

'Keep them safe,' Athene said. 'Keep them all safe,' she said glancing at me. 'You must leave at once, Prince Etienne.'

Etienne nodded.

'We'll all go,' Vergil said firmly. 'After all, he'll be after me too.'

'You're a Blood?' Amalia asked, her face showing her surprise. 'You never said.'

Vergil shrugged. 'I guess it never came up. I'm an Orange, by the way.'

'Could be useful,' Etienne murmured.

'Not until we find a Pellucid, it won't,' he said, his face turning ashen at the prospect. I wasn't sure we'd ever get Vergil to shed blood willingly, or at least with his eyes open.

'Do Yellow Crystals show if someone's a Double Blood?' Amalia asked. 'Only that would be quite useful.'

Athene glanced at me then turned to Amalia. 'No, only that someone is a Crystal Blood.'

I quietly let out a breath. Artem may know about me, but he wouldn't know exactly what I was; even rarer than he already thought.

'Flax may know where the Crystals and Bloods are being taken,' Kit said gazing out the lake window.

'Of course he will, he's a spy,' I said. Flax was a friend of Kit's who only visited Uncle's estate under the cover

Crystal Bloods

of darkness. I'd met him once, by accident, when I'd walked in on the two of them drinking one evening. 'He's one of the Emperor's best, if you believe what he says, but he'll never tell us anything.'

Kit cleared his throat. 'He might tell me. He likes me.'

I raised an eyebrow. I'd always had my suspicions, and now his agitated glance made me suspect I'd been right. '"Likes" you? How much does he "like" you?'

'More than enough to tell me something useful,' Kit said, a rosy blush high on his cheekbones.

'It's a good thing Mother never found out,' I said, rolling my eyes to the ceiling. Why hadn't he told me before? I wouldn't have minded.

'Wouldn't she have approved?' Etienne asked.

'No,' I said emphatically. 'But do you know where to find him, Kit?'

Kit nodded. 'More or less.'

'Priestess, before we leave, I wondered if I might see the Pledging Records,' I said. 'You see, my mother had promised me to a prince, but I don't know who he is – or was – and I need to find out.'

A smile crept across Athene's face. 'You really don't know? I assumed you did.'

I shook my head. 'She never told me before she died. But now I need to know his name.'

'My dear girl–'

Erytheia rushed in. 'Priestess Athene,' she bowed. 'The fleet has landed.'

'Do we have time to leave?' Vergil asked, his muscles tensing.

Erytheia shook her head. 'No. You'll never get through them, there are too many.'

'Then we'll stay and help you defend the Temple,' Etienne said.

Staying sent a shiver down my spine, but it didn't look as if we had much of a choice.

'No, you cannot stay here, it's too dangerous for you all now,' Athene said, heading for a side door. 'You must come with me – we will use the Crystal Aperture to get

139

you away. Get your things and bring the Crystals you shed in the Bolla. Meet me on the first floor.'

'Crystal Aperture? What's a Crystal Aperture?' Vergil asked hurrying after her.

'A gateway, a door to another part of the world,' Athene said as she hurried down the corridor. 'One Crystal of each colour is required to power the Aperture and depending on the order in which they are placed determines which gateway you access. However, the first position is always taken by a Pellucid, the fourth a Red and the seventh a Purple.'

'And the others?' Etienne asked.

'The remaining four crystals can be placed in any combination to access the twenty-four gates – but they are not all functioning. Some have been lost or destroyed, some never explored. Each time an Aperture is opened it uses all the power of the Crystals and so cannot be used again either at a later date or for a return journey. New Crystals are required for each passage.'

'But they're not used now because of the lack of Crystals?' Amalia asked.

Athene nodded. 'The Crystal Bloods of old would use them to travel the lands, but they have not been in use for many years now.'

'But the one here still works?' I asked, suddenly thinking of the room we'd found earlier in the day. Could that be the Crystal Aperture?

Athene nodded as we reached the stairs to our rooms. 'Quickly, get your belongings and meet me in the Aperture Room – you know where,' she said hurrying off.

'You do?' Kit asked, looking at me as we climbed the stairs.

'We were in there this afternoon,' I said.

'Oh – that was the Aperture?' Amalia asked.

We raced to our rooms quickly packing our bags. As I hefted my pack onto my shoulder, my swords already in position on my back, I glanced out the window. Cynric's men were here already. They'd taken up position around the Temple. One moved forward, warily stepping towards the building. Suddenly thrown backwards, he landed hard on his back. Another threw a spear, only to have it rebound. We were safe for now, the Crystals doing their job, but the question was, how long would their power last? An hour, a day, a week? I had no idea.

I met Etienne in the corridor and we moved down a walkway on the first floor, hurrying along the edge of the building, heading for the Aperture; at the far end we turned a corner to make our way along to the far side of the Temple. A balcony looked over the gardens below. A short young man with pale skin, a sharp pointed nose and long brown hair stood looking expectantly at the Temple. His shining gold armour and demeanour meant only one thing.

Prince Cynric, Emperor Taliesin's son.

A smile suddenly broke out on his face.

I paused, wondering why he suddenly looked so pleased with himself. He wasn't getting past the Crystals any time soon.

'At last,' Cynric said, fiddling with his sword hilt.

I paused and moved onto the balcony, peering over the balustrade, trying to see what was happening.

'Sorsha, what the hell are you doing?' Etienne hissed at me.

'Hang on,' I said, gesturing at him to shut up.

Artem walked out to greet Cynric. *Starlight*, he'd somehow managed to evade the priestesses. In his hand he held something that sparkled in the late evening sunshine. No, not one thing, several – the Moon Prince held a handful of the small Purple and Pellucid Crystals that had been sitting in the columns surrounding the Temple.

His betrayal was complete.

'You decided not to go back to Merribor after Steorra?' Artem's voice drifted up to us.

Cynric shook his head. 'No. It wasted too much time, and besides, despite our best efforts, word was bound to spread – and it did. So I brought extra ships with me when we left for Steorra to carry the goods.'

Artem nodded.

'It's a shame about Galatae,' Cynric continued. 'Father won't be pleased, but if we'd persisted, we'd have lost the bulk of the fleet, and he'd have been even less happy about that.'

'Well, they're all yours,' Artem said, gesturing to the Temple. 'But leave the Starlight Princess for me, won't you?'

'I think you've earned her,' Cynric grinned. 'Although we may need to bleed her for Crystals from time to time.'

My blood ran cold at the very idea.

Etienne's eyes widened in horror. 'He's not having you,' he said, grabbing my hand and pulling me back into the Temple. 'I need to get you out.'

I didn't argue.

I could hear the yell of soldiers below us breaching the Temple, rushing into the building as the clash of swords echoed down hallways. The priestesses were fighting back. As we moved along the corridor we passed a stairwell – coming up it at speed was a soldier. He took one look at me and yelled, raising his sword.

I dropped my pack, grabbed my cloak and threw it towards his sword arm, twisting the material as it glided through the air. The cloak landed around the sword, unbalancing it, catching itself around the metal blade. I yanked at the fabric; the entangled sword flew from the soldier's hand. I kicked him full in the chest, something I'd normally avoid for fear of losing my balance, but with the higher ground I made an exception. I sent him tumbling backwards down the staircase and into another soldier who he took with him to the bottom.

'Move!' I said to Etienne as I grabbed my pack and ran down the corridor with him.

'I'm impressed,' he said.

'I said I didn't need a weapon.' I couldn't help the hint of smugness that crept into my voice.

'So you did.'

We ran to the Aperture Room, meeting the others as we got there.

'Artem, he let Cynric's men in,' I said, gasping for air.

'What?' Vergil looked aghast.

'He's taken some Crystals out of the peristyle and let Cynric in,' Etienne said, panting.

'Quickly,' Athene said from her position at the console. 'Give me the Crystals you shed in the Bolla.'

I slipped mine out my pocket and gave them to her before Kit, Amalia and Vergil entered the room. Etienne passed her his Red and Vergil followed him, handing her his Orange. Athene arranged them in the console, except for the Pellucid.

'This will take you to the Asterion Archipelago,' she said. 'You can get a ship from there to Merribor.'

'You can't get us straight to Merribor?' Kit asked. 'It would be so much quicker.'

'Alas the two closest Apertures to Mere City were lost decades ago. This is the nearest gate, unless you want to travel half of the Empire.'

'Not particularly,' he muttered.

The ring of steel and screams drifted up from the Temple below.

'We should stay and help,' I said, my hand going to one of the swords on my back.

'No, Starlight Princess,' Athene said, resting her hand on my shoulder. 'Your destiny is not that of ours here – you have much to do. This has all happened before, the purging of the Crystal Bloods – the circle keeps moving, keeps turning – you must stop it. Now go, all of you.' She placed the Pellucid Crystal in its position. A bright flash of light filled the room and an opening appeared in the granite archway, full of purple mist. The Crystals in the console flared, glowing brightly. The sound of footsteps on the stairways filled the air. 'Hurry. The Crystals will only keep the gate open for so long,' she said, gesturing to the others. 'Princess, take this.' She passed me something cold.

I looked into the palm of my hand. A gold bracelet sat there, with a vibrant red stone.

'A Blood Crystal?'

She shook her head. 'A Red Diamond. It is the Aegis Bracelet.' She glanced towards Etienne who was looking out into the corridor. 'I believe you will have need of it.'

Vergil took Amalia's hand and the two stepped into the swirling mist and disappeared. Kit turned to look at me, his face uneasy, but resigned. He stepped through and vanished. Etienne moved from the door and hurried with me towards the Aperture, a strained look on his face.

I hesitated for a moment, glancing back at Athene.

A brown haired soldier appeared in the doorway, a large scar running down his right cheek. He took one look at the Aperture and lunged towards Athene, running her through. She screamed, blood soaking into her white robe.

'No!' I reached forward towards her, going for a sword hilt.

'Leave!' Athene gasped as she fell towards the console. 'Get out of here, both of you!'

Etienne grabbed my arm, pulling me towards the gateway. My last sight of the Priestess was as the soldier pulled his sword free of her body. She slumped forward onto the console. The soldier had a nasty grin on his hook-nosed face as he looked towards me. The Crystals in the console flared and died as purple mist surrounded me.

Chapter Fifteen

'No! *No!*' I cried as the purple mist around me vanished and a grey dampness soaked into my clothes. I found myself on a hilltop, a black stone arch behind me clearing to an open view across fields and pastures, the grey sea visible in the distance through a fine mist of drizzle. Low cloud scudded overhead. I looked at Etienne who still had a firm grip on my arm, and shivered. This had happened before? *We* had to stop it?

He shook his head. 'There was nothing we could do,' he said quietly. 'It all happened too fast.'

'What happened?' Amalia asked, coming over to us, wrestling to get her cloak out of her pack.

'Athene, sh-she's dead,' I said, struggling to get the words out and contain my emotions.

'What?' Vergil looked horrified as he pulled his hood up. 'What happened?'

'A soldier came in as we were about to step into the Aperture and killed her,' Etienne said.

'She was unarmed,' I said, anger raging in me, burning away the chill air that moved around me.

'He didn't care.'

I shook my head. 'This has to stop,' I said, my teeth gritted.

Etienne nodded silently, his eyes clouded.

'So what now?' Kit asked, trying to put my cloak about my shoulders as Etienne slipped his on.

'We find a ship to take us to Merribor and we finish this,' I said. Taliesin and Cynric would pay – and so would Artem, and if I ever caught sight of that soldier again...

'Agreed,' Etienne said.

'Can anyone see a village or town out there?' Amalia asked. 'We need to find some shelter, it's getting dark.'

'I think I noticed some lights over there,' Kit said, pointing west across the island. 'Maybe they can help us.'

'Does anyone have any money?'

Vergil patted his pack. 'I've got plenty.'

'Good, we may be needing it,' Amalia said leading the way down the hillside, trying not to slip on the damp grass.

The smell of wet vegetation clung to the air, the low cloud mirroring my mood. I pulled my hood up, bent my head down and plodded after Amalia. Thoughts tumbled through my head as I tried to take it all in. Artem, a traitor. The Temple overrun. Athene, and probably the rest of the priestesses, dead. Cynric would likely take all the Crystals out of the Temple columns to bolster his supply – and he'd have some Pellucid, not many, but enough to wreak some sort of havoc. I just hoped the initial defence of the Temple had drained them a little.

After a half-hour walk we reached the lights Kit had seen. They turned out to be a small fishing town on the edge of an inlet, a little rundown perhaps, but obviously the catches here were good. A small inn stood in the middle of the buildings and we made our way along the muddy street and into the quiet building. As my eyes adjusted to the light the smell of stale beer assaulted me – why did inns always smell the same? A few local men sat in the taproom, talking quietly. This was so unlike the rowdy inns of the Citadel where you couldn't hear yourself think. We made our way over to the bar where the dark-haired barmaid bustled about with a sour expression on her face. She didn't look as if she wanted to be there.

'Yes?' she asked, a slight terseness to her voice.

'Five mugs of your best ale,' Vergil said with a captivating smile, enough to even soften the look in the eyes of the barmaid. 'And do you have rooms?'

She nodded then looked at us, her eyes narrowing. 'But we only have two. One of you will have to sleep in a chair.'

'That's fine,' Vergil nodded, still smiling. 'And I don't suppose you do food?'

'Cost you extra,' she said, turning away to pour the ale. 'It's beef stew.'

'Sounds great.'

It wasn't.

The ale was fine, although I only drank it under duress. The stew appeared more like water with a few vegetables floating in it, with two small chunks of beef. When I inspected the bedroom I had to conclude the sheets had probably never been washed. Both Amalia and I remained fully clothed, sleeping on top of the bedding. The boys shared the other room, Kit ending up in the chair because he insisted the princes have the beds, although it may have been because he saw the state of the sheets.

I barely slept, and when I did it was a fitful doze with Apertures, priestesses and a grinning Artem floating in and out of my vision. I gave up as the sun rose, even though no one would be up for a while, and made my way quietly out the inn and down to the harbour. The weather had cleared and the early morning sun glittered on the little waves setting light to the water. I took a deep breath of sea air, salty and fresh. The fishing boats were out and it would be a while before they returned and added the smell of dead fish to the surroundings.

Everything had a calm, peaceful air – at odds with what I'd so recently experienced at the Temple. Athene's words, that we had to stop the cycle of the Blood purges, bit into my soul. How could *we* do that? And knowing it'd happened before didn't fill me with any confidence.

I gazed at the Aegis Bracelet that now adorned my wrist. The sun swept into its clear red stone, and sparkled like fire. Quite why she'd given it to me I didn't know and, if it wasn't a Blood Crystal, why we'd have need of it, I wasn't sure.

The sound of footsteps on the still muddy road made me turn. Etienne walked towards me, a wan smile appearing on his face as I caught his eye.

'I gave up trying to sleep too,' he said. 'Move up, then I can sit here as well.'

I dutifully moved along the crate and he sat beside me. His face appeared pale and drawn in the light – whatever toll this was all taking on me, it was taking a similar one on him too, and my heart twisted.

'Things will never be normal again, will they?' I asked, watching a seagull bobbing on the water.

'No,' he replied softly. 'I don't think they will.'

I sighed, a pang of homesickness and grief spreading through me, and I pushed back the tears that threatened to come.

'But we'll get through it,' he said. 'Together.'

'You sound very sure.'

'Don't worry, it'll be fine – everything will be fine. It might take a while to get there, that's all.'

'Hmm.'

'So how did you find out you were a Double Blood?' he asked, glancing at me.

'An accident,' I said. 'I was six. I fell over in the palace gardens and gashed my knee. Instead of blood, a Pellucid and two Purple Crystals landed on the ground. You should've seen my mother's face when she saw them shining in the sun–' Mother. It brought me up short and I swallowed before continuing. Etienne hesitantly placed his hand on mine. 'She scooped them and me up and had me back in our rooms in an instant, although not before I'd shed two more small Pellucids. She bandaged me up and then swore me to secrecy. Not that I really understood what was going on at the time. That came later. But not long after I went to live with Uncle, out the way, far from Court and theoretically away from trouble.'

'That turned out well,' Etienne said sarcastically.

'Didn't it, though.' I smiled.

'And only your uncle knows?'

I nodded. 'We never told Kit. There were times I wanted to, but it was too dangerous for both of us.'

'And now?'

'Telling him now would be so awkward, trying to explain why I hadn't told him before,' I said, wondering how Kit would take the news if he ever heard. We'd always told each other everything. Although come to think about it, he hadn't revealed his true relationship with Flax until recently, but I suppose knowing his inclinations it wasn't a huge stretch, and in retrospect, I was hardly surprised, really.

'I think you should tell him,' Etienne said.

'What? Why?'

'We may need his help and if he knows it means you won't have to go into deep explanations later when there may not be the time for long discussions,' Etienne said.

I twisted a curl of escaped hair around my finger. 'Maybe.'

'And your First Crystals are in the Starburst Necklace?'

I nodded, my hand instinctively going to my neck. 'Mother hid them in plain sight, but kept them at the palace. Not much need for sparkling necklaces on Uncle's estate. Farming implements, perhaps, but not jewellery.'

'She was a very clever woman, your mother,' he said, squeezing my hand. 'I wish I'd had the chance to know her.'

'So do I,' I said, resting my head on his shoulder. 'What about you, how did you find out?'

'I was seven – fell off my horse when I was hunting with Father,' he said ruefully. 'It was the first time he'd ever taken me out with him and my brothers. He'd decided it was time he fulfil his "kingly duties" as far as my education was concerned in that area. Anyway, my horse shied and I slipped off, gashed my arm on a rock on the way down and sliced it open. Gave everyone quite a turn when they saw Crystals, not blood, on the ground.'

'I bet it did,' I said, smiling.

'Of course, it also reinforced the whole "Etienne's nothing but a nuisance" thing.'

I slid my arm around his shoulders and gave him a little hug. 'You're not a nuisance.'

'Maybe not to you.'

'Definitely not, to me,' I said, my face burning as he glanced at me. 'So you didn't try to keep it secret?'

'No point, really. Too many people had seen what had happened, and without a Double Blood, who were

149

supposed to be extinct,' he said looking meaningfully at me, 'or a random Pellucid turning up, my Crystals were useless.'

'Until now,' I murmured. 'And now they know about us both, and Vergil too. They will come after us, you know.'

'Not sure they'll be expecting us to come to them, though.'

'Maybe not, but we're going to have to be careful – very careful.' I chewed my lip, knowing we were heading into the lion's den, knowing it was dangerous for Etienne and Vergil, and knowing it was even more dangerous for me. But it had to be done. I knew that, too.

Etienne let out a groan, then chuckled.

'What's wrong with you?' I asked, frowning.

'I've just realised,' he said, shaking his head as if he'd been stupid and had suddenly seen the light. 'The Moonweever Fish. By the Sun, you used a Pellucid Crystal to stop the pain, didn't you?'

I glanced at him, then looked away. 'Maybe.'

'You risked everything to help me?' he asked incredulously. 'When you barely knew me? Wasn't that a bit foolhardy?'

I shrugged. 'Probably. But you were in so much pain I couldn't let you suffer like that when I could do something about it. And I had a feeling about you, even then, like I could trust you.'

'I could've found out your secret.'

'But you didn't.'

'That's why you got me to shut my eyes, isn't it?'

I nodded. 'So you couldn't see the glow, although the setting sun actually obscured most of it.'

He looked at me. 'You could've trusted me, you know. I wouldn't have betrayed you or your secret.'

'I know that now,' I murmured. 'I think – I think I even knew it then, too.'

'Did you shed blood for me, on the beach?' he asked softly, rubbing his forehead.

'Luckily I didn't have to,' I said, and told him about the buckle on the saddlebag.

'Would you have done? If you hadn't already had that in your pocket?' he asked, looking intently at me.

Of course I would. 'As long as you'd kept your eyes shut,' I said.

He laughed. 'I'm glad I did as you said.'

'So am I, because I didn't want to spend a cold night out on that beach.'

'Are you saying you really helped me because you wanted to sleep in a warm bed?' He raised an eyebrow, an amused look on his face.

'No. I did it because you were in such awful pain. And I'd do the same thing again,' I said indignantly.

He smiled. 'And I'm extremely grateful for it,' he said, then hesitated. 'You'd really have stayed out there with me? All night?'

'Yes, if I'd had to. But I didn't need to, thankfully.'

'No one's ever put themselves at such risk to help me before. Not like that, anyway.'

'You're welcome,' I said, smiling back at him.

He raised my hand to his lips, kissing me tenderly, lingering as he did so and sending little sparks shooting up my arm. He appeared to let go of me very reluctantly.

He cleared his throat. 'Right then, let's get back to the inn for some breakfast – hopefully it'll be better than last night's stew.'

'Can't be much worse,' I said, making a face.

He laughed and helped me up, leading me back to the inn. We woke the others and after we'd eaten, we headed down to the now bustling harbour and arranged passage for later that morning on a merchant ship heading for a small port close to Mere City. As we waited to make sail, we sat below deck in a large cabin, chatting.

'So Artem was working for the Emperor all along?' Kit asked, sipping at a flagon of mead.

I shrugged. 'I guess so.'

'That's why he wasn't overly keen on sorting out Luna's aid,' Amalia said. 'Too busy searching for Crystals and Bloods for the Emperor.'

'So he knows about Etienne and Vergil. Which means

Cynric and the Emperor will know,' Kit said, shaking his head. 'You two are going to have to be careful.'

Amalia nodded. 'They'll be after you both now,' she said, her hand resting on her dagger.

It was worse than that, but I wasn't going to divulge that information to the three of them at the moment. I glanced at Etienne. Neither was he. But maybe he was right about telling Kit.

'I'm sure Vergil and I can take care of ourselves,' Etienne said. 'Besides, we've got you, Sorsha and Kit to keep an eye on us, cousin.' He grinned and slipped his arm around her shoulders.

'Stop that, Eti, I'm serious,' she said.

'I know you are, and so am I.'

'Poppycock.'

Shortly before noon we set sail. Marsh, the merchant ship's captain, moved around his vessel like a master perusing his estate. He had an air altogether different to Captain Lucian, who was far more affable. Marsh kept to himself. We were just paying passengers.

As the day wore on I lost my breakfast over the ship's rail.

A few days later I'd barely eaten anything other than a few biscuits and a bit of fruit, and my nights had been fitful; the events at the Temple had only helped fuel my nightmares, and although I didn't find myself running out on deck to throw up, I did wake repeatedly in a cold sweat. As I stood on deck Kit came to check on me. I glanced around us. We were quite alone. The Captain was with his men at the helm, Vergil and Amalia at the bow chatting away, and Etienne in the cabin with his book.

'Why didn't you tell me about you and Flax?' I asked, careful not to look Kit in the face.

He shrugged. 'Don't know really. Wasn't entirely sure what you'd think.'

'Seriously?' I was slightly put out by that.

'What I mean is, I knew you wouldn't have worried about it, but I wasn't sure, if it got out, what your uncle or your mother would think. I didn't want to cause any upset between any of us.'

'I would've kept quiet, you know. I can keep a secret.' *How ironic.*

'I'm sorry, I should've told you, Sorsh.'

'While we're making apologies for keeping secrets, I have one big fat apology for you, but you must swear never to tell anyone, and that includes Amalia, Vergil and Flax when you see him – most particularly Flax. Can you promise me that?'

Kit frowned, his forehead deeply furrowed. 'I'm not sure I like where this is going,' he said. 'Wait, does Etienne know?'

I nodded.

'Who else?' he asked.

'Uncle – Mother knew and so did Athene, but no one else has ever known. Well, not until now.'

'Go on,' Kit said, looking sideways at me.

I glanced around to check we were still alone. 'I'm a Double Crystal Blood,' I said. No point in beating about the proverbial bush. I blurted it out – quietly.

'What?' Kit's eyes looked like they were about to pop out of his head. 'What did you say?'

'You heard,' I said, checking once again to make sure no one would overhear.

'Well, I wasn't expecting that,' he said, mulling it over. 'Although that explains why you always panic when you cut yourself and hide your wounds away. But why are you telling me now? And more to the point, why didn't you tell me before?'

'Because it's a dangerous secret to have, particularly now, and I wanted to keep you safe – but I thought you should know, particularly with where we're headed. Artem's Yellow Crystal will have told him that I'm a Blood too, so it follows the Emperor will know fairly soon as well.'

'But not necessarily that you're a Double Blood?'

'No, just a Blood.'

'But that still makes you a possible target. We'll have

to look after you, Sorsh. Maybe you should leave. Go away somewhere safer.'

I shook my head. 'No, I can't do that, I have to stay and help, fight if necessary. I'll be a target, yes, but no more than Etienne or Vergil, at least at the moment.'

'Until they discover what you really are.'

'We'll fall off that bridge when we come to it,' I said, determined not to be sidelined in all of this chaos.

Kit nodded. 'Very well.' He frowned again. 'So Etienne knows?'

'Yes, he walked in when I shed blood into Athene's Bolla – but I think she orchestrated that, to be honest.'

'Maybe she did,' Kit said, nodding.

Chapter Sixteen

I spent a few moments alone after supper out on deck before turning in for the night. The cool, salty air helped to relax me a little, and I stared out at the stars and moon, relishing their familiar company. The others had already gone to their cabins, and were probably fast asleep by now.

I headed below decks to my cabin. Etienne was making his way along the corridor carrying his pack, a pillow and a blanket.

'Where're you going?' I asked. 'Isn't your cabin back that way?'

He nodded. 'It is, but the Captain's cabin is right next door and he's snoring like a thunderstorm. I'll never get to sleep, so I thought I'd try and make myself comfortable in the main cabin. Good night,' he said as he brushed past me.

'That won't be very comfortable,' I said, chewing on a lock of hair.

He shrugged. 'There's nowhere else, unless I go in the hold or out on deck.'

Thoughts tumbled through my mind, but my heart won over my head. 'Share with me.'

He turned and looked at me. 'Really? Are you sure?' he asked, a little frown passing over his face. 'I don't mind the main cabin.'

'If any of the crew use it overnight they'll wake you up. You can share my cabin.'

'All right, if you're sure?' he asked, still hesitant.

'I'm sure.'

I opened the door into my cabin and he stepped in, dropping his pack in a corner as I shut my door.

He looked at the bed. 'It's going to be snug,' he said. 'You won't mind me being so close?'

Of course not.

'You can stop me falling out,' I said.

He grinned at me.

I pulled my boots off as Etienne removed his, then slipped my tunic off leaving my shirt on, and turned around. The prince was already in the small bed, his shirt over the end of the bed, his chest bare. I swallowed again, a mixture of excitement and fear filling me. Had this really been a good idea? I couldn't have left him in the main cabin, though, could I?

Yet again I wished I knew who I'd been Pledged to – and if he was alive or not.

My eyes widened as a thought hit me. Had Etienne taken off his britches too? I glanced back at the end of the bed, but I couldn't see them anywhere. I walked over to the other side of the bed and pulled the covers back to get in. No, he still had them on. For some reason a little wave of disappointment skipped through me, and a strange longing moved in my core. I climbed in beside him, immediately ensconced in vetiver.

'You'll sleep well tonight,' he said, pulling me towards him, kissing my forehead. 'No nightmares, because I'll be here with you, looking after you.'

'You really care about me that much? Like that, I mean?' I asked, a little quiver in my voice. Damn. Why did it have to do that?

The lopsided grin appeared. 'Yes, I do.'

'I thought you didn't like anyone like that.'

'Up until now I haven't, couldn't, really. And I certainly never imagined ever being with anyone. Until you. You've changed all that, Sorsha. Now, for the first time, I can imagine spending my life with someone.'

'Just not me,' I said, with a sigh.

'Why not?'

'You know why not. I can't Pledge myself to you anymore than you can Pledge yourself to me.'

'And if you find out your Pledged is dead? I know you said that Finnar would find you someone else, but the law says you'd be free to choose your own Pledge.'

My eyes stung with tears. 'And what are the chances of that happening, if that were the case? No. With my luck my prince is still alive out there somewhere, and the spitting image of Artem.'

'No, he's not.'

'You can't know that. I don't know who he is, whether he's dead or alive. All I know is he's a sixth child far removed from the throne. He could be on any of the islands waiting for me. What I do know is that whatever I may want, I can't be with you. Especially now – all our islands will need to strengthen our bonds more than ever.' I turned away, facing the door. 'The Pledging Records will still be at the Temple.'

'Assuming they haven't been burnt.'

'Cynric's after Crystals, not paperwork.'

'But what if I–'

'Please, don't,' I said, still looking at the door. Asking him to share my cabin had been a big mistake. This all hurt too much. I had feelings for Etienne. I cared about him, deeply. In truth... I loved him. I'd let it go too far after all. I should never have allowed myself to get close to him again after leaving the Temple. What I needed was a friend, and although he had indeed become a dear friend, he'd also become a lot more to me. He'd wormed his way into my heart and I should never have let that happen; but it was too late. All that lay ahead of me now was pain.

He slipped his arm around my waist, over my silk shirt, his touch making me tremble. Despite my despair, a little shiver of pleasure skittered down my back.

'Are you cold?' he asked.

'Yes,' I lied. I could hardly tell him I was trembling at his touch.

'There,' he said, moving even closer, his warm chest resting against my shirt. I could feel his heart beating through my back as he held me to him. 'Is that better?'

Not really, it just made things worse.

'Thank you,' I forced out.

'Goodnight. And don't worry.'

If only it were that simple.

'Goodnight,' I said, closing my eyes.

#

A few days later, we arrived at a small port a short distance outside of Mere City as dawn broke. According to Captain Marsh the taxes at the main Mere Port had been raised to an obscene level, so he chose to make port here where the fees were cheaper, and he'd receive a better profit for his goods. We collected our packs and made our way down the gangplank, and walked along the quayside.

Etienne was deep in conversation with Kit about something, and Amalia and Vergil were chatting about their respective home isles. I followed them, wondering how to deal with Etienne. I loved him. I knew that much. But I couldn't have him. Somewhere out there was a mystery prince waiting for me. A mystery prince whose family knew about me. A mystery prince I didn't want, but the law, and tradition, said otherwise. I sighed and put my pack down. I retied my hair that had escaped in the breeze.

Someone yelled behind me. I turned to see a man running towards me, a small crate in his hands as two sailors chased after him, shouting obscenities. The man ignored me, ploughing straight into me and sending me backwards. Wind rushed past me as I screamed as much in surprise as anything. Water hit me like a wall, knocking the wind out of me. Air bubbles rushed past me as I sank into the depths of the harbour.

I lashed out, desperate to stop my downward plunge, eventually bringing myself to a halt as the light around me dimmed. How far down had I gone? I drove myself upwards, kicking hard, moving my hands through the water, hoping I'd reach the surface before I drowned. The light grew brighter and my head broke free of the water.

I gasped in lungfuls of sweet air. Then started to cough.

'Sorsha!' Etienne's anxious voice sounded from above. He'd taken his tunic off and looked about to jump in, but Kit and Vergil were restraining him.

'She's all right,' Kit said.

'Look, she's okay, Eti,' Amalia said from beside them, holding on to my pack.

Etienne's face relaxed as he caught sight of me. I trod water for a few moments as my coughing fit subsided, then struck out for a ladder that reached down from the quayside above. Slowly I climbed up towards safety. As I reached the top Etienne grabbed me, pulling me to him into a fierce embrace.

'I'm all right,' I said, starting to cough again.

'I thought I was losing you,' he murmured, still holding me tightly.

'I'm fine. Wet, but fine.'

He finally pulled away and looked into my eyes. 'You're sure?'

I nodded. 'Really. What happened?'

'A man stole a crate of fish and made a run for it,' Kit said. 'He knocked into you while he was being chased. You sure you're all right, Sorsh?'

'Yes.' I started to shiver.

Etienne let go of me. 'Start moving,' he said. 'If you don't, you'll never get warm.'

I rubbed my hands up and down my wet clothes, shifting from one foot to the other as I attempted to get the blood flowing around my body.

'Let's get going,' Vergil said, shifting the axe on his back and leading us north.

Amalia passed me my pack and we set off into the town. The wind blew in off the sea, a cold edge to it making me shiver even more. My hair still dripped even though I'd done my best to squeeze the seawater from it. I hoped I'd dry off quite quickly, but a chill seeped into my bones, taking hold. Etienne and Kit both cast me the odd worried glance, but I smiled reassuringly at them as we left the town behind and headed into the countryside. I followed, my head beginning to ache as the shivering became persistent, cold wracking my body. As we walked along the sun began to rise, partially obscured by clouds, but its milky light did nothing to warm me and my shivering continued for a while, my teeth chattering like a couple of children.

Suddenly the shivering stopped.

Thank the Starlight.

I glanced ahead. Vergil was still leading the way, chatting to Amalia who walked at his side. Etienne and Kit were just behind them, now deep in conversation about something.

As I walked, my arms and legs grew cold, verging on numb, and I found it hard to feel the ground under my feet. I tripped. As time went on, I could barely put one foot in front of the other without stumbling and staying upright became a challenge all of its own. Although I wasn't shivering I still felt cold, and I tried to pull my cloak around me for extra warmth, but my fingers had ideas of their own and refused to function properly. I couldn't seem to get them to do what I wanted. What was going on? I tried bending them, forcing them to take hold of my cloak and wrap it more firmly about my shoulders, but they wouldn't comply. This was getting tiresome.

Still deep in conversation, the others gradually pulled away from me as we walked between golden fields of corn where insects chirped to each other and birds swooped like flying fishermen attempting to catch their dinner. Every now and then we passed a field of green with cows or sheep munching on the lush grass. Where was it we were going again? I couldn't quite remember, but I knew it was important.

All I really wanted to do was sit down and rest. Rest for an eternity. I was so tired from the sea voyage, from the seasickness and lack of sleep, that the numbness growing in my body made little difference. Tiredness was all that occupied my thoughts. Tiredness. Sleep. That's what I wanted. But I'd settle for – where were we going again? I just wanted to sit, that's it, sit for a while, take a breather. In fact, it got to a point where that's exactly what I did do. I found a rock and sat down.

I couldn't be bothered with all this anymore. Couldn't be bothered with walking to wherever we were going. I didn't even know why we were going there. Why couldn't we go back home? I wanted to go back home to the Citadel and see Mother. She'd have some warm clothes for me there, and a four-poster bed, with silken sheets and soft pillows where I could sleep for as long as I liked. What's more, she'd be able to send to the kitchen for food. Plenty of food. I'd had nothing to eat for ages because of, what was it? Oh yes, the seasickness. I had no more energy. My limbs felt like ice and I had no sensation in them at all – so strange. Hard to describe really, not being able to feel your arms and legs.

I tried to take my pack off, but failed miserably. My fingers refused to do my bidding. I looked at them, but they blurred in front of my eyes. I blinked. Blinked again. That was better. No, they were still blurred. I couldn't even take my pack off, damn stupid fingers, why wouldn't they work properly? Totally ridiculous. I couldn't even remember what it was we were doing here. Where was Mother? She'd have all the answers, but I couldn't see her anywhere, too many fields of gold, but she had to be here somewhere.

Etienne came running back to me. 'Sorsha? What's wrong?'

I frowned, trying to remember. 'I-er-um...' I didn't know. Why wouldn't he go away and leave me to rest?

He reached out and touched my face, instantly recoiling. His face blanched and he quickly scanned the countryside, what for, I couldn't tell. Had he seen Mother?

'Come on, get up,' he said, trying to pull me to my feet.

I shook my head. 'N-no. L-leave me alone.' Getting up was the very last thing I wanted to do. I was happy where I was. 'I'm waiting for Mother to take me home to bed.'

His face paled further as the others came running up.

'What's the matter?' Kit asked, looking worried. Kit was funny when he looked worried. His forehead would crinkle and his eyes took on a wild, puppy look.

'Sorsha's ill, she's freezing,' Etienne said, pulling my pack off and giving it to Amalia. Thank the Starlight that wretched, heavy pack was gone. 'We need to get her warm.'

'There's a barn a little way over there,' Vergil said, pointing out across the wheat fields. 'We could certainly shelter there.'

Before I could argue, Etienne had scooped me up in his arms and had started to carry me towards the barn. I wanted to protest but the urge to sleep was stronger and I couldn't be bothered. Where was Mother? Maybe I'd sleep until she came back from wherever she'd gone.

'Oh, no you don't,' Etienne said, giving me a gentle shake. 'Don't you dare go to sleep, Sorsha. Please don't – I couldn't bear to lose you, not now, not when we're...'

I opened my eyes. Why was he being so damned annoying? Why wouldn't he let me sleep – and why couldn't he bear to lose me? He was just a Sun Prince. Nothing to me. Arrogant and proud. Wasn't he? I was finding it hard to remember because all I wanted to do was go to sleep.

'I'm tired,' I protested. 'Leave me alone.'

'I'm sure you are tired, but right now you need to stay awake or you might never wake up again,' he said.

That sounded nice. No, wait. What was he talking about? Never wake up? Nonsense.

'Kit, we'll need warm, sweet tea for her once we get to the barn,' Etienne continued. 'A half full mug.'

'No problem.' Kit nodded.

We finally reached the barn Vergil had pointed out, and Kit set about making a fire and some tea as Amalia started searching through the packs for something or other.

'I-I'm fine,' I said, sitting near Kit's fire. 'J-just, just... um... let me sleep. Stop fussing. Mother will be here soon. Father too...'

'Oh hell,' Etienne murmured.

Kit's face fell as he looked at Etienne. The Sun Prince gave Kit some sort of funny look and took the warm drink from him. What was wrong with them? My eyelids, heavy and achy, started to close.

'No, you can't sleep yet,' Etienne said, passing me the half full cup of warm sweet tea. Too sweet. I didn't like things too sweet – did I?

I looked into the tin cup and frowned. 'It's not full. I don't want it if it's not full. And it isn't hot, it's only warm – in fact I don't think I want it at all.'

'You don't want it too hot, you'll burn your mouth and neither do you want it to be full, now sip it,' Etienne said gently but firmly. I scowled at him, before taking a tentative sip. Too sweet.

'Why did you want me to half fill it?' Kit asked, looking at Etienne with a confused expression.

'Because when she starts to warm up she'll start to shiver like she's never shivered before,' Etienne said. 'And we don't her making herself wet again as she spills it. In the meantime, we need to get her warm.'

Amalia passed him some blankets and he put them over his shoulders – *Starlight*, was he cold too? I thought it was just me – or maybe I wasn't cold anymore? I couldn't decide as I took another sip of tea. Etienne came and sat behind me, straddling me and wrapping his arms around me, the blankets settling around both of us.

'Wh-what are you doing?' I asked. This was embarrassing. 'What do you damn well think you're doing?' I almost dropped the cup.

'Saving your life,' he said. 'Now, sip that tea.'

What a load of fuss. Still couldn't see why they wouldn't leave me alone until Mother came. Still, I did as he said, no point in upsetting a Prince of the Sun Order – after all, we didn't want to go to war with them over a cup of tea and a blanket. And if it meant he was going to hold me like this, even in public, it was worth it. I didn't just like him anymore, I was definitely falling in love with him. Or was I actually in love with him already? My addled brain couldn't decide, but it was one of those. I continued to sip, the sickly sweet tea cloying at my throat as he held me, his body so warm against mine.

I started to shiver.

I very nearly dropped the cup, but Kit wrested it from me before I could spill the last of its contents over me and the blankets. Etienne was finding it hard to hold on to me as my body shuddered like a sapling in the harshest winter storm.

Some time passed and the shivering ceased as a combination of Etienne, the tea, the blankets, and the fire finally warmed me up. I could feel my arms and legs again. What a relief. My fingers and toes began to follow and I wiggled them, finally getting some sort of response from them.

I looked around at the well-constructed wooden barn we were in, with straw strewn across the hard earth floor, except where Kit had cleared it for the fire. A large heap of hay sat at one end where Amalia and Vergil were lying, talking quietly to each other, periodically glancing in my direction with anxious expressions on their faces – what were they so worried about? Kit sat drinking a cup of his brew, while Etienne still held on to me.

'What happened?' I asked weakly, feeling like a newborn lamb in his arms.

Etienne sat up a little. 'You got too cold. What with that and your lack of food and sleep, you got ill.'

'Ill? I've not been feeling good, but Mothe–' I stopped in mid-sentence as I remembered. Mother wasn't coming. She was dead. Dead back on Steorra, weeks ago. How the blazes could I have forgotten that? 'I-I…' I sniffed.

'Don't worry about it, when you get cold like that you can get a little confused,' he said, a reassuring note to his voice. A little confused? He was being very kind.

I nodded slowly. 'I feel so tired, but hungry too.'

'Eat something and then you can rest. Kit, can you find her something to eat?'

Kit grinned and produced two dead, cleaned rabbits from behind him. 'Vergil and Amalia brought these back a little while ago. I'll have something ready for you in no time.'

Rabbit stew wasn't really my idea of a good meal, I didn't really care for it much, but when you haven't eaten properly for days you're glad of anything. I dutifully ate, my stomach rumbling gratefully. Perhaps it wasn't so bad after all.

'Why don't we rest for a while, we can move on later in the day?' Vergil suggested after we'd all eaten. 'We can still be in Mere City before nightfall.'

'Sounds good,' Etienne said. 'Kit, will that fit in with finding Flax?'

Kit nodded. 'I don't see why not.'

We made ourselves soft beds in the hay to rest in for a few hours.

'Etienne, will... will you stay with me, keep me warm?' I asked him. My head told me I was being foolish, but my heart didn't care.

'I was intending to,' he said, snuggling next to me under the blankets as I lay down. 'You can go to sleep now, it's fine to rest.'

'I'll probably not want to nod off now I can,' I said, still slightly peeved at not being allowed to sleep earlier.

However, I was asleep in seconds.

#

No dreams plagued me and I awoke from an inky blackness, Etienne still lying next to me, his arms protectively wrapped around me. I sighed contentedly. For the first time I could actually imagine myself Pledged to someone, and that was quite a feat in itself. Etienne was caring, generous, fearless, and above all, kind. All the things I'd never imagined a Sun Prince to be, and yet here he was, and he seemed to feel similarly about me. My whole train of thought brought me up short – there was a prince out there waiting for me, and it wasn't Etienne. Maybe I'd grown to truly love the Sun Prince, but it was completely hopeless because he could never be mine. I had to stop thinking this way; it was just so, *so* difficult to see him only as my friend now, and nothing more.

'How are you feeling?' he asked, opening an eye.

'Much better, thank you – but how did you know?' I asked. 'I've never felt like that before, never been so cold and confused.'

'Seen it once before when a cousin fell into a pond in winter. He was cold, confused, argumentative, even started seeing things. Then he started taking his clothes off. We tried warming him up, but he constantly fought us. We held him down in the end, but he didn't survive.'

'Oh. I'm sorry.'

'You were lucky,' he said, smiling, his turquoise eyes burning a hole in my heart.

'I wasn't lucky – I had you,' I said, kissing his cheek. His face burst into flame. Why had I done that?

'Maybe.'

'We should think about moving on,' Kit said from where he stood at the barn door looking out over the fields. 'Or we won't reach Mere City before nightfall. We'll want to find an inn before it gets too dark. I'll start looking for Flax tomorrow.'

'You think he'll be easy to find?' Vergil asked, scratching his head as he stood beside him.

Kit shrugged. 'Not sure. But I have a good idea of where to look for him.'

I frowned. 'All those times you said you were on errands for Uncle and you'd disappear off for a few weeks, you were in Mere, weren't you?'

Kit turned towards me, looking like a mouse that had just been caught. 'Not always, Sorsh. But sometimes,' he said, shifting awkwardly. 'Let's get packed up.'

I glanced at Etienne.

He grinned back. 'Your friend is rather a dark horse.'

The look in the Sun Prince's eyes drove any doubts from my mind – I truly and deeply loved him.

'You're telling me,' I said, getting up and going in search of my pack.

'Are you feeling better?' Vergil asked, retrieving his own pack from beside mine.

'I think so, thank you,' I said. I paused a moment. 'Vergil, do you have many princes on Planetae?'

'There's me, Prince Rinn and Prince Jephra, that's it.'

'Are either of them sixth children?'

He shook his head. 'No. They're my uncle's two sons – he has a daughter too, but that's it. Why?'

'Just wondered.'

So my Pledged wasn't a Prince of Planetae. So who, by Starlight, was he?

Chapter Seventeen

We walked through the fields, Etienne inexplicably holding my hand – actually, it wasn't inexplicable. From the little smile lingering on his face, he liked it, but I also had a sneaking suspicion it was also to make sure I didn't wander off or get left behind again. The sun sank slowly to the horizon as we joined the main road into Mere City. Merchants trundled along in their carts laden with spices, materials, vegetables and other goods making their way to the city.

The paved road made walking easier, men rode past on their horses, kicking up dust, and other travellers on foot carrying all manner of packs, plodded along. Periodically we passed little shrines to the Merribor Pantheon. The deities they worshipped here were everything from birds to boots – a weird selection of items, really. It appeared that if someone decided something had brought them luck they made a shrine to it on principle. Thankfully we didn't do that on Steorra – we'd soon have run out of room.

We made our way along the road, the sun kissing the grassy horizon to the west, sending its golden-red fingers across the sky, lighting up the puffy white clouds, staining them with its angry colours. I was tiring quite quickly now. The events of the day were taking their toll, despite the rest we'd had.

I stumbled on an uneven paving stone.

'You all right?' Etienne asked, holding my hand tighter to steady me.

I nodded. 'Just tired.'

'We're almost there – look.'

I glanced up. There in front of us rose the city of Mere, capital of Merribor. Its dark granite buildings with grey slate roofs rose high into the air attempting to scratch the sky, a vast, high wall surrounding the city. No easy way to escape once you were inside. It hugged the coast, a great harbour with ships going in and out in the fading

167

light, lanterns swinging on their masts and the tang of salt intermittently in the air as the wind blew. At its centre rose the palace, a black granite building more like a fortress than anything you'd see amongst the Orders. It had a foreboding look that sent a shiver working its way down my spine. Little pinpricks of yellow light began to illuminate the city's buildings as lamps and torches were lit in readiness for the coming darkness. Night wrapped her skirts around us as we entered the gates.

'Where now, Kit?' I asked.

'We head left, into the Bell Quarter,' Kit said, leading the way. 'There's a quiet little inn there I know. Flax and I stay there quite a bit.'

'I bet you do,' I muttered. He shrugged and wandered off ahead, not hurrying, not drawing attention to us.

We followed him through the narrow streets, the smell of old beer and spices heavy in the air, and as we passed the end of some alleyways, the smell of something far less salubrious. Rats scuttled in the shadows, sending the hairs on the back of my neck standing to attention. After another ten minutes we arrived at a well-kept, if slightly small, establishment. Kit walked straight in and started chatting to the barmaid. I looked around the taproom. There were a few patrons talking quietly, but this was no rowdy inn. We took a table, and quickly had plates of hot meat pie and vegetables in front of us. I ate quickly, not realising before this how hungry I still was, enjoying the taste of the herbs in the pie and the minted potatoes. I drank the honey-mead and then Kit led the way upstairs to our rooms.

'They're not busy tonight, so we have a room each,' he grinned. 'See you all at breakfast,' he said, disappearing into the far bedroom.

'I'm going to sleep for a week,' Amalia said, taking the next room, Vergil opposite her.

I took hold of the next door handle.

'I'd rather not leave you alone after today... would you mind if I stayed with you?' Etienne asked quietly. 'Made sure you were all right tonight and didn't get cold again?'

I swallowed, my heart racing in my chest, slamming against my ribs. No, I didn't need him staying with me tonight; not only was I fine now, but it would just make things so much harder than they already were. But I *wanted* him to be with me.

My heart won.

I nodded, my breathing suddenly shallow and irregular. We entered the room and dropped our bags to the floor, Etienne shutting the door behind us. A little lamp glowed from its holder on the wall, illuminating the room in a soft glow. I glanced at the bed. It wouldn't be as snug a fit for us both as the ship, and at least it looked like the bed had fresh sheets, which was more than could be said for the last inn we stayed at.

I discarded my weapons and sat on the edge of the bed with a sigh. Tiredness made my bones ache and my neck stiff, and I rolled my shoulders to try and ease them. On the other side of the bed, Etienne placed his weapons against the wall and took of his tunic and boots.

'Let me,' he said, scrambling over the bed. He helped me take off my tunic and gently started massaging my neck.

'Hmm, that feels good, thank you,' I said as he released my tense muscles.

'You know, when we met, I couldn't work you out. But once I got to know you, found out about you being a Double Blood, everything made sense.'

I laughed lightly. 'I'm no longer an enigma? Shame.'

He leant forward, resting his head on me. 'Enigma? No. But you'll always be legendary.'

'Stop it,' I said, shifting my shoulder and making him pull back with a laugh.

I looked over at him and he smiled at me, the one that reached from ear to ear, lighting the whole of his gorgeous face and made his turquoise eyes sparkle like diamonds. I sighed, and if I'd been a block of ice, I'd have melted at his look.

'So what about you? You didn't think much of me when we met.' He went back to massaging my shoulders.

I looked forward again and winced, embarrassed by my initial reaction to him. 'I didn't know you then, just the stories I'd heard about the other Orders. With being away from Court so much I never had the chance to meet anyone from outside Steorra for any length of time.'

'And now? What's your honest opinion now?' he asked, sitting beside me and gently turning my face towards him, staring into my soul.

I moved his hair from where it covered his eyes. 'I was completely wrong.'

His eyes softened, his pupils dilated and he leant slowly and tenderly towards me, and for one exquisitely mad moment I thought he was going to kiss me, and I'd let him.

But I couldn't. I pulled back.

He hesitated, his brow furrowed.

'No. I can't,' I said, standing up. 'I won't put you in danger because there's some mystery prince out there expecting to be Pledged to me. It doesn't matter how much I want to. How much I...' I looked at him, before quickly glancing away, my face burning. 'I can't give you what you want.'

'And what do you think I want?' he asked, standing up and reaching out to my chin, forcing me to look at him. He searched my eyes, waiting for my answer.

'Y-you want... are you really going to make me say it?' I stared back at him, but he didn't move, didn't even flinch. 'My heart. My love... And I want to. I want to give you my heart and everything that goes with it, but I *can't* give them to you, not properly. You know that. I have to at least have a chance with this mystery prince, although I think you've already crushed whatever hope there was of that.'

'So you do? You truly love me?' He leant forward, eyes sparkling.

'It doesn't matter what I feel, because I can't.'

'If there was no mystery prince, if we could both make our own choices, would you Pledge yourself to me?' he asked, taking hold of my arm, but I took a step back. 'Would ours be a love match?'

'I-I can't, you know I can't... it's just a wonderful dream we can never have.' I turned away. At what point I'd started to cry, I didn't know, but tears streamed down my face. 'Stop toying with me, Etienne. The Pledging Records may still be at the Temple, and even if they're not, the prince's family will know about me. We can never be together, and this, whatever this is, is too painful. It has to stop before we hurt each other anymore.'

'I never meant to hurt you, Sorsha. I just wanted you to love me like I love you, willingly, because it's what you wanted, not because you felt obliged to.'

He truly loved me. My heart lurched in my chest at his words.

'Of course I love you too, so much it hurts, but it's no use.' I took a step towards the door, my heart thudding uncomfortably. What did he mean: "obliged" to? 'I can't do this anymore, I'm sorry.' I reached for the handle. 'You've ruined me for anyone else.'

'There is no one else. I'm the one you're being Pledged to.'

I stopped dead.

Froze; my hand hovering above the door handle.

He took a shuddering breath. 'It's me, Sorsha. I'm the one your mother had arranged for you to be Pledged to.'

'W-what? How do you know?' I didn't dare turn around in case I was hearing things. Could it possibly be true? A wave of ice, followed by a wave of fire, washed through me as my heart thundered in my chest.

'I was being Pledged to the Seventh Starlight Princess. I just didn't know her name. I wondered about finding out who she was when I first reached the Citadel, but then I thought how it wouldn't make a difference to anything as I couldn't change it even if I wanted to. If she was awful, there wouldn't be anything I could do about it, so I decided I was best not knowing, that I should leave it until we were formally introduced and Pledged – too late to worry about it then. I didn't know who the Seventh was, didn't know that was you, until... until I asked

Finnar before we left the Starlight Citadel the second time.'

I turned around slowly, wiping my eyes with my cuff. 'Mother said my Pledged was a sixth child, far removed from the throne.'

He nodded. 'I'm a sixth child, and removed from the throne – or I was. I don't know now,' he said, eyes far away for a moment. 'I'm your mystery prince, Sorsha.'

'But I thought you were being Pledged to Aster,' I said with a frown.

He shook his head. 'No, it wasn't her. You were all making assumptions.'

'Taran would have said if it was me. He would have loved the opportunity to taunt and mock me, but he didn't. He said he knew who you'd been promised to.'

'Taran lied.'

It certainly wasn't the first time my cousin had lied to my face, but it had been the last.

I swallowed. 'But you said–'

'I said I didn't know her name, not that I didn't know her title. I knew I was being Pledged to the Seventh, but not who the Seventh was. On the way back to Steorra I was already falling hard for you, Sorsha, and after what happened at the Starlight Citadel, well, I decided I needed to know exactly who I was being Pledged to, so I asked Finnar when he came to see us off at the docks. He told me you were the Seventh.' He took a breath. 'It was always you, Sorsha. We were always meant for each other.'

My breath caught in my throat as he moved over to me and took hold of my shaking hands, his own trembling slightly as he gazed into my eyes. I'd seen him talking to Finnar as I'd boarded the ship, but thought nothing of it at the time, too wrapped up in the horror of the attack.

'So it was you all along?' I asked, trying to take it all in. 'Mother did say she'd introduce me properly to my Pledged when I got back. I thought when she said "properly" that it was an odd choice of words.' I looked at him. 'Now I know why.' I reached out to Etienne's face, gently caressing it. Could this really be happening? He grabbed hold of my hand, turned my palm towards him and kissed it, sending sparks through my body. 'She even told me to get on with you – this was why…'

He nodded. 'To begin with, when we first met, I'd assumed all the Starlight Princesses had been named in age order.'

I shook my head. 'No, we're given our titles according to how close we were to the throne. Although the two oldest were the First and Second, but that was coincidence. I'm not the youngest, but I'm the Seventh. I'm surprised your Father would want you bound to me, especially with my reputation.'

Etienne rubbed his forehead. 'I'm not important. I'm sixth in line, dispensable – removed from the throne – as your mother put it. Because of that I was sent to Steorra on this mission. I don't mean to insult you, but I'm at least as irrelevant to Solis as you think you are to Steorra.'

I flinched. 'You're not irrelevant, and I'm not insulted.'

He shrugged.

'I'm irrelevant though,' I said.

'You may not be now. Who knows what will rise from Steorra's ashes?'

'The same can be said of Solis. We don't know what's happened there at all.'

He rubbed his forehead again. 'I know, and it plays on my mind, but statistically speaking, as I said, I have five elder brothers. It's unlikely something's happened to all of them. Some would have survived, as some people survived on Steorra. It's still unlikely to affect me with regards to the throne, which suits me fine.' He sighed. 'My elder brothers were all too important to be sent on this "trifling" errand – that's why *I* was sent to Steorra – royalty, but not important royalty.'

'You're important to me,' I said. *So very important.*

He looked at me, the skin around his eyes crinkling as he smiled. 'I am?'

'Of course you are.'

'I'm not sure I've ever been important to anyone before, not properly.' His eyes sparkled with delight. 'So, does this mean you approve of your mother's arrangements after all?' he asked, slowly slipping his hands onto my hips, giving me time to pull away if I wanted.

But I didn't want to now. I didn't need to anymore. The wall I'd built up between us had been smashed to smithereens, and there was nothing to stop me from embracing the new feelings that were rushing in to take its place. I gazed at him, drinking him in. I nodded. 'She told me I had no choice, that there hadn't been a royal love match for two hundred years…'

'And yet here we are,' he murmured, tilting his head as he leant towards me. 'Have we proved her wrong?' he asked, his lips a whisker from mine.

'Yes,' I said, breathlessly, not pulling away this time. His lips gently brushed mine, and my heart skipped a beat. 'I think we have. I can't believe this,' I said, shaking my head. 'I can't believe you're my prince.'

'I couldn't believe it when I found out the Seventh Starlight Princess was you,' he murmured, his velvet lips brushing mine again and sending sparks through me. 'Knowing the one I was to be Pledged to was you… was amazing. You're everything I've ever wanted, everything I'll ever need.'

'You can be quite romantic when you want to be, can't you?' I asked, sliding my arms around his neck.

He drew back a little so he could look me in the eye, and grinned at me. 'I can try harder, if you like?'

'If you want, after all, there can never be too much romance in the world,' I said, then frowned. 'So you've known it was me you were to be Pledged to since we left the Citadel the second time?'

He nodded.

'So why, by Starlight, didn't you say something sooner?' I demanded.

Chapter Eighteen

Suddenly annoyed, I took a step backwards letting go of him. 'Why didn't you tell me the prince I was to be Pledged to was you? That *I* was your Starlight Princess? You put me through this torture, thinking I couldn't have you, and yet you knew we were to be Pledged – how can you claim to love me and do that to me?'

He flinched. 'Because, like I said, I wanted you to love me for me. Not feel obliged to *try* and love me. I've seen all my brothers in unhappy matches, and I didn't want ours to be one where my wife hated me, cherishing every moment we were apart. I wanted my wife... I wanted *you*, to love me properly, for me, not because you felt forced into it or duty bound and obliged to want me when deep down you didn't. I wanted you to be sure, like I was. I wanted you to love me because that's what *you wanted*.'

My heart fluttered.

He hesitated. 'I suppose it all sounds rather stupid and idealistic, but I wanted you to love me like I love you, to want me like I do you. Before we even got back to Steorra I was falling in love with you. I tried to fight my feelings, but I couldn't. It didn't matter what was being arranged, I wanted you. *You*, Sorsha.'

I'd told him once I'd be shocked if anyone ever wanted me. But now, when it came to it, I wasn't. It seemed so natural that he'd want me. That he loved me and I loved him.

He paused and bowed his head, looking to the floor. 'In truth, by the time Finnar told me you were to be mine, my heart was already yours. I thought you were falling for me too, but you'd gone cold on the way to the Temple.'

'I realised what was happening between us and at the time, I couldn't let it go further. You know that,' I said, wiping an errant tear from my eye. 'Although I did in the end.'

He reached out and tenderly brushed away another tear.

'The fact you thought there was this mystery prince somewhere out there meant you couldn't let your guard down, and I understood that. I respected it, admired your resolve to be true to someone you'd never even met and didn't know. I was honoured that you were being true to me, even though you didn't know it. Because things were good between us again I didn't want to break the spell and possibly spoil things by telling you the truth. I still wanted us to have a chance together for our own sakes, not for the sake of legalities and political alliances, so I kept quiet.'

'You should have said,' I chided.

'I'm sorry,' he said, his eyes clouding. He took a deep breath, raking his fingers through his dark blond hair and making my heart flutter. 'I love you, Sorsha.'

'And you're sure you want *me* because you love me? The sword-wielding, awkward, country bumpkin-princess?' Taran's words rang in my ears making me flinch.

Etienne frowned. 'Your cousin was wrong about you, so wrong. You don't have a single prickle, not really. And you *are* beautiful, not to mention, quite exquisite.'

I sensed blood rushing to my cheeks. His tone of voice told me he was being completely sincere as he spoke. 'But, your feelings, they're really not just out of duty, because of what your parents have arranged?'

'I could never feel the things I do for you because of duty,' he said, shaking his head, an earnest look in his eyes. 'There's no question I love you, for being *you*. You fill my heart, my head, my soul. I had no idea I could feel like this, that some*one* could make me feel like this. But you have. My love for you fills me to overflowing.'

I couldn't begin to put my thoughts in order.

He'd wanted me to love him, *really* love him – like he loved me. He didn't want me from obligation, from duty. I hadn't wanted a loveless match either, but I'd never in my wildest dreams hoped it would be a true love match on both sides. And yet, it was. If I'd been in his position and realised first, wouldn't I have done the same? Given him the chance to love me for me, and not out of duty and obligation?

Etienne's shoulders sagged. 'I should've told you from the moment I found out, saved you from this pain, but I didn't. I just wanted you to be sure. I didn't want to force you and you end up resenting me, like my brother's wives resent them. I was an idiot.'

I shook my head. 'No, you weren't,' I said softly. 'What you did wasn't stupid or idealistic or idiotic, because you did it from love.'

A flicker of hope crossed his face. 'You think you could forgive me one day?'

I knew there was nothing I wouldn't forgive him.

'I forgive you now,' I said.

He stepped forward and took my hand. 'Are you sure?'

I nodded. 'Yes, I'm sure,' I said, reaching out and once again caressing the side of his face.

'I love you, Princess Sorsha of Steorra, my Seventh Starlight Princess,' he said, his eyes full of love, his pupils dilating as he looked at me.

'And I love you too, you silly, wonderful Sun Prince,' I said, my heart thundering in my chest. '*My* Sun Prince.'

He leant towards me, arms slipping around me pulling me close as he tilted his head, his lips once again brushing mine. His breath caught and he pulled back a little.

'Can I – I mean would it be all right if I – may I…' he said, his voice husky.

'I really wish you would,' I said, pulling him towards me. As his velvet lips met mine my brain went into meltdown as flashes swept behind my closed eyes and my veins filled with molten blood. I slipped my hand through his hair, pulling him further towards me as our bodies rested against each other. Yes, I loved him. As he drew back for breath we looked at each other, both embarrassed and emboldened at once.

'I had no idea…' He looked at me, his gaze coming to rest on my lips.

'Was it that bad?' Self-doubt filled me. 'I'll get better at it, I promise.'

A mortified look clouded his eyes. 'What? No! I didn't mean it was bad, I meant it was so *good*.'

'Oh. I see. I haven't done this before, so I don't know what I'm doing really,' I said, suddenly embarrassed.

He ran a finger over my lips. 'I haven't done this before either, so for two people who've never had any practise at this, I think we're doing rather well.'

If my heartrate was anything to go by, he was right.

'And even if we're not, as far as I'm concerned, you kiss exquisitely,' he said.

'So do you,' I said, my voice quavering.

He smiled at me, a lopsided smile that set fire to my soul.

'Be mine,' he murmured, leaning towards me. 'For always.'

He'd crept into my heart and made a home there. I loved him and no one could ever winkle him out.

I nodded, gazing into his eyes, his turquoise irises just rims around his dark, dilated pupils. 'If you will be mine, forever.'

'I will. There's no one else in this world I'd give myself to but you, now. No one I could ever want, but you,' he said, voice hoarse.

He hesitated, swallowed. He took my hands, looked into my eyes, as deep within his the flames of love, desire and longing mixed with want and amazement.

He shook as he spoke, 'I know this is usually done in public because we're royalty, but I don't want to wait for some formal ceremony.' He took a deep breath. 'I-I give myself to you absolutely, of my own free will, and without reservation. I will be your husband from now and forevermore.'

A little shiver worked its way down my spine. He'd spoken the words of the Vow of the Pledging Oath.

'We're doing this now?' I asked, slightly surprised at his eagerness.

He shrugged. 'If everything had been fine in Luna chances are we'd have had the Pledging Ceremony weeks ago, before I'd even had a chance to go back to Solis.

You know what royalty are like when they've got a Pledging to finalise. They do it immediately the two of you are together in the same room before you've even uttered a word to each other. Knowing what we know now, in some ways I'm surprised your mother didn't get us to exchange the Oaths when we first met, before we'd even left for Luna. We've been extraordinarily lucky and got to know each other first.'

He had a point.

He hesitated. 'Unless you want to wait, of course?' he asked. 'I mean, you've only just found out about it being me, and technically, even though we can exchange Oaths just the two of us, royalty usually do it in public. It's just with everything going on I don't know when that will happen for us. But if you don't want to do it now, I'd understand and–'

I placed my finger over his lips, silencing him.

'I give myself to you absolutely, of my own free will, and without reservation. I will be your wife from now and forevermore,' I said, without a trace of doubt. 'I want you, Etienne, my Sun Prince. I give myself to you, and you alone,' I said, and pulled him towards me. 'And I do it now.'

'And I want you, my Starlight Princess,' he murmured, voice hitching.

Our lips met again and this time his tongue gently, but quickly, parted my lips. He started to explore, as did I. His mouth was warm and sweet, and I shivered with the intensity of his touch as he caressed my face with his hands before slipping them around me and pulling me closer, so close I fancied we could feel each other's rapid heartbeats through our chests pressed so tightly together. I kissed him back, losing myself in the sensations, as his breathing deepened and body responded to our love.

Eventually he pulled back, his turquoise eyes glowing in the light as I caught my breath. 'You're beautiful,' he said, his voice catching as he caressed my cheek. 'I love you.'

I took hold of his hand, and kissed it. 'I love you too.'

He smiled at my words. 'I want you to know that I want to show you how much I love you – that I'd like to Seal our Pledge properly.'

My eyes widened as I glanced at the bed. 'You mean…?'

'Yes.'

He really wasn't wasting any time – although, I had to admit that I'd been thinking the same thing, somewhere at the back of my mind in its darkest, deepest depths where I seldom went, seldom explored. I just hadn't been listening to the little voice screaming at me about how much I wanted him, how much I needed him, how much I wanted *that* from him. At the same time I couldn't believe what he was saying, and the whole idea filled me with ice and fire.

'I–' He put his finger to my lips, stopping me before I could say anything further as my heart tried to explode from my chest.

'Just know I want to,' he said, his eyes burning with love. 'But now isn't the time. I-I wouldn't want to get you pregnant with everything so unsure, with everything that's happened – is happening back home – neither of us can risk that, even if we wanted to,' he said, his voice hesitant as he finished, his eyes searching mine. 'And I so want to.'

'I want to Seal our Pledge too,' I said breathlessly, realising how true those words were. 'You know I-I think there are herbal elixirs that can stop me getting pregnant,' I said, mulling the idea over in my mind, surprising myself with my brazen thoughts.

'But aren't they hellishly dangerous?' Etienne asked, frowning.

'They can be sometimes. In fact now I think about it, a girl on Uncle's estate was really ill after she took one a few years ago, never been the same since. And of course they don't always work.'

'Best avoided then – I'll not take any chances with you,' he said emphatically. 'Whatever I, or you, want for that matter. You're too precious.'

I turned his face towards me. 'I love you, we're together, that's all that really matters.'

'I hoped you'd understand,' he said, his eyes sparkling. 'Thank you.'

Of course I understood and I respected him for it, and the fact he wouldn't risk using an elixir, only made me respect and love him more.

'So the idea of being with someone like *that*, doesn't make you feel sick now?' I smirked.

He sighed and smiled. 'Not when it's you, no. Quite the opposite, in fact. Besides, we know each other. It wouldn't be weird at all, especially now when we're in love with each other too.' His forehead furrowed a little. 'It would be... wonderful.'

My heart skipped. 'Yes, it would,' I said, breathlessly.

'The problem is we don't know what we'll go back home to, what we'll have to do to rebuild, and we have to get it right when we do,' he said. 'It's very unlikely, but if-if something's happened to Father and my brothers I'll be...' He suddenly looked far away.

He was worrying about the fact he might have lost all his family, however unlikely that was.

'If I am King of Solis I wouldn't want there to be any arguments about my Queen, about my-my children, if I had any,' he said, looking at the wall.

With such thoughts, such worries plaguing him, I could see that possibly making me pregnant wouldn't be at the top of his list – even if getting me into bed with him was.

'Of course not,' I said. I understood perfectly, and anyway, I wasn't ready for babies yet.

'S-so, what do you think?' he asked, fear colouring his face. 'You're still okay with having Pledged yourself to me? Or would you rather we forget the whole thing?'

'What, on the off-chance you've just made me Queen of Solis?'

In my wildest dreams, or nightmares, I'd never considered becoming a queen. All those formal occasions I wouldn't be able to escape. For a moment terror filled me, and I chewed my lip as nausea rose in my throat and my heart hammered even faster than before. All I wanted was a quiet life in the country away from Court – Starlight or Sun.

He looked awkwardly at me, tensing again. 'Yes,' he said, a little hesitantly. 'It's a lot to ask when we don't know what's happened, but the last few weeks have taught me how much I need you, Sorsha. Whatever lies ahead will be hard, but with you at my side I think I can cope with whatever comes. I love you – I need you, and you already know I want you. And the first thing I'd do, if it happened, would be to revoke the Entombing Law.'

'Oh, good,' I said with a shudder.

'So, are you? Are you sure you're still happy to be Pledged to me?'

It appeared that Etienne, the Sun Prince of Solis, could be quite the romantic. The voice that could melt glaciers reduced me to a puddle. If I had to be a queen to have him, then – I would. No question. Although I think he'd forgotten the tiny fact I didn't actually have a choice as all the documents were signed and filed.

'Yes,' I said, reining in my initial reaction to bolt. Now I'd found him, I couldn't lose him. I'd do anything, even if it meant attending banquets and balls for him. 'A thousand times, yes.'

He grinned and pulled me into a kiss more vibrant than any before. The world vanished and it was just the two of us in a world of our own where we could live and love together, unhindered by any other concerns. His kiss grew deeper, and sensations I'd never felt before rattled through me in a wave of pleasure and desire. Like kissing, I'd not had any experience of relationships, not ones like this anyway, and it made me nervous and excited all at the same time. I also knew he didn't have any experience either, so at least we were both the same. As we continued to kiss I concluded he was right and we seemed to be doing just fine; at least I was definitely enjoying it and he appeared to be too, if the little moans he uttered now and then that sent small shivers down my spine and made me moan once or twice in response, were anything to go by.

When we finally settled down to sleep in each other's arms, I could honestly say I'd never felt so loved or so content in my life. A short while ago I couldn't have imagined myself Pledged to anyone, ever. And yet now, here I was, bound to a Sun Prince of Solis. Life was strange. Etienne was my world now, and my dearest love. We'd do anything for each other. Anything at all.

I'd even become Queen of Solis.

#

I awoke once in the night, a cold sweat covering me as a nightmare faded away. I sighed. Would these dreams never leave me in peace? I glanced over at Etienne in the dim light. He was restless too. Dreams or nightmares, I didn't know, but he didn't appear happy in his sleep and I feared the latter – I didn't like to wake him, though. At least he was resting.

The next morning we agreed to keep our Pledge hidden from the others for now. We wanted a little time to enjoy it just us two, and besides, it wouldn't make any difference to anyone else for now, so we kept it to ourselves.

'You had a nightmare last night?' I asked.

Etienne looked at me and nodded. 'How did you know?'

'I slept beside you.'

'Oh. Sorry, I didn't mean to wake you.'

'You didn't – is it the first one you've had?'

'I've had a couple before, but I think they're getting a bit worse.' He sighed. 'Not knowing what's happened at home, and you not being well too – I think that's just made it worse. And I also guess I'm worried about what Taliesin and Cynric would do to you if they got a hold of you.'

'They'd bleed me dry,' I said with a grunt.

'Exactly,' he said, bowing his head. 'And then there's Artem...'

'I can take care of Artem, don't you worry about him.'

'I dare say you can,' he said, squeezing my hand. 'But it doesn't stop me worrying about him, or you.'

'Like I worry about you,' I said, gently kissing his lips.

He smiled at me. 'Guess we'll have to watch each other's backs.'

'Definitely,' I said with a grin.

Etienne left my room before anyone awoke, so we could avoid any awkward questions, and I ventured downstairs a short while later.

'I thought I might have to come and wake you,' Kit said.

'I've been awake for a while,' I said as Vergil and Etienne arranged our breakfasts. I noticed the Sun Prince giving me a surreptitious wink, and I had trouble suppressing a grin. 'I've been thinking–'

'Always dangerous.' Kit grinned.

'Rude,' I said, glowering playfully at him.

'You really let him speak to you like that?' Amalia asked, eyes wide with surprise.

I shrugged. 'I don't *let* him, he just does it and anyway, he's been doing it for so long now I'll never break him out of the habit.' I gave my friend a sidelong glance.

'Now who's being rude?' Kit asked.

'You started it – look, surely we need to go to the palace – wouldn't Taliesin take the Crystals and Bloods there?'

'Not necessarily,' Kit said, shaking his head. 'Taliesin could be stashing them anywhere. He has several prisons across the country where he could be keeping Bloods. No, we need to speak to Flax first.' He paused. 'What's wrong with you this morning?' he asked, a suspicious look in his eyes.

I frowned. 'Nothing's wrong, why?'

'You've got some weird grin on your face.'

'I have? Can't I look happy?'

'We're in a dangerous city on a hazardous mission. I'm not sure there's much to be happy about,' he muttered.

'I almost died yesterday, I'm just glad to be alive and with you,' I said, slipping my arm through his and giving him a squeeze.

'Get off,' he said, pulling away as Vergil, and Etienne returned with our food.

'What's going on?' Vergil asked, raising an eyebrow.

'Kit was saying how pleased he was that I'm feeling better,' I said with a little smirk.

Kit sighed. 'I'm going to find Flax,' he said, heading for the door.

'What about breakfast?' I called after him.

'I've lost my appetite with you being silly.'

'Please yourself,' I said as he left the inn. Etienne came and sat beside me, Vergil and Amalia on the other side of the table.

We enjoyed a good meal of pastries while we waited for Kit to return, then went back to our room to chat. The morning dragged on.

'Should we get some supplies?' Amalia asked.

'Probably, but we don't know what we'll need yet,' Vergil said. 'I mean, we don't even know where we're going next. The Relics and Bloods could be here in the capital or on the other side of Merribor.'

'Good point.' Amalia nodded. 'We'd better wait.'

The sun was high in the sky when Kit returned.

'Where have you been?' I asked. 'I was beginning to get worried.'

Kit had an anxious look on his sweaty face. 'Flax isn't here. He's in Scorhill, up the coast. We need to leave now. The Emperor's Guard are looking for us.'

'Here? Already?' Vergil asked, his eyes wide.

Kit nodded. 'They don't know where we are. They've been given orders to look for us everywhere along the coast.'

'Damn,' I muttered. 'Do we go now or lay low until night?'

'Rumour has it they're shutting the gates at dusk from now on. Not opening them again until dawn.'

'Then we go now,' Etienne said, standing up. 'Get supplies and horses on the way out of the city, and try and stay out of the Guards' way.'

I took a deep breath and looked at the Sun Prince.

His expression matched Kit's. Troubled.

Chapter Nineteen

We moved along, me with Amalia, and the boys together in a separate group, in an attempt to make us less obvious to any passing Guards. While the others haggled over horses, Amalia and I went in search of supplies. The markets here were full of fruits I'd never seen before, and a vast range of vegetables, fish and meat that sent varying aromas into the air that vied with the spices circulating with them. We quickly stocked up on things that would last on our journey, particularly as we were heading north to warmer climates, as well as light cloaks for sun protection, and water, plus a small wineskin Amalia seemed quite pleased about.

'You rarely get this wine at home,' she said. 'It's Faerlandian – strong and sweet, but so good. Even Etienne takes a sip from time to time and he's not a great one for wine. Talking of which, the two of you are getting on well now.'

Not sure how wine had anything to do with me and Etienne. My heart skipped. Had she guessed?

'I think we are,' I said, studying a cloth merchant's stall.

'He seems very happy, and I'm pleased.'

'What about you and Vergil?' I asked. Their furtive glances and attempts at hidden hand holding hadn't escaped my notice.

She swallowed, a rosy blush appearing on her pale cheeks. 'We're doing fine, thank you.'

'Is it serious?'

'Are you and Etienne serious?' she asked looking intently at me.

I glanced away.

'Well, that answers my question,' she said with a little laugh. 'And so are we. Let's just hope your mystery prince doesn't find out.'

The scarlet uniforms of the Emperor's Guard caught my eye.

'Amalia, quick.' I pulled her along with me into the shadows of a putrid smelling alleyway.

'That was close,' she said, peering after them as they marched along.

'We'd better get back to the boys,' I said, leading the way out of the alley and back towards the stables where we'd left them. Outside the stableyard five horses stood tied to holes in the curbstones, but where the boys were eluded me. I looked into the stables to see if I could find them. A hand gripped my arm.

'We need to leave now,' Etienne whispered in my ear. 'There are Guards all over the place.'

'We saw some a short while ago,' I said as he helped me load the supplies into the packs on our horses, Vergil and Kit had returned and were helping Amalia.

'Which gate?' Vergil asked Kit.

'North, it's the quietest.'

Vergil nodded and led his horse along the main street towards the gate. It took us a while to weave our way through the noisy citizens and to the North Gate. We didn't want to ride and draw attention to ourselves, and every time we saw a Guard we attempted to put the horses between us and them. By the time we finally reached the gate I was getting quite agitated. Every time a red cloak appeared I jumped, convinced we'd been spotted. My nerves were in shreds as we made our way past the Gate Guards amongst a group of wagons laden with fish and oil, and out into the countryside.

Once well clear of the city we mounted up and rode at a decent pace along the well paved road, the sea sparkling like diamonds to our right, the blue water of the Mere lake far off to our left glistening away. Shrines littered the side of the road, becoming less frequent the further we were from the city. Before long we crossed the river linking the Mere and the sea, a great granite bridge spanning the grey, churning waters, but from here marshes spread out on both sides of us. Causeways and low bridges took us across foul smelling pools and stagnant water trapped by sand dunes that rose like small hills between us and the sea, interspersed by mud flats. Mosquitos buzzed around the pools, making an incessant droning that began to get on my nerves.

'We need to be well out of these marshes before evening,' Vergil said, screwing his nose up. 'If not, they'll eat us alive.'

'We have about another half hour's riding,' Kit said, suddenly slapping his arm. 'After that we'll be clear of them. They're a menace, these mosquitos. Flax says they keep saying they're going to drain the marshes. But they never do.'

'I'll be glad to be out of them,' Amalia said, flapping a mosquito away from her horse's ears.

As Kit had said, we soon broke free of the fetid water and marshes, once again surrounded by grasslands with swooping birds and noisy insects which didn't bother me as much as the mosquitos because their calls weren't nearly as menacing. We rode on for another hour until the shadows around us from the bushes and trees became long and the sea disappeared from view as the land pushed it further to the east.

'We'll have to think about making camp soon,' Etienne said, looking towards the setting sun.

I scanned the countryside. 'There's a small copse over there, maybe that would do?'

'Good call,' Kit said, and urged his horse on towards the trees. 'It's a good distance from the marshes and nicely off the road. It'll make a good campsite.'

We allowed ourselves a small campfire to cook our meal, but extinguished it immediately before it became completely dark, to avoid unwanted attention. I wandered out to the edge of the trees and looked out at the road. Periodically a pitch torch could be seen as those more determined travellers continued their journeys, but they were few and far between.

The faint scent of vetiver and travel drifted on the air. Two hands slipped around my waist and Etienne rested his head on my shoulder.

'I wondered where you'd gone,' he said.

'Not far, just thought I'd take a look at the road before we turned in for the night,' I said. 'It all seems fairly quiet.'

'Good,' he said, gently resting me against a tree. 'Now, I have some important business to attend to.' He leant towards me and gently kissed my lips, sending shockwaves through my body as he held me around the waist. I slipped my hands up to his neck, running one through his hair.

'Tell me, now we're Pledged, do you intend to make this a daily occurrence?' I asked, grinning mischievously.

'Would you like me to?' he asked, his eyes glinting in the moonlight.

'I won't say no if you want to,' I said, slowly pulling him towards me until I could feel his breath on my skin. 'In fact I may encourage it.'

I kissed him again, long and deep as we held each other close. Although I'd not had any experience in this area, I was finding that we were muddling along just fine.

#

My nightmares were improving, but Etienne's weren't. I still woke several times in the night, although not as much as I had been, but when I did he wasn't exactly sleeping peacefully beside me. He'd move restlessly, sometimes mumbling something incomprehensible. I'd watch him, gently stoking his hair until he settled a little, then I'd try and get back to sleep myself. The pattern continued.

As we travelled north the weather became drier and warmer – Scorhill sat on the edge of the Great Dune Desert, and the closer we got the hotter the days and the cooler the nights. Etienne took to sleeping under my blankets again, and I noticed Vergil tentatively edging closer to Amalia each night. Even the air itself changed; you could smell the dry desert in it now when the wind came from the north, and it took on a clear, bright quality meaning you could see for miles. Although the nights were cold, the daytime sun became stronger, ready to burn you given half a chance. Kit and Vergil didn't care, Etienne just tanned, Amalia and I burnt – I kept my pale skin hidden as much as possible, the hood of my light cloak up, but still my nose turned red.

'We'll reach Scorhill tomorrow,' Kit said one afternoon. 'There's a village up ahead though. It has a little inn there where we should be able to stay the night.'

'You mean we'll get a bath and a bed?' Amalia asked, rubbing her neck.

Kit nodded.

'Good, my back is killing me from lying on the ground,' she muttered.

'Are you going soft?' Etienne grinned.

'No, Eti,' she said, glowering at him. 'I just prefer not to have a stiff, achy back.'

'Me too,' Vergil said.

The inn was well-kept and clean. We were able to bathe in their bathhouse, and then had a good meal of vegetables and meat, with a steamed pudding for dessert much to Amalia's delight. When it came to retiring for the night, there were only three rooms.

'You girls take one, Etienne and Vergil can take another. I'll have the small one,' Kit said as we made our way upstairs. 'Sleep well,' he yawned, leaving us on the landing.

Etienne gave me a slightly pained look as he grasped the handle to his and Vergil's room.

'Um, would you two mind if you shared a room?' Vergil asked, scratching his head as he looked at me and Etienne.

Amalia raised an eyebrow. 'But we're not Pledged,' she hissed. 'And neither are they.'

'We're only going to sleep in the same room,' Vergil said defensively. 'I'll take the couch, you can have the bed. I just want to be with you.'

I grinned as Amalia's face turned the colour of one of Mother's ball gowns.

Mother.

The thought of her wiped the grin off my face almost immediately.

'If that's what you want, it's fine with me,' Etienne said, a relieved look in his eyes. 'Sorsha?'

I nodded. 'You can take the couch,' I said in a loud voice, slipping past him into his room.

'I can what?' he asked, following me in, closing the door behind us. 'By the Sun, do you really mean that? Even though we're Pledged now?'

'No, silly, I only said it for their benefit.' I kissed his cheek.

He grinned. 'Good. Amalia seems to enjoy Vergil's company.'

'She told me it was serious,' I said, taking off my weapons and removing my tunic, but leaving my other things on, just as Etienne did. I didn't trust the look of the bed sheets, and by the way Etienne squinted at them, I don't think he did either.

'He told me his father was trying to Pledge him to some girl.'

'I told him to ask Amalia to Pledge herself to him, and when he gets home, point out to his father how suitable a match she is. The King can't really object. And if he does, it'll be a bit late.'

'You're a devious woman, Starlight Princess,' he said, getting into the bed.

I grinned at him as I climbed in beside him. 'Aren't I just?'

'And you're all mine,' he said, leaning towards me and kissing me lightly.

'That is also very true.'

'Then Vergil better hurry up and ask her to Pledge herself to him, or he may lose her. She won't wait forever and she's not the sort to put up with him messing about, either.'

We settled into the bed, quickly drifting off to sleep on the soft mattress.

#

A strange sound cut through my dreams, one that made me sit bolt upright, the hairs on the back of my neck standing to attention. There it was again – a groan of such despair and misery that my heart froze. I turned to Etienne. He lay beside me, the moonlight streaming in the window illuminating the glistening sweat beading on his brow like diamonds, as he moved about in a troubled sleep. The look of despair on his contorted face quite upset me.

'No, no don't,' he mumbled.

I gently shook his shoulder – I couldn't leave him asleep this time.

'Etienne, wake up,' I said softly, but his torment continued.

'Leave her alone! Sorsha!' He flung his arm out in the throes of his harrowing dream, catching me on the side of my jaw with his hand.

'Ow!' I muttered, grabbing his shoulders as his head tossed from side to side. 'Etienne,' I said in a louder voice as he tried to move his arms. 'Wake up! I'm here, it's okay.'

He opened his eyes with a gasp. He looked at me, his turquoise irises wildly ablaze, full of fear and terror as he took a moment to register my presence.

'Only a dream?' he asked in such broken tones it clawed at my heart.

Suddenly he pulled me towards him in the most ferocious hug I'd ever experienced. I could feel him shaking under me and over my shoulder, where he'd buried his face in my hair, he let out a strangled little sob. I frowned. Whatever had he been dreaming about? I, of all people, knew how trauma could set these things off, but despite all my nightmares, I didn't think I'd had one quite like Etienne just had.

'I'm here,' I murmured. 'It's okay.'

'I-I didn't mean to wake you,' he said, a catch to his voice. 'It was just a bad dream.'

'A very vivid bad dream,' I said. He nodded as he released me. I sat up and looked at him, his eyes gleaming with unshed tears.

He hesitated a moment. 'They were killing you in

Helios,' he said, his eyes glistening like the sea in the pale moonlight. 'Cynric and Artem were bleeding you dry as the city burned, and they made me watch.'

I took his still trembling hand. 'That will never happen,' I said, kissing his palm before lying back down beside him, resting my head on his shoulder. 'I'll kill them first.'

A little laugh escaped his lips. 'I dare say you would. I love you, Sorsha of Steorra,' he murmured.

I lifted my head and twisted around, planting a kiss on his warm lips. 'I love you, too, my Sun Prince,' I said. 'More than you'll ever know.'

He pulled me back to him and kissed me, a deep kiss full of profound love. My body tingled from head to toe and my face flushed with the burning intensity of his kiss. When we finally parted I was breathless for a moment.

'I love you so much that sometimes it hurts,' he said, gazing into my eyes. 'I find I ache with it.'

I let out a little involuntary gasp. 'S-so do I,' I said, a wry smile forming on my face. 'But it's a lovely ache, one I always want to have.'

'I never want to be without it either,' he said, moving my hair from my face.

'Now, let's see if you can't have some sweet dreams this time,' I said, snuggling up next to him, cherishing his warmth. His trembling had stopped, and as he held me the smell of fresh vetiver filled my senses. Etienne's breathing quickly deepened and in a few minutes he was peacefully asleep.

I sighed thankfully and tried to join him, but sleep wouldn't come.

I took to wondering what we could do now we were Pledged that didn't involve dodgy herbal elixirs, but the sound of low voices drifted in the window. Now what? I just wanted to get back to sleep.

'You're sure they're still in there?' came a harsh voice.

'Yes, they're all in there.' That was a voice I recognised.

Artem.

Chapter Twenty

I sat bolt upright, my heart racing.

'Wake up,' I hissed, nudging Etienne.

'What?' he murmured, still asleep.

'We've got trouble. Artem's here.'

That woke him up. 'Where?'

We both scrambled out of bed and I slipped to the window peering down into the dark street. Two shadows hurried away.

'– at dawn,' Artem's voice drifted back.

'We need to get out now,' I said, pulling my tunic and boots on before grabbing my pack, Etienne doing the same.

We moved out onto the landing.

'I'll get Vergil and Amalia, you get Kit,' I whispered.

'Wouldn't you rather get Kit?' he asked, closing the door quietly behind us.

'No. When he's alone he usually sleeps naked, without covers, and I've had an eyeful of that before – I don't need to see it again.'

Etienne chuckled. 'I hope you won't feel like that about me?'

I gave him a long, steady look as my cheeks flushed. 'Of course not, now go and get him.'

Etienne hurried down the corridor as I moved over to Vergil's door and knocked gently. Nothing. I opened the door. Suffice it to say, Vergil hadn't taken the couch, and neither had Amalia. They lay tangled up in the bed. I just hoped their sheets had been cleaner than ours.

'Hey, wake up,' I said, gently shaking Amalia's shoulder.

Amalia's eyes snapped open and she grabbed a knife from under her pillow before she realised it was me. 'What is it?'

'Artem's here – we need to go.'

'Alone?' Vergil asked, pushing himself up onto one shoulder.

'No, there's at least one person with him. We'll meet in the stables. Hurry.'

I left them, joining Etienne on the stairs.

'I see what you mean,' he said in an amused voice.

'Exactly,' I said, leading the way down the stairs and out the back of the inn to the stable yard. We quickly tacked up the horses as the others arrived, attached our packs and mounted up, riding out of the yard slowly and quietly. We rode in the opposite direction to the one Artem and his companion – had it been Cynric? – had gone, riding straight out into the countryside before heading back in the direction of the road, but staying off it until after the sun had begun to rise. We didn't stop until the late morning, finding a little river valley – more of a stream really – to rest the horses and eat.

'Hey,' Etienne said, pulling me around to face him as the others started getting some food ready. 'What happened to you?' he asked, looking at my jaw. 'You've got a bruise.'

I gingerly reached out to touch it, immediately wincing as I did so. 'Oh, that, it's nothing,' I said, not wanting to tell him the truth. 'Let's get something to eat.'

'Tell me,' he said, holding my wrist and refusing to let me go as he looked directly into my eyes as he demanded an answer.

'Would you believe me if I told you I walked into a door last night on our way out the inn?'

'No,' he replied. 'I was with you and you didn't walk into anything. Tell me.'

I bowed my head. 'If I do you're to promise me you won't get upset.'

'Someone hit you, didn't they?'

'Etienne, promise me not to get upset,' I said, standing firm.

'I'll get them back, don't worry. Now who was it?'

'You'll do no such thing. I'm not telling you unless you promise me that you're not going to get upset.'

He scowled a moment at my insistence, but slowly Etienne's expression turned from determination to a kind of acceptance.

'All right,' he said begrudgingly. 'Just tell me what happened.'

I nodded, looking at him. 'Good. You hit me.'

'What?' his eyes widened in horror. 'I did no such thing! I'd never hit you! Ever. When? I don't remember. Are you sure it was me?'

'Unless someone else has been sharing my bed, then yes, it was definitely you, but it's all right, you didn't mean to and you wouldn't remember anyway. You were in the midst of that nightmare, thrashing about. I didn't see your hand coming in the dark, that's why I got hold of your wrists. It'll be fine in a day or two, don't worry about it.' I took hold of his head and kissed him soundly. 'In the meantime, as far as anyone else is concerned, I walked into a door in the dark.'

'I'm so sorry,' he said, still looking mortified.

'Forget about it – I had until you reminded me.'

He gave me a quick hug. 'I'll make it up to you,' he murmured.

'Don't worry, I'll make sure of it.' I grinned at him mischievously.

We rested a while, but didn't dare tarry too long with Artem on our heels with who knew how many men.

'How long will it take to get to Scorhill?' I asked Kit as I looked out at the horizon of scrubby grass and small bushes.

'We'll be there by this afternoon, Sorsh,' he said. 'But I don't think we should stay. If Artem's on our collective tails we need to get out of there as soon as we've got Flax.'

'Will he know of somewhere we can stay outside the town?'

'Knowing Flax, he's probably got a whole collection of safe houses scattered around. Hopefully he'll have somewhere suitable.'

I nodded. As we readied our horses for the ride to Scorhill, Amalia sidled up to me.

'You won't mention to anyone what you saw this morning, will you?' Amalia asked, her voice low.

'I didn't see anything,' I said. 'Sometimes I'm truly unobservant – it's a failing of mine, I'm afraid. Although I hardly see it matters.'

'Poppycock. You know how things are in the Orders – sleeping together if you're not Pledged is frowned upon, particularly if one of you is a Prince.'

'Do you love each other?'

'You're direct.'

'Well?'

She nodded, her face turning pink. 'Yes, we do.'

'So what's the problem? You're a Royal Lady, he's a Prince, there's no problem there.'

'Vergil wants us to Pledge to each other. I'm just not sure his father will approve if we ask his permission. I think his father is thinking of Pledging Vergil to someone else. So you see, it's probably quite hopeless.'

'Your father was a noble of Planetae. I can't think of a more suitable match. I think the King will agree. Just present it to him in a way he can't argue with.'

'What do you mean?'

'Don't ask permission, just explain to Saros how suitable the match is. If that doesn't work... The Vows are sacred. If you've already Pledged to each other, the King won't go against Order custom. Just don't mention it to him unless he presses the issue. If he doesn't, it won't matter if you have two Pledging Ceremonies, will it?'

'You really think it'll work?' she asked, a thoughtful expression on her face.

I shrugged. 'I don't see why not. Just present it to him calmly. I've already said this to Vergil.'

'He spoke to you about us?' she asked, arching an eyebrow.

'A bit of guesswork on my part, actually, but he confirmed it.'

'You're quite devious, Princess, I hadn't realised.'

I gave her a smug little grin. 'Etienne says the same

thing.' I blushed and looked away. 'I just learnt to think on my feet a long time ago.'

'And you and Eti, are you…?' she left it hanging.

I couldn't tell her the complete truth, we'd agreed to keep our Pledging secret for now. 'Best friends.' *And soulmates.*

'But–'

'Our situation is slightly different to yours and Vergil's.'

She nodded. 'True. I don't want to sound awful or anything, but I rather hope this mystery prince of yours isn't around any longer to get in your way. Nothing would make me happier than seeing you and Eti together.'

I glanced over at Etienne who was climbing into his saddle. My mystery prince was still around, all right, and totally in my way, just where I wanted him. I put my foot in my stirrup, then turned back to her.

'Out of interest, how do you two make sure there aren't any unwanted repercussions?' I asked, curiosity getting the better of me. 'From, you know…'

A little frown formed on her forehead and her eyes filled with unshed tears. 'I can't. So we don't have that to worry about.'

'Oh, I'm sorry,' I said, wondering what Vergil's father would make of that – as the next King, Vergil would be expected to supply heirs. He and Amalia were in for some tough times, I just hoped their love for each other could surmount them. 'Still, makes that side of things easier in some ways since you don't have to worry.'

'True,' she said, a grin slowly forming on her face. 'And I've discovered that it can be such fun, Sorsha.'

'I'll take your word for it.'

She glanced at her cousin. 'Maybe you'll find out, one day.'

Maybe.

We rode on, keeping off the road, approaching Scorhill from the north as the wind picked up sand from the desert making the air hot and dry. I wiped the sweat from my forehead, my coat and tunic long since stuffed in my saddlebag. It was late afternoon, but the fishing town still bustled with ships docking, bringing in their wares and selling them in the market or sending them off in creaky old wooden wagons for sale elsewhere. Kit led us to a rickety looking house in a backstreet. It had seen better days and didn't look particularly inviting. We stabled our horses at a farriers across the street and made our way to the house. Kit knocked on the door, a funny rat-a-tat rat-a-tat-tat. After a moment the door opened a crack.

'Kit? What in the blazes are you doing here? Bugger me, you should've let me know you were coming. Come in, quickly, before someone sees.'

The voice coming from the house had a lyrical tone, and as the door opened I recognised the young man that stood before me – in his early twenties, his skin a light beige colour, his short dark hair slightly unkempt and a scar running down his left cheek. He had a charming aura, just as I remembered, and he could only be described as being handsome, his scar adding to the air of intrigue that he exuded.

'Thanks, Flax,' Kit said as we all entered the house.

As Flax closed the door he turned and hugged Kit, giving him a kiss.

'Princess Sorsha, lovely to see you again,' he said, kissing my hand and bowing extravagantly, much to Etienne's annoyance. 'Now, are these others who I think they are?'

'And who do you think that is?' Etienne asked stiffly.

'You are Prince Etienne, and this is Prince Vergil and the Lady Amalia,' he finished, bowing to each in turn.

'Correct, but how did you–'

'You're wanted across Merribor and I'm sure Kit's already told you I'm a spy. I know these things ahead of everyone else. Now, why are you here, particularly?'

'We need your help,' Kit said, sitting on an old couch in the dusty, dark living room that Flax had ushered us into.

'Kit, you know I can't get involved, however much I might want to.'

'Emperor Taliesin sent Prince Cynric to the Celestial

Isles to take all the Order's Relics decorated with Blood Crystals,' I said as Flax's eyes narrowed and his forehead furrowed.

'He's gathering them all together, along with any Bloods he can find, so he can use the magic in the Crystals,' Etienne said, finally relaxing.

'Not only that, he's razed the Orders' capital cities to the ground, burning and murdering royalty and commoners alike,' Vergil said.

Flax sat down, his face ashen, his knives that he wore on his belt and hips catching. Come to think of it, I'd never seen so many knives on one person before.

'And attacked the Celestial Temple and killed the priestesses,' Amalia added.

'We're going to recover the Blood Crystals and free the Bloods he's imprisoned,' I said.

'We just don't know where they are,' Kit said. 'That's why we need you.'

'I didn't know,' Flax said, his knuckles white as he gripped the arms of his chair.

'What do you mean, you didn't know?' Kit looked bewildered. 'You know everything.'

'Apparently not. I knew something was going on – I knew Cynric had been sent to the Orders, but was under the impression it was for diplomatic reasons. I had no idea he was rounding up Clarets.' He shook his head, then frowned.

'Clarets?' Amalia asked.

'It's what we call Crystal Bloods around here, on account of blood being red,' Flax said. 'What are these Relics, anyway?'

'Magical artefacts of the Orders,' I replied. 'They're powerful, with embedded Blood Crystals. They'd been hidden in our art, in our libraries. Cynric destroyed or stole it all just to find them.'

Flax's forehead furrowed deeper. 'Destroying artwork? That's a travesty in itself,' he said through gritted teeth. 'Art is history, the story of our peoples. To wantonly destroy it is an unspeakable crime.'

I raised an eyebrow. I hadn't taken Flax for an art lover, but I was obviously wrong. He appeared to have a deep passion for it.

'The books too?' Flax asked, looking up.

Kit nodded. 'Anything with a gemstone that could remotely be a Crystal.'

Flax's nostrils flared and a vein rose on the side of his neck. 'Taliesin has gone too far this time. I can't countenance it any longer.' His hand went to the bone hilt of one of his knives, his fingers running over the cold white shaft. 'What do you need?'

I chewed my lip. I hoped Kit was right about Flax, that we could trust him. Kit's intuition about things was generally good, but Flax was a spy – and one of the Emperor's, at that. I took a deep breath, praying we wouldn't later regret placing our trust in him.

'Any idea where Taliesin would take the Crystals or the Bloods themselves?' Kit asked.

'There's only one place, really. The Stronghold. He has a dungeon there – more like a torture chamber really – and vaults. The walls are forty feet high and ten feet deep. Impregnable. And he has a small army stationed there. Taliesin will take everything and everyone there.'

Kit had been right about the palace in Mere City – we'd have put ourselves in danger trying to get in to no avail.

'Where is the Stronghold?' Etienne asked.

'West of here, many days travel,' Flax said.

'And is there a way we can get in?' Vergil asked, shifting his axe slightly.

Flax rubbed his chin. 'I have a contact beyond the Stronghold. She may be able to help us – she probably has enough men to take on Taliesin's.'

'She?' Amalia asked, glancing at Kit.

'Morven. The Ash Bandit Leader. She's an old friend.'

Friend? Not by the look in Flax's eyes. Did Kit know?

'Do you think she'll help?' Etienne asked.

'She's been looking for a way to bring down Taliesin for years and this might be her chance. We'll go and see her,' Flax said standing up. 'I assume you're being followed?'

Kit nodded.

'Then we'd better go now,' Flax said, leaving the room.

'Do you have somewhere we can spend the night?' Kit called after him, a hopeful note to his voice.

'Don't you like camping?'

'Not as much as a warm bed, you know that,' he said, then winced, suddenly remembering he was in company.

Flax came back in grinning from ear to ear. 'I have a house of sorts about two, three hours ride from here, but we'll have to hurry. It'll be dark soon and I don't want one of the horses' breaking its leg in a rabbit hole.'

Chapter Twenty-One

Flax's safehouse was more of a dilapidated barn than anything, but it was watertight – or rather, sandtight – which was just as well because a wind got up, sending the sand from the neighbouring desert swirling around, stinging any exposed skin like a swarm of needles. At one end loose boxes provided stabling for the horses, and we sat at the other, a small platform above us for sleeping.

'Sorsh, I've been meaning to say, Happy Birthday,' Kit said, a big grin on his face.

'What? It's today?' I asked, having no idea what the date was anymore.

Kit nodded.

'What's this?' Etienne asked.

'Sorsha's eighteen today.' Kit grinned.

'I'm sorry I don't have a present for you, but Happy Birthday,' Etienne said, his eyes softening as he took my hand and gave it a lingering kiss that turned my blood molten and my bones to jelly.

'Thank you,' I said back, rather breathlessly.

Flax laughed as he sharpened a knife. 'Get a room, you two.'

My face burnt, and Etienne was doing a rather good impression of a strawberry as he turned to the spy.

'Master Flax, it's quite obvious you know nothing of Courtly Manners,' Etienne said.

Kit didn't help, he just sniggered. 'Or Courtly Love,' he added.

Etienne and I both went redder.

Amalia and Vergil sat in a corner talking softly, totally oblivious to the rest of us.

'Nothing at all,' Flax said, checking his blade for sharpness, 'and long may it stay that way. Although from my experience manners are over-rated. As for love, well, that can become an art form, you just have to work at it, hone it, keep doing it as much as possible to refine it, and if you're lucky, one day you might manage perfection.'

Kit flushed and looked away. Served him right.

'And how would you know this?' I asked primly – he was only interested in Kit, what did he know about me and Etienne?

'Oh, in my role I've had experiences on both sides of the fence and in between,' he said, buffing his fingernails on his tunic in a "know-it-all" kind of way. 'But I think that's over with – no more spying for me. Taliesin has seen to that. And I only have one man in my sights now,' he said, glancing at Kit who flushed even more. Flax grinned broadly.

We settled down to sleep on the platform as the wind howled outside. Etienne wrapped his arms around me keeping us both warm as the cold desert air drifted into the barn. I prayed he wouldn't clobber me again in the night. As it happened, despite the surroundings, we both slept reasonably well, the nightmares only shades at the edges of my dreams.

The next morning we set off at dawn, staying off the road, although parallel to it, on the edge of the desert where scrubby bushes vied with the dry earth-cum-sand. Not easy going for the horses, or us as the sun rose higher and the heat became intolerable. I rode along next to Kit, a little behind the others, although Etienne kept turning around to check I hadn't stopped – he was still a little nervous about me falling behind again.

'Did you know about her?' I asked Kit. 'Morven, I mean?'

He nodded. 'Yes, Flax told me a while ago. I didn't mind sharing him – although I think that might be changing now,' he grinned. 'He's transferring *all* his affections to me by the sounds of things.'

'I wonder what she'll make of that,' I said.

Kit shrugged. 'Don't suppose she'll worry too much. According to Flax she has several lovers on the go at once.'

My eyes widened. 'Isn't one at a time enough?'

'She doesn't think so,' he said. He grinned, a mischievous look in his eye. 'But it would wear me out.'

I tried to give him a friendly punch, but luckily for him he was out of reach. 'You're impossible.'

#

The following day we stopped at a small oasis of five crystal clear pools as night fell. Tall date palm trees quietly moved their great leaves in the gentle breeze. Below them citrus and peach trees hung low with their colourful fruits begging us to try them, soft ferns and grasses sprouted out amongst the sand in little clumps around the bases of the trees. We made a little fire in amongst the dunes and plants, and ate a warm supper.

'I've been working with Morven and her men for a while now,' Flax said, breaking little pieces of wood up and feeding the fire. 'They're intent on bringing down Taliesin because of his persecution of the people, what with high taxes and harsh laws. They'll be even more determined now because of the Clarets – I believe there are a couple amongst her men. And I wouldn't mind a little revenge of my own.'

'Revenge?' I asked as Etienne sat beside me, his hand sliding on top of mine, sending a warm ripple down my spine.

Flax nodded. 'When I was about ten I had a cousin, younger than me. One day we were out in Mere Market when the Emperor and Prince Cynric rode past. Cynric's horse shied, slammed into my cousin, squashed him against a wall. Taliesin didn't care, just told Cynric to hurry up and leave the peasant. Cynric moved his horse away and laughed as my cousin struggled to breathe because of his injuries. Taliesin glared at my cousin as if it was all his fault for holding them up, and they rode off. My cousin died in my arms in excruciating pain. They didn't care. I've been looking for a way to get revenge ever since,' he said bleakly.

'So why did you go to work for him?' Amalia asked, frowning.

'To get close to him, to wait for my chance for retribution, but that chance has never come, until now. You can help me get in and finish him.' Flax's eyes were as hard as agates and a little vein stood out in the taut muscles of his neck.

'Finish him? You want to kill Taliesin?' Kit asked, surprised.

Flax nodded. 'Of course. Why do you think I've spent all these years doing his foul bidding? I've been collecting information, gaining favours whilst passing on information to Morven. I will get him, Kit, I swear it.'

Kit looked genuinely surprised. Flax had been following a dangerous path.

I glanced at Etienne. Flax's fervour made me question my own motives and desires. Looking into the prince's eyes I started to doubt my murderous, vengeful thoughts.

Etienne's hand closed around mine and, as the others continued deep in conversation, we left the camp and wandered between the palm trees and pools until we reached the pool furthest from the others. He led me over to a dip in the sand dunes and grasses beside the small pool. He laid his cloak on the sand, and for a while we sat in silence watching the warm little breeze move the reeds in the water as the moonlight glistened like silk on its surface. Although the desert had lost its scorching daytime heat, the air was still warm enough to make little beads of perspiration break out on my brow. Staring at the cool, inviting water, I stood up.

'Let's go for a swim.'

Etienne sat looking at me, eyes widening. 'Now?'

'Now,' I said, pulling off my shirt.

His eyes widened further as he watched me, his pupils dilating in the moonlight. He swallowed, his face taking on a rosy hue.

'Are you sure?' he asked, getting up and standing beside me, catching my hand in his.

'I said swim, not anything else, we've already agreed that,' I said. 'But we don't have to–'

'I'd love to, it's just… do you mean without anything on? I'd love to do that too, but is that what you mean?'

I guess I hadn't entirely thought this through. The look of the cool water had been too alluring to resist, and now I realised my mistake. Or was it a mistake? We were Pledged. Just because we hadn't been naked with each other before didn't mean we couldn't be now. My heart fluttered.

'Yes,' I said.

He swallowed, took a deep breath and rubbed his forehead. 'All right then. If you're sure.' He let go of my hand and started to take his shirt off.

I turned away slightly, undoing my bodice and slipped it off, my britches and undergarments quickly following. I turned towards him, naked but for the Starburst Necklace and the Aegis Bracelet sparkling in the moonlight. He stood before me without a thing on, gazing at me, at *all* of me, lips parting slightly. For a split second I wanted to grab my clothes, cover myself, but his naked body suddenly mesmerised me, and I stood frozen to the spot, drinking him in. His body was toned, lean and muscular. My heart thudded in my chest as I concluded this was one of the better ideas I'd ever had.

He let out a little gasp. 'Y-you're beautiful,' he choked out, breath hitching.

'So are you,' I said, now flustered. 'Not beautiful, handsome. Actually, you're beautiful too.' My face burnt as I looked at him.

His gorgeous smile appeared, the one that filled his face and lit his eyes like diamonds, before turning to a smug little grin, then faded. His eyes sparkled in the moonlight, now full of love and desire. When he spoke again, his voice was serious and thick with emotion. 'Like I say, you're beautiful.'

I swallowed. Panicked. I raced straight into the pool without looking back. I dived under the water, surfacing in the direction of the sand to see Etienne, waist deep, wading towards me grinning.

'You can be quite wanton, for a princess,' he said as he moved towards me.

I shrugged. 'It's my day off.'

'Really?'

'Aren't you glad it is?'

His lips parted slightly as he looked at me, his eyes dark. 'Very,' he said, a husky quality to his voice. He ducked under the water, coming up and sending spray flying. I laughed as I wiped the water from my face.

He raked his fingers through his wet hair, making my knees go weak. 'You know, I've been wanting to make it up to you, for not having a birthday present for your Coming of Age the other day, and for hitting you that night.'

'Make it up to me? You don't need to do that,' I said, wiggling my toes into the sand as I stood shoulder deep in the water. 'I never expected a present and you can forget about hitting me, I'm fine. Anyway, Coming of Age is sixteen in Steorra, so I'm already of Age.'

'It is? It's eighteen in Solis.'

'I had no idea they were different. I wonder what it is on Luna and Planetae?'

'Anyway, I still think I need to do something memorable,' he said, leaning towards me with a smile. 'I have nothing with me so the only gift I can give you is this,' he murmured, slipping one slightly trembling hand to my cheek and the other around my bare waist, pulling me close, his velvet lips brushing mine. 'If you want me to?'

'I want you to,' I mumbled as I pulled him to me.

The spark he ignited in me as he kissed me set light to my veins and I soaked up the sensations as I kissed him back. I rested my trembling hands against the warm skin of his toned chest, feeling his heartbeat quicken under my fingertips as he let out a happy little groan. He pulled me closer and I slid my arms around his neck, resting against him, feeling him against me. If this was his idea of a memorable present, I wouldn't complain. Slowly, his tongue tenderly parted my lips and our kisses became deeper as I slipped my fingers through his wet hair. Our tongues explored and our breathing deepened. His hand moved to my neck, caressing me as we continued to kiss, then moved a little lower, and the shocks continued down my whole body as the world melted into nothingness. At that moment I didn't care about anything, other than him.

Crystals, Crystal Bloods, Emperors, they all meant nothing. It was just him and me, and the love we shared.

He paused a moment, gazing into my eyes. 'I love you, Sorsha,' he said, his lips pink.

'Just as well, considering what we're doing,' I murmured back.

He smiled his lopsided little smile. 'I can't believe I was Pledged to the girl I've fallen in love with.'

'I could never have imagined this happening either. You know, if Mother had arranged for you to work for Finnar so that you'd have been mostly away and we'd hardly ever seen each other, I would've hated every single minute you weren't with me.' I looked into his moon-bleached turquoise eyes.

He ran a hand over my wet hair. 'Do you think we'd have fallen in love anyway?'

I blinked a little drop of water from my eyelashes. 'I do.'

'Destiny?' He smiled.

'Destiny, fate, whatever you want to call it. I think we were always meant for each other.'

'And I think you're right. I would have loved you whether we'd met like this or been Pledged. I wouldn't have left your side once we were together, whatever your Mother or Finnar had planned. I would've stayed with you.'

'And I would've shared my secret.'

'Which I would have kept forever,' he said softly, hesitantly resting his hand over my heart.

I didn't stop him and my heart lurched in my chest in response to his touch.

'I love you so much,' I murmured.

He smiled, placed his hands on my waist and pulled me to him, claiming my mouth with his and once more tenderly parted my lips with his tongue. His hands caressed me. A little moan escaped me, which only served to encourage him further, and he held me tighter against him, his body warm against mine, and I raked my fingers through his hair again, caressing his back with my other hand, and he only half-stifled his own little low moan of pleasure.

And yes, this was a gift, and one I'd never forget.

#

I'd quickly found out that cloud wasn't something you generally witnessed near deserts. The next day the sapphire sky looked down on us again, the sun scorching us from on high, but as the day went on the sandy, dry earth changed to scrubby plants and low bushes before finally giving way to short burnt grasses then longer, lusher specimens. We travelled on towards the Stronghold, clouds finally appearing in the sky providing intermittent shade as the air took on a less dry note.

I thought about the previous night, about what had happened between Etienne and me, and every time my thoughts drifted off in that direction I found my heart pumping and a strange warm sensation flooding my body. It had been exquisite. He'd given me a "gift" and I wanted to give him something in return, and I knew exactly what it should be.

We camped in the lee of a little hill facing away from the direction of the far off road, near a little spring that gurgled cheerily on the hillside. After tending to the horses and eating I took Etienne to the spring ostensibly to collect some water, as the sun set sending its golden beams across the land, poking through the little puffy clouds littering the horizon.

My thoughts drifted to the previous evening. 'How did you learn to kiss like that?' I asked, my face warming as I spoke and collected the cool water in a waterskin.

'Beginners luck,' he said, crouching down beside me. 'Although Sol gave me a few tips after he was Pledged.'

'So you do talk to each other?'

'Sometimes, but not often. He thought he was being superior, but actually, as it turns out, he was being quite helpful.' He grinned at me.

'I thought for a moment you'd been talking to Flax,' I said.

'There's that too – you know for a spy, he talks a lot.'

'Maybe too much.'

'Not about *that*, though,' Etienne said, arching an eyebrow. 'Clearly it's something I'll have to perfect into that art form he was talking about.'

I swallowed, a little knot forming in my stomach. I didn't know how much that could be perfected. 'It was an extremely memorable evening.'

'I said it would be,' he said smugly. 'And you enjoyed it?' he asked, a hesitant note creeping into his voice.

I nodded, not quite trusting myself to speak as the waterskin overflowed.

'A lot?' he pressed, apparently very keen to find out my true feelings on the subject.

'Yes, Prince Etienne, a lot. If you want me to say it was the most memorable evening I've ever had, and the most exquisite kisses I've ever experienced, then yes on all counts.'

He grinned, then his face tightened. 'You've had a lot of kisses?'

I looked at him. Was he jealous? Jealous of someone that had never existed?

'No, I haven't,' I said primly. I hesitated, looking down at the water. 'You know that. I don't think anyone's ever wanted to kiss me before.'

'Well, I do,' he said lifting my chin, the lopsided smile on his face. 'And I'm glad we're each other's first. And I'm also glad we're Pledged.'

I smiled at him. 'Me too. So glad.'

The Sun Prince of Solis flushed as his pupils dilated, his lips opened slightly and his breath suddenly hitched. 'I-I'd just love to... what I mean is... I love you,' he said, his eyes full of the same longing and desire that I felt.

I smiled, glancing back towards the camp where the others were talking; there really was nowhere to get any real privacy at all. I stood up, pulling him up with me and reached into the pocket of my tunic taking out one of the Pellucid Crystals. 'I want you to have this.'

'But – are you sure?' he asked, holding out his hand as I placed it into his palm, his eyes wide as it sparkled. 'But it's yours.'

'And I want you to have it,' I said. 'You never know when you might need it.'

'I'll treasure it,' he said, his eyes bright. 'You couldn't give me anything more precious than a piece of you.'

I hadn't looked at it like that before – I really was giving him part of me, and it wasn't lost on him. I knew he'd take care of it, and me. He slipped it into his pocket, glanced towards the camp, then leant forward, brushing his lips on mine, before kissing me properly, sending wave upon wave of warm sensations through my core.

'I love you,' he murmured as he pulled away. 'More than anything in this world.'

I caressed his cheek. 'And I you, my Sun Prince.'

'You know, I should've said last night, but I… I don't know, but I was overcome with everything, I suppose. But I wanted to say again, that you're beautiful.'

I arched an eyebrow. 'Is that with or without anything on?'

He swallowed, blushed. 'Both. But even more so with nothing on.'

'I did notice you watching me dress,' I said, suppressing a giggle.

'And you *weren't* taking the opportunity to observe closely as I got dressed?' he asked, an amused look on his face. 'I saw what you were doing.' Now it was my turn to blush.

'Well, I…'

'I enjoyed you looking.'

I sighed. 'I rather liked you watching me, too.'

'I intend to do it from now on, every time I get the opportunity,' he said, taking my hand, brushing his velvet lips against mine.

'Do you indeed? Then I shall have to follow your lead and do the same.'

He grinned, took my hand and led me back to the campfire.

Chapter Twenty-Two

The next day we passed the crossroads where the highways from Mere City, the Stronghold and Scorhill met. From our position on a low hill to the north, it appeared to be a bustling little brightly tented market area where merchants' wagons and carts met and bartered, or just continued journeying on to their destinations. The roads were busy in all directions, and best avoided.

I squinted in the sun, trying to decide if I could see any Guards' uniforms, but we were too far away. Beside me Kit shifted uncomfortably in his saddle.

'Are you all right?' I asked.

'Not really,' he muttered. 'I have the mother of all headaches. And my body is aching. I must have slept in an awkward position. My muscles are just protesting. I really wouldn't mind sleeping for a week.'

I looked at his face. Little beads of sweat sparkled on his skin, although it was fair to say I had to wipe the perspiration off my face from time to time as we rode, and I could also happily spend several days in bed resting.

Flax led us on through the grasslands, a great green wall appearing on the horizon as the afternoon wore on. 'That's the Arbour Forest,' he said. 'Full of ruins.'

'I've never seen a forest here on a map of Merribor,' Vergil said, a puzzled look on his face.

'The old capital of Arbour used to be here, but it was sacked by the Faerlandians a thousand years ago. The Merriborians were so ashamed of their failure to defend their city they deliberately forgot it and left it off maps. They let nature reclaim it and now there are only ruins left amongst the trees.' He glanced up at the sky. 'I think we could be in for some rain, so we'll camp there tonight. It'll give us some shelter.'

We rode on as the sky became crowded with grey, scudding clouds that darkened and became more and more threatening. I glanced over at Kit as we rode towards the trees. His face had a strained look about it, his eyes had taken on a slightly yellow tinge, and he'd begun to cough. I didn't like this one bit. He was getting ill.

Reaching the trees we followed a small animal path into the shadows as rain began to fall. It dripped through the upper canopy, landing on large leaves, making pools before falling in large drops that hit the ferns and low grasses making little pattering sounds. The animals dived for the safety of their burrows and birds chirped in their nests. The smell of damp, earthy soil, a smell I loved, moved around us as I pulled my hood up but not before a large raindrop had skittered off a leaf above me and landed on the back of my neck. Damn, that was cold.

After a half hour's ride along the path I started to see irregular shapes pushing their way up through the vegetation like broken bones. Grey, moss covered stone protruded from the trees and bushes becoming more prolific as we went. My horse's hoofs hit stone, and I looked down to see a paved road, broken and covered in vines and grass. As we rode further the trees drew back and the remains of old buildings crowded around us, some reaching two or three storeys into the sky, their roofs long gone, few with any staircases or proper floors left intact, but it was obvious that they'd been homes once upon a time. Some were blackened, scorched from fires so hot they'd burnt the stones themselves. I shuddered. I'd seen that before, and not long ago.

'Over here,' Flax pointed. 'There's a building that's still fairly intact.' He cast a quick glance in Kit's direction, and frowned.

I looked at Kit – if anything his bent body indicated he'd got worse. Flax bit his lip, and led us to the remnants of a dry building where we stabled the horses. I followed Kit as he led the way up some stone steps to an empty room. He stumbled as he climbed.

'I'll take that,' I said, grabbing his pack before he dropped it.

'Thank you,' he said, his voice scratchy, his chest moving rapidly as he gasped for air. 'I feel awful.'

'Let's get you sat down and something to drink,' I said, helping him across to a corner of the room as he coughed.

'What's the matter?' Vergil asked as he climbed the last of the steps and joined us.

'Kit's not well,' I said as my friend sat down. 'Can you get him his waterskin?'

Vergil nodded and rummaged through Kit's bag. I leant over and felt Kit's sweaty forehead. It felt like the hot embers of a fire.

'You're burning up,' I said, recoiling slightly. I'd never felt anyone so hot with a fever before. I looked more closely at him. The whites of his eyes were yellow. He was obviously tired, sleepy even, he had a cough, and from the scratchy sound of his voice, a sore throat.

Flax came bouncing up the stairs. 'This place is still good for camping – I was worried after last winter's storms if it would still be standing. Etienne and Amalia are seeing to the horses so maybe we shou–' He stopped dead as he glanced across at Kit, then ran over to us. 'How long has he been like this?' Flax asked, taking Kit's face between his hands and making him open his mouth so he could look inside. 'I realised he'd been looking a little peaky, but I just put it down to your long journey.'

'He didn't look well at the crossroads,' I said. 'He's been getting worse ever since.'

Flax felt Kit's forehead and hissed.

'Flax? What are you doing here?' Kit asked suddenly, a strange, empty expression on his face. 'I thought you were in Merri-Merri-Merribor.'

'What's wrong with him?' I asked, fear gripping my heart as I searched Flax's face for an answer.

'Marsh Fever,' he said. 'He must have been bitten by a mosquito outside of Mere City. That area there is rife with infected insects.'

I thought back to our travel through the marshes.

'I didn't know that,' Vergil said uneasily.

'Now I think about it, Kit was bitten while we were riding through the marshes – I remember him killing one that bit him on the arm, but that was a number of days ago.'

'It can take anywhere from ten days to two weeks for Marsh Fever to some out.' Flax shook his head, his face pale. 'He should've known better than to take you that way.'

'We didn't have much of a choice, we were being hunted,' I said, defending my friend.

'Maybe,' Flax said reluctantly.

'How do we treat him?'

'We can't.'

'What?' I shivered at his words.

'Marsh Fever is usually fatal unless you have the right herbs,' Flax said.

'Then we get some,' I said, gritting my teeth. I wasn't about to let Kit die.

'We can't – the closest supply is Mere City. We'd never get there and back in time. He doesn't stand a chance.'

'No, we can't give up. Tell me what to get, I'll head to back to Mere City now and get what you need,' I said, standing up. 'I won't stop to rest, I–'

'He'll be dead before you reach Mere.' Flax looked at me, his eyes glassy. 'There's nothing we can do, Sorsha. I'm so sorry,' he said, shaking his head. 'I'm so very sorry…'

I swallowed, tears stinging my eyes. Vergil moved over to me and placed a hand on my shoulder.

'I-I could get you an Orange Crystal, but I don't have a Pellucid – we can't cure him.'

I chewed my lip a moment, then took a deep breath – this was for Kit. 'I have a Pellucid.'

Vergil looked at me, a mixture of surprise and confusion on his face. 'You're sure it's a Pellucid?'

I took it out of my pocket and showed it to him. He nodded.

'What's that?' Amalia asked, entering the room with Etienne behind her. 'It's really pretty.'

Etienne immediately looked at me with horror, probably wondering what the hell I was doing.

'It's a Pellucid Crystal,' Flax said, narrowing his eyes as he looked at me. 'I won't ask where you got it, but you have an Orange, Vergil?'

'I will have in a moment,' Vergil said, taking his knife from his belt.

I placed my hand on his arm, knowing how this was affecting him. 'Are you sure about this?' I asked, feeling his arm trembling.

'No, but as long as I don't have to look, it'll be fine,' he said, his face ashen at the prospect of shedding blood. 'Will you do it?' he asked, offering me the hilt of his knife.

'You mean you're a Claret?' Flax asked. 'You never said.'

'Yes, I am. It just isn't something I brag about, mainly due to the fact I've been known to pass out at the sight of blood, but Kit has Marsh Fever and if I don't do this now, he'll die. So I don't have a choice.'

Amalia looked towards Kit in shock, and Etienne quickly made his way over to me.

'I thought he looked a little peaky earlier,' Amalia said. 'Can't we find him some medicine?'

'The nearest medicine is in Mere,' I said. 'He'll be dead before we can get it.'

Etienne slipped his arm around me. 'What the hell are you doing?' he whispered in my ear so only I could hear.

'Hopefully saving Kit,' I murmured back.

He nodded. 'So, what do we do?' he asked, his voice back at its normal level.

'We use one of my Orange Crystals and Sorsha's Pellucid to heal him,' Vergil said, as Amalia took the knife from his shaking hand.

'I'll do it,' she said. 'How much blood do you need?'

'Just a drop,' he said, holding out his finger and resolutely looking away.

'All right,' she said. Gently, she nicked the end of his finger. A blob of blood appeared, fell, turning immediately into an orange coloured Crystal. 'Suck your finger, stop it bleeding,' she said, holding the Crystal up to the light. 'It's beautiful.'

'I'll press it, I don't want a mouthful of Crystals.'

'It's not just beautiful, but powerful, too,' Flax said, holding out his hand. She passed it to him and I gave him my Pellucid. He held them both, looking at them in awe. 'Now let's see if we can get this to work.' He placed one in each hand and closed his eyes, reaching out to Kit's head.

'What are you doing?' Kit said, trying to pull away.

'Keep him still,' Flax said in a commanding voice.

I grabbed one arm and Etienne grabbed his other as Flax held the crystals and concentrated, but nothing happened.

'Do you know how to use them?' I asked quietly. I'd only ever used a Pellucid, never two at once.

Flax shook his head. 'I'm making an educated guess,' he said, but nothing happened. He frowned.

'Maybe, if you put the Crystals both into one hand...' Etienne suggested.

Flax looked up and nodded. 'All right,' he said, placing both the Crystals into his right hand.

Immediately they started to glow, a vibrant white and a deep orange.

Flax grinned and placed his hand back on Kit's head – his hand glowed completely orange before the light spread from his hand to Kit, who started to glow. The light nibbled at my fingers where I held on to Kit, tingling and tickling.

'I feel funny,' Kit said, his eyes suddenly going wide. 'W-what's happening?'

'Just sit still,' I said, still gripping his arm.

A minute later the glow faded and Flax opened his eyes, letting go of Kit. He opened his hand – the Crystals looked markedly different. Before, they'd had a kind of lustre to them almost like an internal glow, but now they were dull unless the light caught them – an ordinary diamond and an ordinary topaz.

'We can sell these,' Flax said, his eyes bright. 'They'll make quite a bit.'

I sighed.

'Where did you get them? And why are you two holding on to me?' Kit asked, shrugging me off.

'Feeling better?' I asked.

'I'm feeling fine, why?' His eyes widened. 'What happened?'

'It's a long story, let's eat and we'll tell you,' Flax said with a grin.

Telling Kit was quite amusing. I'd never seen him look so confused, shocked and relieved all at once, and I couldn't help but giggle.

'Thank you, Vergil, I know it must have been very hard for you,' Kit said.

Vergil gave him a little half smile. 'It's fine.'

'You were very brave,' Amalia said, raising her hand to Vergil's cheek from where she sat beside him.

Vergil shrugged. 'I had to – I couldn't let him die.'

'Which makes you very brave,' she said, pulling him towards her for a kiss.

Vergil's face lit up like a beetroot. I glanced at Etienne, who smiled at his cousin's conquest.

'So where did the Pellucid come from?' Amalia asked, looking at the diamond.

I hesitated, glancing to the floor. 'It w–'

'Athene gave it to Sorsha, back at the Temple,' Etienne said, cutting me off. 'She thought it might be useful.'

'It was at that,' Kit said, looking sideways at me. 'If we hadn't had it I wouldn't have survived.'

I smiled, casting Etienne a grateful glance. 'Perhaps Athene knew what was going to happen.'

'Perhaps she did,' Flax said, but the look in his eyes said he didn't believe a word of it. 'We'll eat, and you need to rest,' he said, looking at Kit.

'But I feel fine,' Kit protested.

'I don't care, you rest.'

Kit muttered something under his breath.

Chapter Twenty-Three

We spent the next few days in the saddle, my rear becoming increasingly sore. I'd be glad to have a rest from riding, but I didn't see one coming in the near future, even if we were successful at the Stronghold.

'When we get to the Stronghold we'll check the town, then ride on to Morven's encampment,' Flax said. 'I have contacts there and we can get the latest information on what's happening.'

'Makes sense,' Etienne said with a nod.

That night we camped near a wide, slow moving river where Vergil, Amalia, Kit and Etienne decided to go fishing. I stayed with Flax to start the campfire and prepare the rest of the food.

'That Pellucid was yours, wasn't it?' Flax said out of nowhere.

'What? No, of course not,' I said glancing down.

'Liar.'

'I'm sorry?' I said as indignantly as I could.

'You're lying, Princess. I'm a spy, remember. It's my job to get information out of people, and I know the telltale signs of when someone is lying. When you lie you look down – you have ever since I met you.'

'I do?' I'd have to watch that in future.

'And if you shed Pellucid Crystals you're a Double Blood. Taliesin would pay good money to get his hands on you, but we're going to do our best to keep you away from him,' Flax said, rubbing his chin thoughtfully. 'I guess it's only fair to tell you I'm a Yellow Blood.'

'What?' Flax was a constant source of astonishment to me. 'Does Kit know?' Before I'd even given voice to my question I knew the answer. Yes, he did – how else could Kit have known so much about Bloods?

Flax smiled, seeing I'd worked it out. 'Does he know about you?'

I nodded. 'But I only told him recently. I'd kept it secret to keep him safe, as much as me.'

He nodded. 'So Etienne's a Red and Vergil's an Orange?'

'Yes,' I said.

'Taliesin would definitely like to get his hands on us,' he said, mulling things over. 'But if we pool our resources, use our Crystals we could stand against him, free the other Clarets and recover the Crystals he has. And kill him.'

'You really do want revenge, don't you?'

'You can't tell me it wouldn't be a better world without the Emperor, can you?'

'No, I suppose not,' I said, although I was now rather uneasy at the idea of deliberately killing someone, whoever it was.

'So what colour are your Crystals?' he asked. 'Or have we doubled up?'

'You'll keep this secret, I take it? Other than Kit, only Etienne knows I'm a Double.'

'I'm a spy, of course I can keep a secret,' Flax said, buffing his fingernails on his tunic.

'Purple.'

'They'll come in useful.'

Kit walked over to where we sat carrying three fish, with Vergil and Amalia not far behind him. 'What are you two talking about so intently?'

'You,' I said, trying to resist the urge to glance down.

Flax sniggered.

Kit raised an eyebrow. 'Me? Why me?'

'Because we both love you,' I said, getting up. 'I was just filling in a few blanks for Flax.'

Kit flushed. 'Not too many blanks, I hope?'

'You'll see,' I said, leaving the two alone. I waved as I passed Vergil and Amalia who were holding hands, and went in search of Etienne.

I found him in a secluded dip in the riverbank overlooking the river, gazing towards the languidly moving water, his mind far away, probably back on Solis.

He took my hand and kissed it, and we stood watching the water for some time.

'Do you still want revenge?' he asked suddenly. 'For your mother's death?'

'I…' I took a long breath. 'I've had a chance to come to terms with things over these last weeks, and now I don't want revenge, exactly. Justice is a better word. Taliesin and Cynric need to be held accountable for what they've done and what they're doing. They need to be stopped, but not in a revenge kind of way.'

He nodded. 'I feel the same. I've had time to think about it now too and, whatever's happened back home, they need to take responsibility for it all. It's not revenge, it's just that what they've done is morally wrong and we need to stop them.'

'Spoken like a true prince.'

I took hold of his tunic pulling him to me. I didn't know what the next days would hold and I had to kiss him, just in case. The last thing I saw before closing my eyes was his soft lips and the tender look in his eyes. It was a searing kiss we shared as he slipped one hand around my waist, caressing the back of my neck with the other and sending shivers down my spine. That faint scent of vetiver swirled around me and his warm body made me want to melt as I ran my fingers through his hair. It felt for a moment as if time had stopped, that the two of us inhabited a world where time had no meaning, where there was no coming danger, where we could be together, the two of us, uninterrupted forever; but it didn't last. We both knew it couldn't.

I held him close, felt his heartbeat through his chest in concert with mine. I slid my hands under his shirt, caressing his chest. He gave a little shudder and gasped as his body suddenly stiffened. I paused, wondering whether I'd done something wrong.

'Don't stop,' he murmured, relaxing again.

I smiled and once more ran my fingers gently across his chest and down to his waist, sliding them fractionally under the edge of the waistband of his britches, gently brushing my fingers against his skin from one hip, across his lower stomach, to the other. Once more he went as taut as a harp string, and for a moment held his breath before letting out a soft little moan that set a fire alight in my core. I couldn't believe I had such an effect on him doing something so small, and I let out a happy little sigh.

'Hmm,' he murmured, slipping a finger under my chin and raising my face towards his. 'Enough. Or ...' He gazed deep into my eyes, his eyes dark, accentuated by the turquoise rims of his irises.

'Or what?' I asked, slightly breathless, my brain not really taking in what he was saying.

He looked at me meaningfully. 'Or I won't be able to stop myself from taking you right here, right now.'

I swallowed and my face flushed at the prospect, my heart skipping around like a mad rabbit. 'That sounds so nice.'

He ran a finger over my lips. 'I know, but unless we improvise, I'm not sure there's anywhere nearby that's suitable, or private enough.'

'We could improvise?' It wasn't a serious question, but from the look in his eyes he was very much considering it. 'I'm not sure now is quite the right time,' I murmured, looking back towards where the others were, up over the other side of the dip cooking the fish. 'Even if I would gladly do it now. Anyway, I thought we were waiting,' I said, turning back to him.

'We are, so as much as I'm enjoying you touching me, and I am *really* enjoying you touching me, you'd better stop or you'll force me to take this to its natural conclusion.'

'All right,' I said, giving him a little pout for good measure, moving my hands to caress his neck instead. 'I know you're right, but I really want to...'

'So do I, more than you can imagine,' he said with a smile that lit his eyes. He leant towards me and kissed me again, just to make his point.

'Come on you two, the meal will be ready soon!' Kit shouted from the camp.

Etienne groaned. 'Already? I rather hoped it would take a little longer. I like being alone with you.'

I smiled. 'Me too, and hopefully in the near future we'll be able to be alone properly, but for now–'

'We'll have to be patient.'

'Exactly.'

He slipped his fingers between mine. 'But I still want to.'

'Stop it!' I laughed as we headed back to camp. 'And so do I,' I whispered in his ear making him chuckle.

#

Once again desert began to encroach on our path, and Flax led us towards the main road.

'If we cross and travel south of the road along the side of Blod Mere we'll avoid the worst of the desert,' he said.

But crossing the road didn't turn out to be easy. We waited in a small scrubby thicket of long yellow grasses and brown thorny bushes watching for a suitable moment to cross into a little valley on the other side of the road. We waited and waited as merchants trundled past in their overloaded wagons, and lone riders, their horses laden with packs, moved along the road. A single rider galloped past leaving a trail of dust behind him. I patted my restless horse, his ears flicking at an errant fly that buzzed around them.

'Now,' Flax said, kicking his horse on towards the road. We broke free of the cover of the thicket, my horse shying at a stone of all things, and as I looked up to encourage him after the others a flash of scarlet on the horizon had a shiver of fear sweeping down my back.

'Stop!' I called. 'Guards.' I pointed, urging my horse back to the thicket. The others looked where I'd indicated and wheeled around, joining me in the undergrowth.

'Dismount,' Etienne said. 'We need to stay as low as possible.'

I slid from my saddle, peering out from between the

bushes, patting my horse's nose to keep him calm and looked out towards the road leading from Mere City and Scorhill.

'Did they see us?' Amalia asked, a hint of concern in her voice.

'We'll see in a minute,' Vergil said, watching uneasily, his hand close to his axe handle.

The Guards galloped along the road, clouds of dust billowing around them, two smartly dressed riders at the front of the group, riders that I recognised.

'Cynric and Artem,' I hissed.

Etienne glanced at me. 'Are you sure?'

'That's definitely Prince Cynric,' Flax said. 'I'm not familiar with Prince Artem.'

'That's Artem all right,' Vergil said, his teeth clenched.

The two princes rode on at the head of the group of Guards, apparently oblivious to our presence. We didn't move until they'd disappeared over the horizon.

'If they're at the Stronghold that'll only make things more difficult,' Flax said with a sigh.

'It doesn't matter, we still have to try,' I said, determined not to let Taliesin have the Crystals or Crystal Bloods for a moment longer than necessary.

Flax looked at me, then at Etienne. 'She's tenacious, isn't she?'

'You have no idea,' Etienne said, a look of pride in his eyes that filled me with warmth.

'The way's clear, let's go,' Kit said.

We set out again, this time crossing the road without further incident, and sped our way south for over an hour, wanting to get as much distance between us and the road as quickly as we could, moving closer to the great lake of Blod Mere which finally came into view.

'What is that?' I asked, shielding my eyes from the sun as the light reflected off the surface of the lake. The water was a deep red – I'd never seen anything like it before.

Flax laughed. 'It's to do with the plants living in the lake. It's salt water due to the minerals here, and the rocks and plants in the water turn the lake red – it's like that all year.'

'Hence Blod Mere,' Vergil said gazing at it.

'What?' Amalia asked, looking out over the red water.

'Blod is blood in the old language.'

'Oh.'

'It looks a bit creepy to me,' Kit said. 'Like thousands of souls have had their blood let into the lake.'

I took a sharp breath. Just what the Emperor would do to us – take our blood, but it wouldn't be poured into a lake. Etienne glanced at me. Kit didn't realise what he was saying, but Flax and Vergil caught the irony.

'It's saltwater, you say, so we can't drink it?' I asked, wondering if we should've stocked up on extra water for our journey.

Flax shook his head. 'Poisonous, but there are a few freshwater streams between here and the Stronghold – we'll be fine.'

We rode on, making good time and made camp as the sun set. The next couple of days proved uneventful but the afternoon of the third a small group of buildings, some sort of old farmstead, came into view below a small ridge. Riding towards them were six red cloaked soldiers and two young people, tied up, with heads bowed. One of the prisoners was a young man not much older than myself, the other, a slightly younger girl, her dark hair flying behind her in the wind. They were taken into the farmstead which had a wall running from the back of the barn around a stable on one side and a shed on the other, forming a three sided wall of sorts, the buildings with rundown thatched roofs.

Flax hissed through his teeth as he sucked in a breath. 'Bugger.'

'What is it?' Kit asked.

'That's Sim, one of Morven's men, and his little sister Tiona. She's a Yellow Claret, they must have found her using Taliesin's stolen Crystals.'

'Or someone betrayed her,' Kit said.

'We need to get them out,' Flax said.

'Then let's do it,' Amalia said, drawing her sword.

'Steady,' Etienne said, resting his hand on her arm. 'It'll be dark soon and we can go in then.'

'Etienne's right,' I said.

'If only we could see where they were keeping them,' Kit said, squinting at the buildings into which the little group had disappeared.

Etienne hesitated a moment before speaking. 'I might be able to help with that,' he said. 'Athene said Red Crystals could allow you to see through walls, didn't she?'

'Dermo-optical perception, I think she called it,' I said, nodding.

'I can use a Red and see where they are from outside.'

Vergil shuddered. 'More blood.'

Etienne shook his head. 'I have the one from the Temple I can use,' he said.

'By the Planets, why didn't I think to use the one I shed for Athene rather than shed a new one for Kit?' Vergil looked to the heavens in despair. Amalia patted his shoulder sympathetically.

'We'll still need a Pellucid,' Flax murmured glancing imperceptibly towards me as his fingers caressed a knife hilt.

'Athene gave me more than one,' I said, trying to resist the urge to look down, much to Flax's amusement. Etienne gave me a knowing smile.

'We'll move as soon as it's dark,' Flax said.

Chapter Twenty-Four

The sun seemed to be tarrying in the sky for longer than necessary as we waited for night to fall. Vergil had suggested he stay with the horses so they were ready for our getaway – I knew the real reason though – he didn't want to fight, mainly due to the blood that might be involved. Which made me wonder why he carried an axe of all things.

The sky finally grew dark.

'Just be careful,' Vergil said, making a grab for Amalia's hand as we prepared to leave. 'I don't want to lose my Pledged.'

'You're Pledged?' I asked, grinning.

Amalia's red face was obvious even in this dim light. 'I thought we were keeping it secret.' She gently punched his arm.

'Sorry, I forgot,' Vergil said.

'Congratulations.' Etienne smiled.

'There'll be time for that later,' Flax said. 'Come on.'

We left Vergil in a secluded dip near the lake with the horses and made our way slowly and quietly across the open ground. The grasses swayed as the night breeze swirled around us, a nip in the air snapping at us like a pack of wild dogs. We kept low, glad the moon remained shrouded in cloud as we made our way to the back of the barn and crouched down, keeping to the shadows. We leant against the barn wall. Etienne reached for his Red Crystal and I handed him my Pellucid. He held the two together in his hand, a red glow appearing as he closed his fingers over them. He touched the back of the wall with his other, and shut his eyes. A red glow ran from his hand holding the Crystals across his body and to the hand resting on the wall. Suddenly he opened his eyes wide.

'Oh hell, this really works,' he whispered, closing his eyes and concentrating again. We waited, the grass rustling, somewhere in the distant night birds sang and the regular sound of Blod Mere lapping against the shore mingled with my heartbeat. 'They're keeping them at this end,' Etienne said finally, pointing to our right. 'They're tied up and there are four soldiers in with them.'

'We'd better check the other buildings,' I murmured, and we moved to the stables.

'Just horses,' Etienne said.

We moved back past the barn to the shed.

'Four more soldiers, but they're asleep,' he said.

'Shouldn't be a problem,' Flax nodded.

'So, can we do it now?' Amalia asked, her eyes shining.

Flax nodded and led the way along the side of the wall as we drew our weapons, cautiously turning the corner, but no one was guarding the entrance. They didn't expect any trouble. Why should they?

That's when it hit me.

This was against everything I'd ever been taught, everything I'd ever been trained for.

My heart clamoured in my chest.

The first rule of battle my uncle taught me, was to run. Don't engage. I knew how to defend myself. I knew what to do if attacked. I'd trained so hard that when the worst happened I wouldn't freeze, my muscles would do what was necessary without my brain doing anything. The soldier at the temple had been no problem at all – he'd come at me and I'd reacted. Uncle had trained me well.

At least he'd trained me well on everything except for two things. Two things that were now glaring omissions in my education.

I could defend – but he'd never taught me how to attack, how to be the one moving first, on the offensive. As it turned out, that was entirely different. Someone coming at you and you pre-empting their strike when you knew it was coming was one thing, but being the first to attack, maybe, hopefully, taking the other person by surprise sent my pulse racing, made my palms sweat and my mouth dry as the Great Dune Desert itself.

But what made me want to throw up? The thought of

my swords cutting another person's body, of the metal sliding through skin, flesh and bone. Despite the reassuring grin Amalia gave me, I could now see how woefully ill-prepared I actually was for something like this. I couldn't even prepare a meat dish, in fact if I ever lived alone I'd be vegetarian. I tried to swallow, but my mouth was too dry.

'Are you okay?' Etienne whispered in my ear, his eyes concerned in the moonlight. Trust him to be so empathic at this moment. I nodded, glancing down. I had no choice. I drew my swords.

My training had included fighting, but without the killing. That might be about to change. What worried me most was how that might change me. No one was ever the same after they'd killed, I knew that much. What would it do to me? How would something like that change me?

'Go,' Flax said, sprinting from the gateway, keeping low and to the shadows. Kit and Amalia were immediately behind him, Etienne and I bringing up the rear. I glanced around the yard noting the stables, the closed bar door where the pitch torches threw out pools of orange light, and so areas to avoid.

Flax slipped straight into the shed, not waiting for us. Before Kit and Amalia could follow him he reappeared, his knives bloody, his face smug and satisfied. 'Easier than I thought. They never even woke up.'

I glanced at Etienne, his sick expression mirrored mine.

'What?' Flax asked in a soft voice. 'You don't want to fight unless you have to. The element of surprise is key. Don't give them the chance to fight back.'

'Even so,' Amalia said, her voice cracking slightly.

'He has a point,' Kit said. 'I'd rather they were dead than me.'

'Come on, let's get Sim and Tiona,' Flax said, moving towards the barn.

The sudden glint of steel to my left made me turn instinctively, sidestepping as a soldier lunged towards me, intending to finish me before I could do anything.

But I was ready. The hilt of one of my swords connected forcefully with his nose. I wasn't taking any chances. A hideous crunching sound followed as he fell backwards to the ground like a ragdoll, unconscious. I swallowed. My pulse hammered in my ears, but I had no time to wallow in any thoughts of remorse.

'I'm impressed,' Flax said. He moved over to the soldier and stabbed him in the heart.

'What are you doing?' I asked, totally aghast at the spy's actions.

'You don't want him coming around and skewering you from behind, do you?' Flax asked, a serious look in his eyes.

'We could've tied him up.'

'Waste of time.' He moved off towards the barn as the others looked around the yard for any more hidden soldiers. None appeared, and we continued after Flax.

'I suppose he's right,' Etienne said, giving me a cautious smile I didn't return.

Flax pushed gently on the barn door. It opened slightly, a golden beam of light from pitch torches flooding the yard. Loud snoring filled the air along with the sound of slurping, and a burp.

'Please, let us go,' a young man's voice drifted out the barn – Sim?

'You've been caught in the company of a Claret, boy, the only place you're going is to the Stronghold for execution, and the girly is going to help the Emperor,' a harsh, raspy voice said.

'He'll bleed her dry,' another voice chuckled as drunken laughter echoed around the barn. The snoring stopped.

'But she's so young–' Sim began.

'Doesn't matter. She's a threat to the Empire. This way she'll be helping it.'

My heart beat faster. Righteous indignation filled me. The men's apparent lack of remorse over the fates of the two young people inside rankled, particularly their indifference to a Blood. They were only interested in using her. Or rather, her blood. Emperor Taliesin's cold ruthlessness was like a knife in my own chest. He couldn't be allowed to do this.

'But–' Sim began again.

'Shut it, or I'll kill you now,' the first soldier sneered.

Flax and Kit looked at each other.

Flax silently mouthed, 'One, two, three…'

They kicked open the doors which swung inwards with a crash, smashing backwards into the inner walls.

Sim and Tiona sat tied up on the left side of the barn at the back wall. A soldier stood over them, menacingly brandishing a knife that glinted wickedly in the torchlight. Two men sat in the middle of the barn, wineskins in hand, and another to the right, lying down. They all turned towards us, eyes wide and expressions full of surprise.

Flax and Kit lunged forward. Flax immediately went for the soldier standing over Sim and Tiona as Kit made for the man lying down. Etienne and Amalia sped towards the men in the centre with the wineskins. I moved towards the hostages, intent on freeing them from the rough ropes binding their hands.

A shadow to my right made me pause. From somewhere up in the rafters a soldier leapt towards me. I instinctively dived to the floor, rolling out of the way as my heart pounded, swiftly coming back to my feet. Where had he come from? Giving him little time to regain his balance, I swung one of my swords across my assailant's chest as I sidestepped around him. My sword connected with light chain mail, skittering over the top. This man had thought he was taking me by surprise. Now it was the other way around. He hesitated, his sword now in his hand. I struck at him again. He swiped my sword away in a clumsy fashion, forcing me towards the middle of the barn. I didn't like this. I much preferred my back to a wall where no unseen threats could get me.

He swung at me again, annoyance clear on his face. Another who'd intended to kill me before a fight had even started. I smiled. I wasn't going to be that easy to kill. He lunged. I twisted past him. He yelled in frustration, losing control, swinging wildly at me. I ducked, sidestepping and parrying his next blow; turning as his sword came crashing down I let his momentum drive him forward. But that only angered him more.

He raised his sword high above his head, leering. Before he could bring it down, I rammed my foot into his knees, using all the force I could muster. He stumbled backwards, tripping. His face took on a look of surprise as he fell. It quickly turned to horror and pain as four bloody spikes pierced his body, punching through the chain mail. They'd forced their way through his chest and ribs, and he screamed in agony as his lifeblood left his body.

I gasped, wincing in horror. I hadn't even seen the upturned pitchfork sticking through the layer of straw in the confusion of the fight. I knew I should have. Although whether it would've changed the outcome of the fight, I didn't know. The screaming man cursed, writhed for a moment, then lay still. I swallowed. Nausea rose in my throat.

A sound behind me made me turn. Flax wrestled with the soldier nearest to Sim and Tiona. I forced myself to move over to the two hostages, sheathing my swords and pulling my knife out, quickly cutting their bonds.

'Thank you,' Sim said, his deep green eyes meaning every word.

I nodded and glanced across the barn just as Flax rammed his knife in the soldier's chest right up to the hilt. I shuddered as he pulled it out and slid it in once more, just to be sure. Kit wiped the blood off his sword while Amalia checked her man to make sure he was dead.

Etienne had his sword in one hand and a bucket in the other. Where he'd found that, I didn't know. He parried a sword stroke, swinging the bucket into his soldier's head. The soldier staggered, hitting his head against the barn wall and fell, poleaxed. Etienne turned around, his eyes wild, searching the barn until he came across me. His shoulders visibly relaxed as he saw me, a little half smile appearing on his face. I give him a little smile back, still having palpitations.

'Flax!' Tiona said, running towards the spy.

'Little Tiona. What trouble have you been getting into?' Flax asked with a big grin.

'We didn't get into trouble,' Tiona pouted. 'We were minding our own business when the soldiers grabbed us.'

'They have Yellow Blood Crystals now,' Sim said. 'They hunted us down.'

'But they'd have needed a Pellucid,' Flax said.

'Taliesin has been hunting art and Relics for all colours of Crystal. Rumour has it he found a hoard of small Pellucids in a merchant's house in western Merribor.'

'I thought you were going to say the bugger had found a Double Blood.'

Tiona laughed, her long brown hair flicking as she moved. 'There aren't any Double Bloods anymore.'

'The Emperor would torture them remorselessly for their blood,' Sim said, a sick expression on his face. 'I *pray* there aren't any now.'

I tried to ignore the furtive looks Etienne and Flax sent me.

Sim led Tiona from the barn, out into the yard.

Flax stabbed his solider once more, triple checking he was dead, then moved around to the others, doing the same – even to Etienne's unconscious man. The Sun Prince looked as if he was about to protest, but the look Flax sent him silenced him.

I glanced back at my soldier. Flax hadn't deemed it necessary to make sure he was dead. His blood soaked clothing and the fork prongs sticking through his body had seen to that. I started to shake, and not because of a sudden feeling of cold sweeping through me. I couldn't control it, or the icy sweat now covering me. The smell of blood and death became too much and I rushed out into the yard, leant over a low wall, and threw up.

Chapter Twenty-Five

'You've trained, you're highly skilled, but you've never used any of it in anger, have you? Not like this at least.' Etienne's calming voice helped to still the thoughts swarming in my mind like bees and the churning of my stomach as he gently placed his arms around me.

I shook my head. 'No,' I said, wiping my mouth. I glanced at him. 'Never. But you have?' Another convulsion had me leaning over the wall again, retching. *Starlight*, I'd had no idea what a real, full-on fight would be like, that it would be so hard. Every time I closed my eyes I endured the agonised expression of that soldier as the pitchfork forced its way through his flesh, piercing skin and shattering bone. I shuddered.

'I've fought before, yes,' Etienne said quietly. 'A couple of times defending Father from assassins – the first time was two years ago, the second eighteen months since, but I only knocked them out. Rather like today.' He paused. 'But even that isn't easy, not like people think. Being prepared to hurt someone is bad enough but to take a life, that's a whole different thing,' he said, looking over at Flax who talked quietly with Kit next to the barn door. 'Not sure I could ever do it deliberately – in self defence, yes, but otherwise…'

'Killing isn't that easy, is it?'

'No.'

Flax got up and walked past us wiping his blade with a rag, black glistening patches on it in the torchlight. 'Good thing Vergil wasn't here, he'd probably have fainted,' Flax chuckled, passing Amalia who was sitting on a crate cleaning her own weapon.

She grinned at him.

'That sort of thing, killing I mean, changes you,' Etienne murmured. 'And not necessarily for the better. It can make you cold. I'm not sure I want to go there, and neither do you.'

'I thought you were battle hardened, Sorsha,' Flax said, turning back towards me with an amused smile.

I wiped my mouth. 'Apparently not.'

'You've got some work to do to toughen up. Treat them like you would an animal, it's the only way.'

'Leave her alone,' Etienne said, his arms still around me as he glared at Flax.

Flax laughed and walked off towards where Sim and Tiona were sitting.

'I didn't mean to kill him, you know,' I said quietly.

'I know,' Etienne said, turning me to face him. 'And to be fair, you didn't kill him. He fell. Landed on the fork. It's not your fault.'

'Then why does it feel like it was?' I asked miserably, still trembling. 'I might as well have run him through with my own sword.'

'Stop thinking like that. It was an accident. You didn't set out to kill him – he attacked you. You were only defending yourself.'

'Hmm.'

'Let's get back to Vergil,' Flax said. 'We don't want to be caught here by any more of Taliesin's men.'

Amalia stood up and nodded. 'He'll be worried about us,' she said, moving towards the entrance.

Etienne pulled me to my feet and took my hand. We followed the others, Kit coming to join us as we walked along.

'Are you all right, Sorsh?' he asked.

I nodded, trying to control the trembling and the nausea that still threatened to overwhelm me.

'Why do you love him?' I asked, needing to know why my best friend loved the ruthless spy.

Kit glanced at Flax ahead of us, then back at me. 'Because underneath the cold blooded killer is someone who cares very deeply about the people of this land. Well, people in general, actually.' He looked towards Flax, then lowered his voice. 'We met because he'd been sent to Steorra to kill Prince Taran. His smuggling exploits had reached Taliesin's ears. He turned up during one of your annual visits a few years ago. I happened to stop him just in time.'

I frowned. 'Why didn't you tell me before?'

Kit shrugged. 'I don't know, really. I guess I was a little ashamed at consorting with spies. But you don't really know him, Sorsh. He's actually very kind and caring. Rather like you.'

'I'm not a killer,' I said.

'He's done what he's had to, to survive. Like you.'

Kit didn't know how true that was, but the way Etienne glanced at me I knew that he did.

'Give him the benefit of the doubt, until you know him properly,' Kit went on. 'He did save my life, after all. That has to be worth something.'

I didn't like to mention that Vergil and I both had something to do with that too, but he had a point. Flax did at least care deeply for Kit.

'All right,' I muttered.

Etienne nodded.

I looked at Kit. 'You knew Flax was a Blood all along, didn't you? That's how you knew about Crystal Bloods when we met Etienne?'

Kit glanced towards Blod Mere. 'Yes. I knew what he was. I just didn't want to appear too knowledgeable back then.'

'You certainly fooled me,' I said, giving him a wry grin as he turned back to me.

'We've come a long way since that day, eh Sorsh?' He glanced at Etienne.

'A long way.' I nodded, squeezing Etienne's hand.

It took an age to reach Vergil, who immediately ran to Amalia, checking she was okay. Quite how she was so calm, I didn't know, but Etienne had given me the impression she'd had experience before – after all, you don't get to be a prince's bodyguard without fighting.

'We need to move on, we'll rest later,' Flax said, lifting Tiona up onto his horse. Kit shared with Sim and we all mounted up, moving off along the shoreline with only the moon for company as it intermittently appeared from out the clouds.

Flax called a halt right before dawn and Kit broke out the rations, Sim and Tiona eating gratefully. I refused. I couldn't stomach the thought, let alone the actual presence of food, and wandered down to the water's edge. I noticed Etienne cast me a worried glance as I left, but I gave him a little nod and a smile; I was happy to be alone for a while. I sat on a rock overlooking the gently lapping water as the sun rose, changing the water from dark red to rose gold. I closed my eyes for a moment as exhaustion washed over me. The Pitchfork Soldier immediately appeared in my vision, screaming, bleeding. I opened my eyes. The Mere's red water ran towards the little beach I sat on in small chattering waves. Waves of calm.

Footsteps made me turn. The Prince of Planetae came towards me and sat down.

'Not hungry?' he asked.

I shook my head.

'The others are sleeping, except for Etienne,' he said. 'I expect he won't rest until you go back.'

'I can't, rest, I mean,' I said. 'I'm tired but each time I shut my eyes…'

Vergil nodded. 'Etienne told me what happened,' he said, resting his hand on my shoulder. 'It'll ease in time.'

'Maybe.'

Vergil paused before speaking again. 'I can fight, I just don't like the blood,' he murmured, scratching his head.

'As it turns out, neither do I,' I said ruefully.

'Certainly theory and reality can be quite different,' he said, picking up a small stone and turning it over in his hands.

'So I've noticed,' I said, looking out over the Mere. 'I used to think I could handle any fight. Turns out I was wrong.'

'But when faced with it you were able to react, to fight.'

'Yes, but only because of instinct.'

'Because of your training – if you hadn't trained you'd

be dead right now. It saved your life, just how it was meant to. You didn't fail. You handled it – no one told you how to handle the aftermath, that's all.'

'Or how to actually kill.'

'But you don't need to kill,' Vergil said. 'You knocked one of those soldiers out.'

'True.'

'The other was an accident, from what Etienne said. You could've knocked him out too without killing him.'

'I suppose.' He had a point.

'I confess that's what I try to do if I have to fight. Less blood,' he said, turning to grin at me.

In spite of my melancholy mood I couldn't help but smile back. 'That's a good strategy.'

'Then follow it too.'

'Flax said knocking them out wasn't good enough, they can come back and get you from behind.'

'Only if you don't hit them hard enough,' Vergil said. 'Hit them hard and by the time they come around you'll be long gone.'

I nodded. 'I'll remember that.'

'Try and get some rest,' he said standing up, his axe clanking. 'Etienne's waiting for you.'

I followed him back to the camp. Everyone was asleep except for Etienne who sat next to the small fire, a worried expression on his face. As he caught sight of us approaching he scrambled up and hurried over.

'Are you all right?' he asked taking my hand. 'By the Sun, you're cold. This is becoming a habit.'

'I'm okay, really,' I said.

'You two get some rest, I'll keep watch,' Vergil said, moving towards the fire.

Etienne nodded. 'Our blankets are over here,' he said, leading me to a little heap of bedding. We lay on the dry, mossy grass, Etienne pulling the blankets over both of us, and we settled down to rest. In minutes he was asleep, but every time I shut my eyes, instead of seeing Mother now, I saw the Pitchfork Soldier.

I didn't sleep.

#

We ate a brief lunch – well, the others did – before moving on. We rode into the evening, stopping in a little valley. I picked at our evening meal, still not overly interested in food.

'We'll reach the Stronghold tomorrow afternoon,' Flax said.

'You're sure you want to go into the town?' Sim asked, moving his dark hair from his eyes.

Flax nodded. 'We'll be able to pass on the latest information to Morven.'

'We should never have left her.'

'You wanted to take me to Mother to be safe,' Tiona said.

'That didn't turn out well, did it?' Sim muttered.

Tiona slipped her hand into her brother's. 'Morven said you should – it wasn't your fault we got caught. We didn't know the soldiers had Crystals now.'

Sim sighed. 'You'll be safest back at the encampment,' he said, 'whatever Morven says. I shouldn't have let her persuade us otherwise.'

'I imagine she thought you were safer away from the gang,' Flax said. 'She was probably right, but as things have turned out, going back will actually be safer.'

I lay in Etienne's arms, desperate to get to sleep, but the Pitchfork Soldier soon put paid to that, rearing up in my dreams in the place of my mother once again. I awoke, my heart thudding and covered in a cold sweat. I slipped out of the covers and quietly made my way down to the little cove where the Mere met the land. I sat on an old log with the moon for company.

I had to get over this. I had to get over the whole fight, my guilt. My confidence had, in part, been shaken. My own mistake for never considering the whole implications of battle. None of what had happened, either Mother or the Pitchfork Soldier had been my fault, and yet I still felt guilty. I sighed, trying to turn my thoughts to the next day and our visit to the Stronghold.

Warm arms slid around my shoulders. My first instinct was to strike, but the faint smell of vetiver instantly made me relax.

'You ought not to do that,' I said. 'One of these days I might hit you before I realise it's you.'

Etienne sat beside me. 'Sorry, I wasn't thinking – well, I was, but it was just about how much I wanted to hold you.'

I smiled. 'You really are quite the romantic, aren't you?'

He shrugged. 'I have my moments,' he said, leaning towards me and warming my whole body with a single, velvety kiss. 'Can't you sleep? Nightmares?'

'Nightmares,' I nodded. 'They're back with a vengeance. I wish I could sleep, I'm so tired.'

'It'll come, just be patient,' he said, slipping his arm around my waist and pulling me closer. 'How about I take your mind off it.' I smiled as he caressed my cheek with his warm hand.

I turned slightly and swung my legs over his. He instantly wrapped his arms around me pulling me close, and we kissed again. I ran my fingers through his hair, soaking up every wonderful sensation I could, and all the love he was giving me. My kiss returned his love, and promised him more in time.

'Everything will be fine, you'll see,' he said, his lips pink, his smile melting glaciers.

#

The morning dawned grey and cool. The sun couldn't break through the scudding clouds, and as we approached the Stronghold in the early afternoon a sense of foreboding filled me as I caught my first glimpse of the grey stone structure, the hairs on the back of my neck standing to attention. Blocks of granite formed the fabric of the Stronghold itself – a menacing building with a high stone wall, the rectangular construction inside featuring four corner towers soaring over the shanty town of ramshackle houses nestling against the walls. The town itself looked not much more than a slum – dirt streets and buildings with tiled roofs in dire need of repair – however, it bustled with people: townsfolk, merchants, traders and thieves.

'We'll stay out here,' Sim said. 'We've had enough excitement recently.'

Flax nodded. 'We'll meet you back here in an hour, we won't be long.'

Sim and Tiona dismounted and made their way into the edge of a small wood leading our horses, as we walked the rest of the way to the Stronghold. The first thing I noticed was the graffiti on the walls that had been painted over in a haphazard way, graffiti that was less than flattering when it came to the Emperor. Rebellion swirled under the surface here, but far enough down to be out of reach of the soldiers patrolling the town's market stalls and traders' carts. The smell of herbs and bread mixed with sewage that ran in the open sewers of the cramped alleys, putrid and foul. We passed a spice merchant, and thankfully the malodourous smell subsided.

'Maybe we should stock up on a few supplies while you're meeting your contacts,' I said looking at Kit.

'That's not a bad idea' Kit said. 'We are getting a little low on a few things.'

'All right,' Flax said. 'Vergil, come with me – that axe of yours will keep some of the more light-fingered thieves away.'

Vergil made a face and followed Flax into the stream of humanity that spiralled through the stalls.

'Right, what do we need?' Amalia asked as we entered the busiest part of the market.

Kit led the way. His knowledge of our stores meant he knew exactly what we needed, although I was keen to get hold of a new water skin as mine had sprung a leak. I found a small shop selling them and made my purchase. As I came out Etienne grabbed my hand.

'Oh hell, soldiers, heading this way,' he hissed. 'And I think they've got Crystals.'

'What?' I strained to see down the street.

'Let's move,' he said. We hurried back towards where Kit haggled over some cheese, Amalia at his side.

I turned back. The soldiers were still coming. Heading right towards us.

'You think they know it's us?' I asked.

'I don't know and I don't want to find out,' Etienne said. 'Amalia, we've got to go,' he said, inclining his head towards the soldiers.

She nodded. 'We'll pay fifteen,' she said, handing the trader the money.

'But–' Kit began.

'We have to go,' I said, as Amalia stowed the cheese in her bag.

Kit looked down the street and then back at me, his eyes widening.

'Move,' Amalia said, grabbing Kit's shoulder and pulling him into an alleyway. Etienne and I followed.

'Hey, you! Stop!' yelled a soldier from behind us.

We ran.

Chapter Twenty-Six

We sped through the alleyways of the Stronghold, weaving between the rickety buildings, attempting to lose our pursuers. But rather than lose them, they were beginning to catch up. Their knowledge of the alleys and streets helped their chase. Every twist, every turn we took they matched, and the people of the town only hampered our progress.

'We aren't going to escape them,' Etienne said. 'They'll use the Crystals to follow us and find us even if we hide.'

'Then we stop and fight,' I said, between gasps for air. My hair had loosened and whipped around my head, stinging my eyes.

Etienne shook his head. 'Too many of them. They mustn't get you,' he said as we dashed down a side alley, diving into another.

'What?' I didn't understand what he was saying as we entered a main street full of citizens where a noisy, crowded market was in full swing. They couldn't get either of us.

'They mustn't find *you*,' he said, dragging me to a halt and looking into my eyes, into my soul, gently taking hold of my shoulders. His lips turned down slightly at the corners, his brows raising a little as he spoke, his eyes glistening in the light.

I shook my head as I took in what he was really saying.

'Oh, no. No, you can't! They'll torture you for your Blood Crystals,' I said, peering over his shoulder, my heart threatening to burst as it thudded uncomfortably against my ribs.

'Better me than you,' he said, the lopsided smile appearing. He leant forward and kissed me, those velvet lips turning my bones to liquid gold. 'We're not going to lose them – it's better they find a Single rather than a Double Blood.'

I swallowed, my eyes filling with hot, unshed tears. My heart cracked. I refused to accept what he was saying.

'No-no, you can't,' I pleaded as Amalia and Kit ran towards us. 'They'll kill you – I won't let them kill you instead of me.'

'I'm making this my choice – I want to do this. For you.'

'No!' My chest ached, my palms sprang sweat and my mouth turned dry as the neighbouring Ash Desert despite the water in my eyes. I shook my head savagely. 'Dammit, Etienne! You can't do this!'

'What's happening?' Amalia asked as she reached us. Her face turned ashen as her eyes widened. 'You're giving yourself up?'

'It's the only way, cousin,' he said to her. 'They're tracking me.' He turned back to me.

'But they'll still be able to track me anyway,' I murmured, trembling.

'They'll go after the one they can see,' he said softly so only I could hear. 'And I'll make sure they see me.'

'But–'

'I love you, Sorsha.' He smiled as he stared into my soul, his look stripped bare. 'Always remember that, whatever happens, always remember I love you. Look after her,' he said, looking at Amalia and Kit. Kit nodded as Etienne let go of me, stepped away, but quickly turned back. He pulled something from his undershirt. 'Use this,' he said, thrusting his book into my shaking hands, glancing at Amalia. 'Hide her, keep her safe.'

Amalia nodded mutely, tears standing in her eyes.

Etienne forged into the busy market, making a scene, banging into people who yelled and swore at him.

'No.' I took a step forward as my heart shattered, but a hand grabbed my arm, roughly pulling me back. Kit had a firm hold of me and he yanked me backwards as Amalia gripped my other arm, forcing me into the shadows behind some crates.

The commotion Etienne was making drew the attention of the pursuing soldiers, and once the prince was sure they had seen him, he ran, taking them with him across the market and away from us.

'Don't let his sacrifice for us be in vain,' Amalia said,

her voice strained. I turned to look at her. Tears escaped her eyes as she looked in the direction Etienne had gone.

'Let's go,' Kit said, his voice cracking. 'Before they realise and start looking for you, too,' he hissed under his breath.

I looked back to the market, unable to see clearly, everything in a watery fog. Etienne had long since disappeared taking the soldiers with him. Kit and Amalia dragged me away from the throng. The walls of the buildings around me started to close in. I could barely take a breath as my hands turned sweaty. A feeling of cold dread filled me, my heart thundered in my chest and my vision narrowed.

'No, no!' My voice caught as they dragged me along, glancing over my shoulder for any sign of Etienne. But I saw nothing, heard nothing other than the roar of the crowd, the blood pulsing in my ears and my heart shattering and scattering its pieces to the four Celestial Bodies.

Clutching Etienne's book, I slipped it under my tunic next to my heart as I was bundled towards the open countryside, tears streaming down my face.

We eventually paused for a moment in a small copse as I tried to get my breath back and my heart rate under control, but I failed miserably. The trees crowded in on me and I thought that at any minute I might faint, but Kit and Amalia were either unobservant or unsympathetic, and they forced me on. We broke free of the copse and ran on to the wood where Tiona and Sim were waiting, Kit and Amalia refusing to let go of me until we were in the relative safety of the trees.

Flax and Vergil were already there. It only took a few moments for Kit to fill them in on what had happened. Vergil cast me an anxious look as I fell to my knees, shaking and struggling to breathe, tears running uncontrollably down my face.

'Take deep breaths,' the Planetary Prince said, crouching beside me and placing an arm around my shoulders. 'It's a panic attack. Totally natural, under the circumstances. Just try and steady your breathing. Breath in for a count of four through your nose and out for four through your mouth.'

Easier said than done, but I tried to do as he said, focussing on my breathing rather than the violent sobs that threatened to erupt from my chest at any moment. I faltered.

'Keep going,' he said, rubbing his hand on my back.

Eventually the sensations and panic eased.

'Thank you,' I murmured as numbness crept over me.

I glanced up. Flax's eyes were flint as he gazed in the direction of the Stronghold. My every nerve and fibre screamed at me to go back and get Etienne at once, now, this minute, but the look on Amalia's face and the way Kit started fingering his knife each time I looked back towards the Stronghold told me I wouldn't get more than a couple of steps before a knife lay at my throat and Amalia placed herself between me and Etienne. They were right, of course. I didn't know where he was by now, how to get to him, how to get him out.

He'd done this for me.

Sacrificed himself to save me.

A supreme act of selflessness – *for me*. And while I wouldn't let that be in vain, I wouldn't let him stay there a moment longer than necessary.

\#

I'd started shaking the moment I'd realised what Etienne was doing. And it didn't stop. Several hours later as we rode towards the Ash Desert and Morven's encampment, I still trembled. The tears had long since dried up, but the ache that had begun in my chest replaced the numbness and increased, reaching a crescendo of grief and longing. How could I carry on without him now? But more to the point, what was happening to him? Was he alive or dead? I screwed my face up at the thought of the latter. No, they'd keep him alive to use his blood for as long as they could, surely?

My red eyes ached and nausea became my constant companion. An emptiness began to grow inside me that would never be filled. Not until I had him back. And I *would* have him back. That I swore.

Anger vied with grief. Anger at what Taliesin was doing to all the Bloods. To Tiona, to Etienne. Anger at what he'd already done to the Orders and the Celestial Temple, and to our art and Relics. To Taran. To my mother. To the other Starlight Princesses. Maybe even to Etienne's family. I gritted my teeth. Emperor Taliesin would pay, as would Prince Cynric – and, if I could get my hands on him, Artem too. I wouldn't rest until they were dead, and Etienne and the other Bloods free once more. I swore it.

Justice be damned, it was revenge I wanted now.

It took a couple of days to reach Morven's encampment in the Ash Desert. My nightmares got worse, my sleep less. The nights without Etienne to hold me were torture. His absence tore at my heart. I'd hadn't realised how much, in such a short space of time, I'd taken him and his love for granted, and I hated myself for it. Not having him here – no warm arms to hold me, no vetiver to surround me – cut me to the quick. If I ever got him back – no, *when* I got him back – I'd never take him for granted ever again, not for one damn second.

The arid desert air was unrelenting, dry and harsh. The sands around us drifted in the breeze that sometimes blew in lazily from the west; not enough to give us any respite but enough to send small bits of grit into our eyes. The heat of the day scorched the already parched landscape and we rested in the shadow of dunes as best we could, riding in the cool of night.

As dawn's silver light crept over the golden sands I shielded my aching eyes, looking out over the vast Ash Desert; although still desert, the terrain was changing. Three distant low, cone-shaped mountains rose on the horizon, a beige rather than sandy colour, and between us and them, the golden sand changed to deep black rock that sucked in all the light the sun could throw at it.

'What is it?' Kit asked.

'Ancient lava flows,' Flax said. 'We walk from here, lead the horses.'

'Where would you build an encampment out here?' Amalia asked.

Flax grinned. 'You'll see.'

Vergil glanced towards me, gave me a little half smile, which was kind of him, but I didn't respond, couldn't. We walked out over the black lava, our boots crunching on the hot rock soaking up the sun's rays, the horses' hooves clinking on the hard surface. It appeared the most inhospitable place I'd ever seen. The raven-black lava stretched as far as the eye could see, its oppressiveness doing little to help my mood, or the ache in my chest. In fact, it made me feel even worse, but at least the shaking was beginning to subside, just a shame I now had a headache.

After about a mile or so, Flax led us to the north a short way then stopped. As we caught up with him I saw a gaping hole opening up before us. It dipped a full sixty feet into the ground, and on opposite sides, two great cavernous entrances yawned like mythical serpents' mouths – entrances with pitch torches flickering inside.

'What is this place?' Kit asked, his voice full of awe.

'Morven's encampment,' Sim said smugly.

'No wonder the Emperor's never found her,' Vergil said, leaning forward for a better look.

'Careful, I don't want my Pledged falling in,' Amalia said, reaching out to steady Vergil.

Her words twisted in my chest making the ache more acute. I took a deep breath to steady myself. I would get him back.

'Did they dig them out?' Vergil asked, unperturbed.

Tiona shook her head. 'They're old lava tubes from past volcanic eruptions, but they've left these tunnels twenty feet wide and twenty feet high. You know there are even some lavacicles on the roofs.'

'Poppycock,' Amalia said.

'Lava icicles?' Kit scoffed. 'You made that up.'

'I did not,' she said indignantly. 'They're like stalactites but formed from lava, and they hang down from the tube ceilings.'

Kit made his *I still don't believe you* face. I would have found the whole exchange just as amusing as Amalia and Vergil, if it hadn't been for Etienne's absence.

'So how do we get down there?' Vergil asked.

'Over on the far side,' Flax said pointing. 'There's a path that leads down amongst the rocks – you can't see it from here, it's well camouflaged.' He led his horse around the rim of the opening and we followed him around to the hidden path and down to the floor of the lava tubes.

Inside the left tunnel stood two guards next to a lit brazier. Pitch torches lined the walls spreading back into the tube, although here and there shafts of sunlight poked into the dimly lit space like fingers of light. Small holes peppered the roof of the tube giving natural skylights where the rock had caved in – and there were lavacicles hanging from the roof. This place was truly amazing, I just couldn't get the awe I felt to pierce the black fog engulfing me.

'Flax! My good man, how are you?' One of the guards, his curly dark hair sprinkled with white strands walked over to Flax and shook his hand. His dark eyes and skin sparkled in the firelight.

'Good, Achis, good, and you?' Flax asked.

'Not bad.'

'Vagnar, you're well?' Flax greeted the other man.

Vagnar could have been Achis' twin, except for his hair, which was brown and straight. 'Aye, I'm fine. What about you, Master Spy?'

'I'll be fine when Taliesin curls up and dies.'

Achis frowned. 'That's a dangerous thing for a Master Spy to say.'

'Only if it's to another spy.'

'So you've finally given it up, then?' A smooth rich voice echoed from deeper inside the lava tube. A woman in her mid to late thirties, her loose, deep chestnut hair turning a little white at the temples, stepped into the light. She was armed to the proverbial teeth with blades, her clothes a kind of light armour, and a look of steely determination in her sapphire eyes.

'Morven,' Flax said, walking over to her, and embracing her warmly.

Morven? For some reason I'd expected her to be younger.

'Spying not paying well enough anymore, Flax?' she asked, a big grin on her face.

'It's not that, it's... that old bugger, Taliesin, has finally overstepped the mark, even for me,' Flax said.

Morven frowned. 'Why have you brought Tiona back, Sim?'

'Soldiers caught us on the far side of the Stronghold – they were going to take Tiona back to drain her and kill me. Flax and his friends saved us.'

The Ash Bandit Leader's eyes turned as hard as agate. 'Good thing you were in the neighbourhood then, Flax.'

'We were on our way to see you anyway,' Flax said. 'I should introduce Prince Vergil of Planetae, Lady Amalia of the Sun Order, the Starlight Princess, Sorsha – and this is Kit.' Morven ran her eyes over us as we were introduced, lingering curiously when she got to Kit. 'One of our number, Prince Etienne of Solis, was captured and taken to the Stronghold,' Flax continued, glancing at me as he spoke.

Morven frowned. 'He's of the Blood?'

Flax nodded. 'A Red.'

She sighed. 'Then I'm sorry for him. He's probably already dead.'

Ice filled my veins, followed by a surge as hot as any lava. 'He's not dead and we will get him back.' My hands clenched into tight fists.

Morven looked at me. 'You know what they do to Crystal Bloods now, girl?'

'Yes. And I intend to stop it and free those imprisoned, along with our Relics, and get justice for the massacre of the Orders.'

'What's this?'

'Let me tell you what's been happening,' Flax said, leading her away.

#

'I need to get him out,' I murmured as we sat around a fire that evening, talking quietly. Our meal had been remarkably good; although I'd eaten little, at least I could taste food again.

Kit, who sat next to me, gave me a pained look. 'You heard what Morven said just now.'

'I don't care, I need to get him out.' I stared into space surrounded by a black mist of grief. 'I won't rest until he's free. I'll leave tomorrow.'

'Don't be daft, Sorsh,' Kit said. 'You can't go alone. How would you get him out of wherever he is?'

'It might be possible,' Flax said, scratching his chin.

'Flax, what you're suggesting isn't possible, I've already explained that. I don't have enough men for a full-on assault of the Stronghold. It would be suicide for all of us,' Morven said, a mug of mead in her hand.

'A full-on assault, maybe, but I'm suggesting a covert mission to get in,' Flax said. 'Once inside, once we've freed the prisoners we'll have more than enough help to get out again.'

'No,' the Bandit Leader said, shutting down the discussion. She sighed. 'If we had Blood Crystals, it might be possible, but we don't.'

'He did it for me,' I mumbled as Flax continued to protest. Etienne had been cruelly snatched from me because he valued my life more than his. 'This is all my fault.'

'Don't talk nonsense. I know he wanted to keep you safe because he loved you, but he did it for all of us so we could escape,' Amalia said, resting her hand on my arm.

I shook my head. The time for hiding in the shadows, for keeping out of sight was over.

'No. He only did it to save me,' I said obstinately. 'I'm a Double Blood.'

Chapter Twenty-Seven

'Sorsh!' Kit stared at me, but it was too late now.

The talking abruptly ceased and they all looked at me, most wide-eyed. Vergil gave me an *I did wonder* look, and Flax bowed his head in relief and, maybe, a little pride.

They had to know. Especially now.

'What?' Amalia frowned. 'What are you talking about? You're no Double Blood.'

'Why do you think my mother sent me away from the Citadel, away from the Court? To protect me from anyone finding out. She sent me to my uncle so I could learn to defend myself, and not spill any blood.' I turned to Morven. 'I'm a Double Blood and you can use my Crystals. I'll give you all I can. Anything to get Etienne and the other Bloods out of that damn Stronghold.'

Morven looked at me, her eyes narrowing. 'What colour are you, girl?'

'Purple.'

'Shield Stones.' She glanced at Flax. 'Maybe we could do it after all,' she said, rubbing her chin.

'While we're making confessions, I'm an Orange,' Vergil said as he scratched his head.

'I'm Yellow,' Flax murmured.

'You're what?' Morven couldn't contain her amazement, or the edge of anger in her voice. 'You never told me.'

Flax shrugged. 'Not the sort of thing you yell about, particularly in my line of work.'

Vergil nodded. 'No one at home knows about me, except for my father.'

'Kit, Flax and Eti–' my voice caught. 'Etienne knew I was a Double.'

'He really did – *does* love you, to give himself up like that,' Kit said, his eyes full of sadness. 'Maybe you could've been Pledged to him... if your prince was dead like his princess was.'

I swallowed. 'His princess isn't dead any more than my prince is. As you know, Mother had arranged my Pledging.' I took a deep breath. 'It was Etienne all along.' I hesitated. 'We exchanged the Pledging Oath a while ago.'

'What?' Amalia's eyes narrowed. 'When?'

'Back in Mere City.' The memories of that night threatened to overwhelm me and I bit my lip in an attempt to hold back the tears.

'I knew something had happened,' she murmured, a slight smugness to her voice.

'And you didn't tell me?' Kit looked like a little puppy, lost and alone.

'I'm sorry, Kit, we wanted some time with it to ourselves, that's all,' I said, patting his hand. 'It wasn't to hurt you, and I'd intended to tell you first.'

'Hmm.'

'Etienne was going to tell you, when the time came, Amalia,' I said, not wanting to upset Etienne's cousin. She nodded, satisfied.

'That's all well and good,' Morven said, 'but we need to concentrate on the business in hand.'

'I have a Blue Crystal, a Truth Stone, if it'll help,' Amalia offered, holding out her ring.

'You take what you need from me,' Tiona said, the first time she'd spoken all evening from where she sat next to her brother. Sim smiled at her.

I pulled Etienne's book from my tunic. 'You can use what you need from here,' I said, the Green, Orange and, what I now realised were Pellucid Crystals, glittering in the firelight. The way everyone pulled together brought tears to my eyes, and a warm feeling to my chest.

'This is all a great help, but what we really need are a lot of Pellucid Crystals to make the coloured work,' Morven said. 'There are some in this book, and you can supply us with some, girl, but–'

'I have these too.' I reached behind my neck, unclasping the Starburst Necklace and placed it on top of Etienne's book. A fire burnt within the Crystals, a fire of white light and a fire of purple, twisting and sparking within the stones.

'Your First Crystals?' Flax asked, his eyes wide as he looked at the stones and then up at me.

I nodded.

'Then they'll be really powerful,' Vergil said, gazing at the glowing, twinkling stones. 'If we can cut them and distribute them...'

'We'll have plenty to go around,' Flax grinned.

Morven looked at the Starburst Necklace and then at me, nodding. 'This could work.'

'You're sure about this?' Kit asked. 'I mean your mother, that necklace–'

'Was always too gaudy for me,' I said, stopping him before tears spilled from my eyes. 'She told me to use it, and that's what I'm going to do. I'm going to use it to save Etienne and the others, and bring down Taliesin and Cynric.'

'Well said, girl,' Morven said, an approving smile lighting her face. 'I'll send for Achis – he can start cutting now.'

#

I tried to sleep, but had little success. I wasn't used to sleeping on a hard floor with little padding. The cold also seeped into my bones, and again the ache drilled into my chest, because he wasn't here. I quietly got up and made my way along the tunnel. It was sectioned off into areas for working, cooking, eating, relaxing and sleeping. Morven had about a hundred men here, all told, some with wives and families. I reached a work area where Achis sat with the Starburst Necklace, Vagnar beside him. They looked up.

'Can't sleep?' Achis asked.

'No,' I said, shaking my head.

'If you take the left tube down there you'll find a large skylight – I always find the stars help me think,' Vagnar said.

'Thank you,' I said.

'If you leave your blades with me I'll sharpen them for you – you may need them,' Achis said.

I nodded gratefully and left my swords and knife with him, before heading for the tunnel Vagnar had indicated. A short distance along it moonlight broke through into the darkness of the tube. I walked out into the silver light and looked up at the stars and moon. I took a deep breath of cold night air that drifted down from above. I shivered.

A light flickered to my right. I glanced towards it – was someone coming with a torch?

The light turned into many lights of different colours that flickered and danced in the air. They swirled, blurred, finally coalescing into a form – a human form.

I gasped.

Standing before me was Etienne. But an Etienne I'd never seen before. His face was pale, haggard, and drawn in concentration, his clothes torn and an ugly purple bruise peeped out from his dishevelled hair at his temple. Dried blood smeared his face and neck. Was I really seeing him? And if I was, what had they done to him in the space of a few days?

'Sorsha? Is that you?' he asked, his voice raspy and low.

My heart stuttered and skipped. 'Yes, yes, I'm here,' I said, moving towards his shade. Only now did I see his hand was glowing red. He was using his First Red and my Pellucid to project astrally. How had he managed to keep them hidden? 'What have they done to you?' I asked, my voice catching as I noticed the cuts on his bruised arms.

'Don't worry about that,' he said. 'You mustn't come for me – do you understand? I'll be dead before you get here and you won't be able to do anything. Stay away. The place is too well guarded for you to get in, plus the Emperor's here. He's learnt to use the Crystals – it's just too dangerous. Get away, Sorsha, go as far away from here as you can.'

'And let Taliesin and Cynric win?' I gritted my teeth.

'There's no stopping them, they have too many Crystals.'

'Maybe there's a way to destroy their Crystals.'

'Maybe there is, but you'll have to find that later. For now, get away and be safe. I want you safe.'

'And I want you alive,' I said, tears filling my eyes. 'I'm not leaving you.'

'Please.' Etienne fell to his knees, the effort of keeping his projection going taking its toll. 'Please don't, please go.' His eyes turned glassy as he looked at me. 'There's no hope for me now. I knew this might happen and I did it willingly. Please, promise me you'll stay safe, wife.'

I tried to stifle a gasp. 'All right,' I said, glancing down to the lava floor as I spoke, my heart twisting in my chest, my hands shaking. 'I'll stay safe.'

Etienne visibly relaxed and nodded. 'Good. I-I can't hold this any longer. I love yo–'

'I love you too,' I said, reaching out to the empty tunnel. Tears fell from my eyes, dripping onto the tunnel floor as my pulse rushed in my ears.

'Liar.'

I spun around to see Flax standing not far away, his expression grim. 'I–'

'You lied to him to make him happy,' Flax said. At least he'd seen Etienne too and I hadn't imagined the whole vision. 'You did the right thing. But I know you have no intention of going anywhere, other than back to the Stronghold.'

I wiped my eyes. 'Of course I'm going back – there must be a way in.'

'Maybe. Depends on what you're willing to do.'

'Anything.'

'Will you kill?'

'For Etienne?' I swallowed. 'If I have to, yes.'

#

'We'll leave at dusk,' Morven had said that morning.

'You all need to shed what blood you can.'

I joined Vergil, Flax and Tiona, and made a cut in my hand, letting the Crystals fall into a wooden bowl. Vergil looked decidedly ill, facing away from all of us as his blood fell and Amalia collected his Orange Crystals.

'You've all done enough,' Morven said a while later. 'We don't want you weakened so you can't travel tonight.'

'I can do more,' I said.

'No,' Kit said, covering my cut with a clean bandage.

'I'd give my life to save him.'

'That's what I'm worried about. Look, you'll be no good to him if you're half dead when you get there. We have enough Crystals now.'

'I just want to make sure–'

'Enough,' Kit said, his deep brown eyes brooking no argument.

Flax collected the Crystals and along with the ones from Etienne's book and the newly cut stones from the Starburst Necklace, started handing them out amongst Morven's men, grouping them into those that would search for Bloods, those that would look for Relics, those who would fight and others who would heal those that became injured.

As the sun slipped towards the sandy horizon, I collected my weapons from Achis.

He passed them over to me and I looked at them in surprise. The previously plain hilts, now contained Purple and Pellucid Crystals. If I grasped the hilts properly the Crystals would burst into life, protecting me from physical and magical weapons, at least for a while. They also looked quite beautiful in their new forms.

'Thank you,' I said, the failing light glinting off the sharpened blades as I carefully placed them in their sheaths so as not to activate the Crystals.

Achis smiled. 'And take these too,' he said, passing me a pair of black suede gloves. 'Wear them until you want to use the Crystals.'

I nodded.

'I saved these from your friend's book,' Vagnar said, handing me a Green and an Orange Crystal.

The ache in my chest increased for a moment as the two Crystals landed in my palm. I nodded, not trusting myself to speak as I placed them in my pocket.

'And you'll probably want this back too,' he said, passing me the red leather-bound book embellished with gold and silver symbols. It looked strange now without the Crystals, just little indentations left to show what once rested there.

'Thank you,' I said quietly, returning it to my tunic.

We gathered the new provisions that Morven's men had arranged, and along with the Bandit Leader and her men, led our horses up and out of the lava tubes onto the black rock as the sun finally set.

'Sorsha, take this,' Amalia said, passing me something. I opened my hand to find a small Blue Crystal sitting there. 'Achis cut my ring into several stones – I've got another, but you never know, you might need to get someone to tell the truth.'

'Thank you,' I said, carefully placing it in my pocket.

'We will get him back,' she said, her jaw set. 'Whatever he says.'

'Flax told you?'

She nodded. 'Eti has always been a little too set on duty and honour for his own good. This time we're ignoring him. If we die getting him out, we die getting him out, but I won't leave him to rot in the Stronghold anymore than you will.'

'That's good to know. Thank you, Amalia.'

She shrugged, smiling slyly at me as we led our horses towards the distant golden sands. 'Don't worry, my Pledged has enough healing Crystals for us all.'

I hoped he had.

Chapter Twenty-Eight

The journey back to the Stronghold took longer than it had on the way to Morven's camp. The fact we had a hundred men with us slowed us down, but having them with us increased my confidence. We needed numbers. On our own we couldn't possibly hope to defeat Taliesin and his men.

'We need to approach at night, or we'll be seen,' I said to Morven the day before we reached the Stronghold.

'I know, and we'll rest into the morning tomorrow, before slipping into the Stronghold in groups during the evening,' she said.

'I'll go in first with Kit, Amalia, Vergil and you, Sorsha,' Flax said. 'Morven will follow with Achis, Vagnar and Sim.'

I wondered how Tiona felt being left behind with the few families that remained in the lava tubes, but she was too young to join us in this fight.

'The others know their orders,' Flax continued. 'Our first group will head to the gatehouse under the pretence of bringing in a Claret.'

'Me,' Vergil said with a grin on his face.

'They'll know we're telling the truth if they decide to use Crystals to check. We'll open the gate and let everyone else in. The various groups will then search the building for Clarets, art and Relics.'

And I'll search for Etienne.

'The Relics are likely to be in the upper storerooms, but the prisoners will be down in the lower levels,' Flax continued.

'We'll have to be careful if they all know how to use the Crystals,' I said.

Morven nodded. 'But we'll have our own to counter them. Just leave Cynric and Taliesin to me and Flax.'

I glanced at Flax who had an excited glint in his eye. I shuddered. What they intended to do with them, I didn't know, but they'd have to get there before me.

I slept a little more that night, but still the nightmares encroached on my rest, a pale, sunken faced Etienne leaving me gasping for air as I awoke. I managed to eat some breakfast and then checked my horse was ready for the afternoon's ride.

'Whatever happens I'm staying with you tonight,' Kit said, walking over to me.

'I'll be fine,' I said, patting my horse's nose.

'Of course you will, you'll be with me.'

'Wouldn't you rather make sure you stay with Flax than me?'

'Flax can take care of himself. Besides, after he's got us in he and Morven have their own plans once they're inside.'

'Has he broken things with her, or is he waiting until after tonight?' I asked, curious to know.

'She'd already guessed,' Kit said. 'She told him she knew the moment she realised he'd brought me along.'

'And she's all right with it?'

Kit nodded. 'She's fine. I think Achis and Vagnar are enough to console her,' he smirked.

'Stop it,' I said, elbowing him in the ribs.

'You asked.'

'I know I did, and I greatly regret it.'

Morven sent scouts out to check we weren't seen by any of Taliesin's men as we rode through the afternoon, keeping to valleys and trees, but hiding a hundred men wasn't going to be easy. I watched the sun heading for the western horizon, my heart beginning to skip with anticipation and anxiety. Was Etienne still alive? Would I get to him in time? I had to cling to the hope that I would.

Whatever he had said.

A cold sweat sprung up over my body as the sun set, turning the sky to red and gold before darkness shrouded the land as we crested a tree-lined ridge overlooking the Stronghold. Pitch torches and braziers already lit the town, and lights flickered at the windows of the Stronghold itself, the dark, brooding building throwing out a challenge to me. A challenge I gracefully accepted.

'Get the men into their groups,' Flax said to Achis. 'Then follow us at two minute intervals.' Achis nodded and moved back towards the main throng of men taking Vagnar with him.

'Take care of yourself, Flax,' Morven said. 'And I'll see you inside.'

'You know me,' Flax grinned.

'Only too well.'

I slipped Achis' gloves on. Not only would they warm my freezing fingers, but I wouldn't activate any Crystals if I touched them. We left the horses and hurried through the long, damp grass, cold air nipping at our heels, and made our way down into the town, the hoods of our cloaks up, keeping to the shadows where we could. We stayed in the smelly back alleys, avoiding the noisy inns and various eating places that the bulk of the citizens frequented in the evening. We twisted and turned, but the Stronghold itself loomed large above us, casting its ominous gloom over us. Finally we reached the outer wall, skirting along it until the gatehouse came into view.

'Are you ready?' Amalia asked, looking at Vergil.

He nodded. 'Ready as I'm ever likely to be.'

'Here,' Flax said, forcing something into my gloved hand.

'What–' I began.

'It's one of my Crystals – use it to find Etienne.'

'Thank you,' I murmured.

'And if you have to kill to get him out, don't hesitate. You don't want him to die because you have a few scruples.'

Scruples? I wasn't sure taking a life could be classed as a mere scruple, but I let it go.

We edged closer to the gatehouse. Flax and Kit took hold of Vergil and marched him towards the entrance. I drew a sword, hiding it under my cloak.

'Bugger, there's more of them than usual,' Flax hissed.

I looked up. The gatehouse was lit by flickering torches that stuttered in the evening breeze illuminating six guards. Were they expecting us? I shuddered as my heart clamoured in my chest.

We reached the entrance way.

'Halt!' a guard said stepping forward. 'What do you want?'

'Wait, they've got one with them,' said a guard from behind him, his hand glowing yellow.

'We're here to hand over a Claret,' Flax said.

'Flax, is that you?'

'Yes, Zel, it's me,' Flax nodded, pulling his cloak back.

'Let him in,' Zel said, ushering us in.

'Sorry about this, Zel.'

'Sorry about wha–'

But Flax's knife was already slitting Zel's throat. Amalia lunged forwards with her sword as Vergil pulled his axe from under his cloak and Kit slammed into a guard. I pulled a sword free and smashed the hilt into the face of the closest guard. He yelled, his nose broken and blood streaming down his face as he fell backwards against the wall.

Flax whirled, forcing his knife into another guard's chest as the others finished their men. Vergil rendered his man unconscious with the handle of his axe, before looking into the courtyard beyond the gatehouse. Avoiding blood again?

Flax began his ritual check to make sure everyone was dead.

'No, wait,' I said as he reached my man who was still semi-conscious. 'Perhaps he can tell us where Etienne is.'

'I won't tell yer nothing,' the guard said, glaring at us.

'Oh, I think you will,' Amalia said, pulling out a Blue and Pellucid.

The guard shrank backwards against the wall. 'Stay back, bitch.'

'I suggest you watch your language,' I said. 'Now tell us where Prince Etienne is.'

'Nev–'

Flax held his knife at the man's throat as Amalia held the two Crystals together and placed a hand on the guard's head.

'Where is Prince Etienne?' she asked.

'Lower level.'

Crystal Bloods

'Taliesin, is he here?' Flax asked.

'In the Royal Apartments, upper floors.'

'Alone?'

'With Prince Cynric and Prince Artem.'

My mouth dried and my heart skipped. All of them here at once?

'The Relics?' Flax pressed.

'Upper levels,' the guard said.

'Thank you,' Flax said, and cut his throat.

Amalia jumped back as blood fell to the ground. 'Do you mind?' she muttered. 'You could've given me warning.'

'Amalia, I–' Vergil's voice sounded from the entrance to the courtyard.

'Stay back, Vergil, you don't want to come in here,' she said, moving towards him.

Flax cleaned his knife on the guard's tunic.

'You need to curb your murderous side,' Kit said, a disapproving tone to his voice.

'I will, my lover, once Taliesin and Cynric are dead.' Flax grinned.

I shook my head, resolutely looking away from the bloody bodies and followed Amalia. Morven appeared in the gatehouse doorway with Achis and Vagnar.

'You've been busy, Flax,' she said.

'I aim to please,' Flax said, giving a little mock bow. 'Taliesin and Cynric are in the Royal Apartments upstairs with the Relics. The prisoners are in the lower levels.'

Morven nodded. 'Let's go.'

The courtyard lay quiet – they probably didn't expect anyone to breach the gatehouse.

Morven and her men moved swiftly towards the main entrance to the Stronghold. Flax gestured to a doorway on the left hand side of the courtyard – I nodded as the spy joined the Bandit Leader.

I glanced at Kit who watched Flax disappear into the building. 'You can go with him,' I whispered.

Kit shook his head, tearing his eyes from Flax. 'No, I'm staying with you.'

I gave him a little half smile and led the way towards the

271

entrance to the lower levels, one sword in hand – I wasn't sure how much room there would be inside to wield two. We paused at the opening, listening for any soldiers, then slipped quietly inside, although I did wonder if anyone would hear my heart thumping loudly away in my chest.

A guard stepped out of the shadows, sword in hand. Kit swept towards him, striking at him, bringing him down quickly. Another appeared. Amalia twisted behind him, slapped her hand over his mouth and stabbed him in the back. She let him slide to the floor. I hadn't realised quite how ruthless and efficient my friends were, and now was definitely the time for it.

I cautiously moved on, now holding Flax's Yellow and one of my Pellucid Crystals in an ungloved hand.

'This way,' I said, heading down a set of stairs that descended into yawning darkness. As I reached the bottom of the steps I might as well have been entering hell itself. The stench of unwashed bodies was overpowering and I gagged. A rat scuttled past and a heartrending moan of pain rushed up to me like a wave. I swallowed. I moved my hand, the Crystals glowing more brightly as I swept them to the left.

'We have to let out every Blood we find,' I said, moving along the corridor and down another level. The dimly lit corridor stretched out in front of me, the torches scattering ugly shadows across the rough, damp stone walls as we walked along. 'Here,' I said, stopping in front of a door with a small grill. I peered in but could see nothing and no one. The Crystals were glowing brightly now, someone had to be inside – but was it Etienne?

Kit turned the handle – locked.

'Allow me,' Vergil said, wielding his axe. He swung the blade down at the handle and the wood shattered. He pushed the door open. A groan from inside had me grabbing a torch from its holder on the wall and charging into the small cell.

'Etienne?' I called, more in hope than because I expected him to be in the first cell we came to.

'Ah, lassie,' a guttural voice croaked. 'Are you here to

kill me at last?' An old man, his white hair long and bedraggled, just like his beard, looked at me through red eyes. His clothes were little more than rags, and he had cuts up his arms. A few had healed; one looked infected.

'No,' I said, sickened to the core.

'We're here to get you out,' Kit said, moving over to the old man and helping him to his feet.

'Get me out? Can this be true?' he asked, his deep green eyes widening.

'Come with us,' Amalia said.

We moved out of the cell and down to the next, where once again Vergil used his axe. Inside was another Blood, this time a young girl, her pale skin streaked with dirt and blood. She hurtled past me.

'Grandfather! Grandfather!' she wept, falling into the old man's arms.

'It's all right, my dear, all is well now,' he said.

I thought his optimism a little overdone – we weren't out of the Stronghold yet.

Vergil cut into another cell where a man in his thirties, in relatively good condition, came out and went over to help the old man. Another Blood released.

I shook my head. Butterflies flapped in my stomach. Something was wrong here. This was all too easy – I looked at Kit.

'I know what you're thinking, Sorsh,' he said. 'And you're right. Where are all the guards? There should be more than two, surely?'

'Maybe they think the Stronghold is so secure they don't need many,' Amalia said brightly.

'That isn't the impression Flax gave me.'

'Let's keep going while we can,' Vergil said.

We released another five Bloods before I turned to Kit. 'Take them up and out of here – Morven's men should be here now.'

'I'm not leaving you,' Kit said firmly.

'I'll take them,' Vergil said.

'I'll go with you,' Amalia nodded. 'We'll be back in a few minutes.'

The Bloods murmured their thanks and joined Vergil and Amalia, heading back up to the courtyard.

The old man looked at me. 'Put them all together,' he said. 'For clear, and all. It's in your hand, now. Destroy them all.' He turned away and followed the others with his granddaughter walking beside him.

'What?' Kit frowned.

I shook my head. The old man seemed too lucid to be talking gibberish, but what he meant? I hadn't a clue – and didn't have time to worry about it now. 'I don't know – I don't understand.' I took a deep breath and looked at the failing Crystals in my hand. Their light was dimming already, not that we needed them; every cell had a Blood inside. The lights flickered and went out, their power drained. I replaced my glove. 'Let's go.'

We ventured down to the next level. I'd kept the torch with me – and just as well, as there was little light down here. The smells grew worse, threatening to overwhelm me and return my last meal, but I held it down.

We got to the first cell door, locked, of course.

Kit groaned. 'We should've borrowed Vergil's axe.'

'He'll be back soon, but for now we'll have to use our swords,' I said.

'Mine's bigger,' Kit said, and he began to hack at the door.

By the time Vergil and Amalia returned with some of Morven's men, we'd released another eight Bloods, but no Etienne. I was starting to worry. A lot.

'There's fighting up there now,' Amalia said. 'I think we must have hit the changing of the guard, that's why it was so quiet – they were all in their guardrooms.'

'Can you take these people up?' I asked one of the bandits.

He nodded, and led the free Bloods along the corridor.

'They're freeing others on the upper levels,' Vergil said.

'Good,' I said. 'Well, let's carry on.'

'I'm glad you've brought your axe back,' Kit said. 'Hacking open a door with a sword is hard work.'

Vergil chuckled.

We made our way down another level – the last, by the looks of things. I chewed my lip as I held my torch up to the grill on the first cell, but couldn't see anyone. Vergil broke his way in, and a woman with a small child hesitantly came to the door. Amalia smiled, and helped them out into the corridor.

Two more cells yielded more, badly injured, Bloods.

'We'll take them up. You keep looking,' Kit said as he and Amalia led the prisoners back the way we'd come and up the stairs to where the bandits waited.

Where was Etienne?

Desperation filled me. I moved along the corridor to the next cell and Vergil dutifully smashed open the door. I raised my torch, peering into the cell.

Chained to the wall, huddled up, was the broken body of a young man, his once rich clothes tattered and torn to the point of hanging off his gaunt frame, his arms and wrists peppered with cuts, some red and raw, dried blood smeared on his bare arms and neck. His dark blond hair was matted and lank. I could just make out the side of his haggard face where an ugly bruise peeped out of his hairline.

Etienne.

I ran over to him.

'Starlight,' I swore kneeling beside him. I knew he'd be bad, but not this bad. Relief, horror, nausea and happiness all vied for my attention at once.

Etienne looked up, face white and smudged with dirt and blood, his gorgeous turquoise eyes sunken and dim. He blinked in the bright torchlight, and the ache in my chest returned as I wondered what he'd endured because of me.

'Sorsha?' His voice came out raspy and weak. 'Sorsha! What the hell are you doing here? You shouldn't be here, it's too dangerous.' He pulled impotently at his chains, his eyes now alive, frightened and panic-stricken. 'By the Sun, go now. Leave me, before it's too late!'

Chapter Twenty-Nine

'No,' I said, slipping my arms around him.

Vergil, his face strained, came over and raised his axe, breaking Etienne's chains. They slid free of his manacles, leaving the ugly metal bands chaffing his bleeding wrists. A drop of blood fell to the floor and a Red Crystal glittered in the light. My heart twisted. It could've been a knife in my chest. I slipped his Crystal into my pocket.

'Vergil, get Amalia,' I said. There was no time to allow for an Orange Crystal to heal Etienne now; it would take too long and we had to get out of here.

'Certainly.' He nodded and hurried away.

I looked back at Etienne. His haunted eyes filled me with a kind of terror I'd never felt before. What had he been through? What had he seen? And would he ever be my Etienne again?

'Come on,' I said, pulling him to his feet. *By Starlight*, he was like a leaf – one cough and I feared he'd crumble. My blood pulsed through my veins, heating until it boiled with the kind of rage I'd never felt before. This wouldn't go unpunished – not the Emperor's treatment of Etienne, or that of the other Bloods.

'I c-can't,' he gasped, sinking back to the ground. 'Everything hurts too much.'

I gritted my teeth. Taliesin would pay for this.

I had to do something, and quick. I had only one option. I removed a glove and slipped out my knife. I nicked my fingertip. A little drop of blood appeared. I let it drop into my palm. A small Pellucid Crystal winked at me in the dim light. I quickly stemmed the blood flow, put my glove back on and resheathed my dagger, holding the Crystal in one hand and Etienne with the other. My hand began to glow white, and I wrapped my arms around him, willing his pain to ease. I knew the little Pellucid wouldn't last long, neither would it heal Etienne, we didn't have the luxury of time, but I hoped I could take the edge off his pain as I had on the beach weeks ago.

He took a deep, shuddering breath. 'What did you do?'

'Nothing you wouldn't have in my position,' I said. I wasn't convinced it was enough. I could do nothing for his physical state. This would have to suffice until we could heal him properly.

'A Pellucid?' he asked, surprise in his thin voice. His brow furrowed, eyes darting about as he tried to take it in. 'Y-you bled for me? You…'

'I'd walk into hell for you.'

'I-I think you have.'

I flinched. 'Can you get up?'

'I think so.'

I managed to get him to his feet and guided him to the door, out into the passageway, his dirty clothes giving off a powerful odour of sweat. As we reached the corridor he almost passed out from the exertion rather than the pain.

'You found him then?'

I turned. Prince Artem stood further down the corridor, a grin on his face, his eyebrow twitching.

'He's held up quite well, all things considered,' Artem continued conversationally. 'Others like him have only lasted a couple of days. His will to live is as strong as his body.'

'Stay back, Artem,' I spat, glaring at the turncoat. 'Go back to Cynric.'

He laughed. 'I'm going back to Luna to rule. But first, I'm going to deal with you.'

I hastily propped Etienne up against the wall. There was little room in the corridor – no room for swords.

I faced the Moon Prince, one foot slightly in front of the other, and raised both my hands in a kind of surrender pose. But this was no surrender. From here I could strike at him in various ways, depending how he came at me.

Artem grinned. 'I'm going to enjoy this.'

Not as much as I am.

He tensed, his eyes narrowed as a shoulder dropped and he prepared to punch. But I was ready. As he lunged towards me I ducked and twisted around. His fist connected with the unforgiving stone wall. He yelped in pain, but I was in no mood to give him any quarter. I struck at his kidneys, my elbow connecting with his back. He yelled again as I knitted my hands together and slammed them sideways with all my strength into the side of his head. He fell to the ground, unconscious.

I stood for a moment, my heart racing, hands sweating. I shook, but whether it was from the fight or from the sight of Etienne slumped on the floor, I couldn't tell. I rushed back to the Sun Prince, shifting his hair from his eyes.

'You're very good at that, you know,' he murmured, his turquoise eyes no more than slits.

'Anything for you,' I said. 'Let's get out of here.'

Amalia and Kit came running down the corridor.

'Is he all right?' Amalia asked, a strained look on her face.

'Barely,' I said. 'Help me get him up, would you?'

Taking an arm each, we pulled him up with Kit's help.

Vergil ran up to us. 'I found Taliesin's men. They were waiting to pounce on us in the courtyard and stop us from escaping, but the bandits and Bloods are fighting back,' he said. 'I think some of the townsfolk are getting in to help too.' He glanced at the prone figure of Artem. 'I see you've made a start here.'

'Didn't have much choice,' I said. 'Can you get Etienne out of here and heal him as best you can?'

'Of course,' Vergil nodded without hesitation.

'Aren't you coming?' Kit asked, a sudden look of fear in his eyes. He knew exactly what I was going to say.

'I have some unfinished business,' I said, looking up towards the centre of the Stronghold. Taliesin and Cynric needed to be stopped. Their persecution of the Bloods had gone on long enough. And I wanted our Relics back, particularly the Amaranthine Rose, not to mention our stolen artworks.

'But Sorsh–'

'I'll go with her,' Amalia said.

'No, I have to do this alone,' I said. 'I don't want anyone else getting hurt.'

'You can say what you want, but I'm going with you, and besides, Etienne would never forgive me if I let you go alone.'

'He'll never forgive you for letting her go full stop,' Vergil said, looking at the semi-conscious Sun Prince.

Amalia shrugged and handed Etienne to Vergil. 'Tough, we girls have to stick together and besides, the two of you are more than capable of looking after Eti. You can produce the Crystals to heal him, Vergil. I can't, and neither can Sorsha.'

'Let's get up to the courtyard,' Kit said, his forehead furrowed. He wasn't happy, but it didn't matter. With Etienne between him and Vergil, Amalia and I led the way up the steps and back up to the prison entrance, pausing just inside in relative safety, as Morven's men headed back to the lower levels to make sure we hadn't missed anyone.

I peered out – the courtyard had erupted in fighting. Taliesin's soldiers fought against Morven's men, the Bloods healthy enough to wield a weapon, as well as some of the townsfolk who had come up from their rundown houses to help. The ring of steel and the smell of blood filled the cool air.

I gently kissed the half-conscious Etienne on the head and turned to Vergil.

'Look after him – please heal him, if you can,' I said, before exiting the door and running along the edge of the courtyard, making for the entrance to the upper levels of the Stronghold. If I hesitated now I'd never leave Etienne. Amalia followed in my wake, after giving Vergil a hasty kiss.

We entered the Stronghold proper.

'Which way?' Amalia asked as I drew both swords.

I gawped at my surroundings. This wasn't a utilitarian building; this was a palace. A great sweeping staircase rose up from the hallway we'd entered, a deep red carpet lining the staircase that featured a gold leaf bannister.

Tapestries and paintings hung on the walls with beautiful candelabras illuminating the artwork. I stopped and squinted. One of those paintings used to grace Finnar's study back at the Citadel. A little pang of homesickness suddenly filled me, but I forced it back down. No time to think about home now.

A small group of Morven's bandits appeared at the top of the stairs carrying books and a couple of paintings. They nodded to us as they passed, heading for the courtyard.

'The Royal Apartments are supposedly on the upper floors, so let's head there,' I said.

'Wouldn't be surprised if Flax and Morven have already taken care of business,' Amalia said, her sword at the ready.

'Maybe.'

As we reached the top of the staircase the sound of clashing metal made me turn back. Soldiers fought some of the bandits in the lower corridors, spilling out into the hallway. Sim was with them, fighting well.

'We'd better keep going,' I said. I didn't really want to get tangled up with that.

'What do you reckon, up again?' Amalia asked, looking up the next staircase.

I nodded. 'The main staircase does seem to indicate we go up again.'

We climbed to the top where a landing swept around to a pair of huge oak doors. That looked promising – some kind of hall or throne room?

A flash of steel to my right caught my attention.

'Look out,' Amalia yelled.

But I was already twisting to one side, my twin swords blocking a soldier's swinging blade. As I took a step back I recognised the soldier's large scar running down his right cheek and his hook nose; this was the man who attacked me and Etienne at the temple. Who killed Athene.

He snarled at me like an angry dog, but I gave him no time to think. I lunged, feinted, then sidestepped his clumsy swipe and let his weight carry him forwards. He hit the smoothly plastered wall, his nose connecting with the white paint, leaving a bloody mark. This time he growled. Now he lunged at me. I twisted behind him, letting his momentum drive him past me to the top of the staircase where he turned, grinning at me. Amalia shouted at him. He turned to look at her. I broke one of Uncle's rules, and I kicked him squarely in the chest, sending him backwards into thin air. He fell, bouncing on the steps during his descent, slamming his head against the wall at the bottom and didn't move again.

Had I killed him?

Achis appeared from a room off the lower landing, saw the soldier and ran over to him, ramming his sword into his chest. He'd obviously been taking lessons from Flax. If I had killed the soldier I'd never know now – whatever the case, Achis *definitely* had.

Achis nodded to us and ran off down another corridor.

'Good man.' Amalia smiled.

Killing still wasn't my thing – despite the fact I wanted Cynric and Taliesin dead. It made me uneasy. It suddenly occurred to me I hadn't actually killed Artem when I had the chance. I was definitely conflicted on the matter, but at least with this soldier I'd acted in self-defence.

A groan of pain made me pause.

'Did you hear that?' I asked.

Amalia nodded. 'It came from over there,' she said, pointing to a side room.

We hurried over and I gingerly opened the door, ready for this to be some sort of trap. Lying on the floor with a bloodied shoulder, was Morven.

'What happened?' Amalia asked bursting into the room and crouching beside the Bandit Leader.

'I got careless, girl,' Morven muttered. We helped her to sit up, her pale, grimacing face showing the pain she was in.

'A soldier?' I asked.

She shook her head. 'Cynric.'

I looked around. 'Where did he go?' I asked.

'I don't know. Flax and Vagnar went straight after him.'

'Probably dead then,' Amalia said.

'Let's hope so,' I murmured.

Amalia slipped under Morven's shoulder and let her lean on her as we made our way back to the door.

'Get her out,' I said. 'Maybe Vergil can do something.'

Amalia frowned. 'What about you?'

I looked towards the ornately carved oak doors with vines and thistles embellished on them. 'I'm going that way.'

'We were going to stick together.'

'That was before we found Morven injured. I'll be fine alone.'

Amalia hesitated, then nodded. 'Be careful, then, or Eti will kill me.'

'I will – and Amalia, give Etienne my love,' I said, looking at my friend.

'I will, although you can give it to him yourself properly, later.'

'I certainly hope so,' I murmured, watching the two women slowly make their way down the stairs.

I took a deep breath, took my gloves off and readied my swords. I walked over to the doors and heaved them open. They grated, setting my teeth on edge and the hairs on the back of my neck to attention. I stepped into the vast room. A great hall opened up before me with a huge fireplace at one end, the fire flickering angrily, and at the other a raised dais with an ostentatious gold throne decorated with a rainbow of gemstones. Deep red drapes hung at the windows where the sky could be seen just beginning to lighten in the east. Chandeliers filled with flaming candles illuminated the vast space, its wooden floor varnished and polished to a mirror shine, and the tapestries on the walls depicting epic battles.

'Do you like my hall, Princess Sorsha?' a deep, granite-like voice asked.

Chapter Thirty

I turned back towards the fireplace, only now noticing a figure coming out from the shadows at the far end of the room. He was tall, over six feet. His salt and pepper hair contrasted with his pale skin making him look ghost-like. His sharp nose and chin cast shadows across his red velvet jacket and black britches. A golden crown sat across his temples and in his hand he held a great golden sword.

'It's a little overdone for my taste, ostentatious,' I said, walking into the room, the smell of freshly varnished wood assaulting me. So, this was Emperor Taliesin of Merribor. 'You murdered my mother.'

Taliesin laughed. 'I didn't do it personally.'

'You might as well have done,' I said, walking over to the window and glancing out. There was no escape from here, just a drop down into a cold, grey stone yard.

The Emperor adjusted his cuff. 'I wanted your Crystals.'

'Perhaps you should've asked.'

'And would the Orders have given them to me willingly?' he asked, moving slowly towards me.

'I guess we'll never know now,' I said, holding my ground.

'I read about Crystal Bloods years ago, but dismissed them as myth. It turns out I was wrong – and once I realised that, it became obvious I needed to collect all I could find, to consolidate my position.'

'I wasn't aware your position was threatened,' I said, watching him as he moved across the smooth, polished floor.

'When you rule you're always in jeopardy.'

'Sounds very lonely.'

He scoffed. 'It's intoxicating. Ruling an empire, everyone at your whim. No one else in Merribor would be capable of ruling as I have, controlling everything and everyone, as I have. They would all fail miserably and the empire would fall. I am the only one capable of keeping the Empire of Merribor intact and great. Your Crystals will see to it that I can rule unchallenged, in sole command. Merribor is, and will stay, great.'

'Not sure your people see it like that,' I said, noticing a closed door at the throne end of the room – there were no other doors for anyone to surprise me through. I rather wished the oak doors were shut too.

'My people love me,' he said, waving his hands in a grand gesture, slightly hampered by the golden sword he held.

'Your people hate you – you're a tyrant, a cold-blooded killer who had my mother murdered, the people of the Orders killed, the priestesses of the Celestial Temple massacred and the Bloods you caught butchered for their Crystals.'

Taliesin's face began to turn an interesting shade of purple as a vein popped up in his neck. 'You don't know what you're talking about. It has all been done for the glory and greater good of Merribor,' he rumbled.

I shook my head, gritting my teeth. 'It's all been done so you can rule absolutely and keep the people under your thumb, no better than slaves.'

'Merribor is great.'

'Merribor is little more than a third rate land.'

Taliesin stopped dead, tilting his head slightly, his fingers clenching around his sword hilt. 'And I'd thought I might ask you if you'd be my new Empress.'

'But we've only just met,' I said sweetly, placing one foot in front of the other and readying my swords for the onslaught to come.

'That matters little in Royal Circles.'

'I'm already spoken for, sorry.'

'He can be dealt with.'

'You've already tried and failed,' I said, my own hands gripping my hilts a little tighter, weighing him up. His sword was bigger than mine, but I could handle that. His strength would be my main problem – I'd have to be fast.

Taliesin's forehead wrinkled, his eyebrows almost knitting together. 'Of course,' he said, nodded, 'that Sun Prince. His Crystals have been most useful.'

I gritted my teeth again, not answering.

'But I understood he was past help,' the Emperor said, moving towards me again.

'Looks like you were mistaken – again.'

Taliesin's face looked like thunder now, thunder and lightning rolled into one. He was riled. And when people get riled they make silly mistakes.

'I would ask you to stop your persecution of the Bloods, to let them go and return the Relics to the Orders, but I have a feeling you won't do that,' I said.

Taliesin laughed. 'And you'd be right. I don't intend to stop – to protect my position I'm going to find more. To protect Merribor I may even invade Faerland.'

Definitely no talking him down.

I took long, deep breaths through my nose, preparing myself. My mouth had gone dry, but I ignored that. I flexed my fingers, readying myself, closing my hands around the Pellucid and Purple Crystals – I hoped they worked.

Taliesin narrowed his eyes as he looked at me. 'I hear you can fight.'

'I guess we'll see, won't we,' I said, noting the knife at his waist as he moved, partially concealed under his jacket. I tensed as he approached.

He pulled his sword arm back.

I didn't wait.

I swung straight at him with one sword, sidestepped, twisted around and swiped at his back with the other. His sword, already on a downward trajectory, glanced off my leg as if it were made of diamond. The Crystals in the hilts of my swords were working, saving me from injury – but it was obvious Taliesin had some of his own, or my strikes would have bitten into his body.

He backed away, grinning horribly. 'It looks as though we'll have to see whose Crystals run out first.'

Crystals were all very well, but if I could goad him into a mistake, wear him out first, I still stood a chance.

'No Cynric?' I asked conversationally.

Something flickered in his eyes. 'Cynric is safe.'

'I heard he was dead,' I said, glancing to the polished floor. Thank goodness Flax wasn't here.

'Cynric has Crystals of his own, he'll be quite safe.'

'You hope.'

Taliesin growled like a dog, slicing his sword at me; I met his blade. Twisted. I let his momentum take him forward. I struck at the back of his neck with my hilt, but it once again glanced off.

Taliesin was breathing heavily now. 'This is going to get very tiresome, very quickly.' He rolled his shoulders and adjusted his cuffs.

'Then surrender,' I said, watching him closely.

A muscle feathered in his jaw.

'Never.'

This time I swung at him before he could move, but the Crystals he had were too powerful. I couldn't break through their shield. My swords glanced off his chest. Damn. He swung at me. I blocked with both swords. Stepped back. As I parried his next blow his sword glanced off my shoulder. Stupid. I was too slow. Maybe over confident.

I moved back warily, sweat beading on my brow. I tried to keep my breathing under control, but it was hard.

I lunged at him. Feinted. Twisted behind him.

His sword caught my left arm. Pain spiralled up the limb. I sucked a breath in through my teeth, dropping my sword. *Starlight*. My Crystals were spent already.

I backed away towards the window, aware of a Purple landing on the floor beside me, followed by a Pellucid.

'A Double Blood?' Taliesin narrowed his eyes. 'You're more valuable than I thought.'

What could I do? I was a sword down and had no protection. Taliesin had working Crystals. Confidence. I was running out of options fast – in fact, short of just going for it, I had no options. If only I could destroy his Crystals, make things even again.

I glanced at the Crystals on the floor, absently thinking how I now had a full set. *Put them all together… Destroy them all.* The old man. Was he right? Was it possible to destroy all the Crystals in existence? Or were they the ramblings of an old, slightly delirious, injured man?

I looked at Taliesin who was happily circling me, knowing full well he had the major advantage now.

For clear, and all.

No – not 'for' but 'four'. I needed four Pellucid *and all* the colours, too. All in my hand at once. I hoped this was going to work. I slit my hand on my sword edge. Two large Pellucid fell. A Purple. Another Pellucid.

I grabbed them all from the floor, including the two Crystals shed from my arm, clutching them in my still bleeding hand. I dropped my sword, pulling the other Crystals I'd collected from my pocket.

'What are you doing?' Taliesin asked, his eyes narrowing further, his eyebrows knitting together.

'I'm not sure,' I said, dropping them all into one hand.

'No,' Taliesin yelled. 'You don't know what you're doing!'

'I think, maybe I do.'

His reaction told me it was the right thing to do. I clasped my hand around the Crystals, forcing them together.

The explosion of light blinded me. The shock wave that sprang from my hand sent me backwards into the wall behind me as the building shook. It sent Taliesin careering across the wooden floor, his golden sword skittering to one side. A loud thundering echoed in my ears – although that could have been my pulse.

The Crystals in my sword hilts disintegrated into a sparkling black mist and vanished, leaving behind the empty indentations where they'd once sat.

'You fool! What have you done?' Taliesin screamed at me.

Levelled the playing field. I hope.

I slipped my glove over my cut hand for protection and scrambled to my feet, grabbing one sword, lunging for the other. Taliesin pulled himself up and retrieved his sword, but I gave him no time to compose himself. I was straight on him, landing blow after blow after blow. He struggled to block them, taken by surprise by the flurry of strikes.

Taliesin's movements began to slow. I didn't. The

Emperor's movements became predictable, even. I smiled. Taliesin's eyes widened as fear clouded his eyes. I forced him back past the oak doors in the direction of the fireplace.

'You won't kill me,' he hissed.

I hesitated. Despite all my vengeful thoughts after Etienne had been taken, I couldn't kill. He was right. I'd fail. There was no way I could finish him, and capturing him seemed incredibly unlikely; maybe I could knock him out? But then, would we want to keep him as a prisoner? Waiting for someone to break him out, let him loose on the world again? I swallowed, ice filling my chest.

'You're too weak,' he said, curling his lip. 'Like your Sun Prince.'

Etienne. That hit a nerve. Taliesin would've had no qualms about draining my Pledged dry and finally killing him. If Etienne had stayed his prisoner much longer, I had no doubt he would've died in excruciating pain.

Pure anger filled my veins.

'He's not weak. He survived your torture,' I said.

Taliesin laughed. 'But for how long? I'll capture him again and he'll beg for death before I finish with him. No, he's weak, just like your Orders.' A vicious smile spread across his face, reaching his eyes as he smoothed a cuff.

Mother.

Anger turned to rage.

He raised a hand, his fingers flicking, goading me on.

I lunged at him with a scream, catching him across the chest. He yelled in surprise, as much as pain. He swiped clumsily at me. I sidestepped around his back, ramming my hilt into the back of his neck. He fell to his knees. I slashed at his unprotected back, and he fell to the floor, blood seeping from the wound. Not moving.

I stepped backwards, stumbling as I went. I gasped.

What had I done?

I'd killed Taliesin.

Nausea filled my chest. A cold sweat suddenly covered my body.

Had I done the right thing?

Of course I had. I'd probably just saved hundreds if not thousands of lives. Etienne was right, though. This would change me.

I moved away from the Emperor's body. I looked out the oak doors, but didn't feel ready to face anyone yet, so I staggered backwards a bit further before falling to my knees with exhaustion, both physical and emotional.

My swords clattered to the floor and as I sank to my knees, I started shaking – not a mild trembling, but a full on shaking as a headache started up in my temples. I struggled to breathe for a moment, and my vision started to go sparkly, but I took control as Vergil had shown me, breathing in through my nose and counting to four, holding it, breathing out for four, until I finally regained a clearer head. I clasped my arm, the pain worse than the wound itself which had long since stopped bleeding, but now I'd stopped fighting the pain drove into me.

Footsteps hurried up the staircase. I prayed it wasn't another soldier, or worse, Cynric. I didn't have much energy left, and definitely not enough for another full on fight. A figure moved into the hall, stepping into the dawn sunlight streaming in through the windows.

Etienne.

I gasped, except it came out somewhere between a gasp and a sob, a weird, rather embarrassing sound.

He looked towards me. He still wore the same torn, dirty clothes, but his drawn face and sunken eyes were no more. He didn't look quite his normal self, but he was a lot better than when I'd last seen him. Even his cuts appeared to have been mainly healed, although dried blood still smeared his arms, neck and face, and his hair still looked like it could do with a good brush.

The relief that flooded his face turned to joy as he smiled at me, his turquoise eyes lighting up.

'Sorsha!' he said, starting towards me.

Behind him a hulking shadow rose, its golden sword raised above its head preparing to strike.

Chapter Thirty-One

With my last remaining strength I slipped my knife from my belt, dragged myself up on one knee and threw the blade. It missed Etienne's head by inches as he ducked, smoothly rotating twice before burying itself in Emperor Taliesin's chest. He dropped his sword. He staggered backwards, plucking at the blade until it came out of his chest – and his life's blood followed after it. This time there could be no doubt. As he hit the ground, a pool of scarlet surrounded him. He was dead.

Etienne, wide-eyed, looked back at the dead Emperor and then at me. 'Sunlight,' he swore.

I slumped to the floor. Nothing left. Shaking.

'Thank you,' he murmured.

As he got to his feet his face drained of all colour. He grabbed his sword, lunging towards me.

I didn't need him to tell me someone had entered the hall from the door beside the throne. I could *feel* it. The hairs on the back of my neck rose up, my muscles tensed, but other than twisting slightly to see who it was, my body had nothing left to give. If I was about to die, I was about to die.

Two metal blades met above my head, the sound as they came together sending ice through my veins. Artem scowled at Etienne as he tried to push his blade down towards me and my unprotected body. Etienne forced him back. He struck at the Moon Prince, making him retreat. Artem clumsily tried to block Etienne's strikes, but he wasn't doing a very good job, to my trained eye. The Sun Prince soon had Artem frantically trying anything to stop his advance, by accident making Etienne stumble. Artem raised his sword high for a final strike, but Etienne was ready. He lunged forwards, his sword running Artem through.

'I-I didn't think you had it in you.' Artem looked down at the blood leaving his body.

'By the Sun, I'd do anything to save her,' Etienne said, a fierce expression covering his face. 'Even kill.'

'I should – I should have kno–' Artem fell to the ground. Dead.

Etienne gave him no more of his time and ran back to me, propping me up, his face now full of concern.

'You-you killed him for me,' I managed to get out.

'Hell, I didn't do anything you hadn't already done for me,' he said, his eyes clouded.

'But you said killing changed a person.' I could already feel guilt riddling my mind as I gazed at the dead Emperor.

Etienne glanced reluctantly at Artem. 'It does – it will,' he said with a little sigh and shook his head. 'But we're already so changed by these last months, we'll never be the same people we were when we first met and set off for Luna Isle.'

No, we weren't the same people, not even close.

'And besides, Artem was going to kill you, and I couldn't have that,' he said, a little lopsided smile playing at the corners of his lips.

I managed a little wan smile in return. 'And I couldn't let Taliesin kill you,' I said, reaching out and touching his cheek. 'He'd tried once in the cells, I couldn't let him succeed now.'

Etienne shrugged. 'Self defence. We didn't set out to kill them.'

I wasn't so sure.

'After you were taken I-I wanted to make Taliesin and Cynric pay. I *wanted* to kill them,' I said, looking up at him through my eyelashes. 'Artem too.'

He gave me a sympathetic smile. 'I wanted the same – but ultimately our personal feelings didn't matter. We had to stop them from what they were doing to the Crystal Bloods, to our Orders. I don't believe for one moment Taliesin would ever have stopped voluntarily. Do you?'

I shook my head. 'No, he wasn't going to stop.'

'Then what choice did we have? The same with Artem.'

'Taliesin goaded me – with you, with Mother,' I said, guilt still wracking me.

'Then more fool him,' Etienne said. 'He deserved what he got in the end. I wouldn't have done anything different.'

'I know, I just…'

'It's all right, we'll get through this together, Sorsh.'

He hadn't called me that before, and a little thrill cascaded down my spine at his use of my nickname. But it didn't last. Everything suddenly overwhelmed me. A black wave rushed towards me. My body slumped, the floor cold and hard under my back and head.

'Sorsh? Sorsha!'

I could hear Etienne, but I couldn't respond to him. Everything was dark, but I could feel him pick me up and move me from the throne room. I had the sensation of being carried down stairs, and then a cool breeze with the smell of morning swept over me, and the warmth of sunlight on my body.

'Eti! Over here!' Amalia's voice cut through the darkness, but still I couldn't see or react.

Etienne took a few more steps and the sun's warmth vanished as a dim light surrounded me and he put me down on something less than soft. Not that I could protest.

'Is she…?' Amalia left it hanging.

'No, she passed out,' Etienne said. 'But she needs healing.'

'After all the Crystals vanished Vergil shed as much blood as he could to help but we only had one Double Blood, and he was an old man we found in a side cell. He gave what he could, but he was already dying. I have no Pellucid left – I saved an Orange to heal Vergil, and I have one other, but we can't use them. Eti, Vergil's really ill.'

I felt someone take hold of my hand.

'Maybe–'

Dragging myself from the sea of darkness I'd slipped into I forced my eyes half open. 'T-take what you need,' I said, waving my cut hand at Etienne.

He gently pulled the bloodstained glove off my hand, and a small Pellucid fell out onto the floor.

'That's all I need,' Amalia said.

'Take it,' I murmured.

She nodded, passed Etienne an Orange, and hurried out the room.

The very act of taking off the glove had reopened my cut, and in moments a Purple and a Pellucid had fallen into Etienne's hand. He quickly tore a strip of cloth from his shirt to bind my wound before replacing the glove, then set the Orange and Pellucid in his hand. The orange glow was quite comforting, and as he placed his hand on my forehead a tingling started to spread through me. The warm sensation seeped into every muscle, nerve and extremity. I felt a certain level of strength returning, the cuts on my hand and my arm started itching as they healed.

I felt more alert. I looked at Etienne. I'd been wrong. His face was still drawn, but not like it had been when I'd first found him in that ghastly cell. His cuts had healed, but some he would carry as scars forever. As the power of the Pellucid failed I knew that I still had healing to do, we both did, and strength to regain but it had started the process, and for that I was grateful. But there was a hollow feeling inside me, as if I'd lost something.

Was *that* the cost of killing? I'd lost a part of me?

But if I hadn't, if I'd lost Etienne, I'd have lost an even greater part of me. There was a cost to killing – but maybe in these circumstances, for these reasons, it was a price worth paying.

I gingerly sat up, noticing that I was sitting on a heap of half empty sacks.

Etienne's eyes, now I looked deep into them, had that same hollowness that I felt inside and I pulled him to me, hugging him, giving him as much love and reassurance as I could, taking the same from him. Then tears came, and wouldn't stop. They streamed down my face while my whole body shook as I sobbed. Then I realised Etienne's body shook like mine. Everything from these last few hellish days had become too much for him too. After a while I pulled away and looked into his red-rimmed eyes – mine would be even worse, with my colouring a couple of tears made my eyes and nose go red and my face blotchy, highly embarrassing and not particularly attractive.

'We'll get through this together,' I murmured, echoing his words and moving his hair from his eyes.

He nodded, a wan smile on his lips. 'Together we can do anything.'

'Just don't leave me again, however noble you want to be,' I said.

'Next time we'll run, together.'

'Let's hope there isn't a next time,' I said, as he pulled me towards him for a kiss. A kiss that was salty and wet, and as he gently parted my lips with his tongue and my bones once more turned to liquid gold, we drew what comfort we could from each other.

A cough sounded at the door.

'Is this really the time?' Kit asked.

I turned and looked at him. 'I can't say I can think of a better one.'

My oldest friend grinned at me. 'I'm glad you're all right, Sorsh.'

'Thanks to Etienne.'

Etienne frowned for a moment then smiled an embarrassed little smile. 'Thanks to each other.'

Flax appeared next to Kit. 'Vagnar's dead. We went after Cynric, but Vagnar was taken by surprise. I tried to help him… I shouldn't have hesitated. Cynric got away.'

'You did the right thing,' Kit said, patting Flax's shoulder. 'Morven will be grateful, and so will Achis.'

'Hmm.' Flax shrugged.

I sighed. I'd hoped the Prince of Merribor had at least been detained.

'Don't worry, Sorsha,' Flax said. 'Cynric won't be back – he knows the country isn't safe for him anymore. And if he does return, my blades will be waiting for him.'

'So who'll take over?' Etienne asked.

'Sim suggested Flax,' Kit smirked.

Flax dug him in the ribs. 'I'm no emperor – but there's talk of Morven assuming command.'

'She's all right?' I asked.

'She was healed before all the Crystals in the Stronghold building vanished.'

'Vanished? Disintegrated, more like,' Kit said, screwing his nose up. 'There was that earthquake and they all turned into sparkling black smoke.'

'Do you know what happened to them?' Etienne asked, looking at me.

I bowed my head. 'That was me. I destroyed them all, although I didn't know how far-reaching the effects would be.'

'Just the Stronghold it seems like, and a good thing you did,' Kit said. 'Some soldier was about to kill me with a Purple.'

'How did you do it?' Etienne asked, raising an eyebrow.

'You remember that old man and his granddaughter, Kit?' I asked. Kit nodded as I turned back to Etienne. 'He was an old Blood, he said to put all the Crystals together to destroy them all. I didn't understand at first, but then I realised he meant I needed one of every colour and four Pellucid with which to do it. It got to a point I had no choice but to try and see it if worked.'

'Well, it worked, and I'm grateful it did,' Kit said, nodding.

'Do you know where the old man went?'

Kit shook his head. 'I last saw him heading into the town with the girl, but that was some time ago. After that, I don't know where he went.'

I nodded. How had the old man known what to do? I really wished he hadn't left – I would have loved to have talked to him.

'We know Cynric got away,' Kit said. 'I think Artem did too. I went back down into the cells and he'd gone.'

'He's dead,' I said quietly. 'In the throne room.'

Etienne looked at the stone floor.

'He was dead when I found him, but I added a couple of blows myself, just to make sure,' Flax said, buffing his nails on his tunic. 'I finished what you'd started, wasn't about to take any chances with a traitor like him – or Taliesin for that matter. He's definitely dead too.'

'Wasn't it already finished?' Etienne asked with a slightly sick look.

Flax shrugged. 'It is now.'

In some ways I couldn't say I was sorry.

#

Morven spent the day setting up camp outside the Stronghold and its town. We tended to the injured, and I shed a little blood to help those most in need. I saw Vergil in the afternoon, and his pale face indicated he still didn't like the sight of blood, but at least he was feeling better. Amalia didn't leave his side, fussing around him like a mother hen – something I understood. I hadn't left Etienne since the throne room.

The camp was quiet and subdued. Despite our win over Taliesin there was an air of exhaustion about the place. Sim rode off with a few of the other men to relay news of the success to the Encampment. Morven sent others to relay the news around the Empire. She was the obvious choice to take control and she quickly began organizing things with Achis' help. Vagnar's death had hit them both hard, and they too, were rather subdued.

I helped Etienne wash and change. I was shaken by the dried blood I found on his back, but he didn't say anything about it. We took advantage of an early night, sharing a tent, but neither of us slept much. We lay holding each other, both anxious we'd wake to find our reunion a mere dream, but the natural vetiver scent of Etienne's now clean body swirling around me once again, became reassurance enough for me. We kept waking each other with our nightmares though, and by morning our eyes were even redder than they had been the previous day, if that was possible.

We dressed slowly, both aching from the previous day's exertions.

'Here, this is yours,' I said, passing him his book.

He reached out and took it from me. 'The Crystals were helpful?'

'They helped save you and free the Stronghold.'

He nodded. 'I wasn't sure I'd see it again,' he said, his eyes misty as he turned a few pages. 'But I suppose I should've realised you'd take good care of it.'

I gave him a wan little smile. 'Of course. It belongs to you.'

'Thank you.' He hesitated. 'I also wanted to say thank you for shedding blood for me, when you found me. I wasn't really taking everything in at the time, but now I realise what you did, how you took away the pain, just like you did with the Moonweever Fish.' He looked at me, eyes still misty. 'It was your love that helped me to survive that hellish place, you know, your love sustained me. I knew I'd never escape there, especially once they started bleeding me – I didn't have the strength. All I could focus on was the thought of surviving long enough for you to find me. It was all that kept me going.'

I raised an eyebrow. 'But you told me to stay away? Why did you think I'd come for you?'

He glanced at the ground, then into my eyes. 'Because I know you. Because I knew, whatever I might say to you, that you'd come for me. I know I told you to go – and I wanted you to, so you were safe, but I also knew deep down you wouldn't, anymore than I would've done if our positions had been reversed. I knew you'd come, and you arrived just in time. I don't think I could've held out much longer.'

'Then it's a good thing I ignored you,' I said with a wry grin, and kissed his forehead.

'I trust you won't make a habit of ignoring me completely, *all* the time?'

'Only when it involves saving your life. And maybe the odd, other occasion, depending on what it is.' I winked at him.

A little smile flickered on his lips. He nodded. 'Sounds good to me,' he said, pulling me in for a hug.

We went out and sat at a campfire not far from our tent. Kit noticed us and smiled. He brought us some breakfast, but I refused a plate.

'You have to eat, Sorsh,' he said. 'Etienne is.' He nodded to the prince who was wolfing his food down.

'And I will, when I'm ready,' I said.

My head hurt, my limbs ached and my energy levels were pretty non-existent. Every bang made me flinch, every new face reminded me of a dead one. I felt at a loose end. I didn't really know what to do now. Lost, was the only word that came close to how I really felt. I hadn't taken the time to think beyond getting Etienne back. Should I go home, back to Steorra? What was the point? Mother was gone, the Citadel destroyed. But I still had my uncle to consider.

On the other hand, I couldn't let Etienne return to Solis alone. I had to accompany him there first, even if I returned home later.

We stayed at the camp a few days, resting and recovering from our various ordeals. Morven set about collecting up the various Relics and returning them to their rightful owners. Kit appeared one afternoon looking very pleased with himself. Once I'd spotted what he was carrying in his hands, I realised why. He held the Amaranthine Rose.

'I thought you might like to keep hold of this yourself,' he said. 'The other Steorran Relics are being sent back to King Finnar in one go, but I figured you'd like to hang on to this one.'

I nodded, taking the small silver rose from him. 'Thank you, Kit. Thank you for everything,' I said, looking at him. 'You didn't have to stay with me and get involved in all this, but I'm so grateful you did.'

He grinned at me. 'I may have been paid to accompany you to begin with, but money's had nothing to do with it for years. You're my friend, Sorsh. Probably my best friend – just don't tell Flax. You and I have been through a lot together, and I'd do anything for you. You don't need to thank me,' he said, squeezing my hand.

I grabbed hold of him and gave him a hug. 'Maybe not, but thank you anyway.'

#

Etienne ate far better than I did, and I was glad. He needed to get his strength back having been half-starved. Vergil's Orange Crystals could heal wounds, but not restore energy, and neither could they heal the mental wounds and emotional injuries, which meant that for both of us sleep came infrequently because of bad dreams. After a few nights my nightmares receded. Etienne's did not. The fifth night we lay in our camp bed. I had been dozing a little when he roused me with a jerk. His chest was heaving as he breathed, sweat on his brow as he groaned.

'No, no more,' he mumbled. 'You've taken enough, you've taken…'

He shifted restlessly, not the violent movements of his last fearsome nightmare, but still there was a deep despair and pain to his voice.

I pulled myself up on one shoulder, running my hand down the side of his face.

'Etienne, it's all right, it's a dream,' I murmured gently.

He groaned again, a sound of such anguish my eyes pricked with tears.

'Etienne, it's a dream, my love, just a dream,' I said.

'W-what? Sorsh?' He opened his eyes, eyes that sparkled in the flickering flame of our nightlight. He let out a shuddering sigh, his tense body relaxing. 'A dream. Another dream?'

'Yes, my love,' I said, stroking his damp hair. 'A dream. I'm here, you're safe.'

He took a deep breath and pulled me to him. 'Thank you,' he murmured as he kissed my head.

I snuggled into him and, arms around each other, we both slipped off to sleep again, and I held him close through the night.

The morning of the sixth day, as the sun rose into a clear blue sky, Etienne sat next to me looking out across the camp and the Stronghold beyond. A few people had started to drift away, heading for their homes, spreading the news across the Empire that Taliesin and Cynric had been overthrown.

Etienne had been very quiet since the battle and I couldn't help but worry about him.

'What is it?' I asked gently, slipping my arm through his and resting my head on his shoulder.

'Just thinking about home, about what awaits us there,' he murmured.

My heart lurched slightly as he said 'us'. He was expecting me to go with him, and a burst of warmth ran through me. And a little fear.

'You think it's time to go and find out?' I asked.

He nodded. 'Don't you?'

'Yes,' I said, 'it's time.'

'I was wondering when you were going to leave,' Morven said from behind us. We turned and looked at her. 'You were right to wait until you were both stronger, but I don't think you'll do much more healing here. It's going to take you both some time to get back to full strength, and you might as well do that back home.'

'If we have a home to go to,' Etienne said.

Morven smiled at him. 'That you have to go and find out, my brave prince.' Morven had really taken to Etienne, especially after his heroic self-sacrifice. He liked her, too, and they'd struck up a strong friendship. She looked at me and glanced at my arm where the Aegis Bracelet sat. 'You do know what that bauble is, don't you, girl? What it does?'

'It doesn't do anything, as far as I know. It's not a Blood Crystal, it's a Red Diamond,' I said with a shrug. 'It was just a gift.'

'No, it's not a Blood Crystal, and you're right, it's a diamond. But it's a Red Norglinder Diamond.'

'What's that?' Etienne asked.

She smiled. 'A Red Diamond from Norglinder on the

north-western coast of Merribor, lad. They only ever found two, and this is the largest of them. They're both powerful. Once, many years ago, they were both in my family.'

I looked at the Red Diamond with renewed interest. 'So it's not just a pretty bracelet?'

'No, girl, it's not,' she said with a sigh. 'I'd have thought you'd have been told that when it was given to you.'

'Priestess Athene gave it to me as we escaped the Temple. She said it was the Aegis Bracelet, but I didn't know what that meant.'

'To be under the aegis of something is to be under its protection,' Morven said. 'And in this case, if you are under the protection of the Aegis Bracelet itself...' Morven looked at us both. 'I guess the priestess knew about the two of you.'

Etienne frowned. 'I think she knew more than we did at the time.'

Morven nodded and smiled. 'That's probably why she gave it to you then, girl. To protect you from him.' She nodded at Etienne, who flinched.

'What?' he asked incredulously. 'I'd never hurt Sorsha.'

I stood up. 'What do you mean protect me from Etienne? I don't need protection from him.'

'Calm down, both of you. And sit down, girl. I don't mean for a moment that you'd hurt her, lad. What I meant was... Athene obviously knew the two of you were falling in love, and so she gave that to you, Sorsha, in case, or rather, for when you realised your true feelings and acted on them.'

I sat back down and shook my head. 'I still don't understand. Why would I need protection from Etienne?' I chewed my lip in confusion.

Etienne's eyes widened and his face turned red. 'Oh. I think I understand.'

'Thank goodness, I really didn't want to spell it out any further,' Morven said, scratching her head.

'And you're sure it'll work?' Etienne asked. 'It'll protect her from... you know?'

'You'll have no trouble, lad, just as long as she wears it the whole time you're...' Morven waved her hands about.

Etienne went even redder. 'She will. I'll make sure of it.'

'I will what? What are you two talking about?' I asked, frustrated with the way they were both carrying on. 'Would you stop talking in riddles and tell me?'

Etienne leant towards me and whispered in my ear. 'It's to stop you from getting pregnant.'

I swallowed, face flushing. 'It is? Does everyone know that's what it does?' I asked, wide-eyed.

Morven laughed. 'No, not everyone by a long way. Just as long as the two of you know what it can do, that's what matters.'

'If it was in your family, do you want it back?' I asked.

'No, you keep it,' Morven said, shaking her head. 'Just remember to wear it for as long as you decide you need to.' She walked away, chuckling to herself.

'Looks like we won't have to worry about herbal potions after all,' Etienne said with a wicked glint in his eye.

Chapter Thirty-Two

The next day we said our goodbyes to Morven and Achis. Flax had taken control of organizing the return of the artworks and Relics, and Kit, after much soul-searching, had decided to stay with him.

'I should really go with you,' he said. 'I'm supposed to protect you.'

'I think you can relinquish that role now,' Etienne said. 'I'm pleased, no honoured, to take it from you.'

'I suppose,' Kit said, nodding. 'But I did promise.'

'Kit, I release you from your vow – you've protected me well these last years, but now you need to look after yourself, and Flax,' I said, giving him a hug.

'If you're sure?' he asked, a little smile flickering on his face.

'I'm sure.'

Vergil and Amalia accompanied us back across Merribor. As we went the feelings of guilt slowly lifted as I came to terms with what had happened, and Etienne also became lighter in spirit, although his nightmares continued, though to a slightly lesser extent. We reached Scorhill and took a ship to the Asterion Archipelago, and from there Vergil and Amalia headed to Planetae and we sailed on another ship to Solis. The weather was fair and we made good time.

'How are you feeling?' Etienne asked as we watched a pod of dolphins from the ship's rail, a day out from Solis.

I frowned. 'Fine, why?'

'You haven't been sick once since we left Scorhill.'

My eyes widened. He was right. 'Damn.'

'What?'

'Maybe Kit was right after all – my seasickness is all psychological. Don't tell him, I'll never hear the end of it.'

Etienne laughed. 'Don't be too unhappy about it if that's right,' he said.

I looked at him. It was the first time he'd properly laughed since the Stronghold.

'What?' he asked, his forehead furrowing.

'It's good to hear you laugh,' I said quietly.

He slipped his arm around my shoulders, pulling me close. He looked out over the water. 'I haven't had much to laugh about lately,' he said, pausing. 'I never told you what happened in the cells.'

'And you don't have to, if you don't want to.'

He hesitated. 'I want to.'

He took me below deck to our cabin and he told me everything, even about the cuts on his body. I cried more than once, and so did he, but afterwards he looked less strained, less as if the world rested on his shoulders, although until we reached Helios and found out what had happened, there was still fear resting behind his eyes.

During the afternoon, we'd both taken advantage of a bath offered to us by the First Mate in the Captain's private quarters. It was good to feel fresh again after several days on board. That night we turned in early after a delicious fish supper and a steamed pudding the ship's cook had produced from somewhere, all washed down with honey mead. The ship rocked gently as I took my weapons off, letting them drop to the floor. I rolled my shoulders, before realising Etienne was watching me, his weapons already discarded.

'What is it?' I asked.

'I… I wondered how you might feel about… whether tonight we could finally Seal our Pledge?' His voice caught as his breathing hitched. His eyes were dark, desire flickering deep within them as he held his hand out to me.

'Oh,' I said, blood rushing to my face. 'You want to Seal it tonight?'

He nodded and smiled tenderly at me as I took his hand. 'I do,' he said, his darkened eyes searching mine for an answer.

'Are you sure you're strong enough now? After what you've been through, it's still going to take you a while to properly recover, even after healing with the Crystals,' I said, worried about him as I reached out and brushed his hair from his eyes.

'I'm fine – at least, I'm fine enough to do this. But only if you want to, truly want to, and you're ready, otherwise–'

I placed a finger over his warm, velvet lips, then gently kissed him, the taste of him intoxicating. I knew now that with the Aegis Bracelet I ran no risk of getting pregnant. We were Pledged. There was nothing, Royal, law or otherwise, to stop us.

My heart skipped a beat.

I gazed at him. Something flickered in his eyes that made me pause in my answer. I knew him now. I knew him well. He was worried about what we'd find back at Solis Isle tomorrow; as was I. Maybe he wanted the comfort, the love to sustain him until we got to his home and found out what had happened. What it would mean for us. I didn't blame him. In fact, I craved that solace too.

He bowed his head slightly as if reading my mind. 'Tomorrow we'll reach Helios City and… who knows what's happened there, what awaits us. I just thought… with things the way they are we may not have another chance to Seal it for some time, depending on what's happened at home. This isn't the most romantic of settings for our first time, I know, but I wanted us to do it before we got back. When it was just the two of us, before we face whatever lies ahead. A moment for us. And I think… I know… I *need* this, Sorsh. I need *you*. I've wanted you for so long and although we've said our Pledge Vows, I…' He paused, rubbing his forehead. 'This may sound a bit stupid, but I want to make you mine properly. I want you to make me yours. And Sealing our Pledge – it's what I've longed for, to truly show you my love and how much you mean to me.' He glanced at me through his tousled hair, setting my veins alight with the look in his eyes. 'I'm strong enough now, really, and you've got the Bracelet, so there'll be no awkward repercussions. And, we can take it slow,' he said, and swallowed.

I wasn't sure he'd be able to take it that slowly, whatever he said, and I wasn't sure I wanted him to. I'd waited an age for this day, and now I needed this just as much as he did.

'And I want to do this,' he went on, 'but only if you're ready, too?'

I swallowed. Such a declaration wasn't what I'd expected from him, and I melted at his words, my body trembling in anticipation.

'None of that sounds remotely stupid,' I said, taking his other hand, heat pooling inside me. 'Yes, I'm ready, and I want to. I want to so much, and I've wanted to for so long. And... yes, I need it too. I need *you*. I'll always be yours, and you mine.'

He smiled. 'Well, then...' He looked into my eyes, his irises vibrant turquoise rims around black pupils. Want, desire flickered there, and as he brought me to him, his mouth claiming mine, there was a hunger to his kiss that there had never been before, and I gave myself to it, and to him, completely. He let out a soft little moan into my mouth, and I pulled him even closer in response.

We both needed this. Needed each other. Wanted to claim each other fully.

'You know that I haven't...' I winced.

He slipped his finger under my chin and raised my face so he could look me in the eye. 'And you know I haven't, either. Don't worry, we'll work it out together. Of course, Flax has given me a few suggestions...'

I narrowed my eyes at him.

He laughed and tucked an errant curl behind my ear. 'We'll be fine. *It* will be fine. We're together. Whatever happens, it will be special,' he said, his hand lingering on the side of my face.

I nodded.

He pulled me to him, gathering me into his arms and holding me close as vetiver swirled around us. My heart raced; he had to be feeling it through my chest as we held each other tightly, bodies pressed against each other, just as I could feel him. I raked my fingers through his hair eliciting a low moan from him that only served to heighten my own desire and, as we kissed and I tasted his tongue, still lingering with sweet traces of the honey mead, I couldn't help but let out a little moan of my own.

I started to pull my tunic off.

'No, let me,' he said, and took hold of the hem, gently pulling it over my head. He took his off, and his shirt, before removing mine.

My heart was doing flips now. Suddenly the longing I had for him, the yearning, was almost too much. Ever so slowly, his hands shaking slightly, he worked to undo the laces of my bodice as he kissed my neck, making me let out another little moan, before he moved down to my shoulder, kissing it as my bodice fell away. I gasped as he gently removed my other clothes. He quickly discarded his and kissed my lips again, ardently, intensely, before moving me towards the bed. Still kissing, we fell on to it, holding each other tightly.

'You're beautiful, you know, and I absolutely adore you,' he said, voice catching as we lay on the bed, both quite naked, except for my Aegis Bracelet, his gaze slowly taking me in.

'You're quite breathtaking too,' I murmured, running a hand over his warm, toned chest as I drank him in.

He let out an odd little gasp, one that turned into a happy groan as I moved my fingers, one that made me shiver. He pulled me to him.

'I'm going to show you exactly how much I love you, Sorsh.'

'And I'll show you how much I love you, Eti.'

He smiled as I used his nickname and kissed my fingers, then moved in closer, tilting his head, his warm lips meeting mine, tongues gently exploring as instinct and love took over our bodies, and we claimed each other, finally Sealing our Pledge. Slowly, just as he'd said, we drew each other to the edge and beyond.

#

In the early hours we lay in each other's arms, bodies tangled up with each other, moulded together, content and warm, my head resting on Eti's shoulder.

'That was… amazing,' I murmured, as I languidly ran my fingers over his bare chest in the flickering golden light of the little lamp in our cabin, periodically pausing to place a little kiss on his warm skin. He'd been nothing but tender, gentle and considerate.

'Hmm, it was for me, too,' he said softly, leisurely winding a lock of my ginger hair around his finger. 'Maybe Flax is right, and we can refine things to the point it becomes an art form – although that was pretty exquisite for a first attempt.'

I raised an eyebrow and paused what I was doing, turning towards him. 'Refine it?'

He shrugged, still twirling my hair. 'I'm happy to try refining things if you are?'

'What, again? Right now?'

'Right now.'

'You're sure you're not too tired?'

He stopped twirling. 'For this? For you? Never. So?'

I grinned at him. 'I've nowhere else to be,' I said, running my finger across his chest.

He smiled and pulled me towards him. His lips brushed mine.

'In that case, how about we refine things a little more, then we'll sleep,' he said huskily as he changed position, rolling me onto my back, and intertwined the fingers of his right hand with mine. He ran his left hand down my side making me tremble, leaning in to kiss me again, his warm body resting against mine as his mouth met mine with a fiery intensity. Once more, we gradually drew each other on to ecstasy, not stopping until we were both finally exhausted, love satiated, and our energy utterly spent.

It was the first night since the Stronghold that Eti didn't have a nightmare, but whether that was because he'd shared his burden or because we'd finally Sealed our Pledge, I didn't know, but I thought it was probably a bit of both.

#

Hot lips pressed against mine. A warm tongue gently tried to prise them apart. I opened my eyes.

Eyes closed, brow furrowed, Eti slipped his hand into my tangled hair as he leant against me. I closed my eyes, let out a contented little sigh, and let him explore my mouth, my own tongue tasting him as I wrapped my arms around him, and pulled him even closer.

Eventually he released me.

'Good morning,' he said, voice hoarse.

'Good morning to you, too.'

He gazed into my eyes, giving me a smile that reached from ear to ear, lit his whole face and made his eyes sparkle like turquoise coloured diamonds. I hadn't seen him smile like that since we'd rescued him. He was almost back to my Etienne, and with more time and love, he would get there.

'I just wanted to say… last night was… the best night of my life,' he murmured. 'Thank you.'

'You're thanking me?' I raised an eyebrow in surprise.

He shrugged. 'We've Sealed our Pledge and… well… I needed it. I needed you. And it was amazing.'

'I think we did all right for our first time, didn't we?' I smiled.

'We did exquisitely for our first time,' he said, kissing my nose. 'And even more so for our second.'

'Hmm, well I needed you as well. So thank you, too.'

'I'm looking forward to many more nights like that.'

'Are you indeed?' I asked, unable to suppress a giggle.

'I am.' He stroked my hair. 'And every morning I think we should wake like this,' he said, smiling at me.

'You'll have no complaints from me if we do.' I grinned back.

'Good…' He leant towards me for another kiss. This

time when he pulled away his face was more serious. 'We'd better get dressed, we don't know when we'll reach Helios.'

I nodded. 'It'll be all right, Eti. I'm with you,' I said, interlacing my fingers of one hand with one of his. 'You won't face this alone.'

His fingers grasped me back, the cloud lifting slightly from his face.

'I know, and it's only because of you today will be bearable.'

I gave him a little kiss and smiled at him. 'I'll be beside you all the way.'

We got out of bed, dressed, but couldn't stomach much in the way of breakfast. It wasn't until the early afternoon we finally sailed into Helios' busy harbour. Building materials and food were being unloaded and taken up into the city from the many ships at the port. As we walked along the docks a familiar face appeared at the side of a ship.

'Prince Etienne!' Captain Lucian shouted, waving to us.

Eti looked up and waved. The Captain made his way down the gangplank and shook hands with us.

'I'm pleased to see you both,' he said, although his voice was strained and his face grim.

'What news?' Eti asked, his face suddenly pale and tight, his muscles tense. I slipped my hand into his and squeezed it.

'Your parents are well,' Lucian said.

I felt Eti relax a little.

'And my brothers?'

Lucian's face told us all we needed to know. 'I'm so sorry,' he said, shaking his head. 'They were all killed either defending your parents or their wives.'

Chapter Thirty-Three

Eti gripped my hand almost bringing tears to my eyes. 'All of them?' he asked, almost choking on the words.

Lucian nodded.

'I'm so sorry,' I murmured, knowing full well what this meant for both of us. We were no longer free to do as we wished. Duty and honour now required Eti to step up, to take on the mantle of heir to the throne. I swallowed.

'Overall Solis has faired better than Steorra or Luna,' Lucian continued. 'King Saros held off Prince Cynric's fleet. They eventually gave up and left Planetae for the Celestial Temple, as you probably already know.'

I nodded. 'Did any of the priestess' survive?' I asked, glancing anxiously at Eti who had been tense since the news of his brothers' deaths.

'A few escaped,' Lucian nodded. 'They've taken refuge with King Saros.'

'Thank you, Captain,' Eti said. 'I think we'd better get up to the palace.'

The Captain gave a little bow and we left the docks.

We walked up through the streets where building repairs were well underway, Eti still firmly grasping my hand. Every now and then one of the people would recognise their Prince, voices would lower, and they'd bow to him as we passed. He gave then a little nod in return.

A cold wave passed through me. Everything would change now, but what scared me most was the thought of meeting the King and Queen of Solis. I took a deep breath, suddenly filled with terror. What if they didn't like me? If they disapproved of me? But they couldn't, surely, after all they'd arranged our match with my mother. Despite that, anxiety welled inside me. I looked at Eti.

'I'm the heir now,' he murmured, looking straight ahead, eyes red and glassy.

'I know,' I said quietly as we navigated blocks of stone and bales of straw.

'If you don't want to stay bound to me, I'll understand.'

'What? You need me more than ever now,' I said, trying to lighten the mood with a little smile.

'You don't know how true that is, Sorsh,' he said, stopping. 'I know how much you prefer to keep out of the limelight, so do I for that matter, but this will change everything for both of us. Are you sure you want to do this? You don't have to – I won't force you.'

'Don't you know by now I'd do anything for you?' I asked, moving a wisp of hair over his ear. 'I've told you before, I'd walk into hell for you, in fact, in some ways I already have,' I said, gazing into his anxiety-riddled eyes. 'This will be easy by comparison. Although to be fair, we've been officially Pledged, the documents have been filed, and we've exchanged the Pledging Oath, so really you're stuck with me whether you like it or not.' I leant towards his ear, my lips brushing his cheek. 'And we've Sealed our Pledge now, too, so you can't escape me.'

His pupils dilated as a wan little smile flickered on his face. I slipped my free hand to his cheek, guiding his face to mine and brushing my lips against his.

'Just get rid of that damn Entombing Law when you become King,' I said, letting go.

He nodded and smiled. 'I will. I'll do it before then. In fact, I'll do it today.'

I frowned at him. 'How?'

'Wait and see. But you're absolutely sure about doing this?'

'Absolutely sure, Eti, in fact, I've never been more sure of anything in my life than I am at this moment of staying by your side,' I said, my heart welling with love. 'Whatever happens and however many social events I have to endure, I'll do it for you so I can be with you because I love you.'

'I think we'll be each other's strength and support through all those banquets and balls.'

'I think you might be right.'

'By the Sun, I don't deserve you,' he said, kissing me on the forehead and giving me a quick hug.

'I'm not sure about that, but whether we were Pledged now or not, you wouldn't be able to get rid of me,' I said. 'I won't ever leave your side, so you'd better get used to it.'

He gave me a little smile. 'Thank you,' he murmured. 'I love you so much.'

'I can assure you the feeling is mutual,' I said, giving him a little smile in return and a peck on the cheek. I took another deep breath and grasped his hand again. 'Now come on, I guess I ought to meet your parents.'

He smiled back and we continued on towards the palace.

The guards at the entrance started shouting as they saw us approach.

'Prince Etienne!'

'It's the Prince. Tell King Aelius and Queen Helene immediately, Prince Etienne has returned!'

Eti was greeted by the guard and they ushered us through the gatehouse, across a courtyard full of wooden scaffolding and brick, and up the marble steps into the palace. The hallway was a beautiful, warm honey marble, and the gold and silver leaf accents on the doors and walls gave the whole place an elegant air. We walked on, following one of the guards to a room off the main corridor.

'Your Majesties,' the guard said bowing low. 'Prince Etienne.'

My heart raced and my vision narrowed as I tried to control my breathing.

'Etienne?' Queen Helene rushed across the room and hugged Eti before he'd taken more than a step inside the room.

'Mother,' he said, his voice thick with emotion.

Queen Helene pulled back from him, her face streaming with tears. 'We thought you were dead. We didn't know what had happened to you. Where's Amalia? Is she all right?'

Eti nodded, his eyes bright with tears. 'She's well. She's with Prince Vergil of Planetae – they're on their way back to Galatae.'

'Prince Vergil?'

'They're Pledged.'

Queen Helene couldn't disguise her surprise.

'It's a very good match for Amalia,' King Aelius said, walking over to Eti and shaking his son's hand. 'I'm very pleased to see you, son.'

'And I you, Father,' Eti said. 'I-I heard about… about the others.' All his brothers, other than Tyr, may have bullied him, but it didn't mean he didn't care about them.

Queen Helene bit her bottom lip. 'They all died saving others,' she said. 'They were outnumbered and unprepared. We all were.'

'I'm sure they were all very brave,' Eti nodded.

'As I'm sure you have been.'

She didn't have a clue what her youngest son had been through – but I'd make sure he told both his parents at least some of the harrowing details. Eti's own bravery and courage had at least equalled his brothers', if not surpassed it, and the King and Queen would need to know this.

'You are heir now,' King Aelius said. 'I'm sure you'll be able to rise up and take my place in due course.'

'Not for a while yet, Aelius,' Queen Helene said, patting her husband on the shoulder. She turned and looked curiously at me. 'And this is?'

'This is Princess Sorsha of Steorra, who more than once over these past months has saved my life,' Eti said. Did I detect pride in his voice?

King Aelius raised an eyebrow. 'Princess Sorsha? You are welcome here, my dear.'

'Thank you for saving my son,' the Queen said, stepping over and giving me a hug.

'Mother, Father, there's something you need to know – Sorsha and I are Pledged,' Eti said, it all tumbling out as he took my hand.

King Aelius looked aghast. 'Pledged to Princess Sorsha? But–'

'Not only is she my choice – and I hers – but she's also the Seventh Starlight Princess, Father, the one you had arranged for me to be Pledged to anyway,' Eti said, his hand gripping mine now.

'Princess Sorsha is the Seventh Starlight Princess? I didn't know,' the King said, glancing at his wife whose face was a mystery. Had she known? Had she been the one who'd corresponded with my mother? 'But her reputation, other than her swords – does she even have one? She's never at Court. Is she really suitable queen material now your circumstances have changed, Etienne?'

'It's already done, Father,' Eti said, a firm note to his voice. 'We've sworn and Sealed our Pledge, and it can't now be undone. And Sorsha will make a fine queen, when the time comes.'

Blood rushed to my face as he squeezed my hand.

'You knew about this?' the King asked his wife, staring at her. 'That Princess *Sorsha* was the Seventh Starlight Princess?'

'Of course,' the Queen said, looking from me to Eti and back to me. 'Your mother and I thought you would be a good match, princess – and it appears we were right,' she said, a little sparkle in her eyes. King Aelius didn't look convinced. 'As you know, husband, I'd arranged their Pledging before Etienne even left here to go to Luna.'

'I didn't know Princess Sorsha was the Seventh,' Aelius said with a frown. 'If I'd have known–'

'What exactly would you have done? Etienne needed a good match. A girl of similar disposition who would understand him. I think we can safely say she does, as he does her.' She turned towards us. 'You love each other?'

'Yes, Mother, we do,' Eti said, as I nodded in agreement. 'Very much.'

'There, Aelius. It was the perfect arrangement. This may not have started as a love match, but I'm pleased it's turned out that way, and the throne will be all the stronger for it.'

'It did start as a love match,' Eti said. 'You hadn't told

me the name of the girl I was to be Pledged to when I left the island. In the end I fell in love with Sorsh before I even knew she was the Seventh.' He turned and gazed at me, love filling his eyes. 'And she fell in love with me before she knew who she'd been officially Pledged to as well. If we'd been Pledged to others, we wouldn't have gone through with those Pledges.'

I nodded as I gazed back at him. I'd been worried the prince I'd been promised to would insist on me honouring that Pledge, but I knew deep down I wouldn't have. Not if Eti had wanted me. Maybe we'd have run away together. I didn't know what we'd have done, but I did know he was right. Ultimately we wouldn't have gone through with those Pledges. We were destined to be together.

'I was away from Court because my mother was keeping my identity as a Double Crystal Blood secret, Your Majesty, but that need has now passed,' I said, smiling sweetly at the King, my hands going cold and sweaty – I hoped Eti didn't mind, but he didn't let go of me.

'A Double Blood, you say?' King Aelius rubbed his chin thoughtfully.

'A Starlight Princess is of noble birth and quite acceptable, and you did say you wanted him Pledged as soon as possible,' Queen Helene said, looking at her husband. 'Especially now. And besides, can't you see they're happy?'

King Aelius looked at us and nodded. 'I did say I wanted him Pledged, and, yes, I'd rather he was happy with his new wife than not, the Sun knows the others weren't. Well, things will change for you now, Etienne, now you're the heir. I hope you don't intend to shirk your responsibilities?'

Eti set his jaw. 'Of course not, Father.'

'What, now that you need him?' I couldn't help muttering.

'What was that?' King Aelius asked.

Eti tensed beside me and his face went ghostly white, his eyes almost popping out on stalks. I didn't care. It had to be said. Eti, and Amalia for that matter, had lived with this all their lives, lived in the shadows. Now the King wanted something he expected Eti to comply without question, and although he would, I didn't see why Aelius should get away with it too easily. I was an outsider and probably the only one who could ever say anything, and if I was going to do it, it had to be now.

'You heard me.'

King Aelius winced and Queen Helene took on a pained expression.

'You're... right, of course, Princess,' Queen Helene said, moving towards us. 'Etienne was never treated like his brothers – we couldn't. The others, being closer to the throne, had to be taught so many things, they had so many responsibilities but now they're all gone,' she sniffed, her eyes filling with tears. 'I'm so glad you weren't here, Etienne. So glad.' She reached out and squeezed his free hand. 'But your father is right. You will have to take over now. If we'd done our job properly we'd have treated you all equally, my son, so if this horrific situation had ever occurred you'd have been prepared. But in our hubris we never considered it a possibility and instead we listened to your stupid father,' she said, turning to Aelius.

'He only suggested we do what he thought was right,' King Aelius said bowing his head. 'But he'd not had as many children to consider. He said to train up the others and leave you to your own devices, Etienne, because you were so much younger.'

'Not because I was a mistake, then?' Eti stood, jaw set. I could feel him trembling slightly as I held his hand. Maybe my own boldness was rubbing off.

Queen Helene blanched. 'Oh, my dear, is that what you really think?'

'Isn't that right?'

'Of course not. You were so much younger, we just wanted you to not have the cares of the others.'

'So you pushed me away, always took their part in everything even when Tyr told you they were bullying me?' Eti's eyes sparkled, but I wasn't sure if it was with unshed tears or anger. 'Sent me to school in Merribor rather than here.'

King Aelius sighed. 'No, son, we didn't treat you differently because you were a mistake. If anything you were born of our great love for each other. One that came later in our union than we might have hoped. Ours was not a love match. It took time for us to grow to love each other, although we do now, very much. And it's a love your brothers never got to experience, but I think you and Sorsha already have.'

'We didn't think we could have any more children after Tyr, but we were wrong,' Queen Helene said. 'We thought by distancing ourselves from you a little we would stop your brothers from resenting you, a new baby in their midst, when they were all secure in their places. Of all of them, I'm reluctant to say this, but you were our favourite, born from our love, not from duty.'

'But we were wrong about that, too,' Aelius said, shaking his head. 'We did try to curb your brothers by sending you to Merribor, but we failed.'

'We never realised how wrong we'd been.'

'We have some work to do to make it up to you, Etienne, but I hope you will at least let us try,' Aelius said. 'I very much regret what we've done. I can see now how wrong we were, and not just because of your brothers' deaths.'

Eti stood, pale faced and quiet. He took a deep breath.

'I accept your apologies,' Eti said. 'We must all work together to rebuild the Celestial Isles. And I will be your heir, but I have one condition,' he said, standing tall.

The King's eyebrows knitted together. 'And what condition is that?'

'That the Entombing Law is revoked from today, this minute, never to be brought back.'

Queen Helene's shoulders dropped in relief. 'I really wish you would, Aelius. That's the one thing that's hung over me all these years, and I don't see why poor Princess Sorsha should have to endure that torment too.'

Aelius looked to his wife, and nodded slowly. 'Very well. I should have done it long ago, I suppose,' he said, bowing his head.

'Yes, you should.'

He flinched, then turned to look at me. 'I can see you'll be a forthright queen, when your time comes, Princess Sorsha – perhaps in the meantime you'll help to keep us on the straight and narrow,' King Aelius said, stepping forward and giving me a hug. 'I can already see what a good influence you are on my son.'

My heart was hammering in my chest – I was half expecting to be sent off to the dungeons, assuming there were any here, not just for my own words but for being a bad influence on Eti. But I had to stand up for him when he couldn't. I nodded and curtseyed, as best I could with my weapons on my back.

'We'll have to find you some more appropriate clothes, my dear,' Queen Helene said, drawing me off to one side.

I groaned internally. 'Did you know my mother?' I asked.

She paused. 'We were acquainted and did meet a couple of times. She was a lovely woman – I was very sorry to hear what happened to her.'

That wasn't exactly what I'd meant.

'We'll send news to King Finnar of your return immediately,' she said.

'When you do, could you send this to him?' I asked, fishing the Amaranthine Rose out from my tunic and handing it to her.

She looked at it, holding it up to the light. 'It's quite beautiful.'

'It's one of the Steorran Relics. It used to have Purple Crystals embedded in it where the petals are, but they've gone now.'

'I'll make sure it gets to Finnar. Do you have any other relatives?'

'My uncle,' I said, nodding.

'We'll send for him to come straight away.'

That filled me with joy, and a warmth spread through

me at the thought of seeing him again. I might even wear a dress.

Early that evening Eti retrieved me from his mother's ministrations and took me to his room, but not before she'd shoe-horned me into a purple silk dress I could barely breathe in. The prince's chambers had been newly redecorated after the sacking of the palace and everything smelt fresh and clean. The main room had a sitting area, and on one side a door led to a bed chamber with a large, sumptuous looking bed with silky sheets and plumped up pillows. Steam drifted from a side room and I caught a glimpse of a bath tub. Eti shut the door behind us and locked it.

'I told Father we'd be sharing my chambers from now on,' he said, glancing at me. He looked away and rubbed his forehead.

'Oh, you did, did you?' I smirked. 'And what did he say?'

'I'm not entirely sure he was happy, mumbled something about the legalities, exchanging Oaths in public, and the formal Royal Solisian document not being signed yet, particularly as I was now the heir. But it's already official between us, seeing as the main documents have been filed and we've exchanged the Oath, so he backed down, just said we needed to get things formally signed in the next day or two, and went in search of his Chamberlain. You know, when you said what you did this afternoon, I... I'm glad you did. I think things will be different with my parents now. Better. And he's already revoked the Entombing Law for us. I've also spoken to him about a Refuge Room in the palace – he thinks that's a good idea, too.'

I took hold of his hand and squeezed it. 'I'm glad. I do seem to remember you telling me once everything would be fine in the end.'

'I did, didn't I?' he said, looking rather smug. The grin faded. 'Father did mention the prospect of heirs just before I left him.'

I swallowed. 'Already?'

Eti grinned. 'No need to mention the Aegis Bracelet to him.'

I smiled back. 'No, indeed.' I hesitated. 'But you want children, one day?'

He took hold of both my hands. 'One day, Sorsh, but as far as I'm concerned, that day is a long way off. We have a lot of work to do before we start worrying about babies.'

'Good. I want them too, one day, but not yet.'

He smiled. 'Let's have some time together, alone, first. Time for just the two of us, to enjoy each other. We'll worry about a family later.'

I nodded, smiling back. I paused. 'I wanted to say again, how sorry I am... about your brothers.'

He nodded, sadness creeping into his eyes for a moment. 'Despite how they treated me, I'll miss them – especially Tyr.'

'Of course you will. But you still have your parents, I'm sure together you'll give each other strength now.'

'You give me strength most of all. If I hadn't had you to cling to in that dungeon, I wouldn't be here now,' he said, his expression taking on a haunted look. 'I only survived because I knew you loved me, and because I loved you and wanted to be with you, too. And I was also quite desperate to get back to you to finally Seal our Pledge.' His cheeks flushed, an impish sparkle now filling his eyes.

I grinned, reaching up and cupping his face in my hands. 'And you did.'

'Only because you came to rescue me,' he said, quirking his lips into a crooked smile.

'That's true – but I couldn't leave you there a moment longer. It was tearing me apart.' I ran a finger across the back of his hand, along a white, shiny scar. The evidence of most of his wounds had gone, but a couple of scars lingered and would never leave him. The emotional scars would take more time to heal for us both, too. 'Did you tell your Father, about what happened to you?'

'A little of it. He was truly shocked, and I haven't told

325

him the worst of it yet – I thought you might like to be there with me when I do?'

'Of course,' I said. 'I'll do anything I can to help you, but I think your mother should know as well.'

He nodded. 'Father said he'd tell her, but maybe the rest should be told to them both together.'

'And I'll be there when you tell them. They need to know of your full bravery and selflessness. And your great courage.'

Eti's face grew rosy. 'I wasn't brave.'

'Utter rot. You put yourself in danger for me, hell, you almost died for me because of your selflessness and self-sacrifice, and they need to know it. It was very courageous.'

'It wasn't courage,' he said, looking me in the eye, 'it was love.'

I reached out to his red cheek. 'I know. And they need to know that too. You're my hero and you always will be.'

The lopsided grin appeared. 'Thank you. And you're mine for coming to my rescue.'

I smiled and gave a little shrug. 'You saved me, I saved you. It's how it should be.'

'It is.' He took a deep breath. 'They do need to know all of it, of course, Mother too. But after that we need to put it behind us. Just look ahead to, hopefully, better and happier things.' He reached out and touched me, his hand tenderly caressing the side of my face and setting off sparks inside me. 'You look quite gorgeous in that dress, you know. It shows you off in all the right places.' His face flushed a little.

'Oh, really?' I stepped a little closer to him. 'And what would those places be, exactly?' I asked, arching an eyebrow.

He swallowed. 'Well, your waist and your shoulders and your...' His eyes travelled to my chest and lingered.

'I see.'

He looked at me. 'Will you be wearing dresses like that all the time from now on? Because if you do, I'll have to have a word with my mother about your necklines – I don't want too much of you on display or the men of the Court might start having designs on you, and I'll have to take steps to fend them off.'

I grinned at him and slipped my arms around his neck. 'Are you saying you'd defend my honour?'

'Always. Although I imagine you'd get there before me.'

'Hmm, you have a point there,' I said, kissing his nose. 'I've already worked out a couple of places in this to hide knives, but I'm hoping to stay out of dresses as much as possible.'

'Have you met my mother?'

I grimaced. 'Are you saying this is going to be a regular occurrence, because I only put this on today to humour her?'

Eti flinched. 'I reckon so.'

I groaned. 'Could we live away from Court somewhere?' I asked hopefully. 'Like I did in Steorra?'

'I'm heir to the throne now, Sorsh, I can't and you know that.'

I reined in the urge to swear and settled for pouting at him. 'Yes, I know it. But I thought I'd ask anyway. Maybe I could start a new trend in pretty tunics and britches or leggings? After all, Amalia had some highly decorated ones...'

'I'll leave that to you, the Royal Dressmaker and Mother,' he said with a laugh. 'I don't want to get involved – other than to say you look beautiful whatever you wear, but in that dress, you're exquisite.'

I blushed and smiled winsomely at him.

He swallowed again, shook his head before once more rubbing his forehead.

'Now, seeing as we're alone for the rest of the evening, I thought a nice bath and then...' he looked towards the large bed. 'It'll be more comfortable than last night.'

'I enjoyed last night,' I said, pouting again.

He grinned, and ran a finger down the side of my face, triggering more sparks. 'So did I, and in some ways I don't think anything will ever surpass it – but we'll have more room to… manoeuvre here, and like I said, it's about refinement and making it an art form, so we'll just have to continue to strive for perfection. With any luck it'll take us a lifetime.'

I raised an eyebrow. 'Really?' I asked.

A mischievous glint sparkled in his eyes. 'Yes, really.'

I chewed my lip for a moment. 'And you want to start refining things now? Even though you only indulged a few hours ago?'

He nodded, his eyes darkening. 'I think indulging in that particular activity together is going to become an extremely regular event, and a somewhat addictive one. As long as you feel the same way?'

'Oh yes, I feel the same,' I said, sliding my arms down and around his waist. 'Well, where's that bath?' I tilted my head and brushed my lips against his. He started to move closer, but I pulled back and put a finger over his mouth. For a moment he looked disappointed. 'But it's on the understanding I have the pleasure of undressing you, this time.'

The disappointment vanished as his pupils dilated. 'Can I still undress you?'

I put on a show of considering his request for a moment, then smiled. 'I suppose that would be acceptable, my Prince.' I pulled off his jacket.

He grinned. 'Excellent, my Princess,' he said, leaning forward and kissing me with those velvet lips. My heart thudded and I trembled at his touch. He drew back, lips still slightly parted, his breath hitching as he looked at me and reached out towards my dress. He slowly took hold of the laces and started to undo my bodice, increasing his speed as he went. My dress fell to the floor, leaving me with very little on. 'Dresses do have their advantages,' he murmured as he gazed at me.

'I suppose they do,' I said, fluttering my eyelashes at him. I grabbed his shirt, slid it free of his britches, pulled it off and started to lead him towards the steaming bathtub.

328

He laughed. 'You're very keen – I didn't realise Starlight Princesses could be so shameless,' he said, pulling me back to him, his irises brilliant turquoise rims around his fully dilated pupils.

'Did you not?' I grinned at him, undoing his britches. His breaths became deeper, heavier as he stepped out of them. 'I thought you might have by now.' I leant forward and kissed his bare chest. I smiled as he went taut as a harp string, and I drew a little moan of pleasure from him. 'You see sometimes I need a break from being a princess.'

'I'm quickly coming to realise that, and it's something for which I shall be eternally grateful,' he said, his voice almost cracking as he tried to keep it steady. He slipped my remaining clothes off and pulled me close, our bodies resting against each other.

'Then it's lucky for you that today is one of my days off.'

'It certainly is,' he said, running his thumb over my lips. Leaning in he kissed me, his tongue parted my lips and explored my mouth as I kissed him back. He caressed me as I raked my fingers through his hair. Pulling back slightly, he gazed into my eyes. 'I think we should get started,' he said, voice husky now.

'I thought we had?'

'I haven't even begun to get started, yet...'

I could see that with Eti, I was going to need a lifetime of days off.

Acknowledgements

My husband has been encouraging (and enduring) my writing for years. Without his support this book wouldn't be here now. My daughter's cheerleading and enthusiasm has been a constant source of motivation without which Sorsha and Etienne may not have travelled the road that they have.

To my wonderful editor Sofia (Elsewhen First Officer) – thank you! I have really enjoyed working with you to perfect *Crystal Bloods* and make Sorsha and Etienne's journey the best it possibly could be. You have been a steady pair of hands, and I look forward to working with you again sometime.

I must make special mention of two of my writer buddies. Emma Bradley and Estelle Tudor have been sounding boards, inspiration and such great supporters of my work that my stories wouldn't be here without them. Thanks also go to Stuart White and his excellent WriteMentor team who continue to encourage and support me and so many other writers with the WriterMentor Hub out in the writing community.

To my readers, I hope you enjoy Sorsha and Etienne's story, the twists and turns, and above all, their love story. You never know where else it may lead them…

Alison Buck (Elsewhen Captain) has produced a beautiful cover for *Crystal Bloods*, with such gorgeous details representing the Celestial Orders, the Bloods and the fantasy of the story. She has also drawn the most wonderful map of the Celestial Isles that really brings the world to life. Thank you so very much!

Peter Buck (Elsewhen Chief Engineer), thank you for believing in my book and for being the guiding light that you are. Without you and Alison my dream of seeing this book out in the world would never have happened; thank you so much!

If you want to know more about my writing and books, then please visit my website www.aerinapeltun.com where you can sign up to my Readers' Newsletter!

Take care,

Aerin

Author and Elsewhen Payload Specialist

Elsewhen Press
delivering outstanding new talents in speculative fiction

Visit the Elsewhen Press website at elsewhen.press for the latest
information on all of our titles, authors and events; to read our blog;
find out where to buy our books and ebooks; or to place an order.

Sign up for the Elsewhen Press InFlight Newsletter at
elsewhen.press/newsletter

THE MAREK SERIES BY JULIET KEMP

1: THE DEEP AND SHINING DARK

A Locus Recommended Read in 2018

"*A rich and memorable tale of political ambition, family and magic, set in an imagined city that feels as vibrant as the characters inhabiting it.*" **Aliette de Bodard**

You know something's wrong when the cityangel turns up at your door

An agreement 300 years ago, between an angel and Marek's founding fathers, protects magic and political stability within the city. A recent plague wiped out most of the city's sorcerers. Reb, one of the survivors, realises that someone has deposed the cityangel without replacing it. Marcia, Heir to House Fereno, stumbles across that same truth. But it is just one part of a much more ambitious plan to seize control of Marek. Meanwhile, city Council members connive and conspire, manipulated in a dangerous political game that threatens the peace and security of all the states around the Oval Sea. Reb, Marcia, the deposed cityangel, and Jonas, a Salina messenger, must work together to stop the impending disaster. They must discover who is behind it, and whom they can really trust.

ISBN: 9781911409342 (epub, kindle) / 9781911409243 (272pp paperback)
Visit bit.ly/DeepShiningDark

2: SHADOW AND STORM

"*never short on adventure and intrigue... the characters are real, full of depth, and richly drawn, and you'll wish you had even more time with them by book's end. A fantastic read.*"
Rivers Solomon

Never trust a demon... or a Teren politician

The new Teren Lord Lieutenant has an agenda. A young Teren magician being sought by an unleashed demon, believes their only hope may be to escape to Marek where the cityangel can keep the demon at bay. Once again Reb, Cato, Jonas and Beckett must deal with a magical problem, while Marcia tackles a serious political challenge to Marek's future.

ISBN: 9781911409595 (epub, kindle) / 9781911409496 (336pp paperback)
Visit bit.ly/ShadowAndStorm

3: THE RISING FLOOD

"*Fantasy politics with real nuance ... a fantastic read*" **Malka Older**

Hope alone cannot withstand a rising flood

A darkness writhes in the heart of Teren, unleashing demons on dissenters. Marek's five sorcerers with the cityangel can expel a single demon, but Teren has many. Storms rampage across the Oval Sea. Menaced by the distant capital, dissension from within, and even nature itself – will the rising flood lift all boats? Or will they be capsized?

ISBN: 9781911409984 (epub, kindle) / 9781911409885 (392pp paperback)
Visit bit.ly/TheRisingFlood

4: THE CITY REVEALED

"*Eminently satisfying epic fantasy*" **Juliet E. McKenna**
"*An absorbing fantasy set in a richly imagined world*" **Una McCormack**

Independence brings self-determination but also threats

Marek is newly-independent. Teren's expelled Lieutenant threatened to return with soldiers & war sorcerers. The common folk of Marek demand representation. Marcia, Fereno-Heir, agrees with them. She and sorcerer Reb, her lover, must convince the Council of the truth of magic, whilst her sorcerer brother, Cato, rushes to build some sort of defence.

ISBN: 9781915304315 (epub, kindle) / 9781915304216 (344pp paperback)
Visit bit.ly/TheCityRevealed

Bookworm series by Christopher Nuttall

Bookworm

Elaine, an inexperienced witch in Golden City, has her life turned upside down when she triggers a magical trap to end up with all the knowledge in the Great Library stuffed inside her head. Avoiding the Inquisition she tries to understand what has happened to her. But she is a pawn in the dark plans of one who wants the Grand Sorcerer's power.

Bookworm won the Gold Award in the Adult Fiction category of the 2013 Wishing Shelf Independent Book Awards.

ISBN: 9781908168320 (epub, kindle) / 9781908168221 (368pp, paperback)

Visit bit.ly/Bookworm-Nuttall

Bookworm II – The Very Ugly Duckling

Not every ugly duckling becomes a swan ...

In the wake of the disastrous attack on the Golden City, Lady Light Spinner has become Grand Sorceress and Elaine, the Bookworm, has been settling into her positions as Head Librarian and Privy Councillor. But any hope of vanishing into her books is negated when a new magician of staggering power appears in the city, one whose abilities seem to defy the known laws of magic.

ISBN: 9781908168382 (epub, kindle) / 9781908168283 (432pp, paperback)

Visit bit.ly/Bookworm2-Nuttall

Bookworm III – The Best Laid Plans

Elaine and Johan prepare to leave Golden City, with Daria and Cass, to search for the Witch-King. But Elaine is arrested on the orders of a new Emperor, puppet of the Witch-King. She must escape and destroy him. Privy Councillors and Heads of the Great Houses have bowed to the Emperor. Only Elaine and her friends can prevent an all-out war.

ISBN: 9781908168764 (epub, kindle) / 9781908168665 (400pp, paperback)

Visit bit.ly/Bookworm3

Bookworm IV – Full Circle

Until now the Witch-King had remained hidden as a lich. But Elaine was intent on his destruction. Bonded to the unknowingly powerful Johan, she was the only other magician who understood the deeper layers of magic. As they slowly made their way towards the catacombs in Ida where his lich was hiding, he had to rely on the new Emperor to stop them.

ISBN: 9781908168948 (epub, kindle) / 9781908168849 (416pp, paperback)

Visit bit.ly/Bookworm4

All now available as audiobooks from Tantor

Other Elsewhen Press titles that you might like

The Vanished Mage

Penelope Hill and J. A. Mortimore

A vanished mage…
A missing diamond…
The game is afoot.

"*From Broderick, Prince of Asconar, Earl of Carlshore and Thorn,
Duke of Wicksborough, Baron of Highbury and Warden of
Dershanmoor, to My Lady Parisan, King's Investigator, greetings. It has
been brought to my attention that a certain Reinwald, Master Historian,
noted Archmagus and tutor to our court in this city of Nemithia, has this
day failed to report to the duties awaiting him. I do ask you, as my
father's most loyal servant, to seek the cause of this laxity and bring word
of the mage to me, so that my concerns as to his safety be allayed.*"

The herald delivered the message word-perfect to The Lady
Parisan, Baroness of Orandy, Knight of the Diamond
Circle and Sworn Paladin to Our Lady of the Sighs.
Parisan's companion, Foorourow Miar Raar Ramoura,
Prince of Ilsfacar, (Foo to his friends) thought it a rather
mundane assignment, but nevertheless together they
ventured to the Archmagus' imposing home to seek him. It
turned out to be the start of an adventure to solve a
mystery wrapped in an enigma bound by a conundrum and
secured by a puzzle. All because of a missing diamond with
a solar system at its core.

Authors Penelope Hill and J. A. Mortimore have effortlessly
melded a Holmesian investigative duo, a richly detailed city
where they encounter both nobility and seedier denizens,
swashbuckling action, and magic that is palpable and, at times,
awesome.

ISBN: 9781915304186 (epub, kindle) / 9781915304087 (212pp paperback)
Visit bit.ly/TheVanishedMage

The Harlequin: The Draper's Reel

J. A. Mortimore and Penelope Hill

Question my honesty if you must, but nobody, and I mean nobody, questions my skill.

I've never paid much attention to the gods, which may be why I foolishly agreed to steal Pardeem's reel. It seemed a straightforward enough challenge for a master trickster like me, but with things like this you never know.

Leaving my cosy retirement isn't difficult. Wearing the Harlequin's hat again feels right. However returning to Emor holds challenges. Old friends and enemies wait in the shadows; maybe I can turn that to my advantage. But now my own god seems to be paying me far too much attention. This isn't going to be straightforward.

But that's the thrill, isn't it? To dance with peril, to spin with the twists, to confound expectations and to embrace the trick for its own sake. The Harlequin doesn't give up at the first hurdle.

If I can carry this off, it will be the heist of a lifetime.
Failure might cost me everything.

ISBN: 9781915304551 (epub, kindle) / 9781915304452 (226pp paperback)
Visit bit.ly/HarlequinDrapersReel

Other Elsewhen Press titles that you might like

AN ORCHID IN MY BELLY BUTTON

KATY WIMHURST

Offbeat short stories that explore our fragile world

These stories savour the surreal, flirt with magical realism, dabble with dystopia. A boy sees the ghosts of dead crabs. A girl with a fox tail is bullied. A disenchanted woman sprouts orchids from her belly button. Fashion models pursue the trend of having plants as hair. Electronic goods amassing all over London herald an apocalypse. Darkness and wonder, the strange and the ordinary, interweave to offer an environmental and social portrait of our times. Guaranteed to evoke a response, whether a giggle, a gasp, or a nervous gulp, these stories will stay with you, enriching your perception of the world.

Surreal, absurdist, magical realist; Katy Wimhurst writes speculative fiction that meditates on our reality. Although bleak themes are examined – dystopian futures, the climate crisis, bullying – a quirky imagination and wry humour lift the tales above the 'realm of grim'.

ISBN: 9781915304797 (epub, kindle) / 9781915304698 (160pp paperback)

Visit bit.ly/AnOrchidInMyBellyButton

About Aerin Apeltun

Aerin Apeltun is an English writer based in the East of England. Aerin started writing stories as a child, and always loved reading about fantasy worlds, imagining herself within those worlds and joining in the adventures with the characters. She now loves to develop and write about her own worlds and mythologies.

Having been listed in a number of writing competitions, her debut YA Fantasy trilogy was acquired by SmashBear Publishing, and *The Amethyst Talisman*, the first in *The Cursed Weapons* trilogy, was published in July 2023. The second book, *The Malachite Quest*, followed in April 2024.

A Second Class Archer, Aerin has had various careers in school/university administration and insurance, as well as a stint at the local library, but writing is her passion. She also loves to draw, and is a keen fantasy cartographer, designing maps for her worlds. Aerin enjoys travelling, taking inspiration from nature and landscapes for settings and characters in her books.